AN UNOFFICIAL GRAPHIC NOVEL
FOR MINECRAFTERS

REDSTONE JUNIOR HIGH

WHEN PIGMEN FLY

BOOK 6

CARA J. STEVENS

ART BY MITCHELL CREEDEN

Sky Pony Press
New York

Copyright © 2019 by Hollan Publishing, Inc.

Minecraft® is a registered trademark of Notch Development AB.

The Minecraft game is copyright © Mojang AB.

Sky Pony Press books may be purchased in bulk at special discounts for sales promotion, corporate gifts, fund-raising, or educational purposes. Special editions can also be created to specifications. For details, contact the Special Sales Department, Sky Pony Press, 307 West 36th Street, 11th Floor, New York, NY 10018 or info@ skyhorsepublishing.com.

Sky Pony® is a registered trademark of Skyhorse Publishing, Inc.®, a Delaware corporation.

Minecraft® is a registered trademark of Notch Development AB.
The Minecraft game is copyright © Mojang AB.

Visit our website at www.skyponypress.com.

10 9 8 7 6 5 4 3 2 1

Library of Congress Cataloging-in- Publication Data is available on file.

Cover design by Brian Peterson

Print ISBN: 978-1-5107-4110-2
Ebook ISBN: 978-1-5107-4129-4

Printed in China

REDSTONE
JUNIOR HIGH

MEET THE

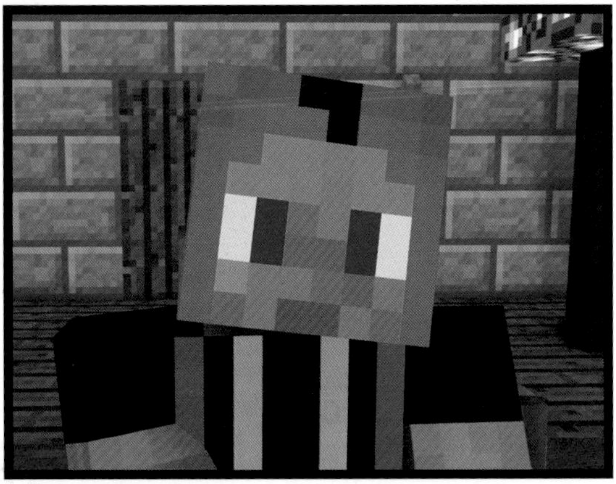

PIXEL: A girl with an unusual way with animals and other creatures.

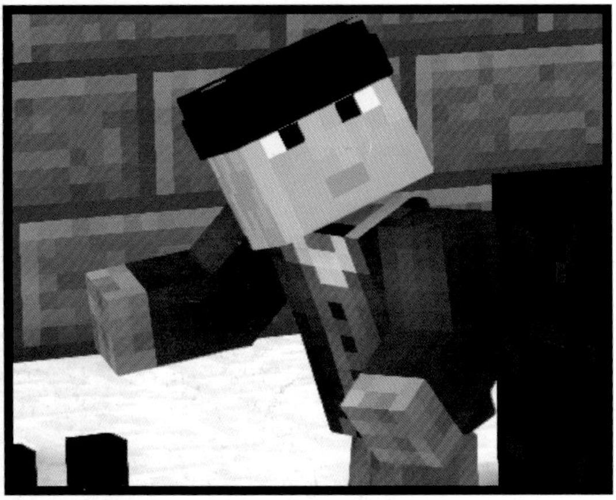

SKY: A redstone expert who is also one of Pixel's best friends at school.

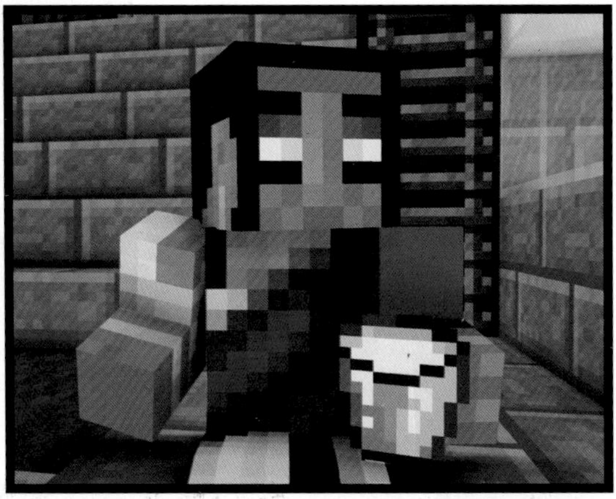

UMA: A fellow student at Redstone Junior High who can sense how people and mobs are feeling.

CHARACTERS

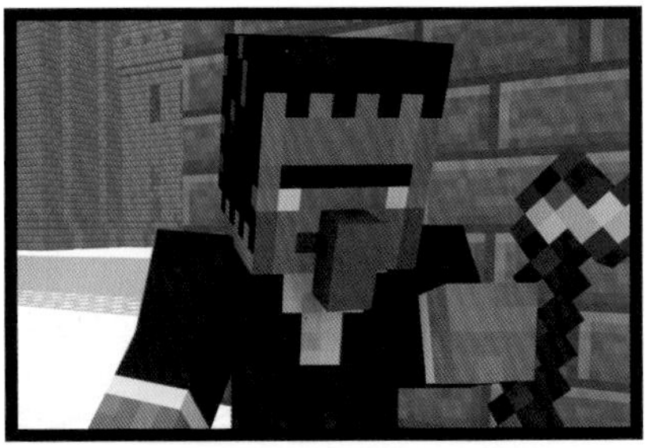

MR. Z: A teacher with a dark past.

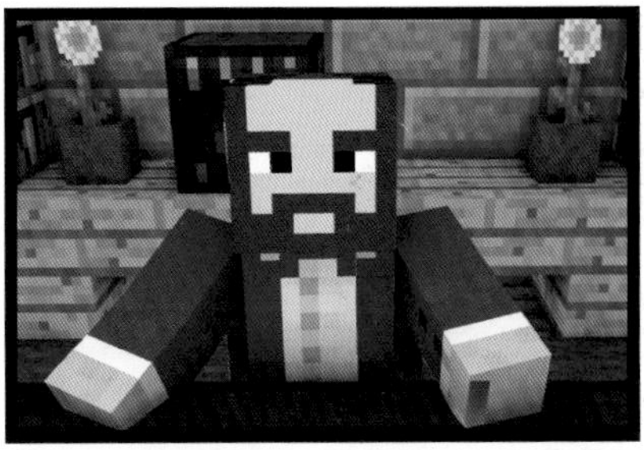

PRINCIPAL REDSTONE: The head of Redstone Junior High.

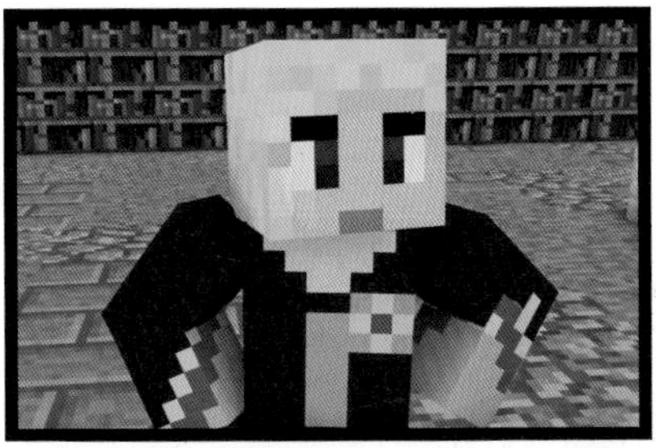

TINA: Pixel's nemesis.

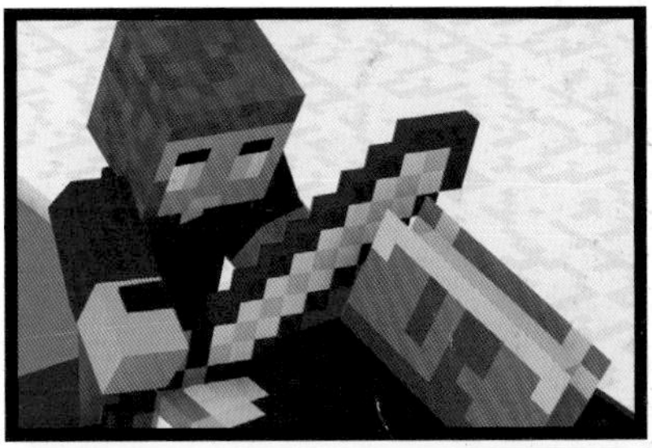

VIOLET: A student with amazing enchantment and conjuring skills.

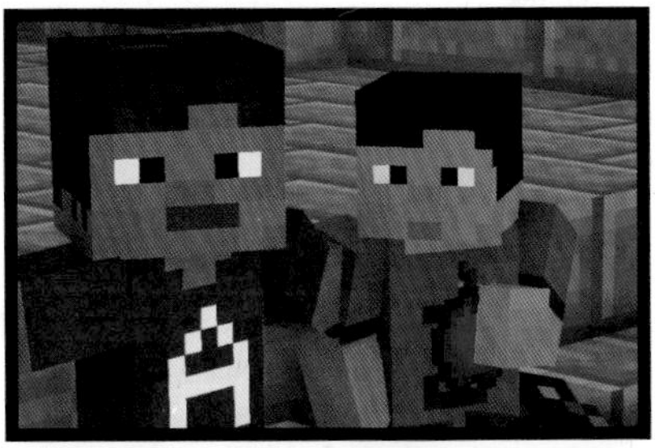

ALPHA AND ZEB: Tina's battle-ready friends from Combat School.

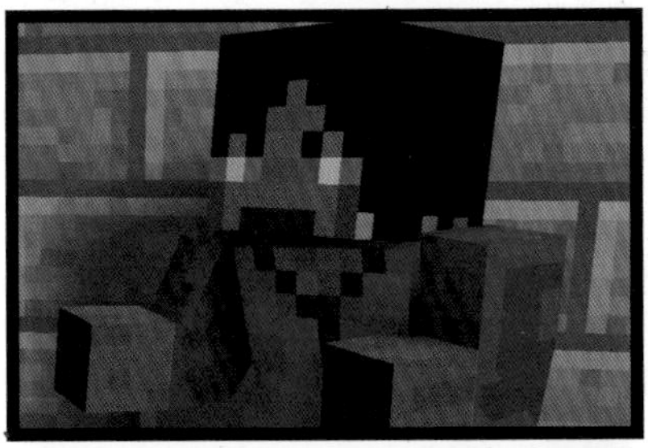

PENNY: A former zombie girl who is not happy about being "cured."

INTRODUCTION

If you have played Minecraft, then you know all about Minecraft worlds. They're made of blocks you can mine, creatures you can interact with, and lands you can visit. Deep in the heart of one of these worlds is an extraordinary school with students who have been handpicked from across the world for their unique abilities.

The school is Redstone Junior High. When our story opens, it is winter. The students, including a new mysterious student with a dangerous and secret past, are returning to the school after their holiday break for the last time. In their final year, the students are each required to do something that makes the school a better place than when they arrived. They are also tasked with a nearly impossible and dangerous final project—one that will lead them all down a dangerous path to the End. It is a field trip that will require them to work together, and succeed together or fail together.

Will Pixel and Tina finally get along? Will Sky finally win a tournament? Will the kids be able to graduate without being destroyed? It all seems about as impossible as seeing pigmen fly…but maybe, just maybe, they can find a way to work together and make the impossible a reality after all.

PROLOGUE

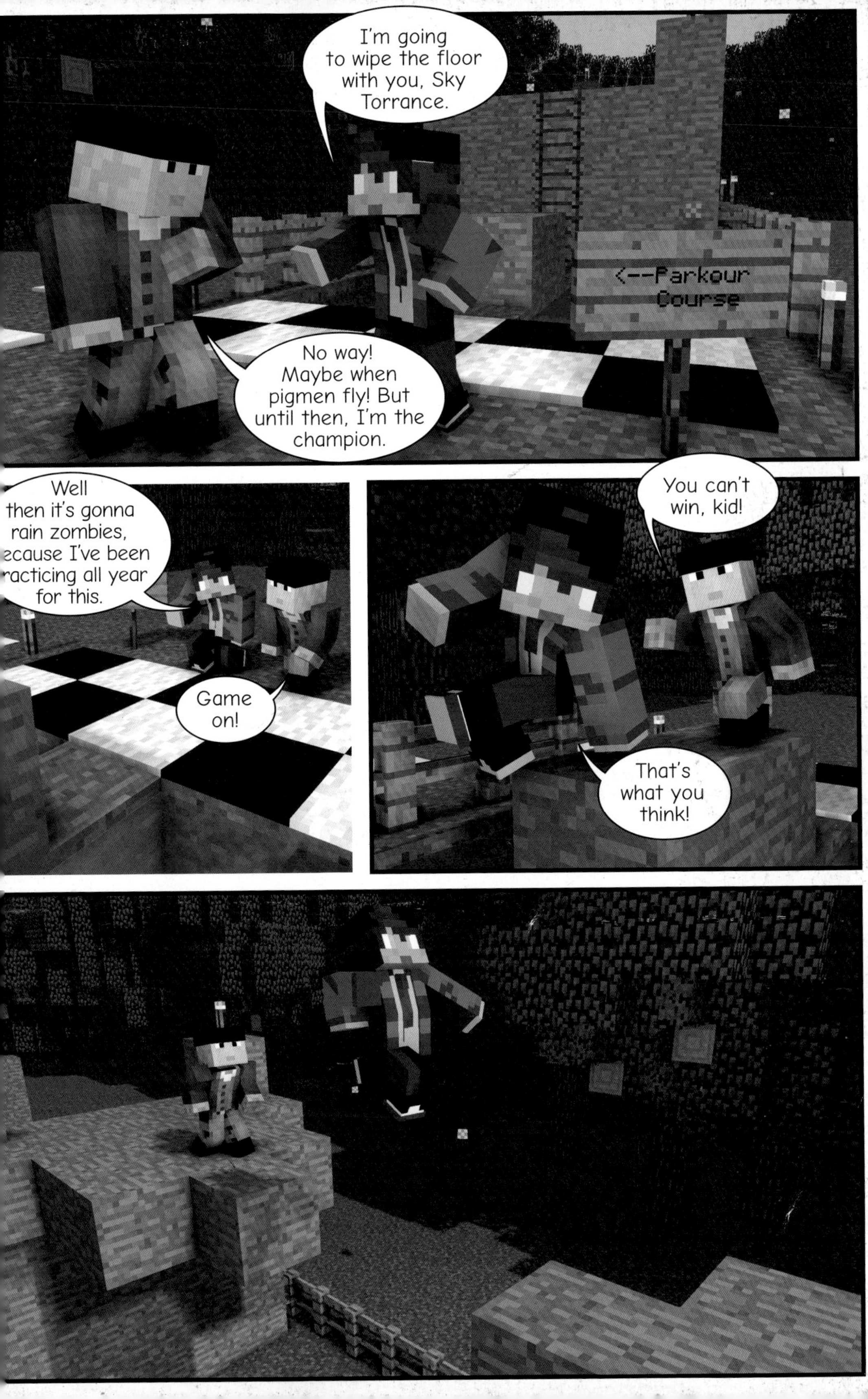

I'm going to wipe the floor with you, Sky Torrance.
<--Parkour Course
No way! Maybe when pigmen fly! But until then, I'm the champion.
Well then it's gonna rain zombies, ecause I've been racticing all year for this.
Game on!
You can't win, kid!
That's what you think!

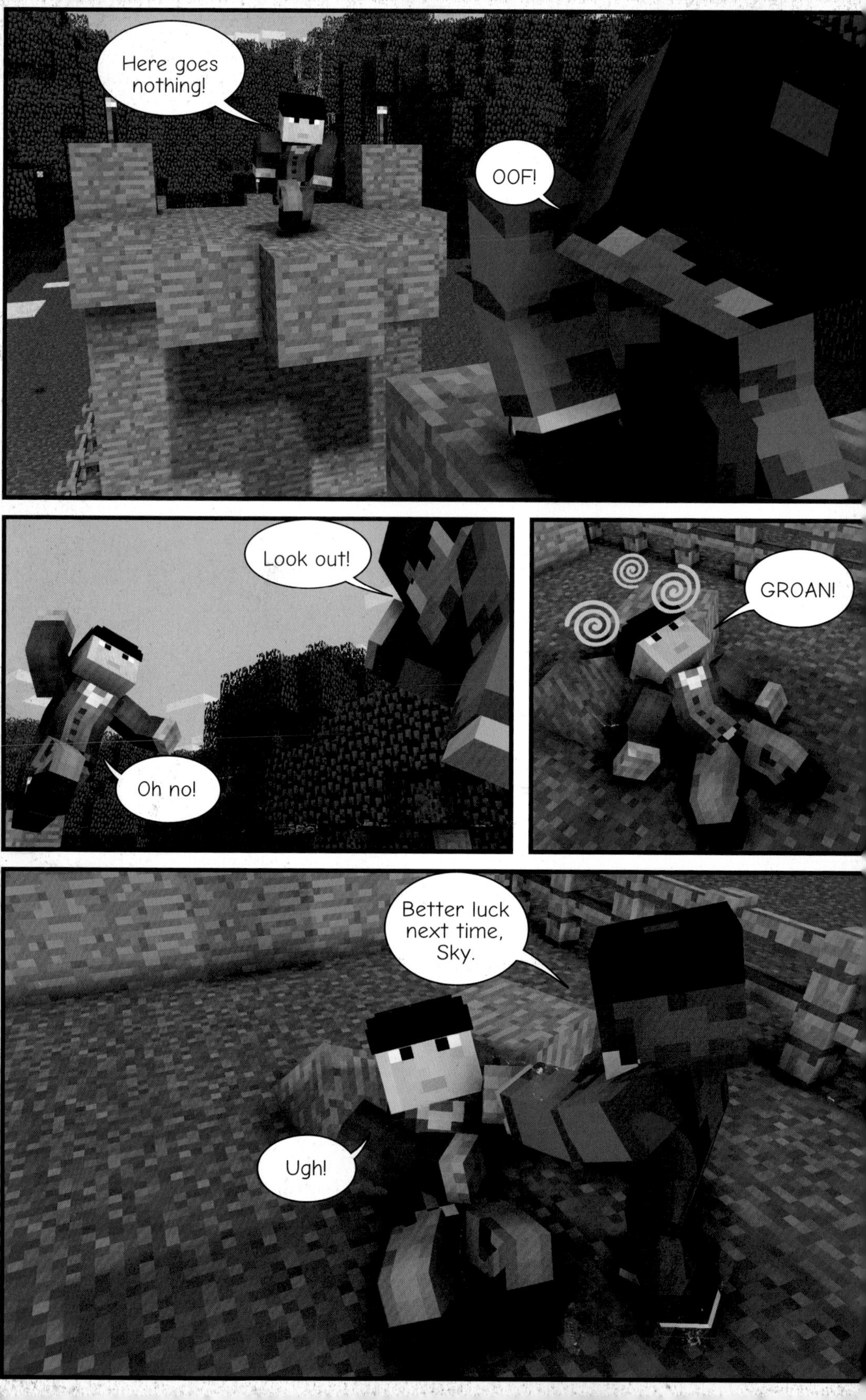
Here goes nothing!
OOF!
Look out!
Oh no!
GROAN!
Better luck next time, Sky.
Ugh!

CHAPTER 1

PENNY

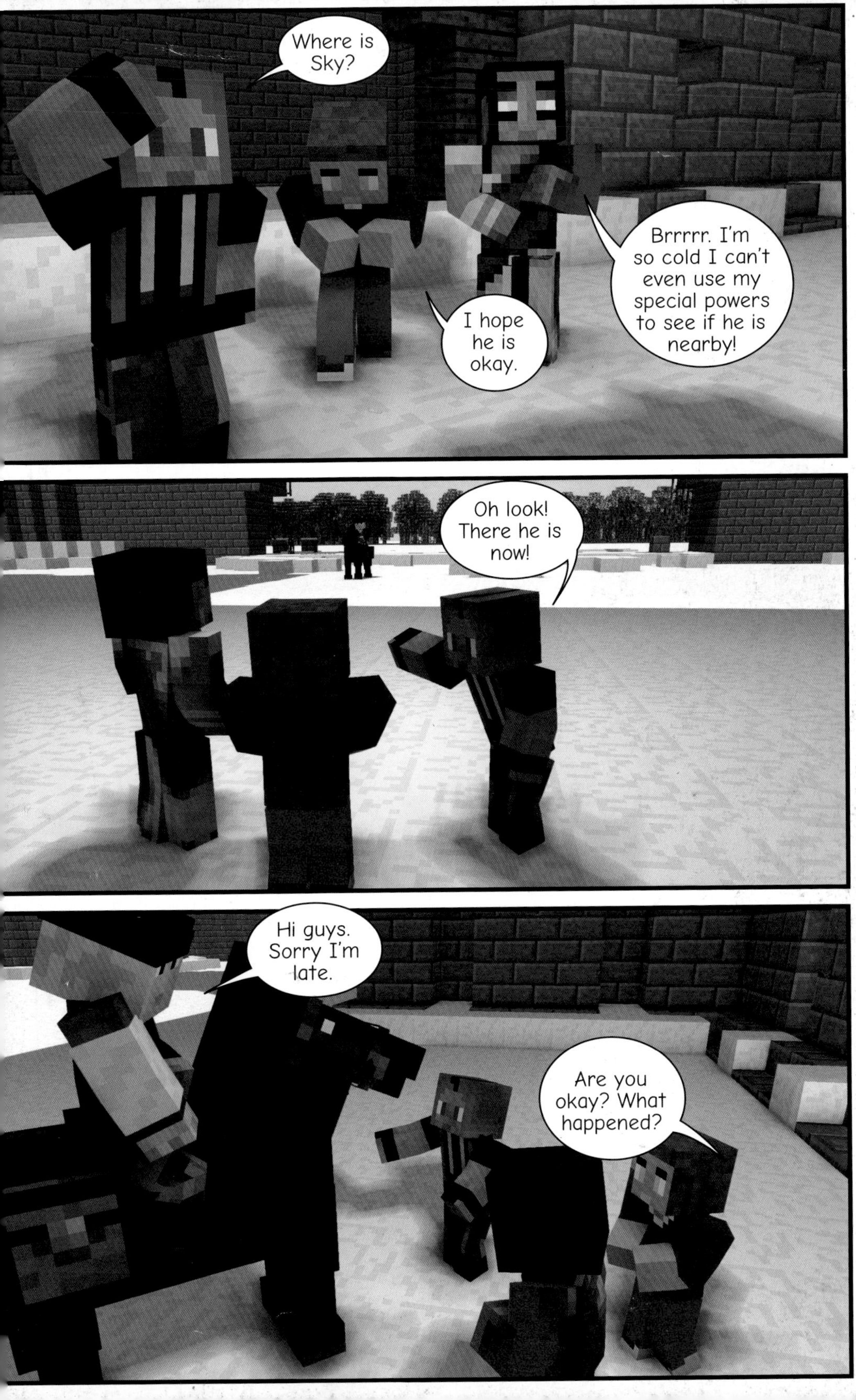
Where is Sky?
Brrrrr. I'm so cold I can't even use my special powers to see if he is nearby!
I hope he is okay.
Oh look! There he is now!
Hi guys. Sorry I'm late.
Are you okay? What happened?

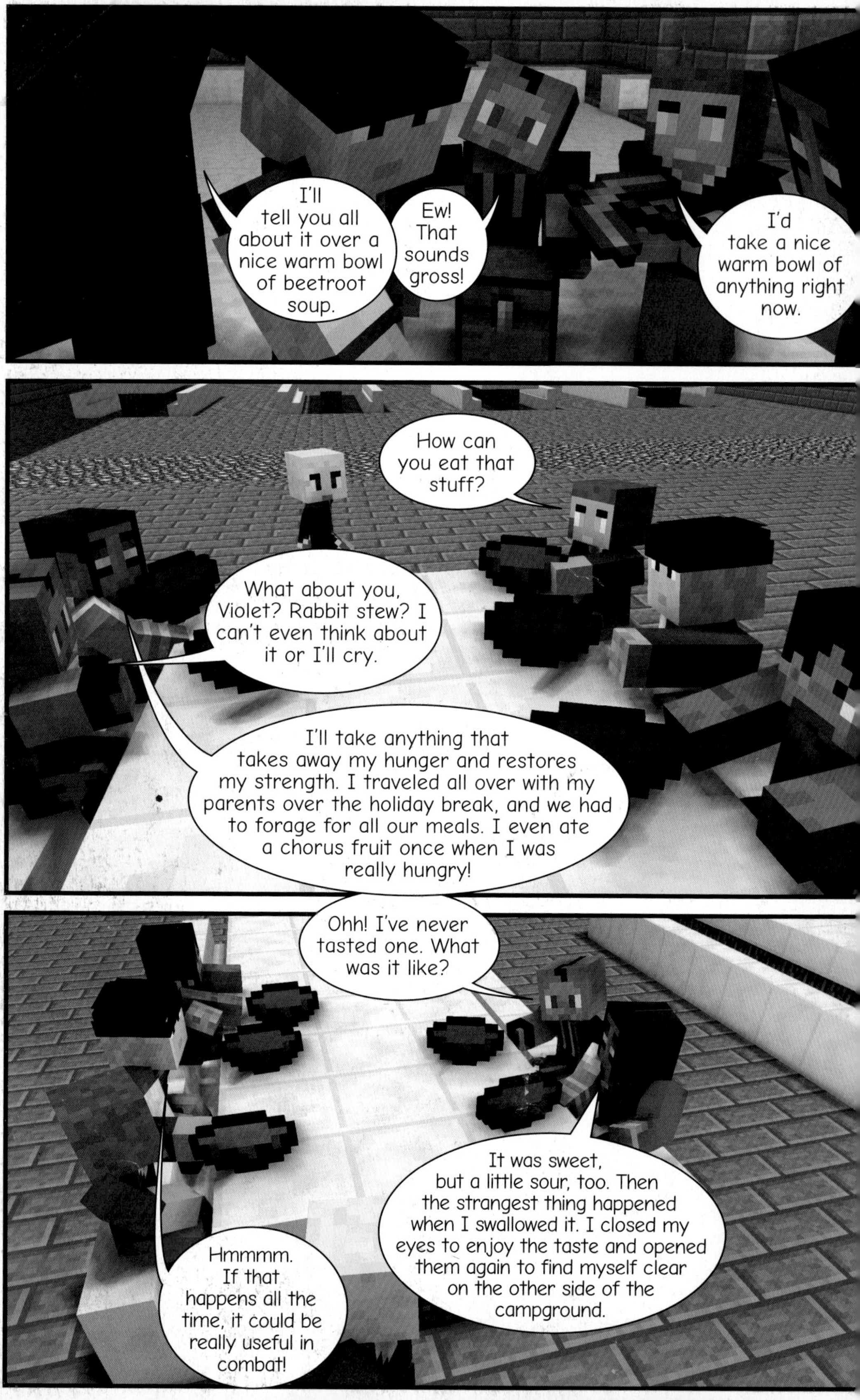
I'll tell you all about it over a nice warm bowl of beetroot soup.
Ew! That sounds gross!
I'd take a nice warm bowl of anything right now.
How can you eat that stuff?
What about you, Violet? Rabbit stew? I can't even think about it or I'll cry.
I'll take anything that takes away my hunger and restores my strength. I traveled all over with my parents over the holiday break, and we had to forage for all our meals. I even ate a chorus fruit once when I was really hungry!
Ohh! I've never tasted one. What was it like?
It was sweet, but a little sour, too. Then the strangest thing happened when I swallowed it. I closed my eyes to enjoy the taste and opened them again to find myself clear on the other side of the campground.
Hmmmm. If that happens all the time, it could be really useful in combat!

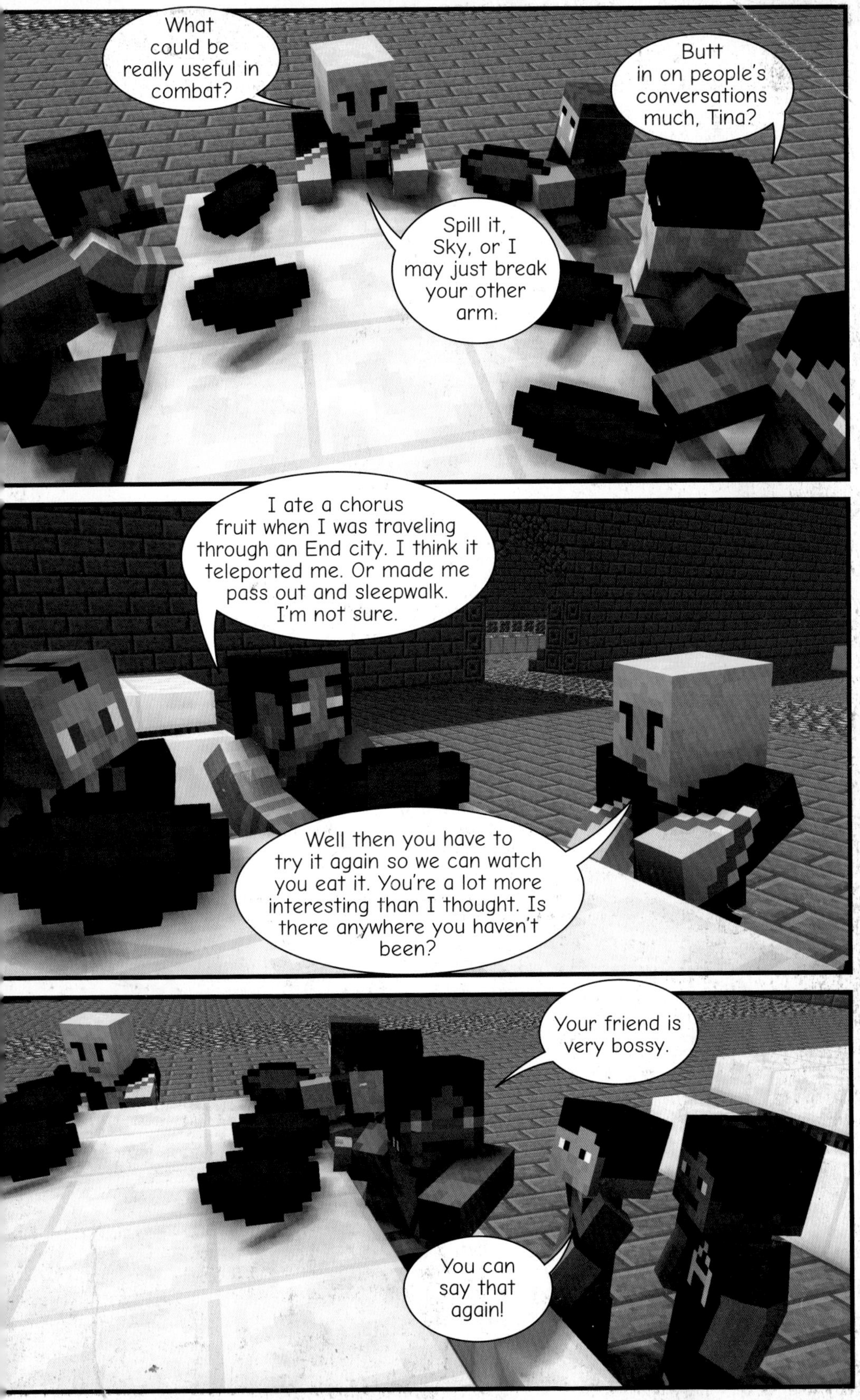
What could be really useful in combat?
Butt in on people's conversations much, Tina?
Spill it, Sky, or I may just break your other arm.
I ate a chorus fruit when I was traveling through an End city. I think it teleported me. Or made me pass out and sleepwalk. I'm not sure.
Well then you have to try it again so we can watch you eat it. You're a lot more interesting than I thought. Is there anywhere you haven't been?
Your friend is very bossy.
You can say that again!

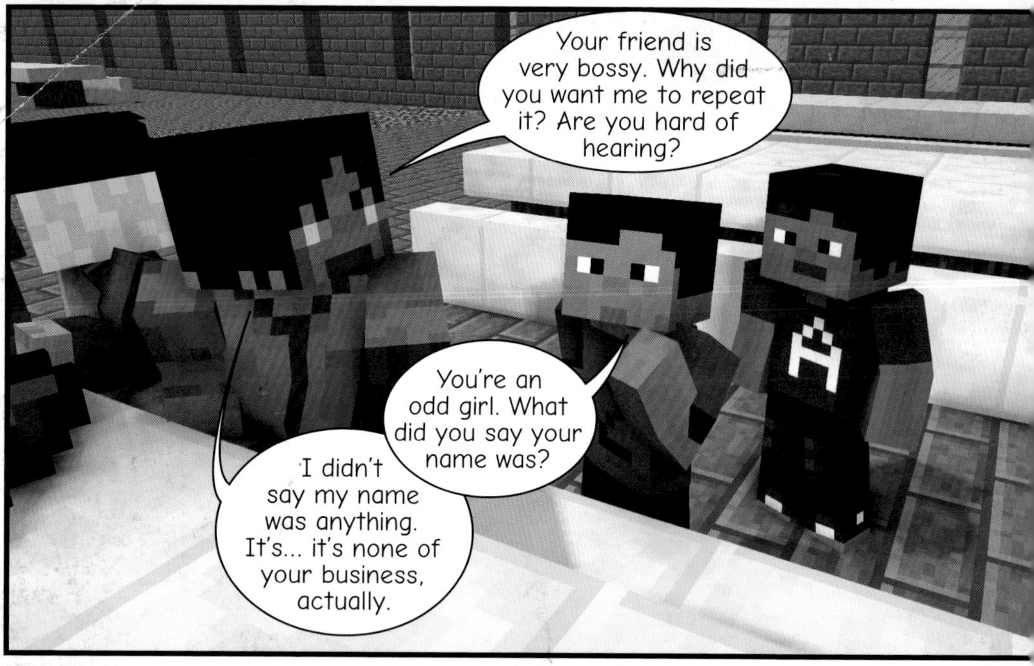
Your friend is very bossy. Why did you want me to repeat it? Are you hard of hearing?
You're an odd girl. What did you say your name was?
I didn't say my name was anything. It's... it's none of your business, actually.

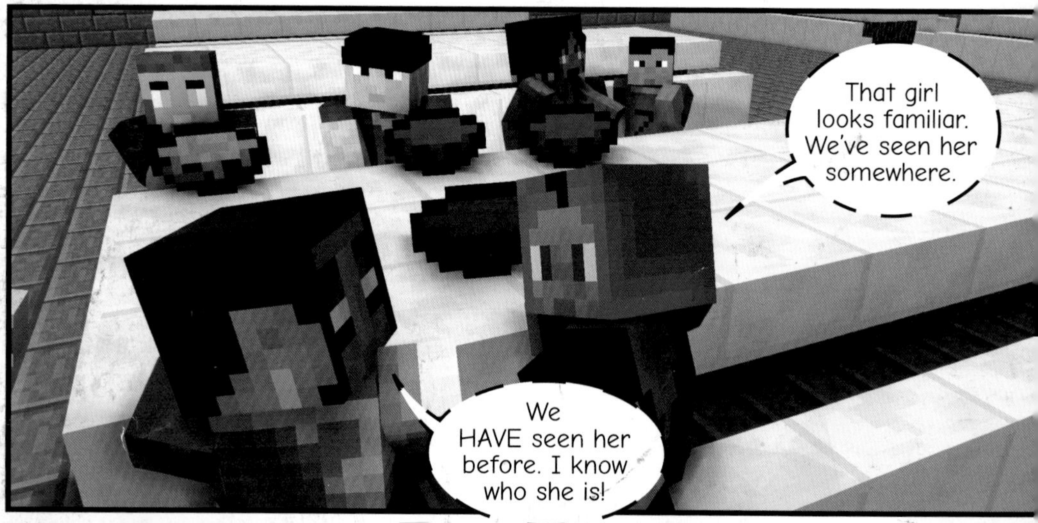
That girl looks familiar. We've seen her somewhere.
We HAVE seen her before. I know who she is!

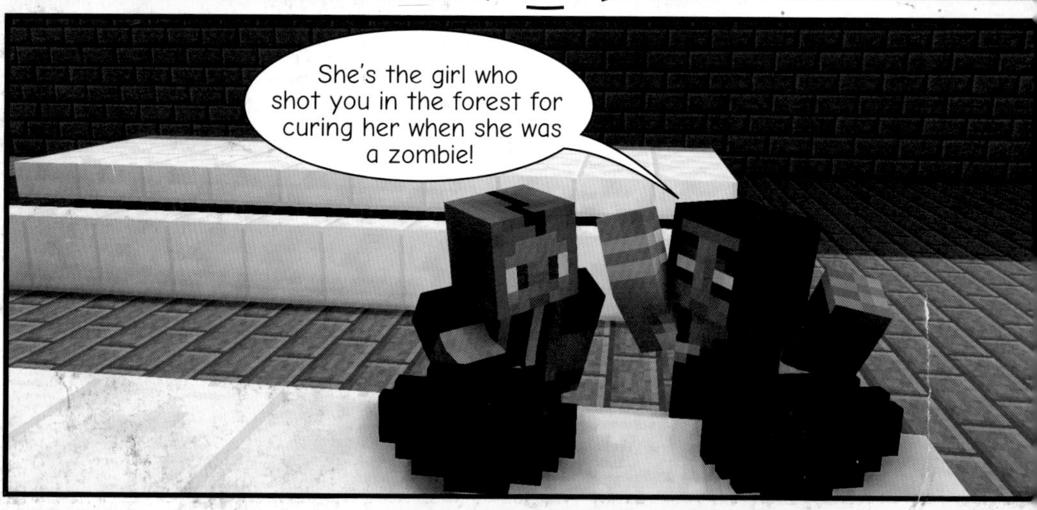
She's the girl who shot you in the forest for curing her when she was a zombie!

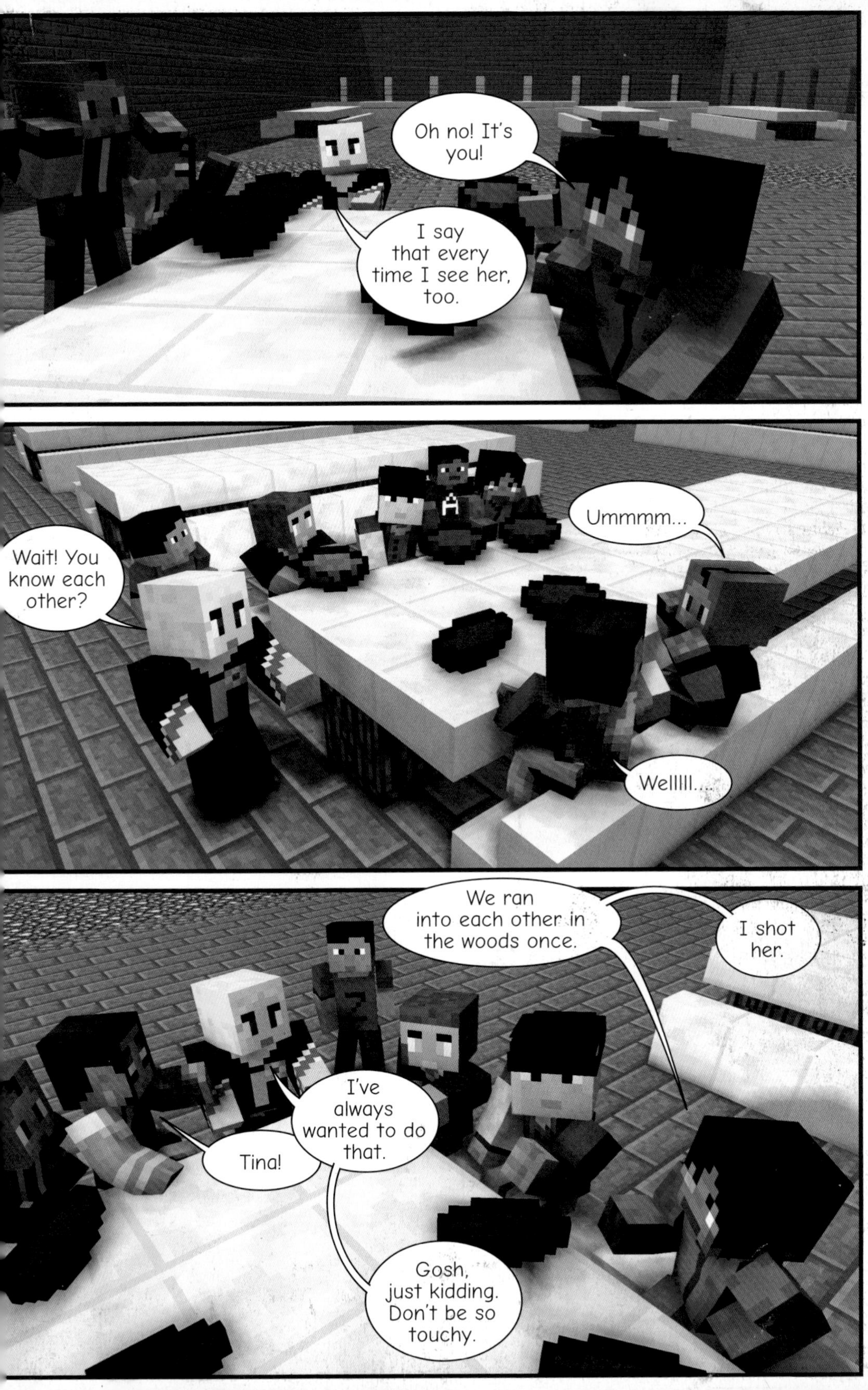
Oh no! It's you!
I say that every time I see her, too.
Wait! You know each other?
Ummmm...
Wellll...
We ran into each other in the woods once.
I shot her.
Tina!
I've always wanted to do that.
Gosh, just kidding. Don't be so touchy.

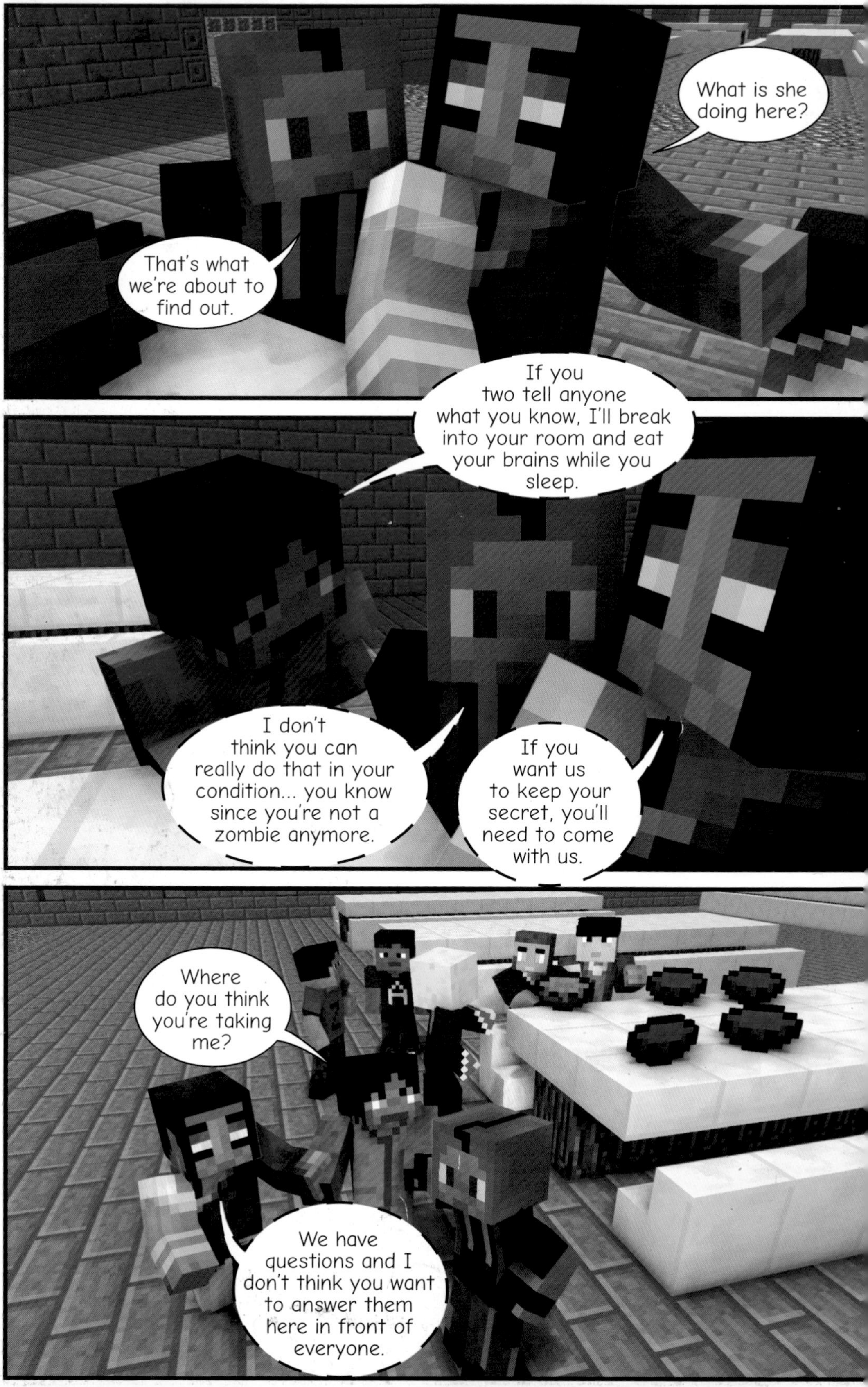
What is she doing here?
That's what we're about to find out.
If you two tell anyone what you know, I'll break into your room and eat your brains while you sleep.
I don't think you can really do that in your condition... you know since you're not a zombie anymore.
If you want us to keep your secret, you'll need to come with us.
Where do you think you're taking me?
We have questions and I don't think you want to answer them here in front of everyone.

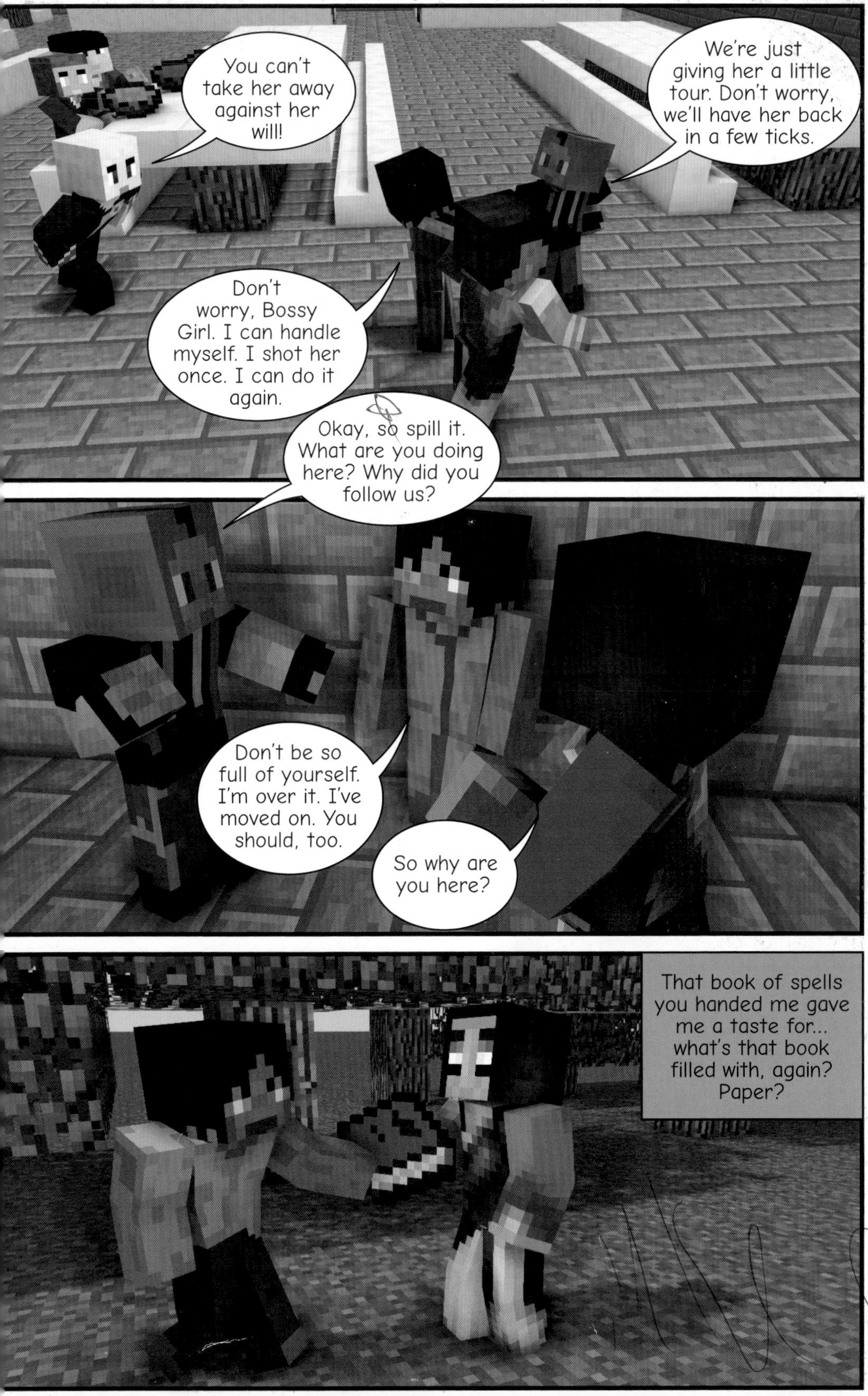
You can't take her away against her will!
We're just giving her a little tour. Don't worry, we'll have her back in a few ticks.
Don't worry, Bossy Girl. I can handle myself. I shot her once. I can do it again.
Okay, so spill it. What are you doing here? Why did you follow us?
Don't be so full of yourself. I'm over it. I've moved on. You should, too.
So why are you here?
That book of spells you handed me gave me a taste for... what's that book filled with, again? Paper?

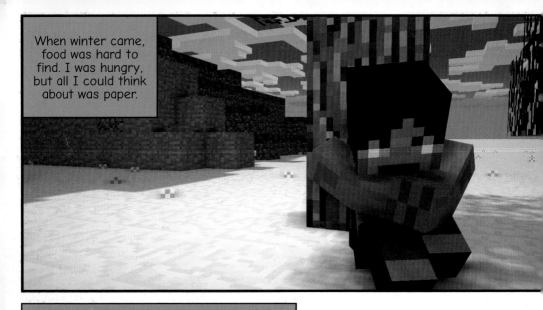

When winter came, food was hard to find. I was hungry, but all I could think about was paper.

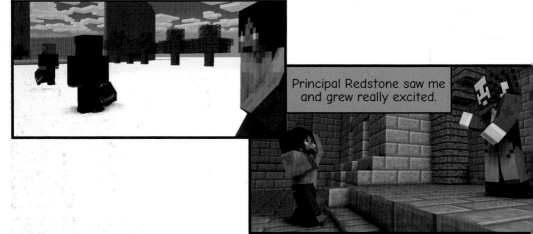

I found some kids who had books with them and followed them to the school.

Principal Redstone saw me and grew really excited.

He said he saw something in me—something special—and he invited me to join the school.

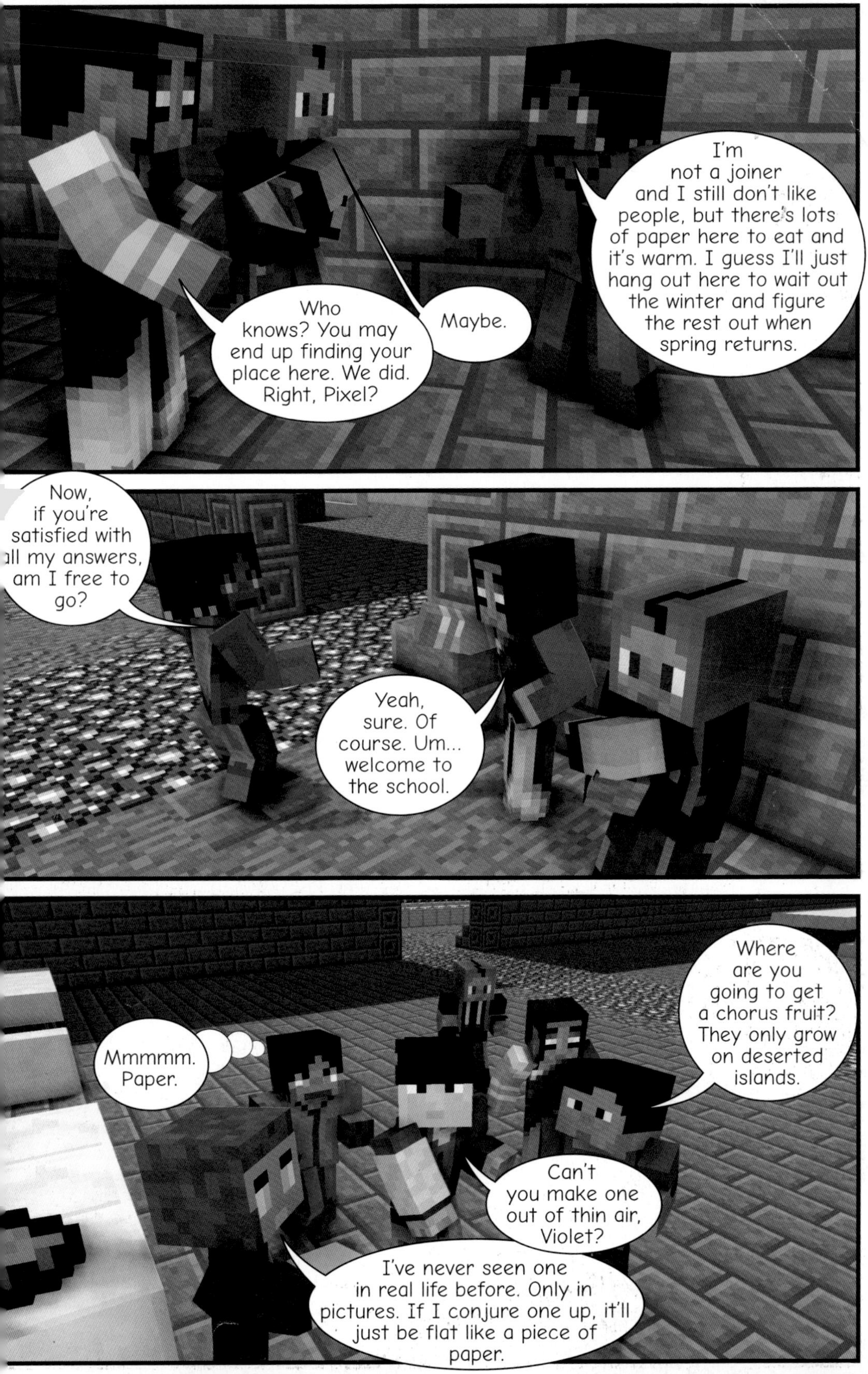

Who knows? You may end up finding your place here. We did. Right, Pixel?
Maybe.
I'm not a joiner and I still don't like people, but there's lots of paper here to eat and it's warm. I guess I'll just hang out here to wait out the winter and figure the rest out when spring returns.
Now, if you're satisfied with all my answers, am I free to go?
Yeah, sure. Of course. Um... welcome to the school.
Mmmmm. Paper.
Where are you going to get a chorus fruit? They only grow on deserted islands.
Can't you make one out of thin air, Violet?
I've never seen one in real life before. Only in pictures. If I conjure one up, it'll just be flat like a piece of paper.

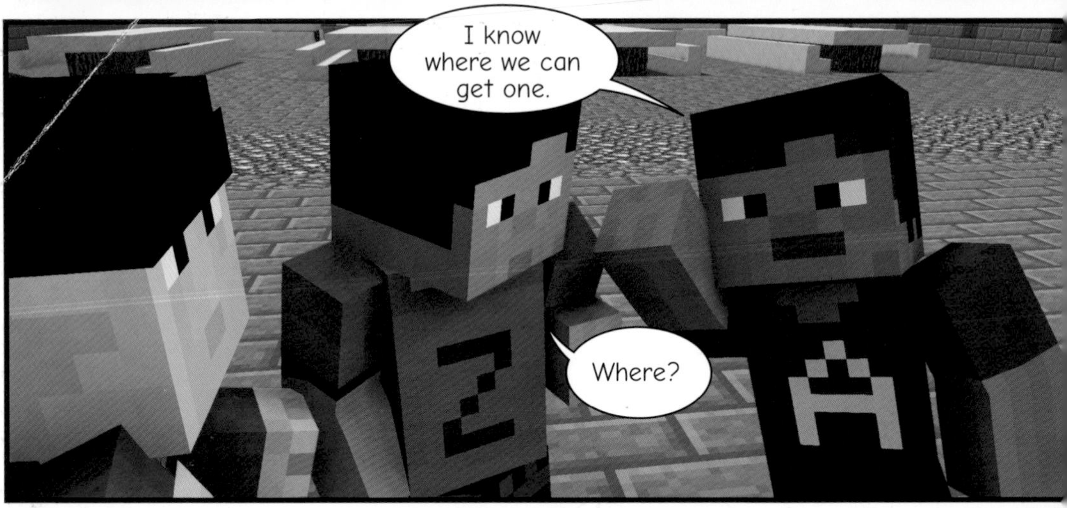
I know where we can get one.
Where?
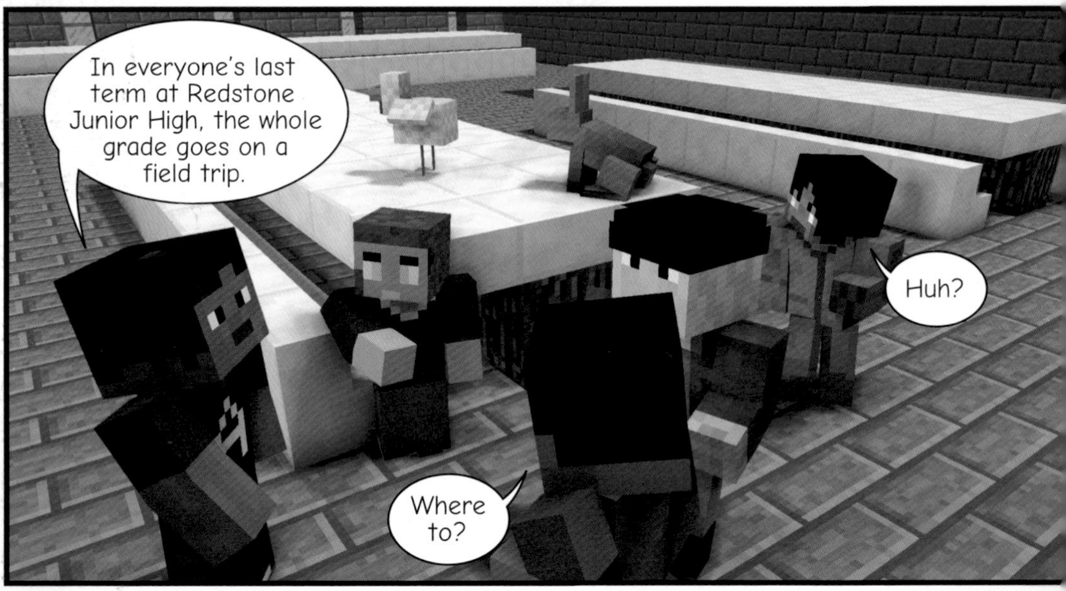
In everyone's last term at Redstone Junior High, the whole grade goes on a field trip.
Huh?
Where to?
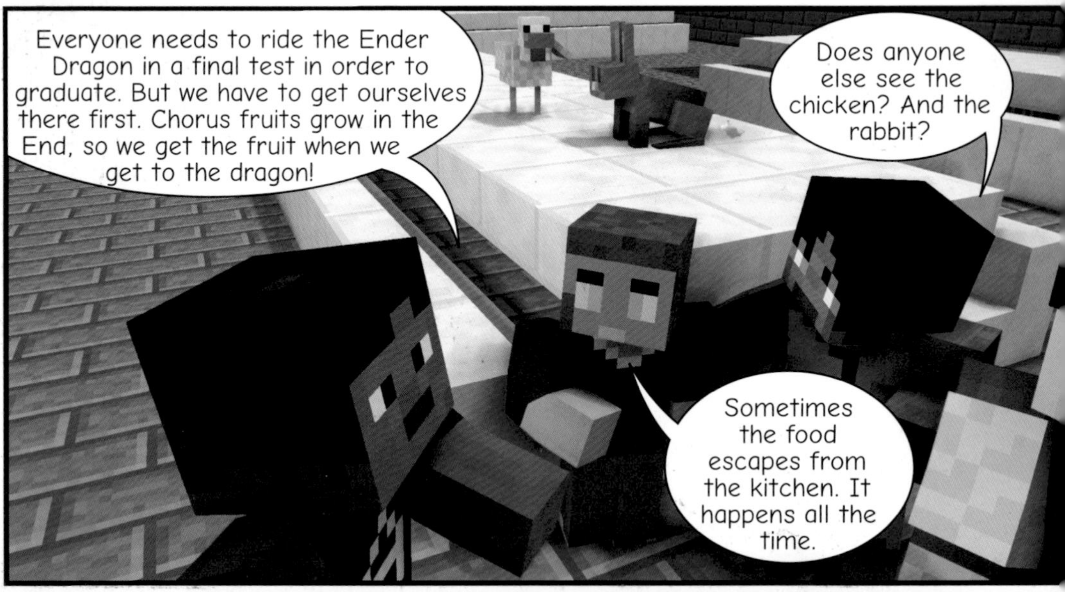
Everyone needs to ride the Ender Dragon in a final test in order to graduate. But we have to get ourselves there first. Chorus fruits grow in the End, so we get the fruit when we get to the dragon!
Does anyone else see the chicken? And the rabbit?
Sometimes the food escapes from the kitchen. It happens all the time.

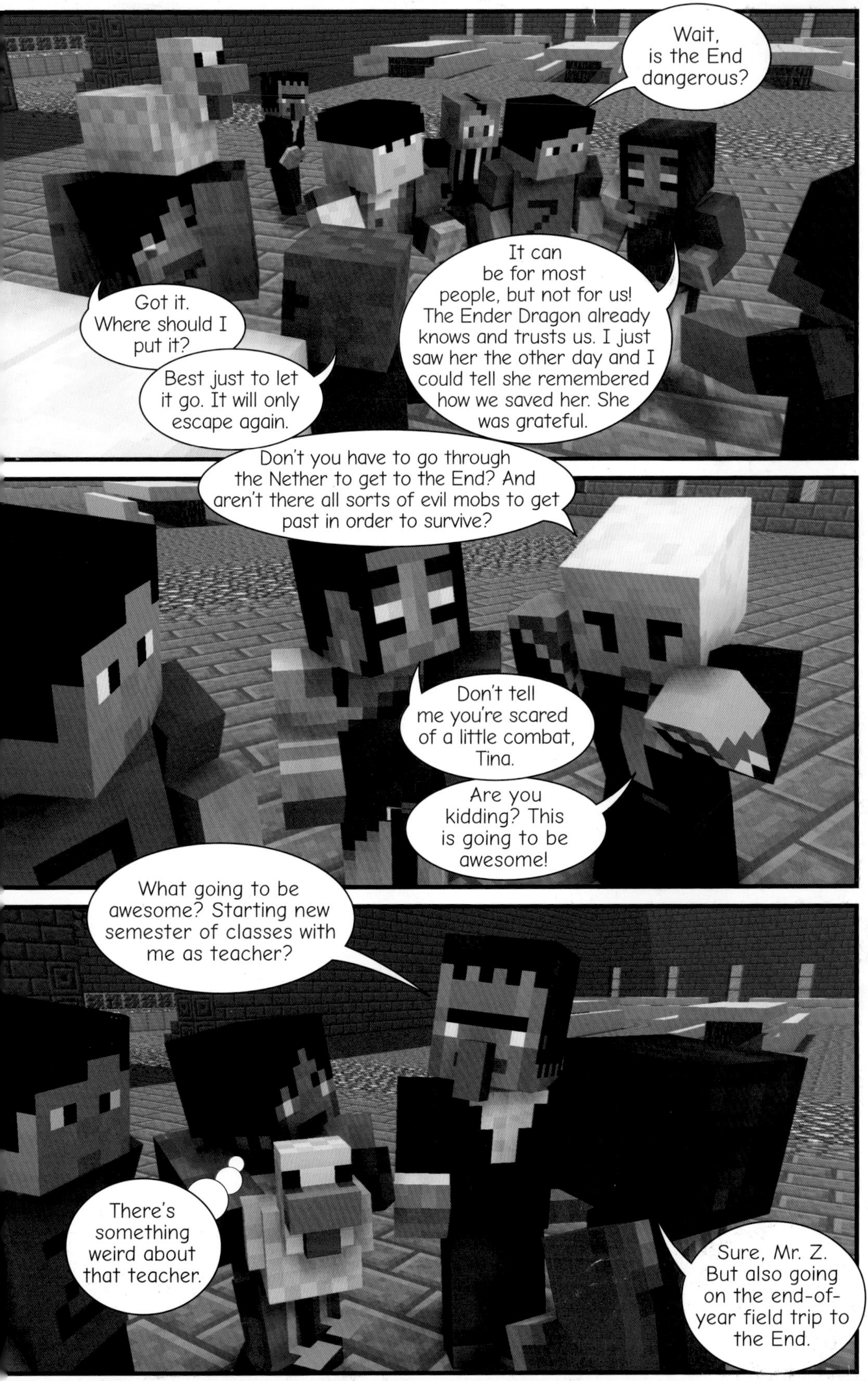
Wait, is the End dangerous?
Got it. Where should I put it?
Best just to let it go. It will only escape again.
It can be for most people, but not for us! The Ender Dragon already knows and trusts us. I just saw her the other day and I could tell she remembered how we saved her. She was grateful.
Don't you have to go through the Nether to get to the End? And aren't there all sorts of evil mobs to get past in order to survive?
Don't tell me you're scared of a little combat, Tina.
Are you kidding? This is going to be awesome!
What going to be awesome? Starting new semester of classes with me as teacher?
There's something weird about that teacher.
Sure, Mr. Z. But also going on the end-of-year field trip to the End.

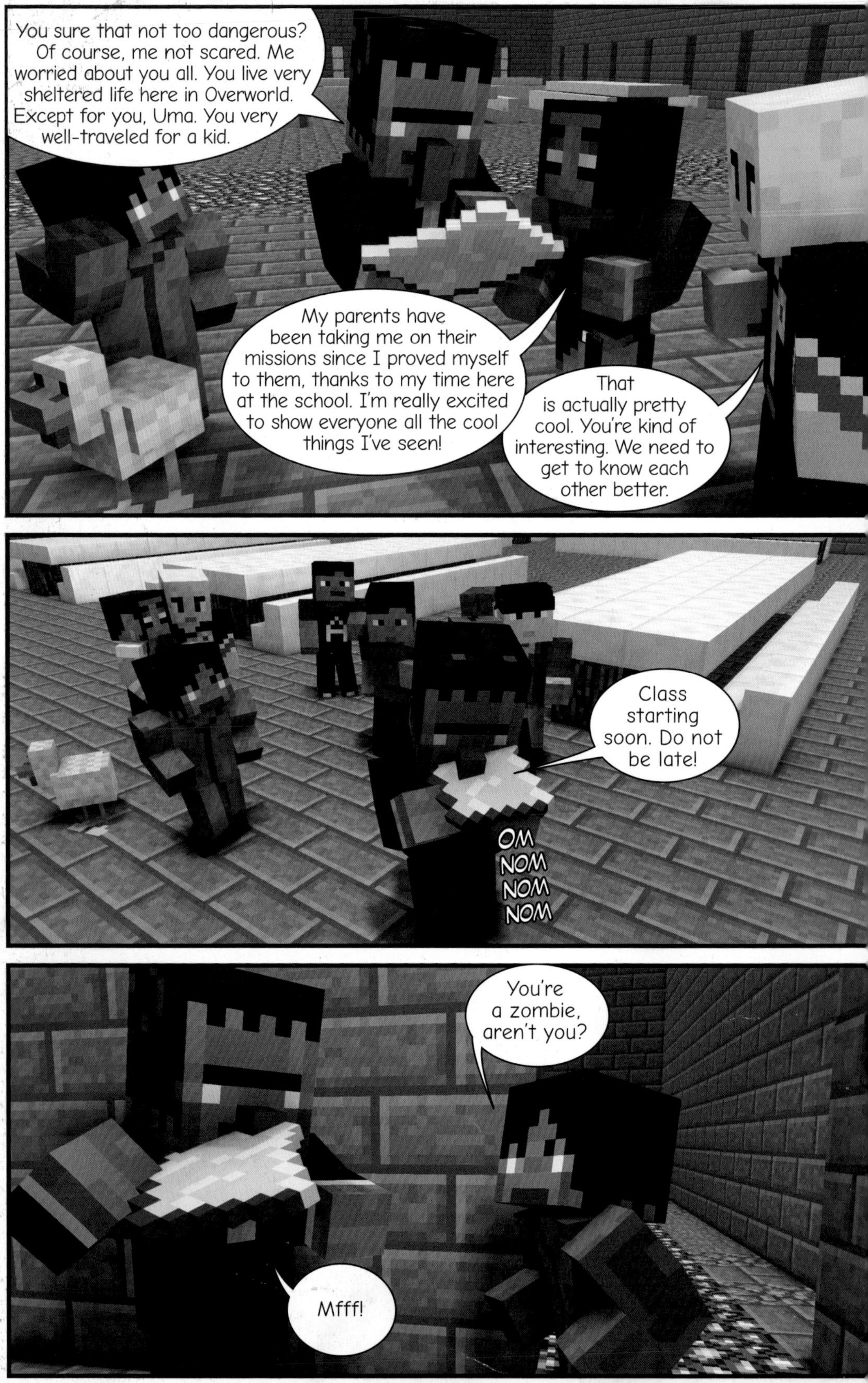
You sure that not too dangerous? Of course, me not scared. Me worried about you all. You live very sheltered life here in Overworld. Except for you, Uma. You very well-traveled for a kid.
My parents have been taking me on their missions since I proved myself to them, thanks to my time here at the school. I'm really excited to show everyone all the cool things I've seen!
That is actually pretty cool. You're kind of interesting. We need to get to know each other better.
Class starting soon. Do not be late!
OM NOM NOM NOM
You're a zombie, aren't you?
Mfff!

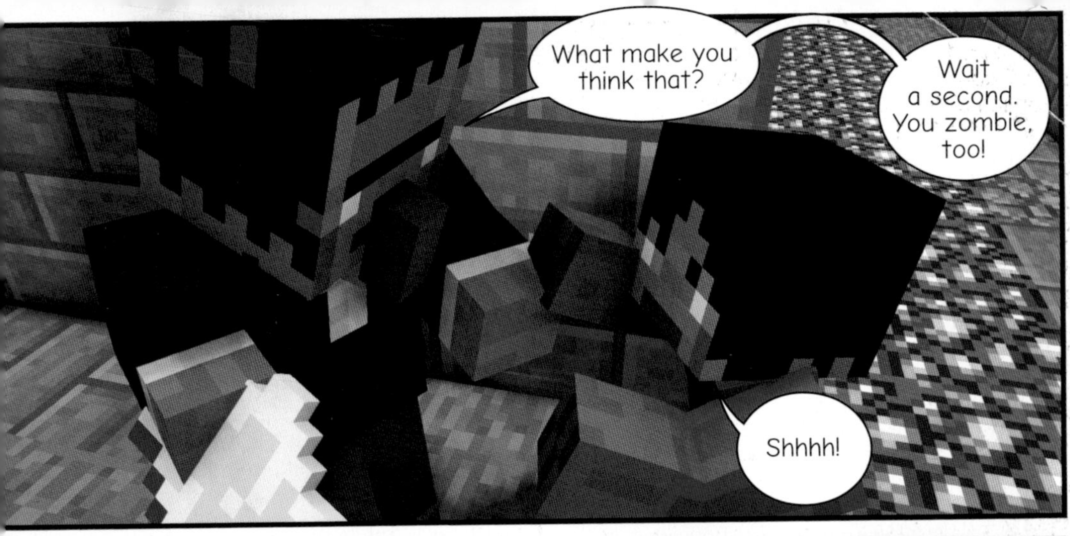
Wait a second. You zombie, too!
What make you think that?
Shhhh!

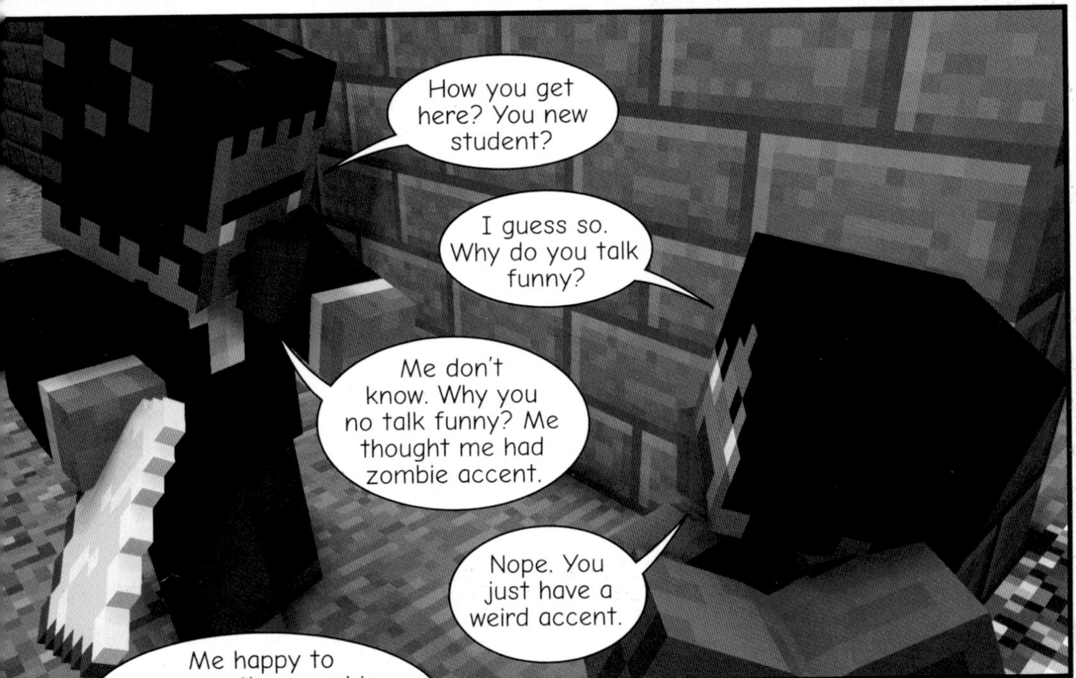
How you get here? You new student?
I guess so. Why do you talk funny?
Me don't know. Why you no talk funny? Me thought me had zombie accent.
Nope. You just have a weird accent.

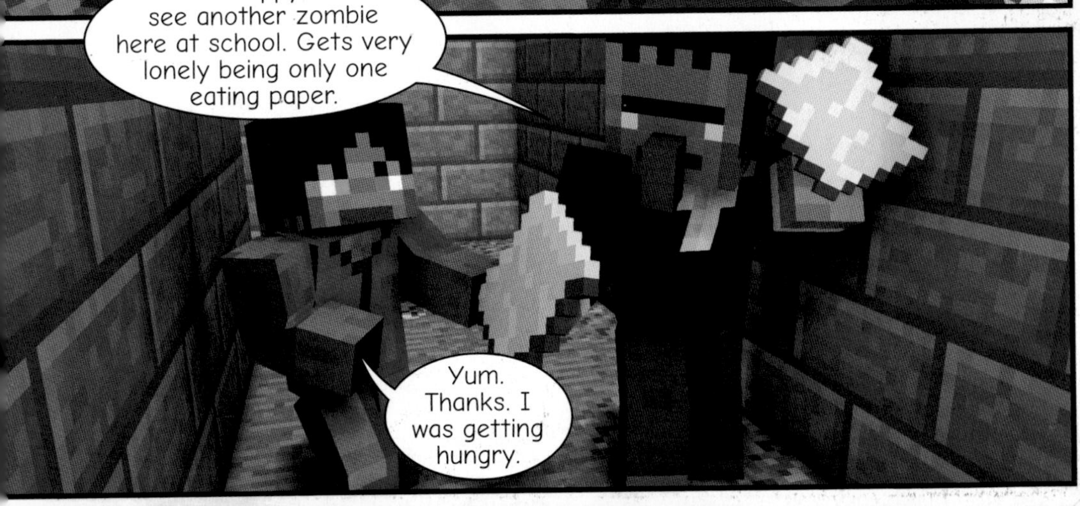
Me happy to see another zombie here at school. Gets very lonely being only one eating paper.
Yum. Thanks. I was getting hungry.

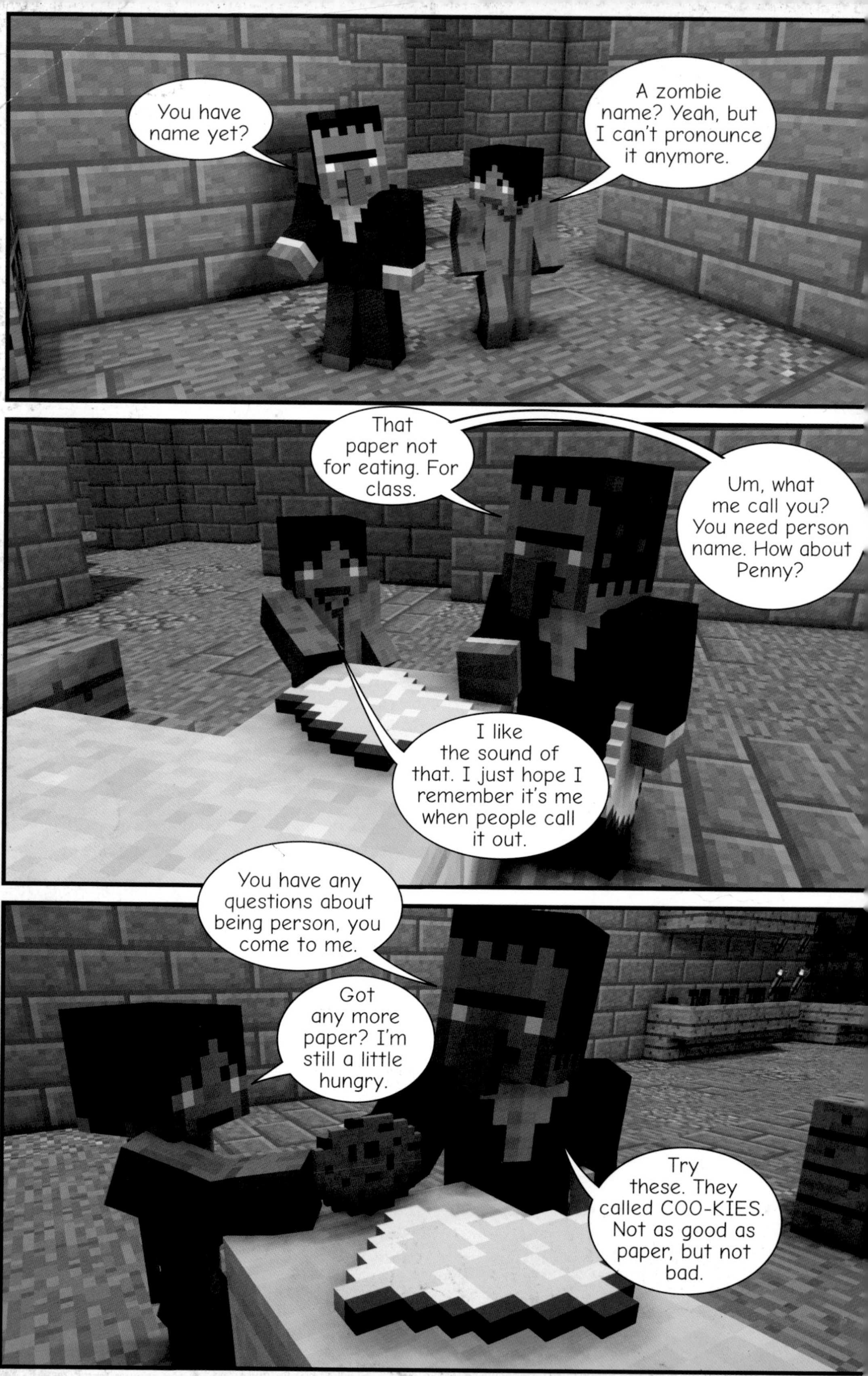
You have name yet?
A zombie name? Yeah, but I can't pronounce it anymore.
That paper not for eating. For class.
Um, what me call you? You need person name. How about Penny?
I like the sound of that. I just hope I remember it's me when people call it out.
You have any questions about being person, you come to me.
Got any more paper? I'm still a little hungry.
Try these. They called COO-KIES. Not as good as paper, but not bad.

CHAPTER 2

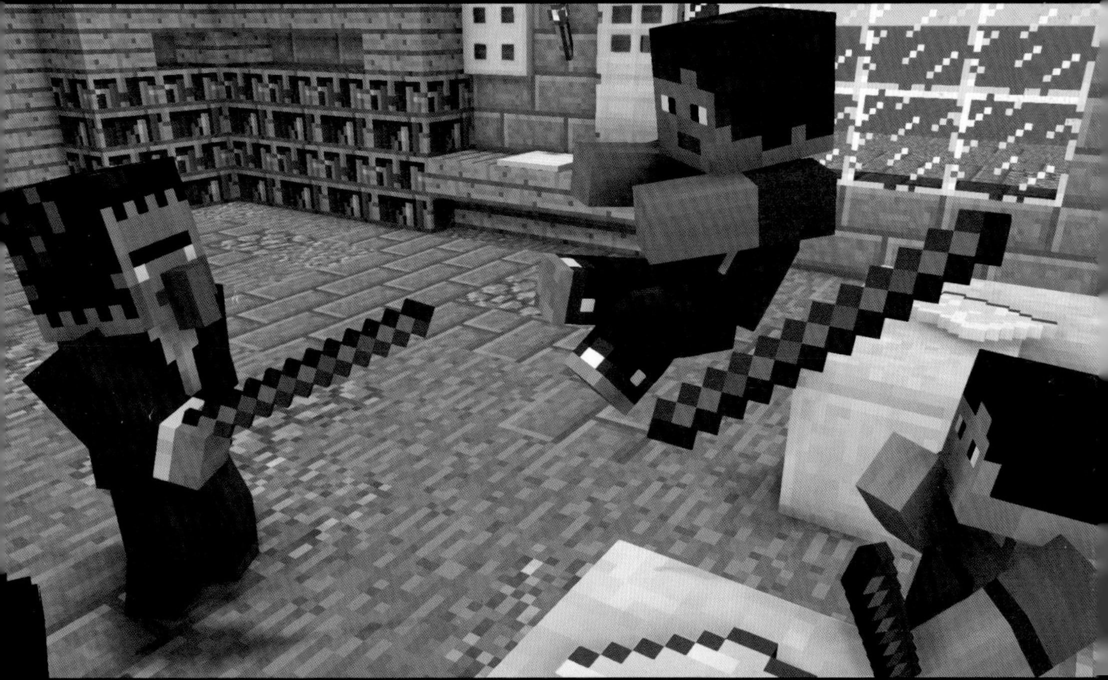

KNOCKBACK

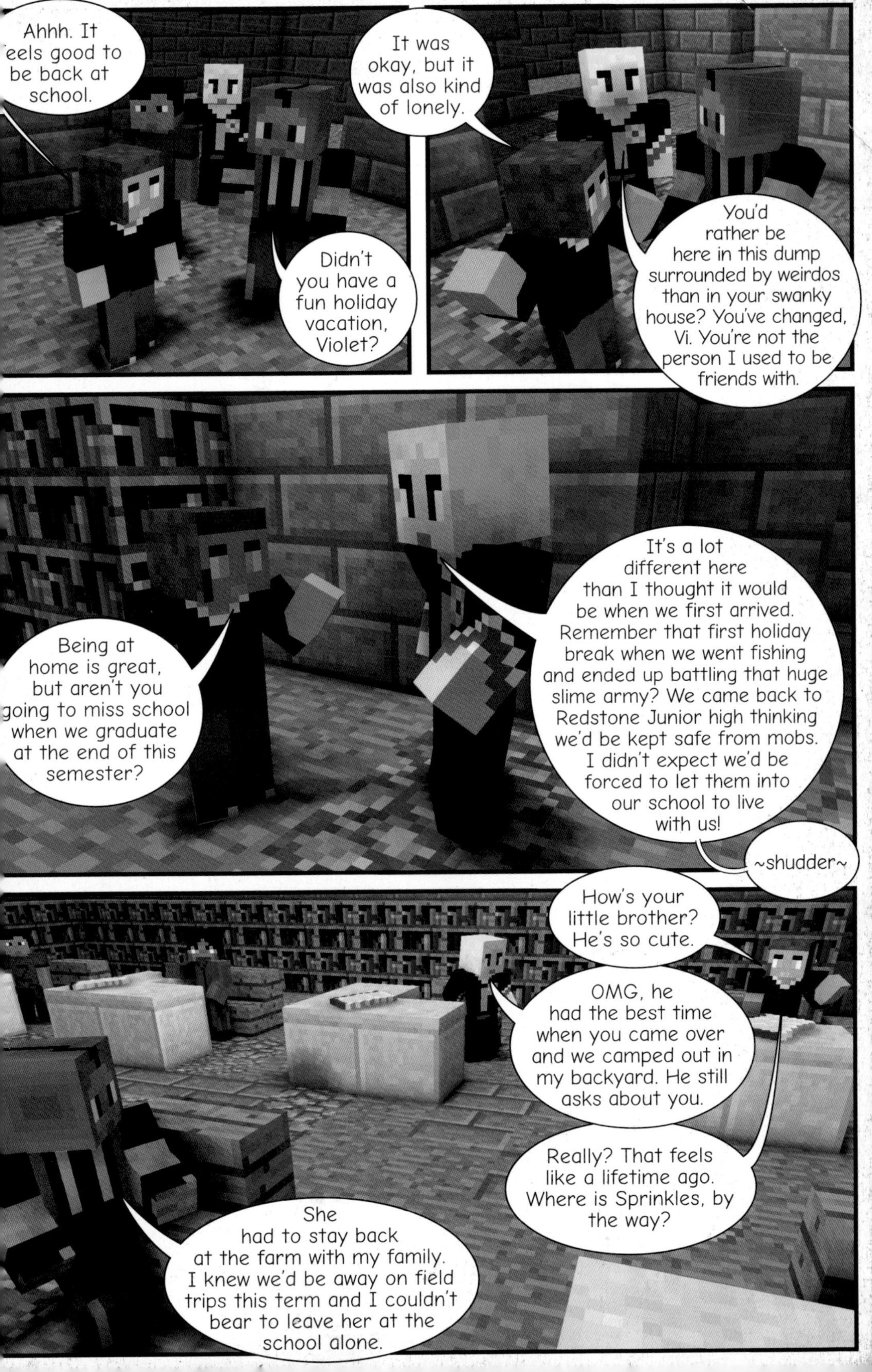
Ahhh. It feels good to be back at school.
Didn't you have a fun holiday vacation, Violet?
It was okay, but it was also kind of lonely.
You'd rather be here in this dump surrounded by weirdos than in your swanky house? You've changed, Vi. You're not the person I used to be friends with.
Being at home is great, but aren't you going to miss school when we graduate at the end of this semester?
It's a lot different here than I thought it would be when we first arrived. Remember that first holiday break when we went fishing and ended up battling that huge slime army? We came back to Redstone Junior high thinking we'd be kept safe from mobs. I didn't expect we'd be forced to let them into our school to live with us!
~shudder~
How's your little brother? He's so cute.
OMG, he had the best time when you came over and we camped out in my backyard. He still asks about you.
Really? That feels like a lifetime ago. Where is Sprinkles, by the way?
She had to stay back at the farm with my family. I knew we'd be away on field trips this term and I couldn't bear to leave her at the school alone.

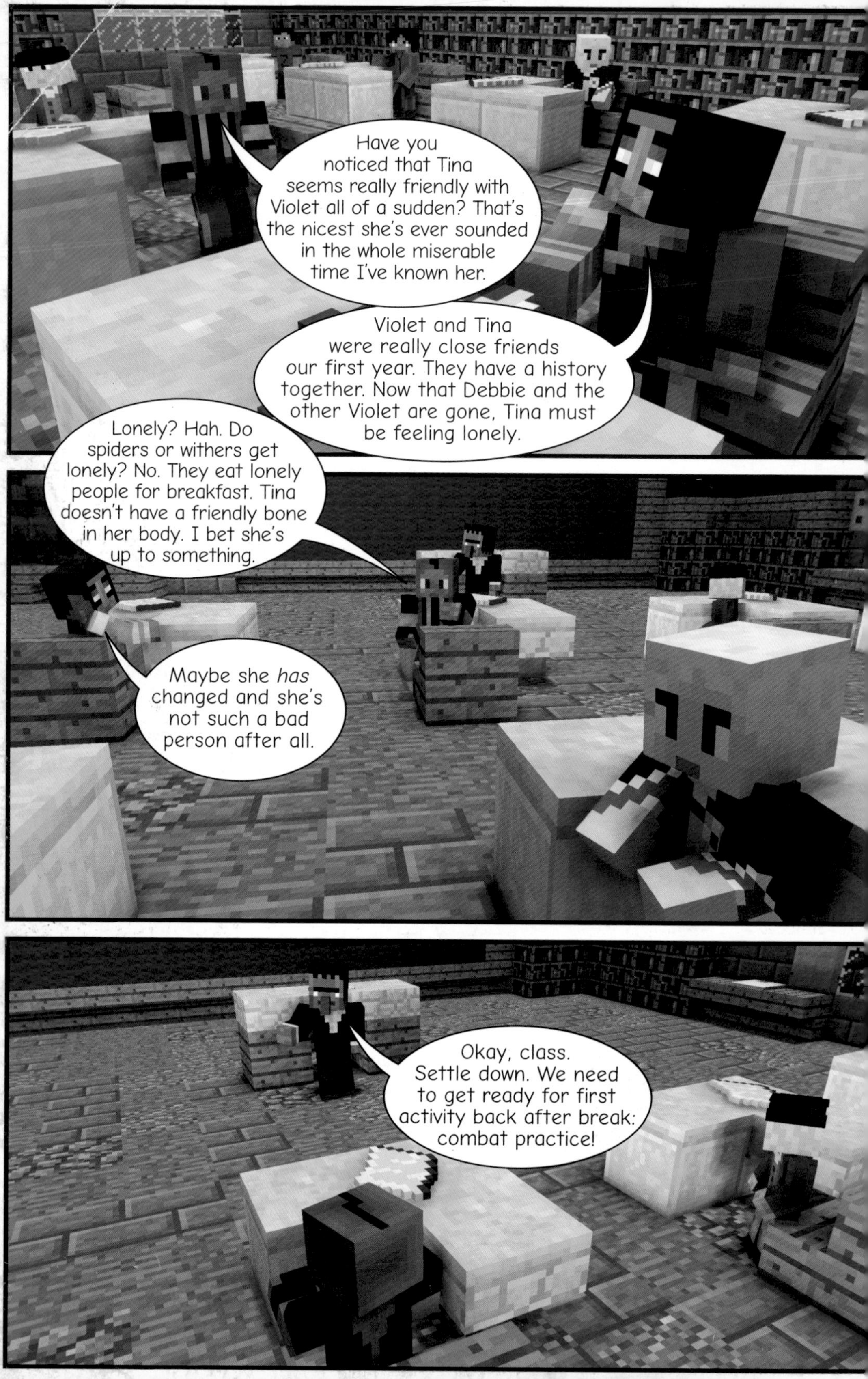
Have you noticed that Tina seems really friendly with Violet all of a sudden? That's the nicest she's ever sounded in the whole miserable time I've known her.
Violet and Tina were really close friends our first year. They have a history together. Now that Debbie and the other Violet are gone, Tina must be feeling lonely.
Lonely? Hah. Do spiders or withers get lonely? No. They eat lonely people for breakfast. Tina doesn't have a friendly bone in her body. I bet she's up to something.
Maybe she *has* changed and she's not such a bad person after all.
Okay, class. Settle down. We need to get ready for first activity back after break: combat practice!

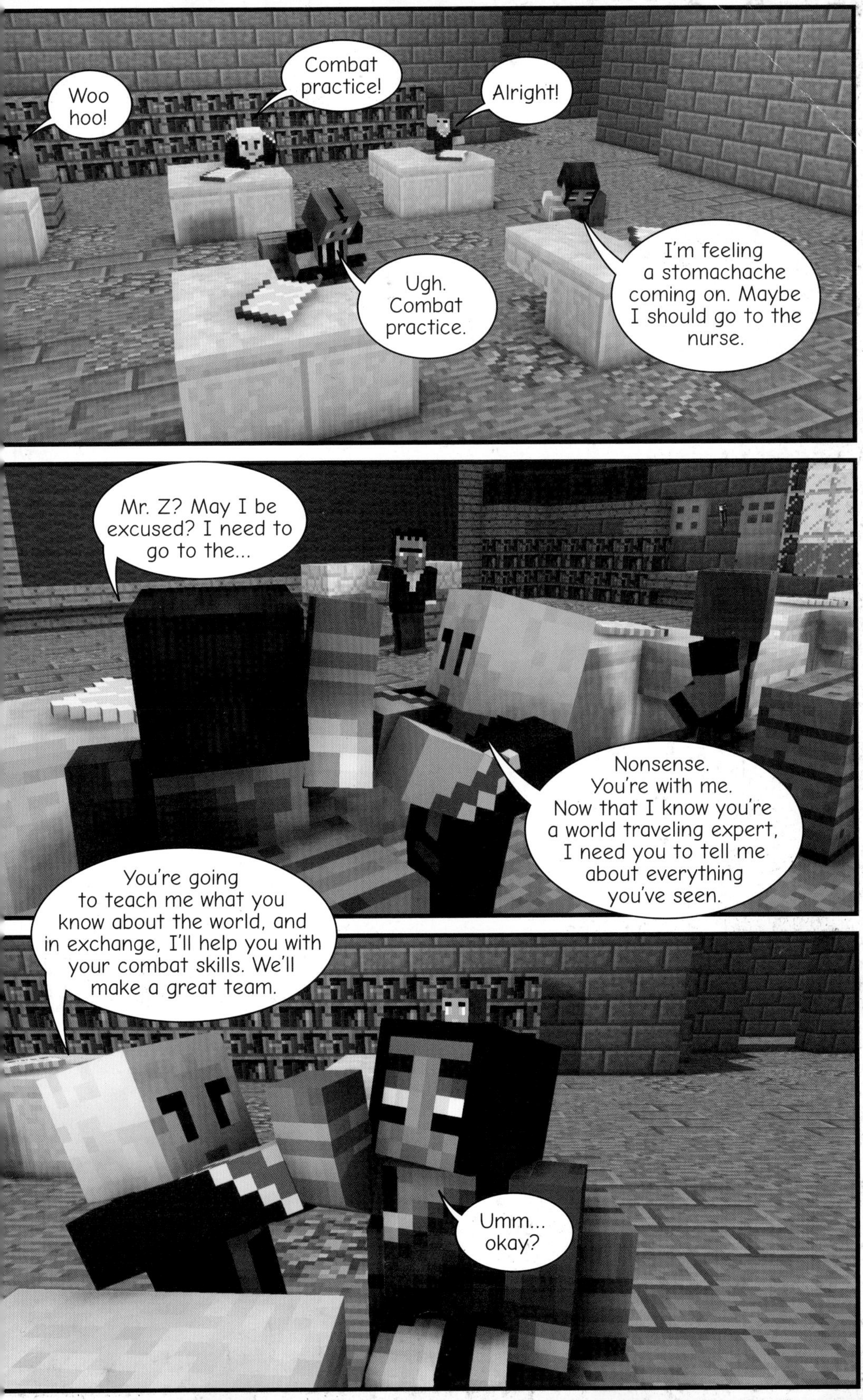
Woo hoo!
Combat practice!
Alright!
Ugh. Combat practice.
I'm feeling a stomachache coming on. Maybe I should go to the nurse.
Mr. Z? May I be excused? I need to go to the...
Nonsense. You're with me. Now that I know you're a world traveling expert, I need you to tell me about everything you've seen.
You're going to teach me what you know about the world, and in exchange, I'll help you with your combat skills. We'll make a great team.
Umm... okay?

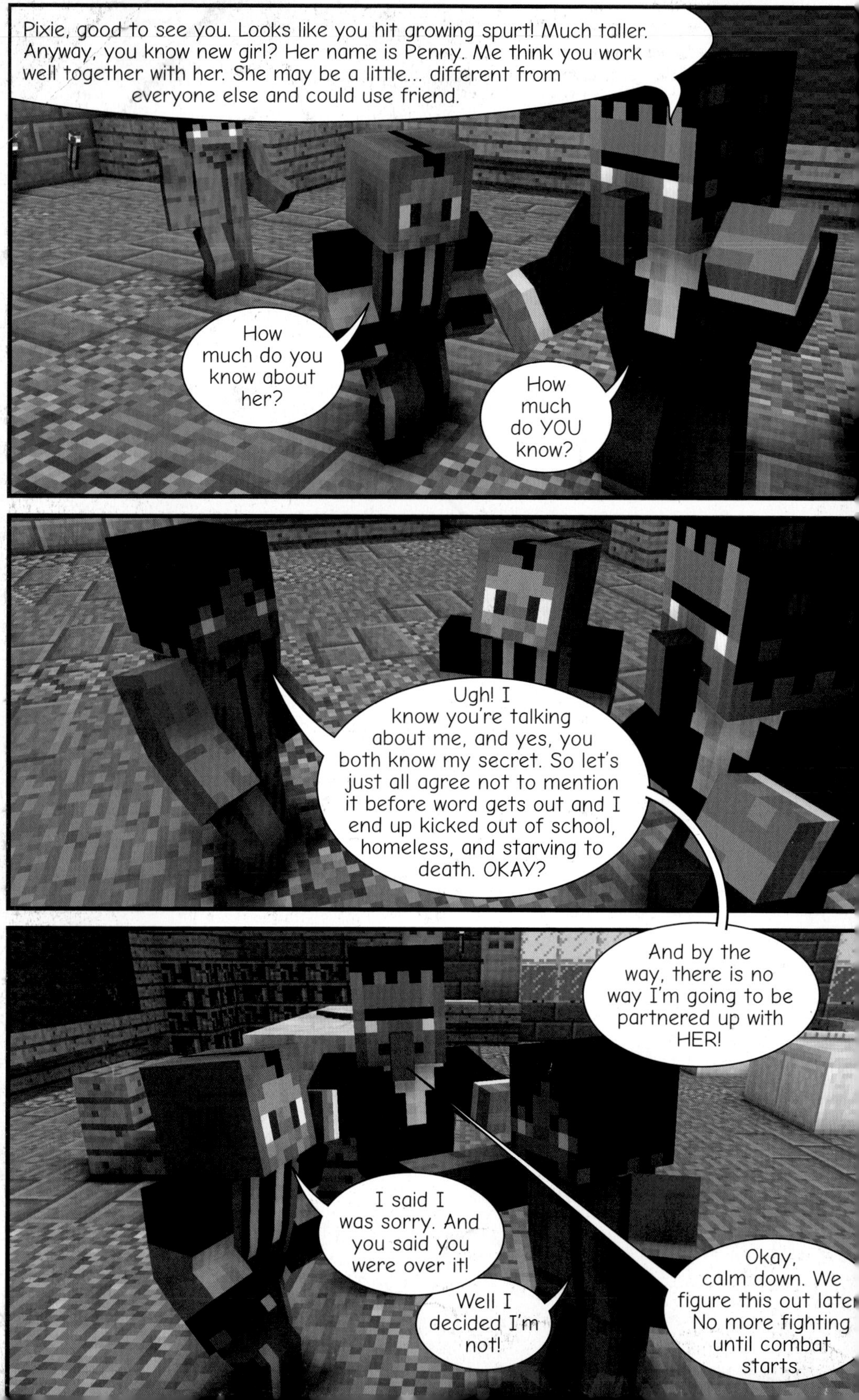
Pixie, good to see you. Looks like you hit growing spurt! Much taller. Anyway, you know new girl? Her name is Penny. Me think you work well together with her. She may be a little... different from everyone else and could use friend.
How much do you know about her?
How much do YOU know?
Ugh! I know you're talking about me, and yes, you both know my secret. So let's just all agree not to mention it before word gets out and I end up kicked out of school, homeless, and starving to death. OKAY?
And by the way, there is no way I'm going to be partnered up with HER!
I said I was sorry. And you said you were over it!
Well I decided I'm not!
Okay, calm down. We figure this out later. No more fighting until combat starts.

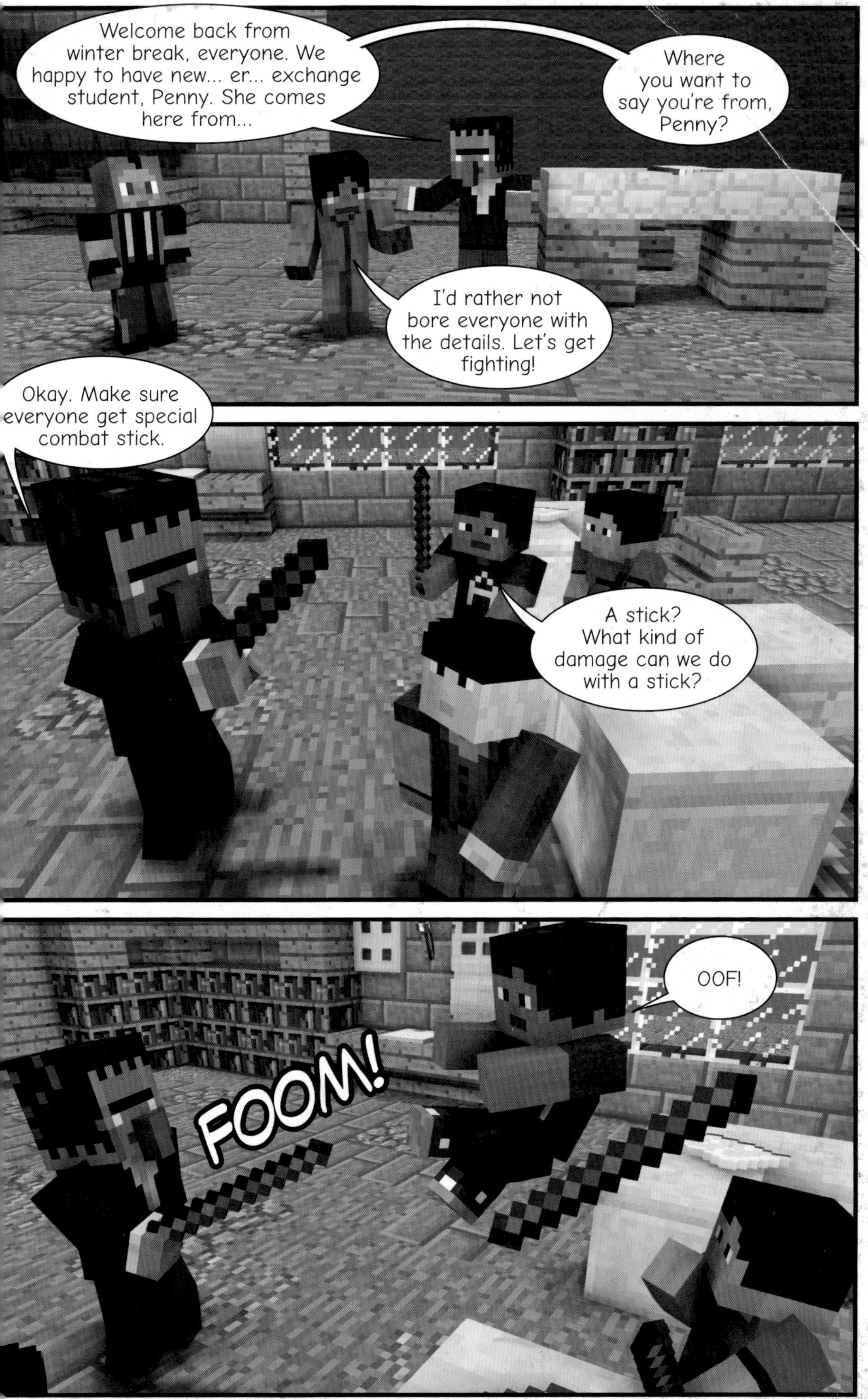
Welcome back from winter break, everyone. We happy to have new... er... exchange student, Penny. She comes here from...
Where you want to say you're from, Penny?
I'd rather not bore everyone with the details. Let's get fighting!
Okay. Make sure everyone get special combat stick.
A stick? What kind of damage can we do with a stick?
FOOM!
OOF!

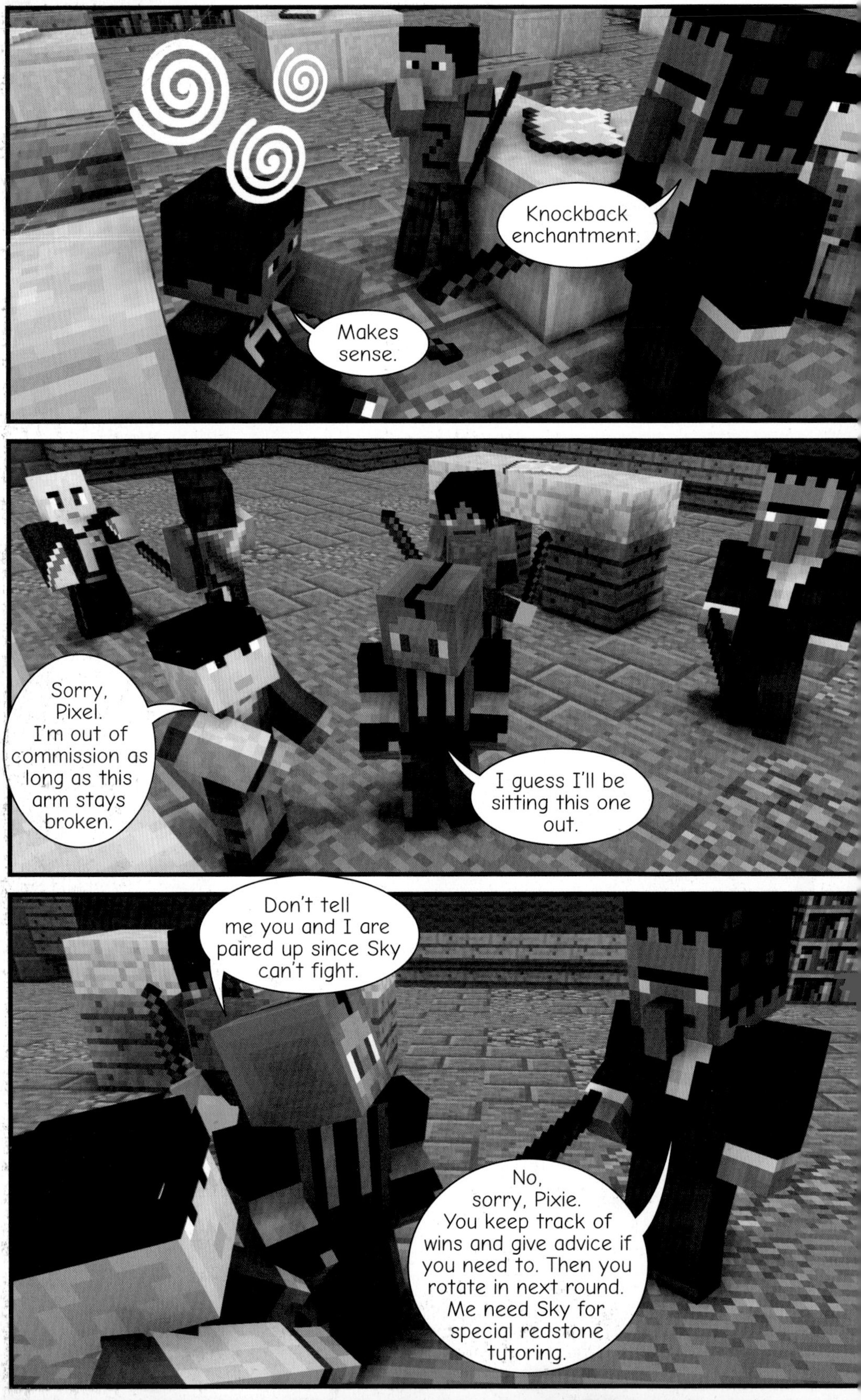
Knockback enchantment.
Makes sense.
Sorry, Pixel. I'm out of commission as long as this arm stays broken.
I guess I'll be sitting this one out.
Don't tell me you and I are paired up since Sky can't fight.
No, sorry, Pixie. You keep track of wins and give advice if you need to. Then you rotate in next round. Me need Sky for special redstone tutoring.

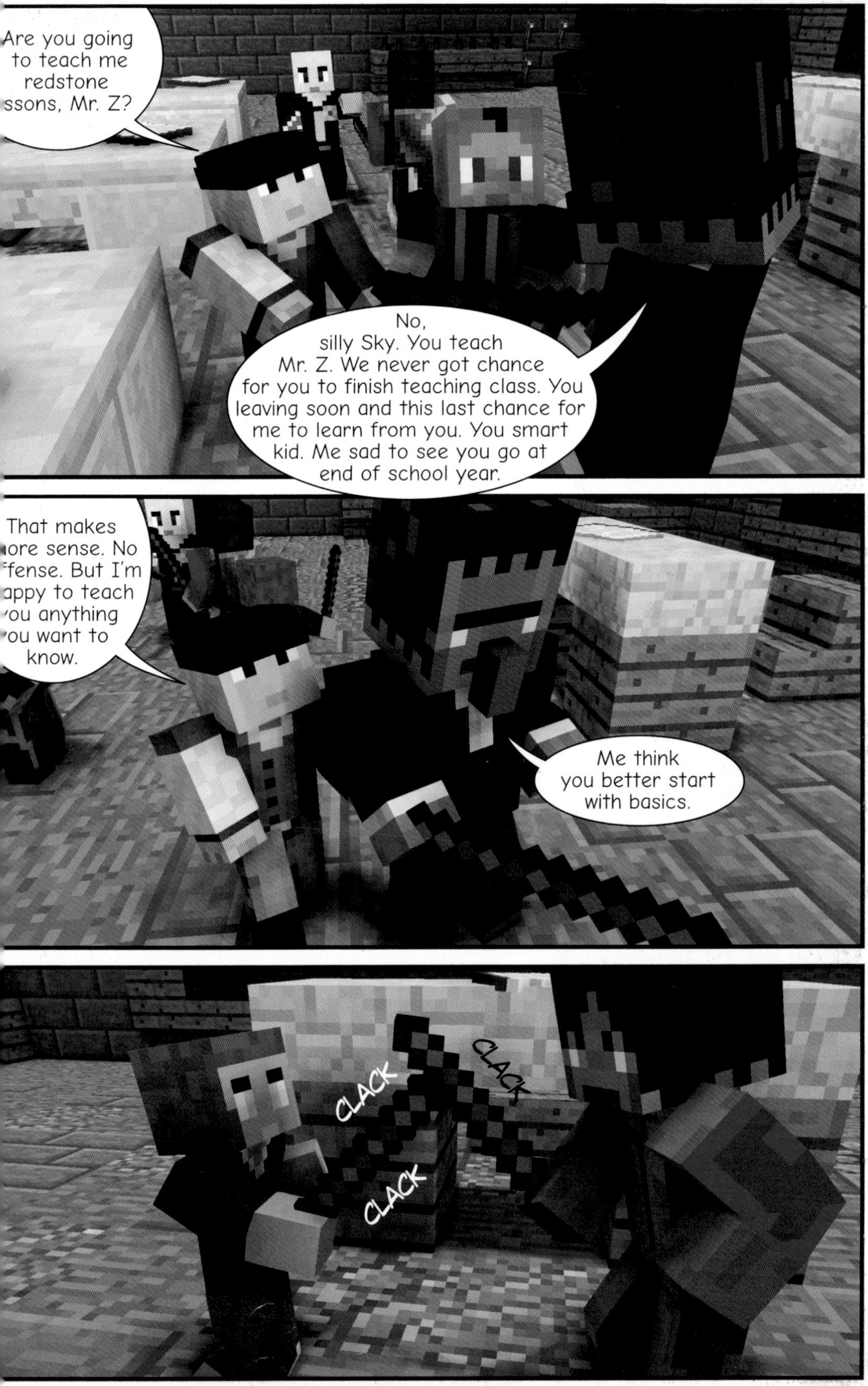
Are you going to teach me redstone ssons, Mr. Z?
No, silly Sky. You teach Mr. Z. We never got chance for you to finish teaching class. You leaving soon and this last chance for me to learn from you. You smart kid. Me sad to see you go at end of school year.
That makes ore sense. No fense. But I'm appy to teach ou anything ou want to know.
Me think you better start with basics.
CLACK
CLACK
CLACK

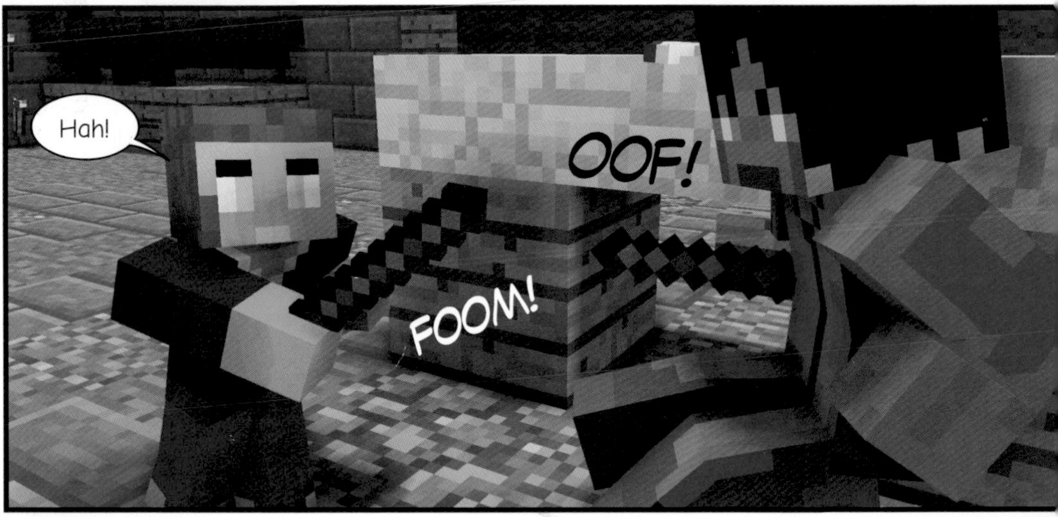
Hah!
OOF!
FOOM!
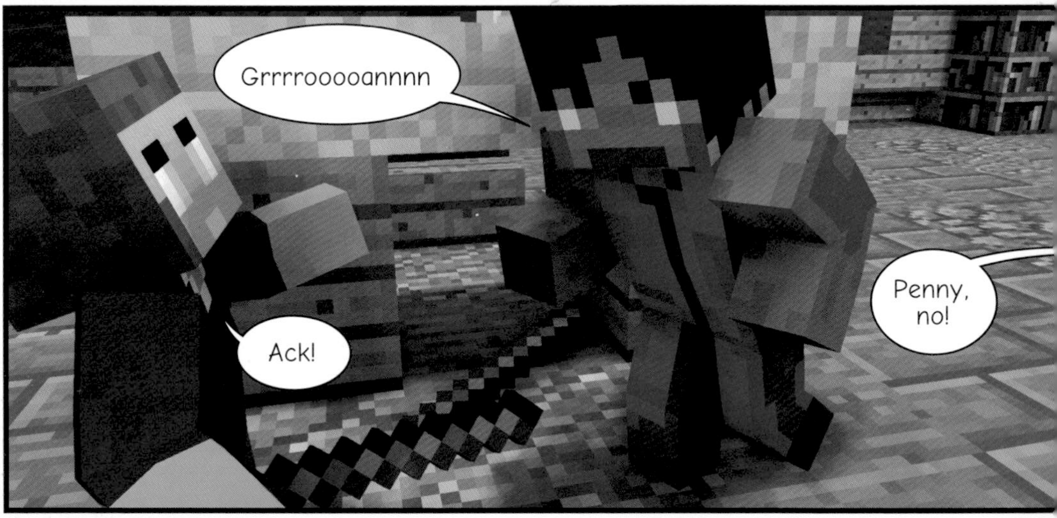
Grrrroooooannnn
Ack!
Penny, no!
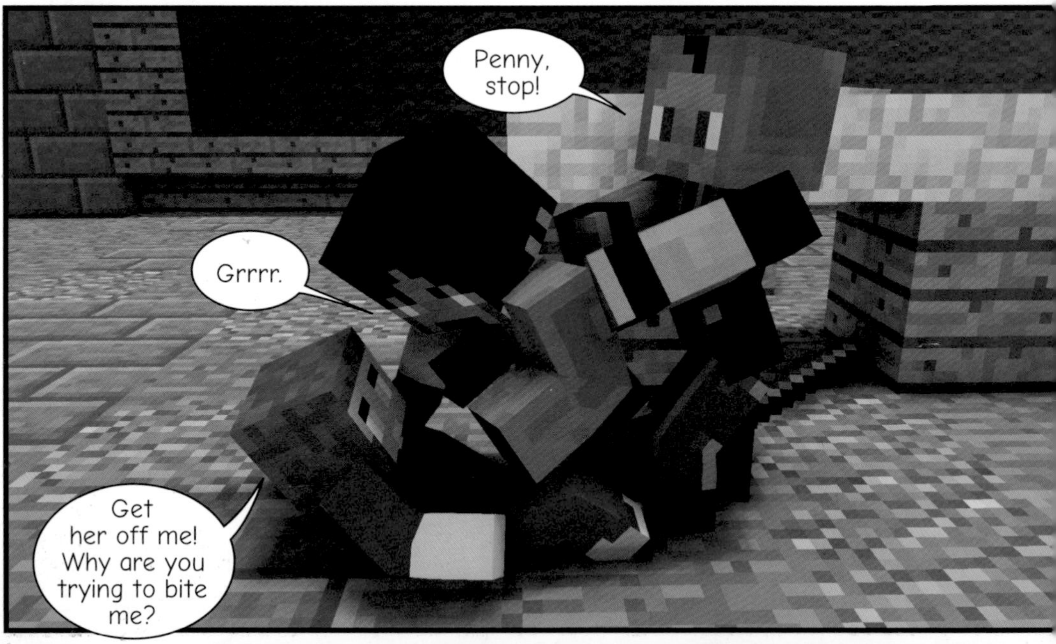
Penny, stop!
Grrrr.
Get her off me! Why are you trying to bite me?

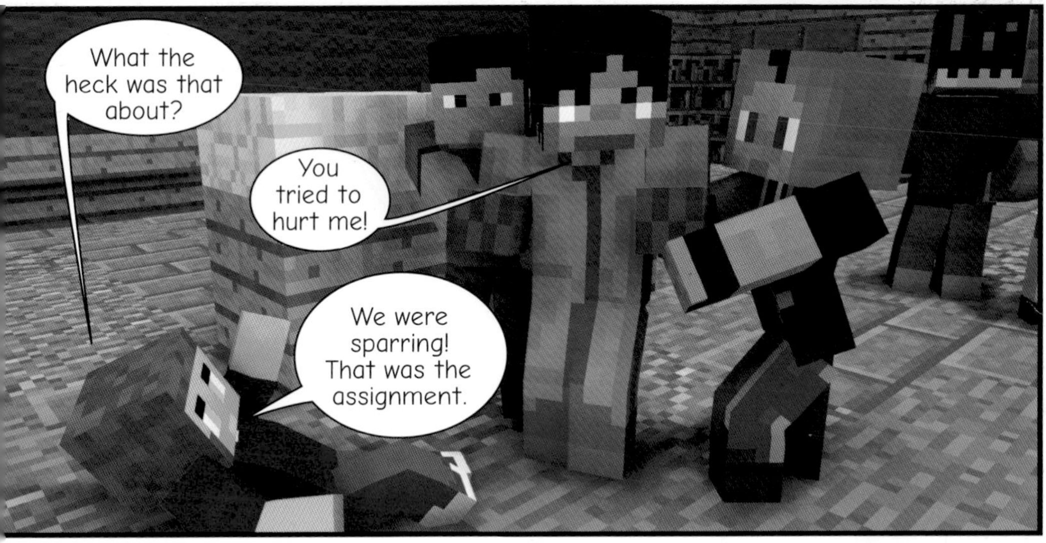
What the heck was that about?
You tried to hurt me!
We were sparring! That was the assignment.

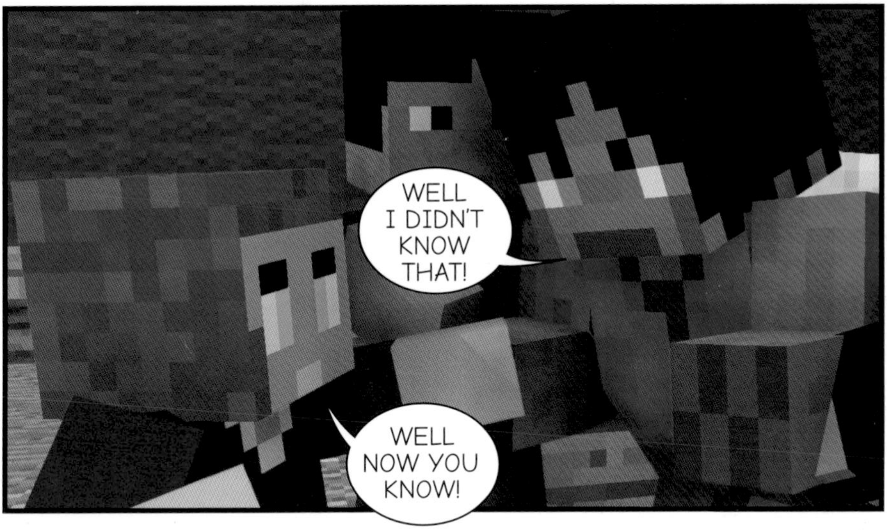
WELL I DIDN'T KNOW THAT!
WELL NOW YOU KNOW!

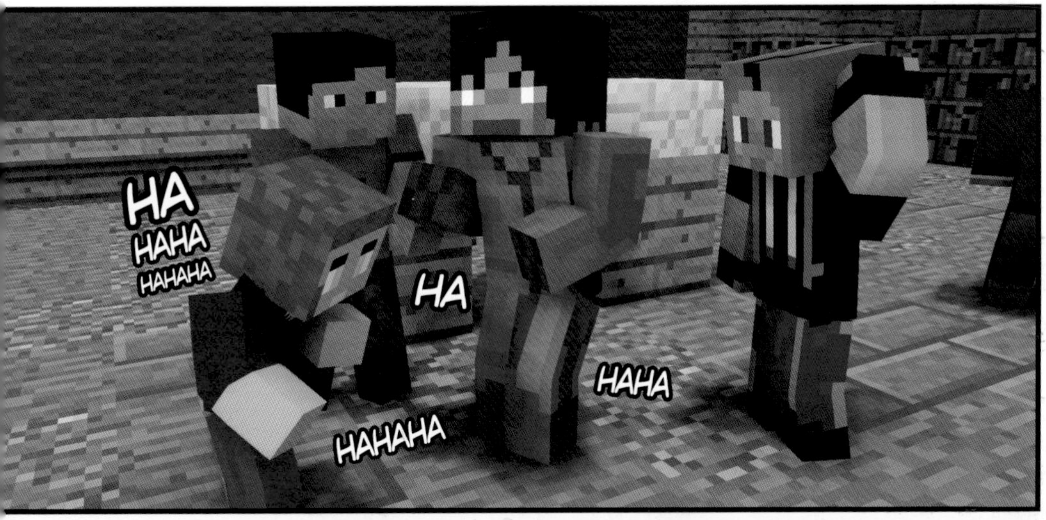
HA
HAHA
HAHAHA
HA
HAHA
HAHAHA

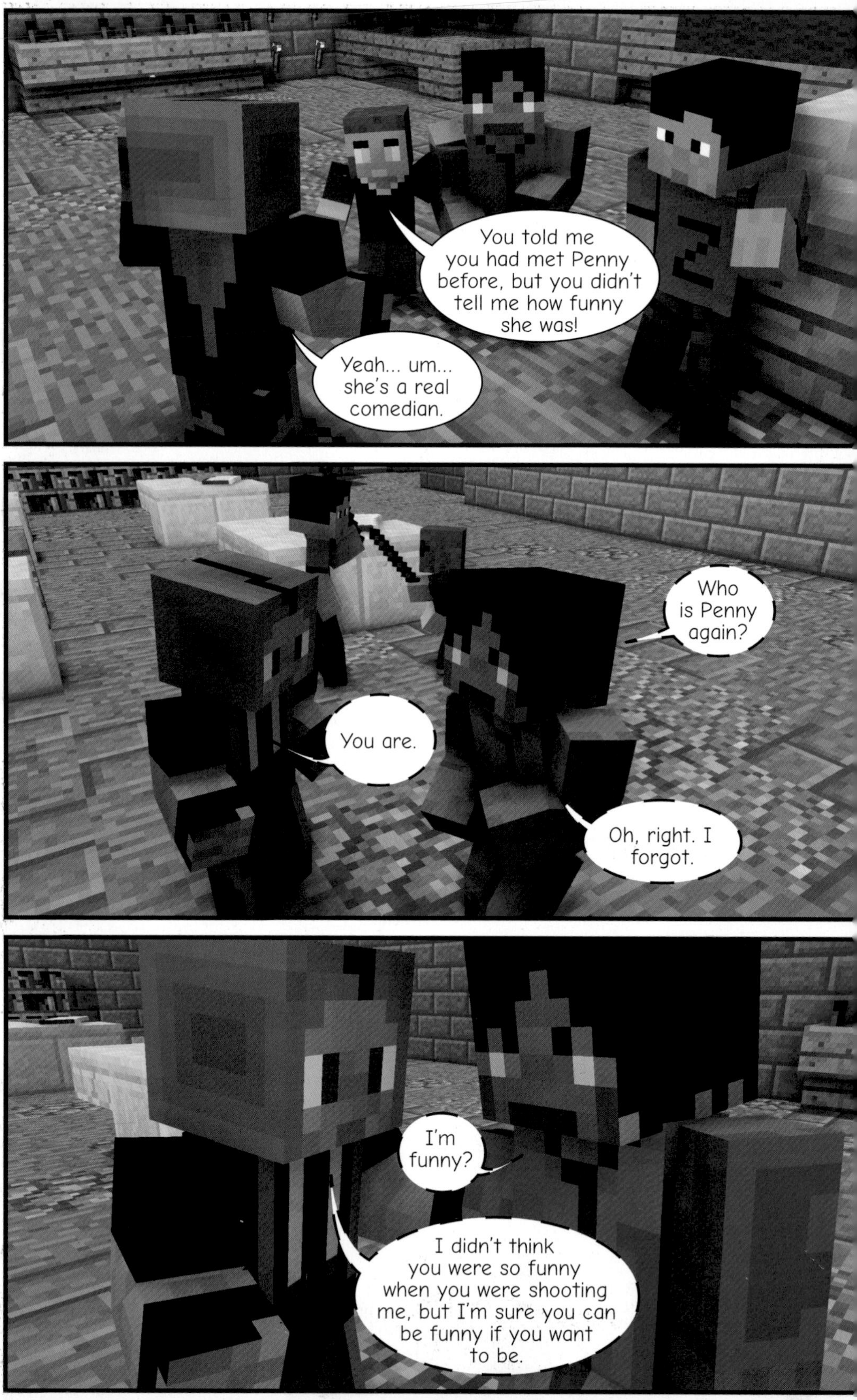
You told me you had met Penny before, but you didn't tell me how funny she was!
Yeah... um... she's a real comedian.
Who is Penny again?
You are.
Oh, right. I forgot.
I'm funny?
I didn't think you were so funny when you were shooting me, but I'm sure you can be funny if you want to be.

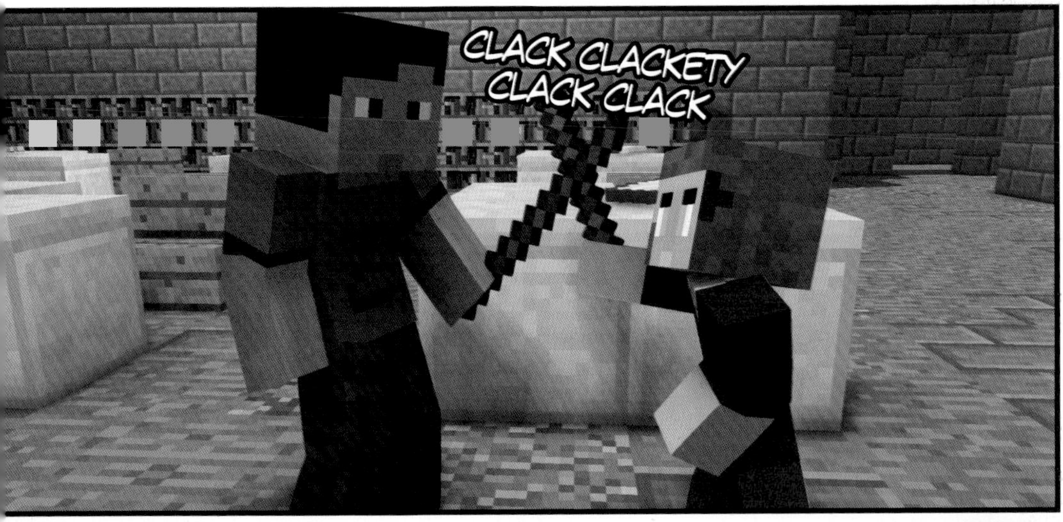
CLACK CLACKETY
CLACK CLACK

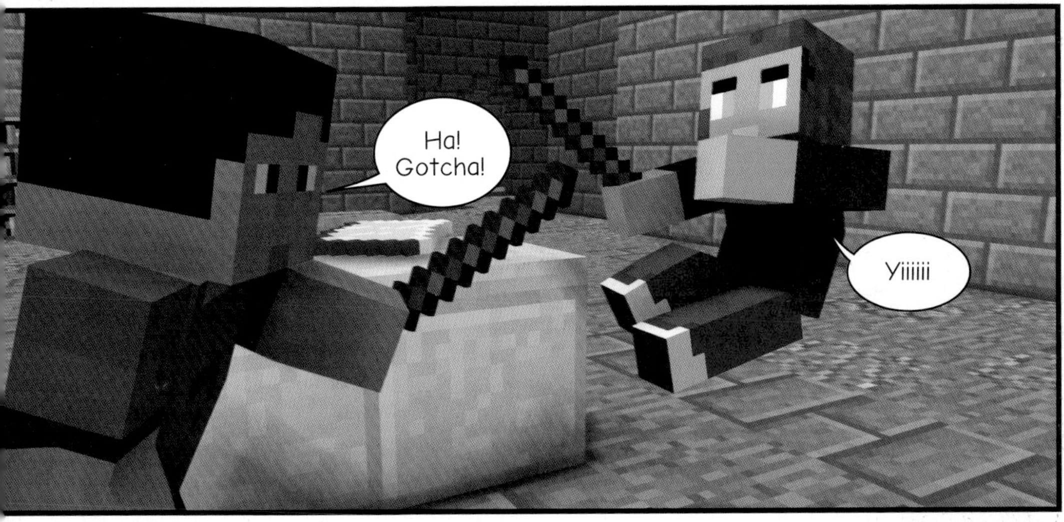
Ha!
Gotcha!
Yiiiii

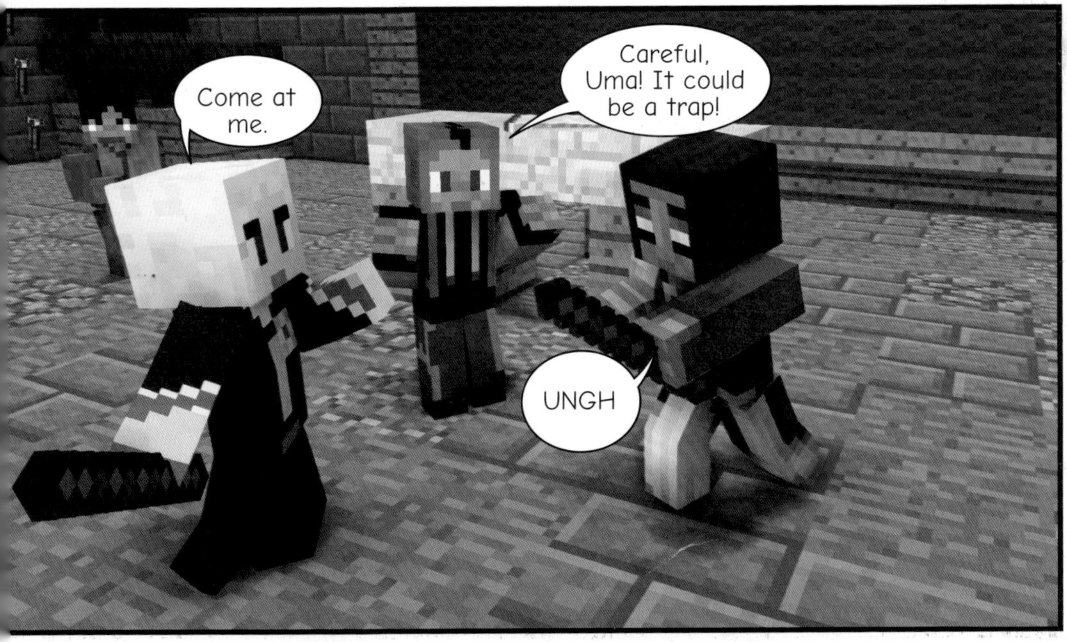
Come at
me.
Careful,
Uma! It could
be a trap!
UNGH

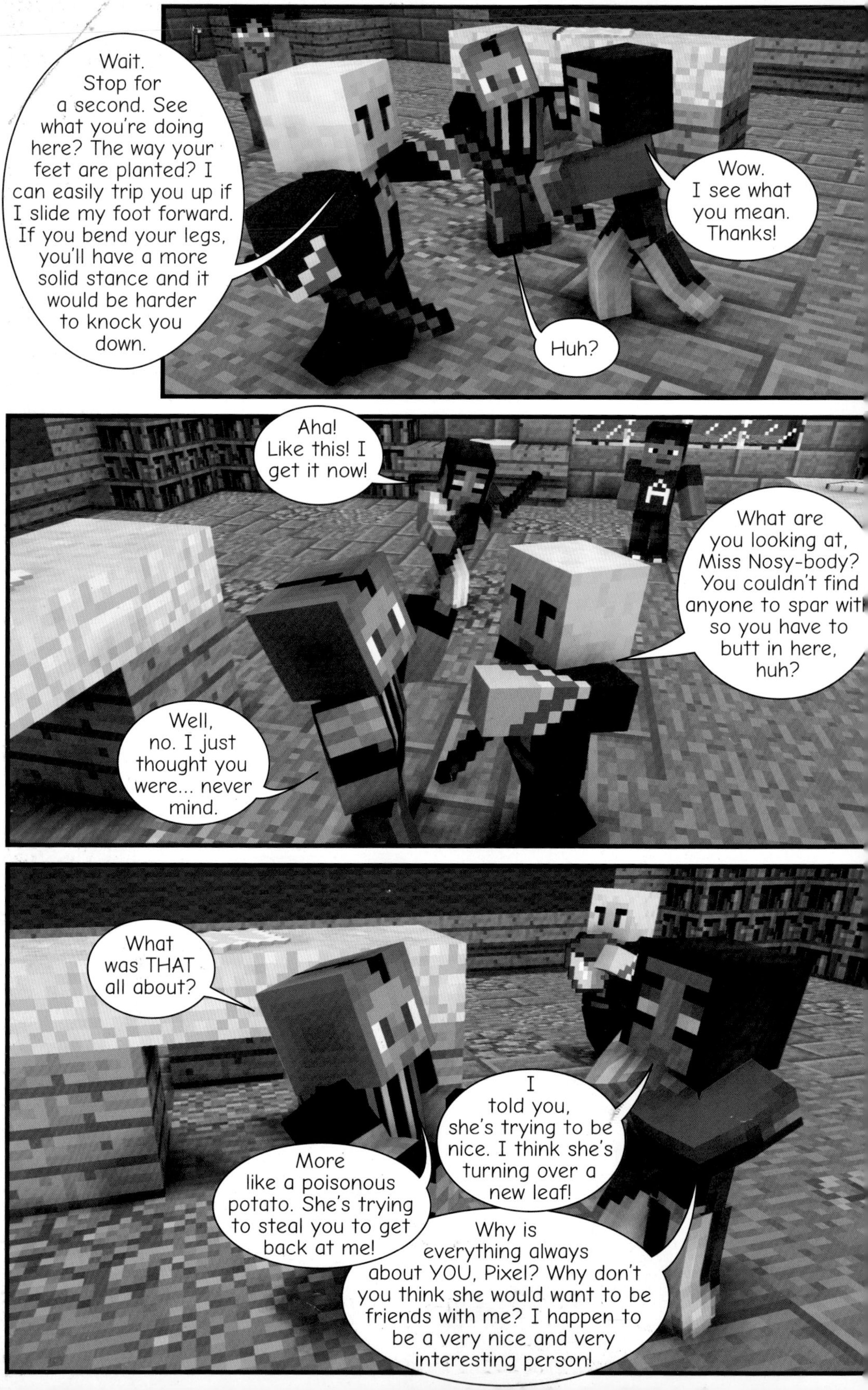
Wait. Stop for a second. See what you're doing here? The way your feet are planted? I can easily trip you up if I slide my foot forward. If you bend your legs, you'll have a more solid stance and it would be harder to knock you down.
Huh?
Wow. I see what you mean. Thanks!
Aha! Like this! I get it now!
What are you looking at, Miss Nosy-body? You couldn't find anyone to spar with so you have to butt in here, huh?
Well, no. I just thought you were... never mind.
What was THAT all about?
I told you, she's trying to be nice. I think she's turning over a new leaf!
More like a poisonous potato. She's trying to steal you to get back at me!
Why is everything always about YOU, Pixel? Why don't you think she would want to be friends with me? I happen to be a very nice and very interesting person!

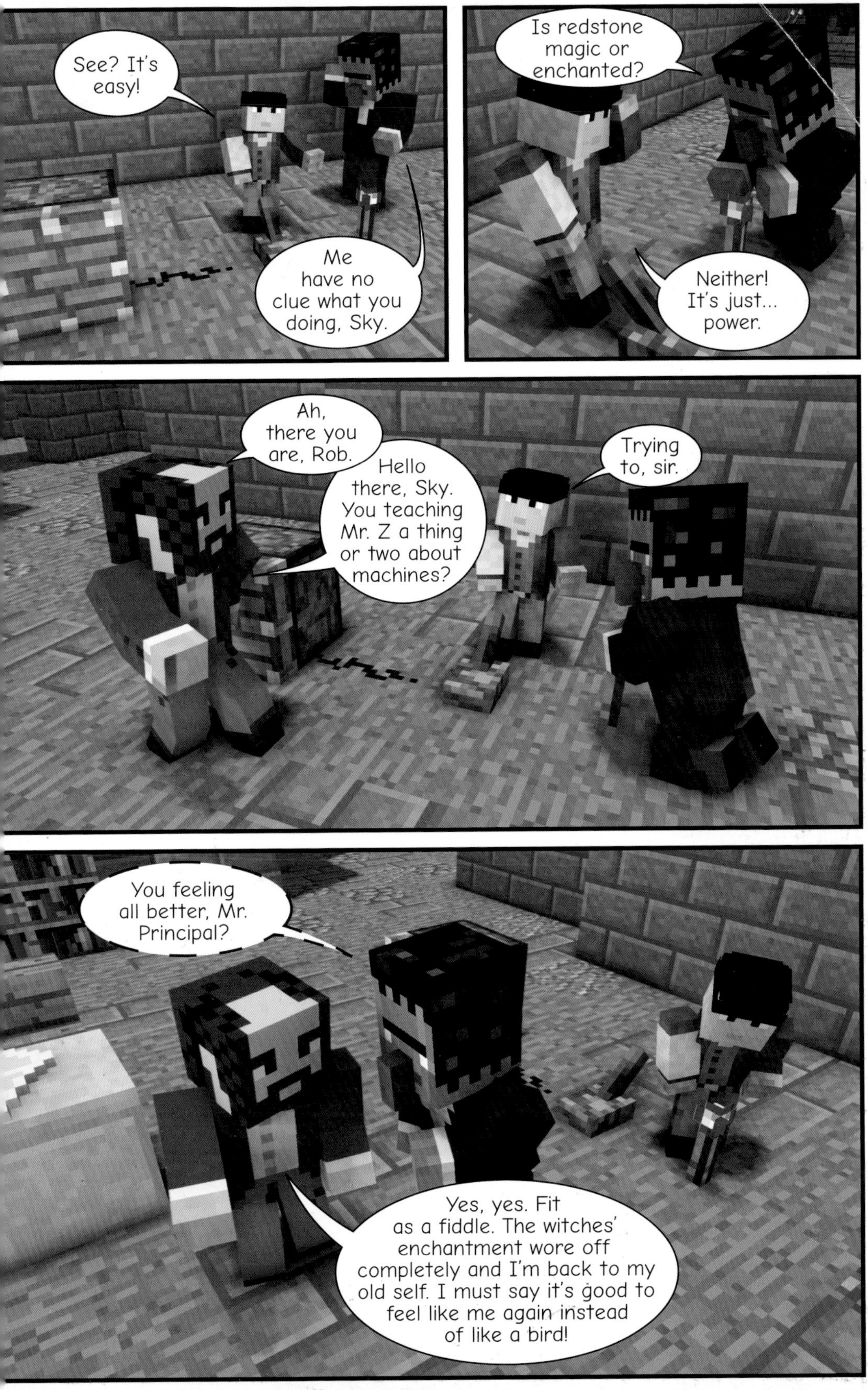
See? It's easy!
Me have no clue what you doing, Sky.
Is redstone magic or enchanted?
Neither! It's just... power.
Ah, there you are, Rob.
Hello there, Sky. You teaching Mr. Z a thing or two about machines?
Trying to, sir.
You feeling all better, Mr. Principal?
Yes, yes. Fit as a fiddle. The witches' enchantment wore off completely and I'm back to my old self. I must say it's good to feel like me again instead of like a bird!

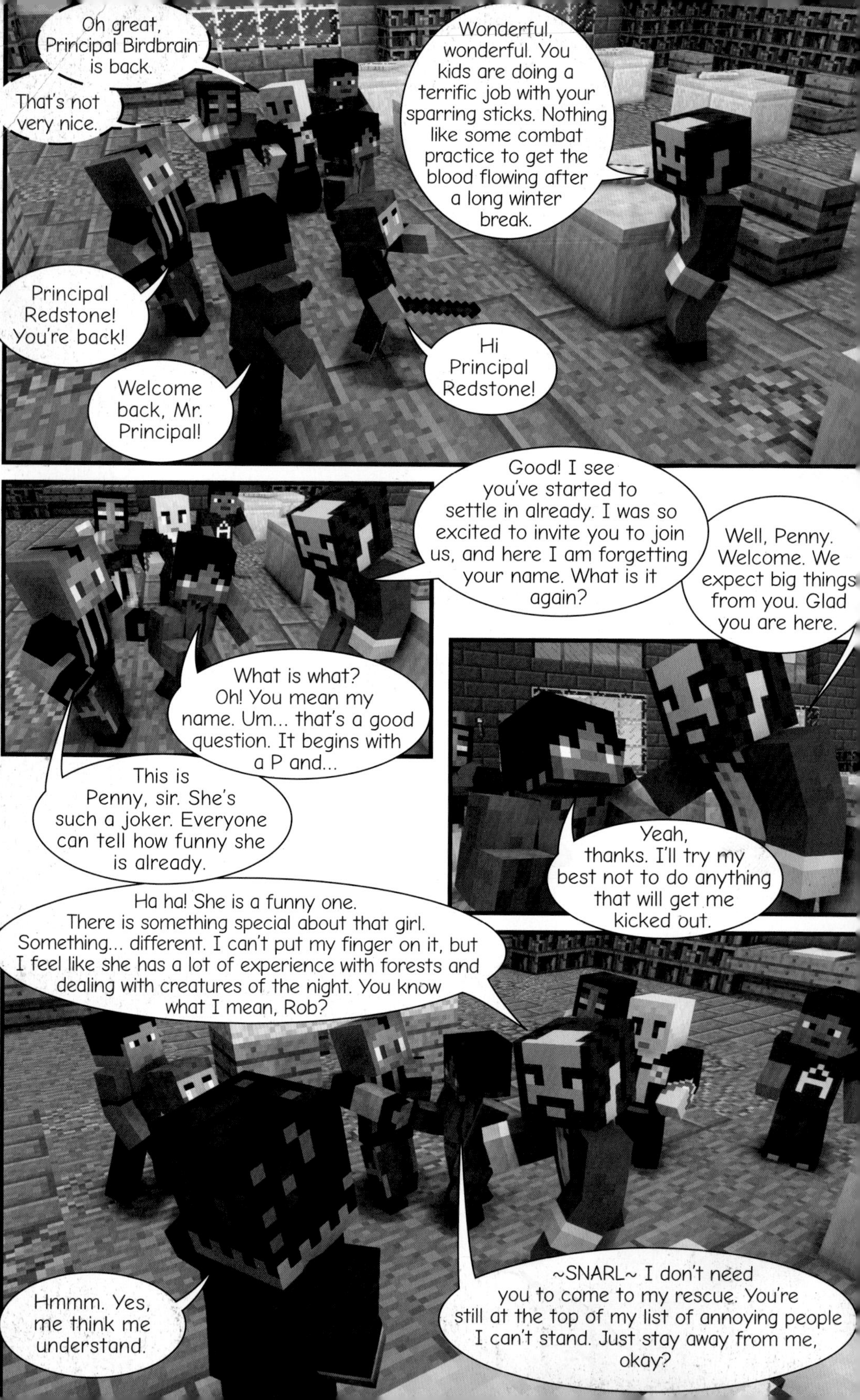
Oh great, Principal Birdbrain is back.
That's not very nice.
Wonderful, wonderful. You kids are doing a terrific job with your sparring sticks. Nothing like some combat practice to get the blood flowing after a long winter break.
Principal Redstone! You're back!
Hi Principal Redstone!
Welcome back, Mr. Principal!
Good! I see you've started to settle in already. I was so excited to invite you to join us, and here I am forgetting your name. What is it again?
What is what? Oh! You mean my name. Um... that's a good question. It begins with a P and...
This is Penny, sir. She's such a joker. Everyone can tell how funny she is already.
Well, Penny. Welcome. We expect big things from you. Glad you are here.
Yeah, thanks. I'll try my best not to do anything that will get me kicked out.
Ha ha! She is a funny one. There is something special about that girl. Something... different. I can't put my finger on it, but I feel like she has a lot of experience with forests and dealing with creatures of the night. You know what I mean, Rob?
Hmmm. Yes, me think me understand.
~SNARL~ I don't need you to come to my rescue. You're still at the top of my list of annoying people I can't stand. Just stay away from me, okay?

CHAPTER 3

A BETTER
PLACE

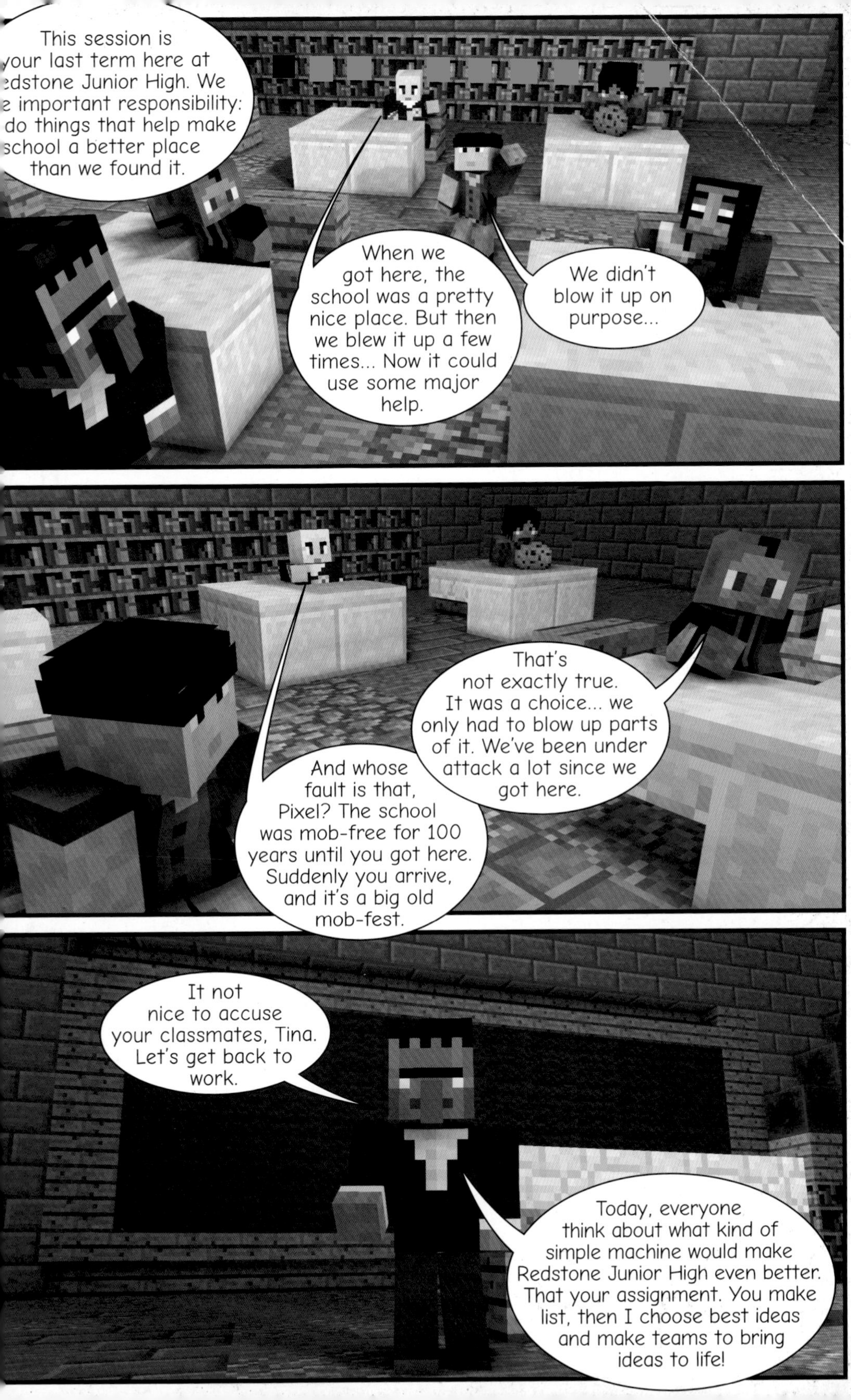

This session is your last term here at edstone Junior High. We e important responsibility: do things that help make school a better place than we found it.
When we got here, the school was a pretty nice place. But then we blew it up a few times... Now it could use some major help.
We didn't blow it up on purpose...
That's not exactly true. It was a choice... we only had to blow up parts of it. We've been under attack a lot since we got here.
And whose fault is that, Pixel? The school was mob-free for 100 years until you got here. Suddenly you arrive, and it's a big old mob-fest.
It not nice to accuse your classmates, Tina. Let's get back to work.
Today, everyone think about what kind of simple machine would make Redstone Junior High even better. That your assignment. You make list, then I choose best ideas and make teams to bring ideas to life!

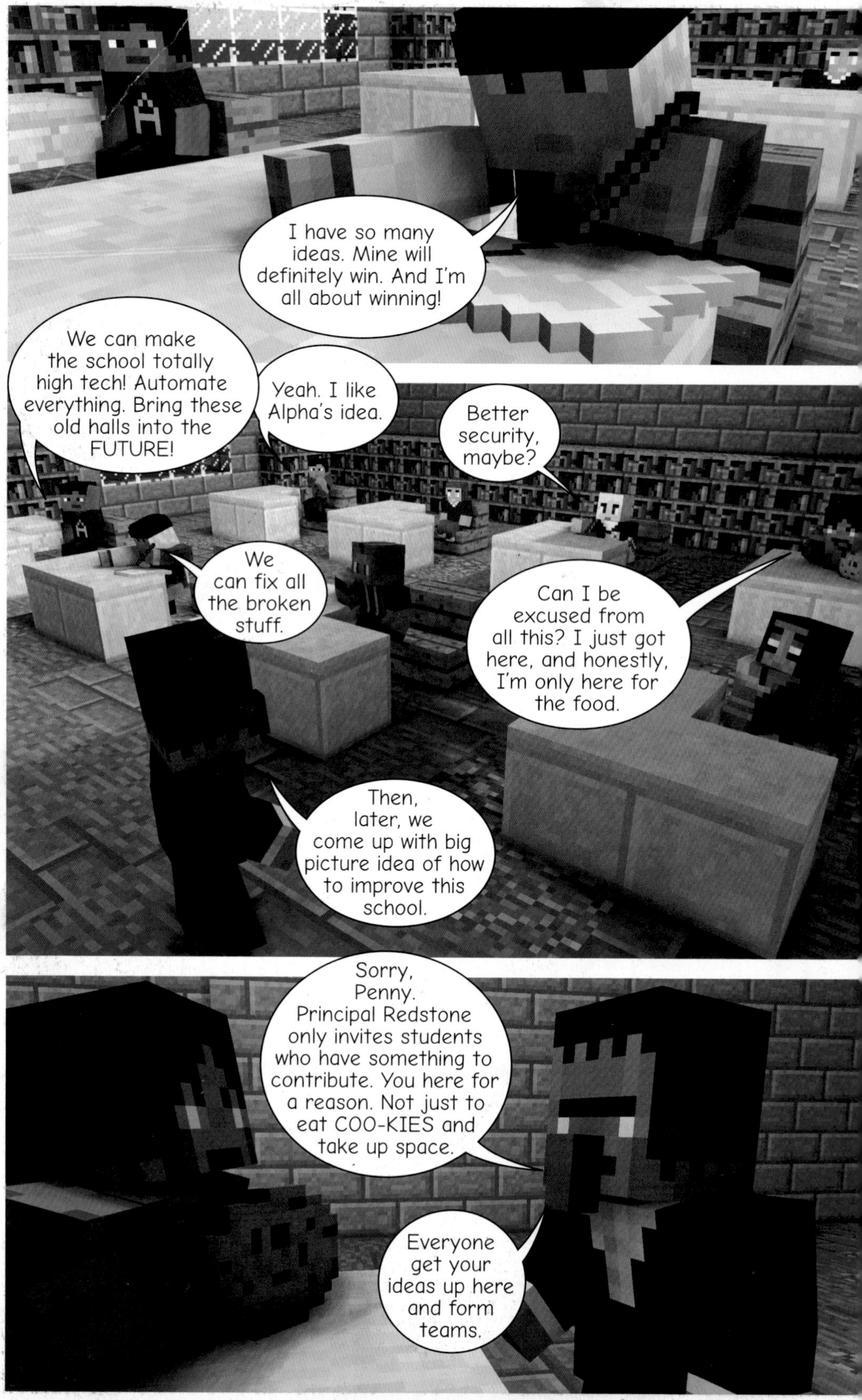
I have so many ideas. Mine will definitely win. And I'm all about winning!
We can make the school totally high tech! Automate everything. Bring these old halls into the FUTURE!
Yeah. I like Alpha's idea.
Better security, maybe?
We can fix all the broken stuff.
Can I be excused from all this? I just got here, and honestly, I'm only here for the food.
Then, later, we come up with big picture idea of how to improve this school.
Sorry, Penny. Principal Redstone only invites students who have something to contribute. You here for a reason. Not just to eat COO-KIES and take up space.
Everyone get your ideas up here and form teams.

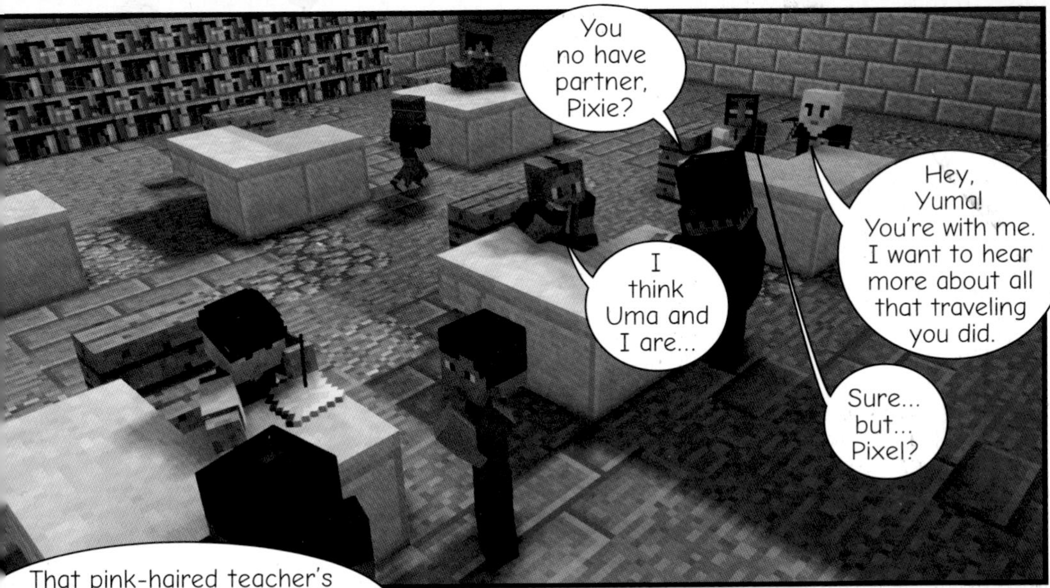
You no have partner, Pixie?
Hey, Yuma! You're with me. I want to hear more about all that traveling you did.
I think Uma and I are...
Sure... but... Pixel?

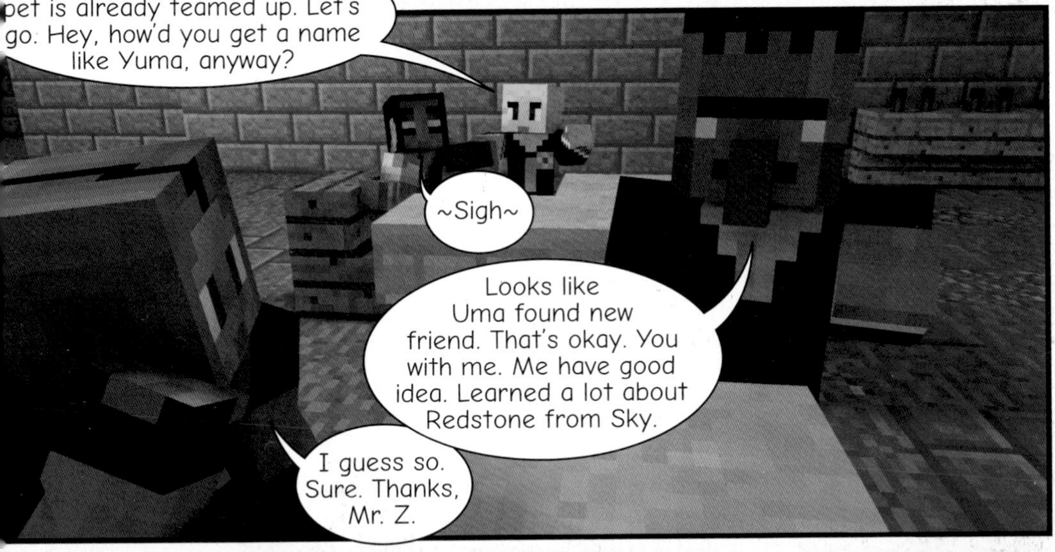
That pink-haired teacher's pet is already teamed up. Let's go. Hey, how'd you get a name like Yuma, anyway?
~Sigh~
Looks like Uma found new friend. That's okay. You with me. Me have good idea. Learned a lot about Redstone from Sky.
I guess so. Sure. Thanks, Mr. Z.

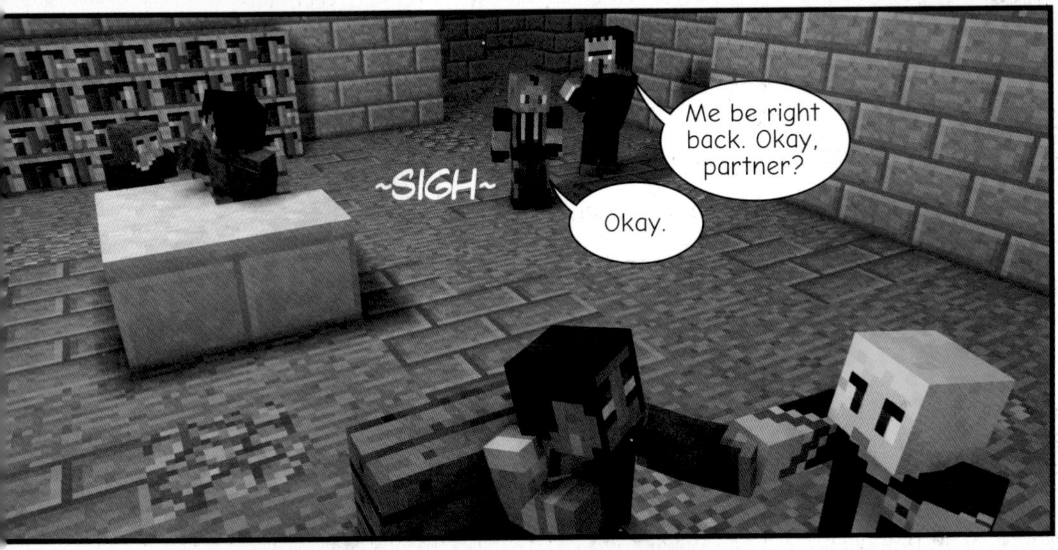
Me be right back. Okay, partner?
~SIGH~
Okay.

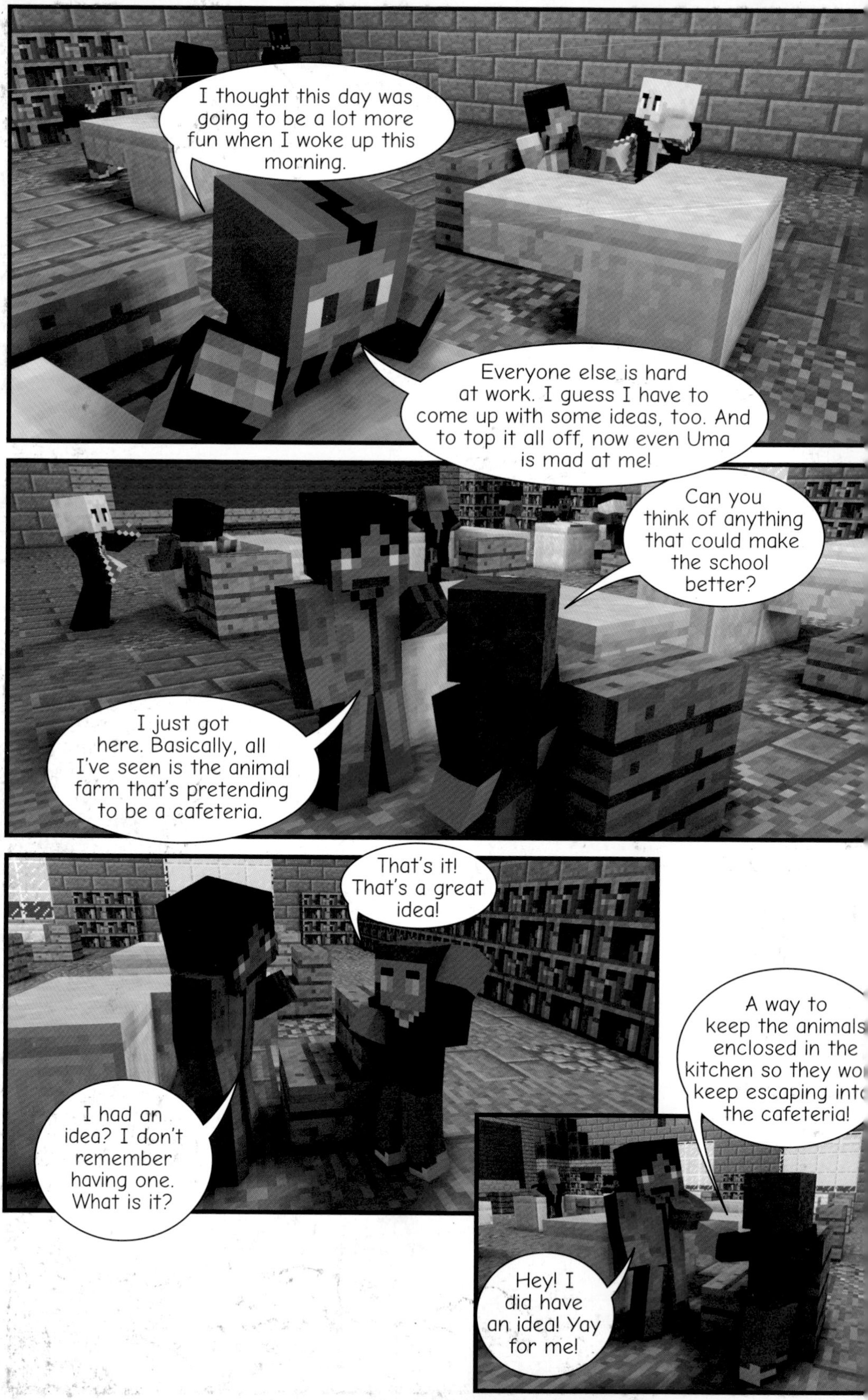
I thought this day was going to be a lot more fun when I woke up this morning.
Everyone else is hard at work. I guess I have to come up with some ideas, too. And to top it all off, now even Uma is mad at me!
Can you think of anything that could make the school better?
I just got here. Basically, all I've seen is the animal farm that's pretending to be a cafeteria.
That's it! That's a great idea!
I had an idea? I don't remember having one. What is it?
A way to keep the animals enclosed in the kitchen so they wo keep escaping int the cafeteria!
Hey! I did have an idea! Yay for me!

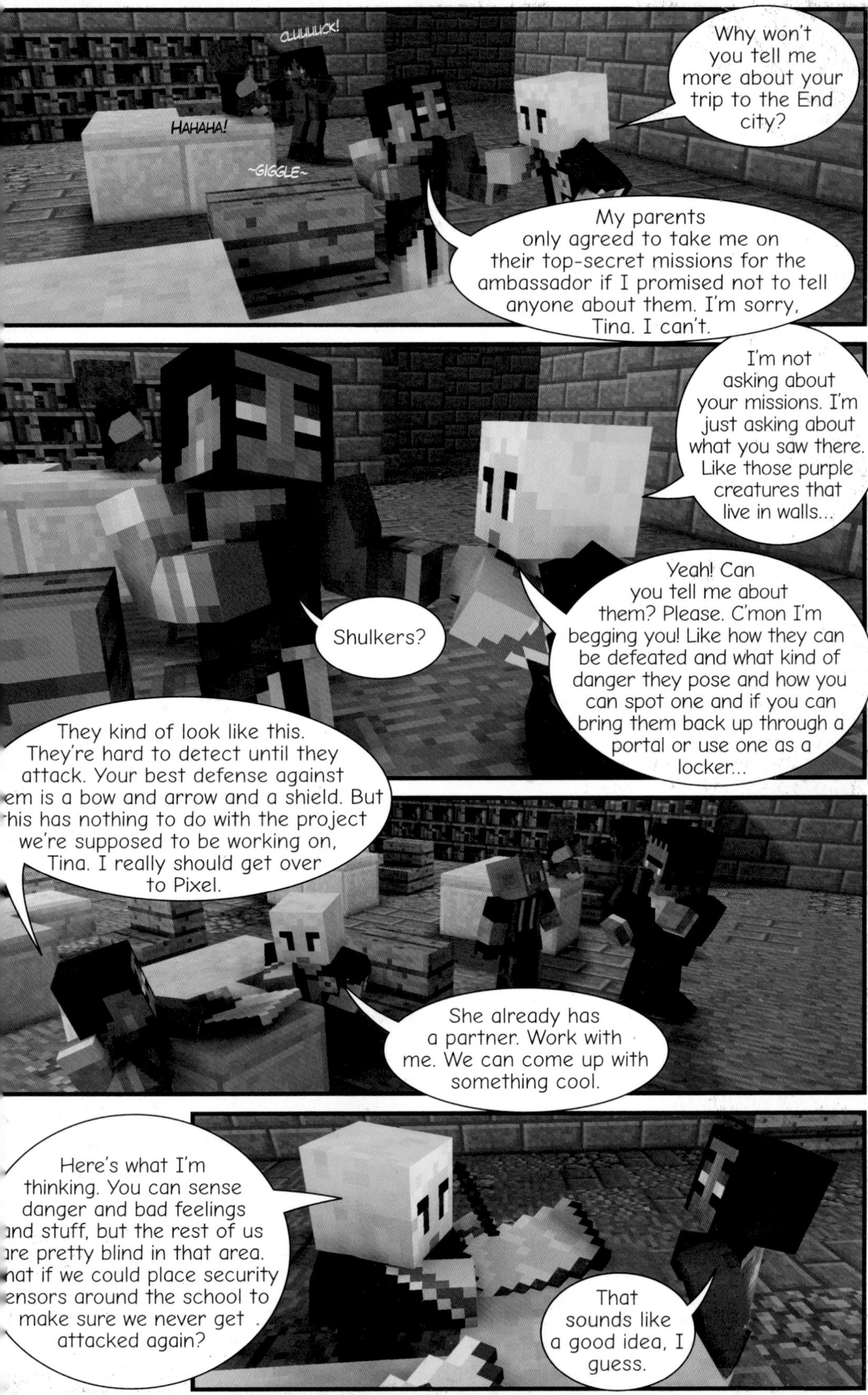
CLUUUUCK!
HAHAHA!
~GIGGLE~
Why won't you tell me more about your trip to the End city?
My parents only agreed to take me on their top-secret missions for the ambassador if I promised not to tell anyone about them. I'm sorry, Tina. I can't.
I'm not asking about your missions. I'm just asking about what you saw there. Like those purple creatures that live in walls...
Shulkers?
Yeah! Can you tell me about them? Please. C'mon I'm begging you! Like how they can be defeated and what kind of danger they pose and how you can spot one and if you can bring them back up through a portal or use one as a locker...
They kind of look like this. They're hard to detect until they attack. Your best defense against em is a bow and arrow and a shield. But his has nothing to do with the project we're supposed to be working on, Tina. I really should get over to Pixel.
She already has a partner. Work with me. We can come up with something cool.
Here's what I'm thinking. You can sense danger and bad feelings and stuff, but the rest of us are pretty blind in that area. hat if we could place security ensors around the school to make sure we never get attacked again?
That sounds like a good idea, I guess.

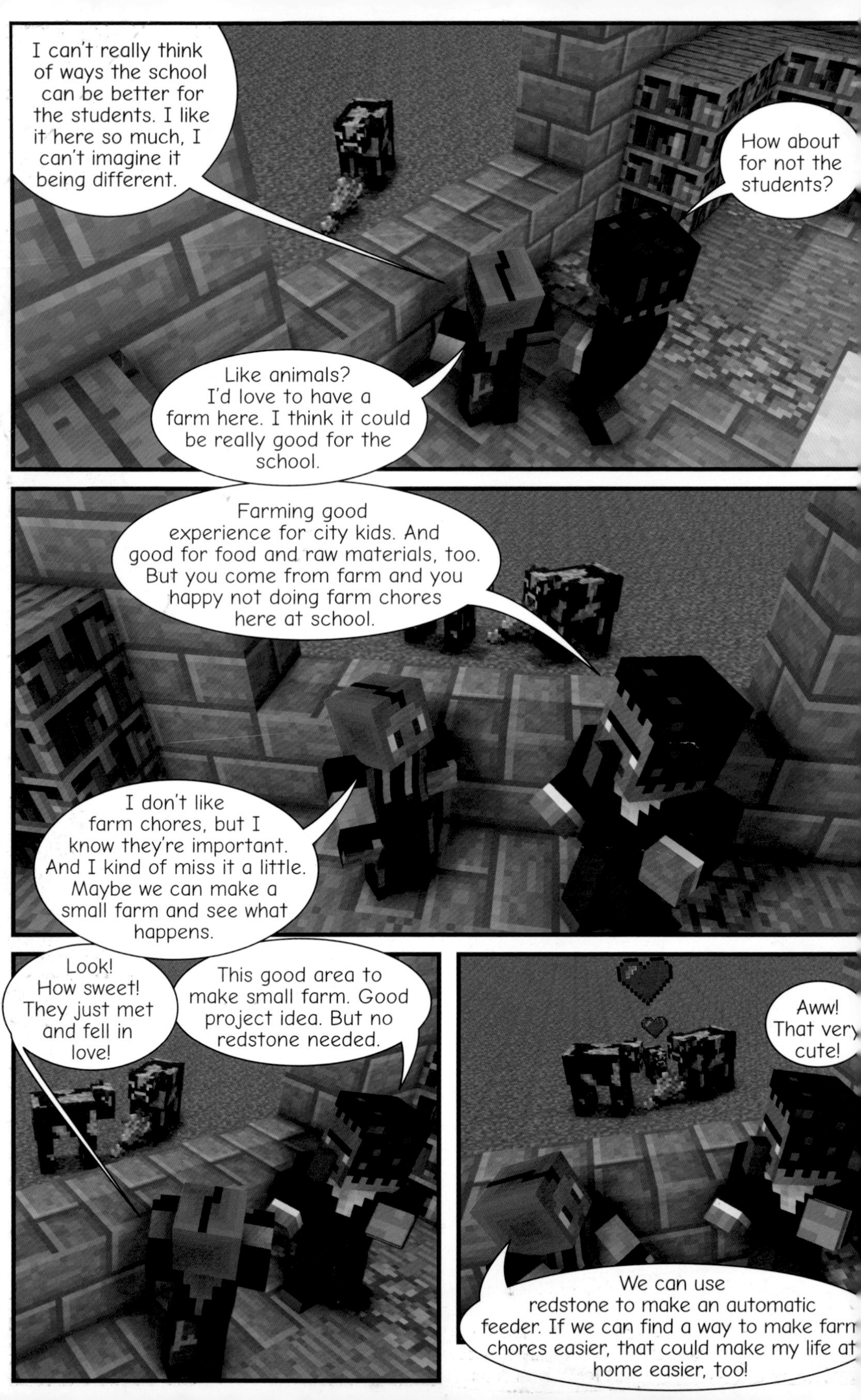

I can't really think of ways the school can be better for the students. I like it here so much, I can't imagine it being different.
How about for not the students?
Like animals? I'd love to have a farm here. I think it could be really good for the school.
Farming good experience for city kids. And good for food and raw materials, too. But you come from farm and you happy not doing farm chores here at school.
I don't like farm chores, but I know they're important. And I kind of miss it a little. Maybe we can make a small farm and see what happens.
Look! How sweet! They just met and fell in love!
This good area to make small farm. Good project idea. But no redstone needed.
Aww! That very cute!
We can use redstone to make an automatic feeder. If we can find a way to make farm chores easier, that could make my life at home easier, too!

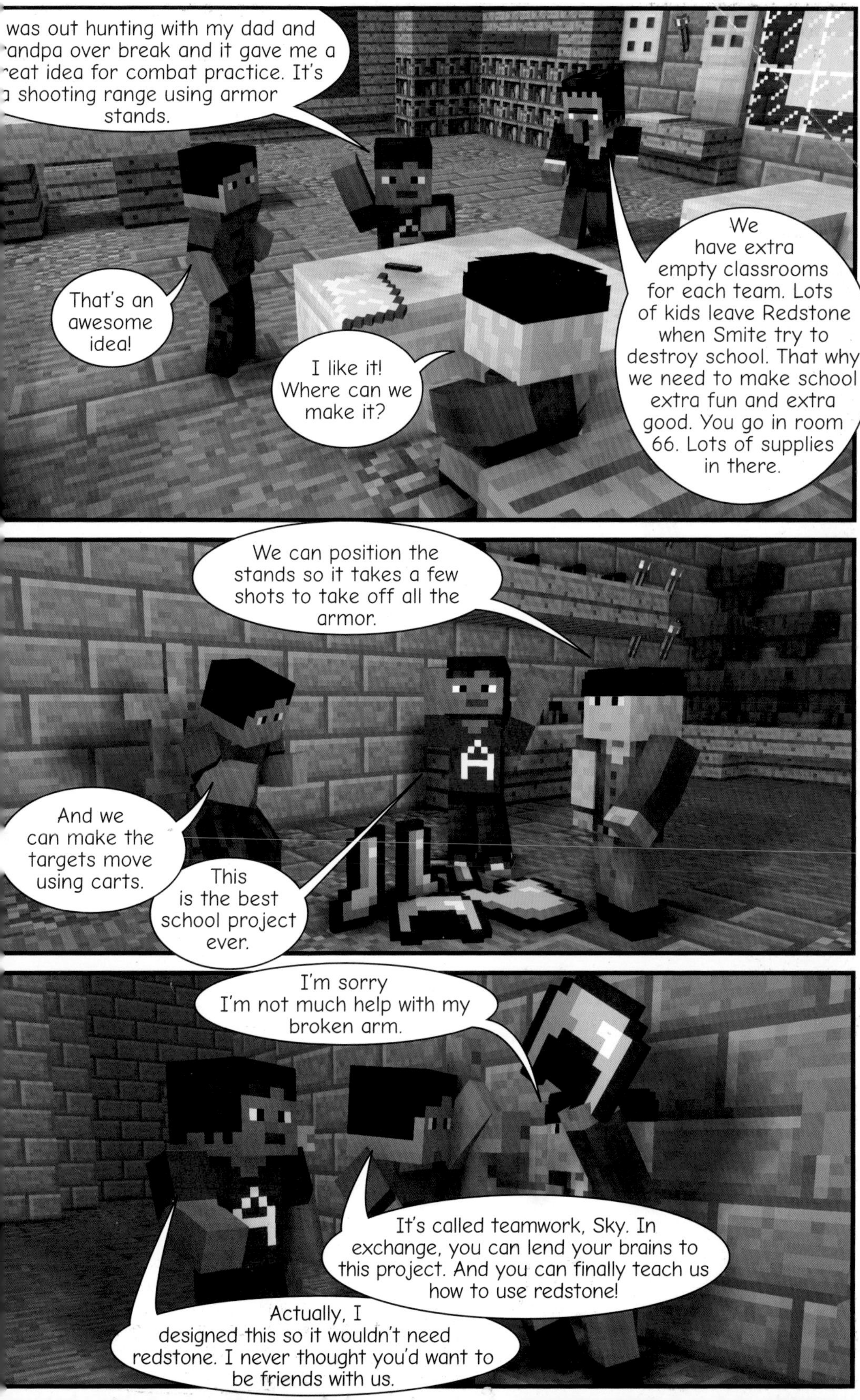
was out hunting with my dad and andpa over break and it gave me a eat idea for combat practice. It's a shooting range using armor stands.
That's an awesome idea!
I like it! Where can we make it?
We have extra empty classrooms for each team. Lots of kids leave Redstone when Smite try to destroy school. That why we need to make school extra fun and extra good. You go in room 66. Lots of supplies in there.
We can position the stands so it takes a few shots to take off all the armor.
And we can make the targets move using carts.
This is the best school project ever.
I'm sorry I'm not much help with my broken arm.
It's called teamwork, Sky. In exchange, you can lend your brains to this project. And you can finally teach us how to use redstone!
Actually, I designed this so it wouldn't need redstone. I never thought you'd want to be friends with us.

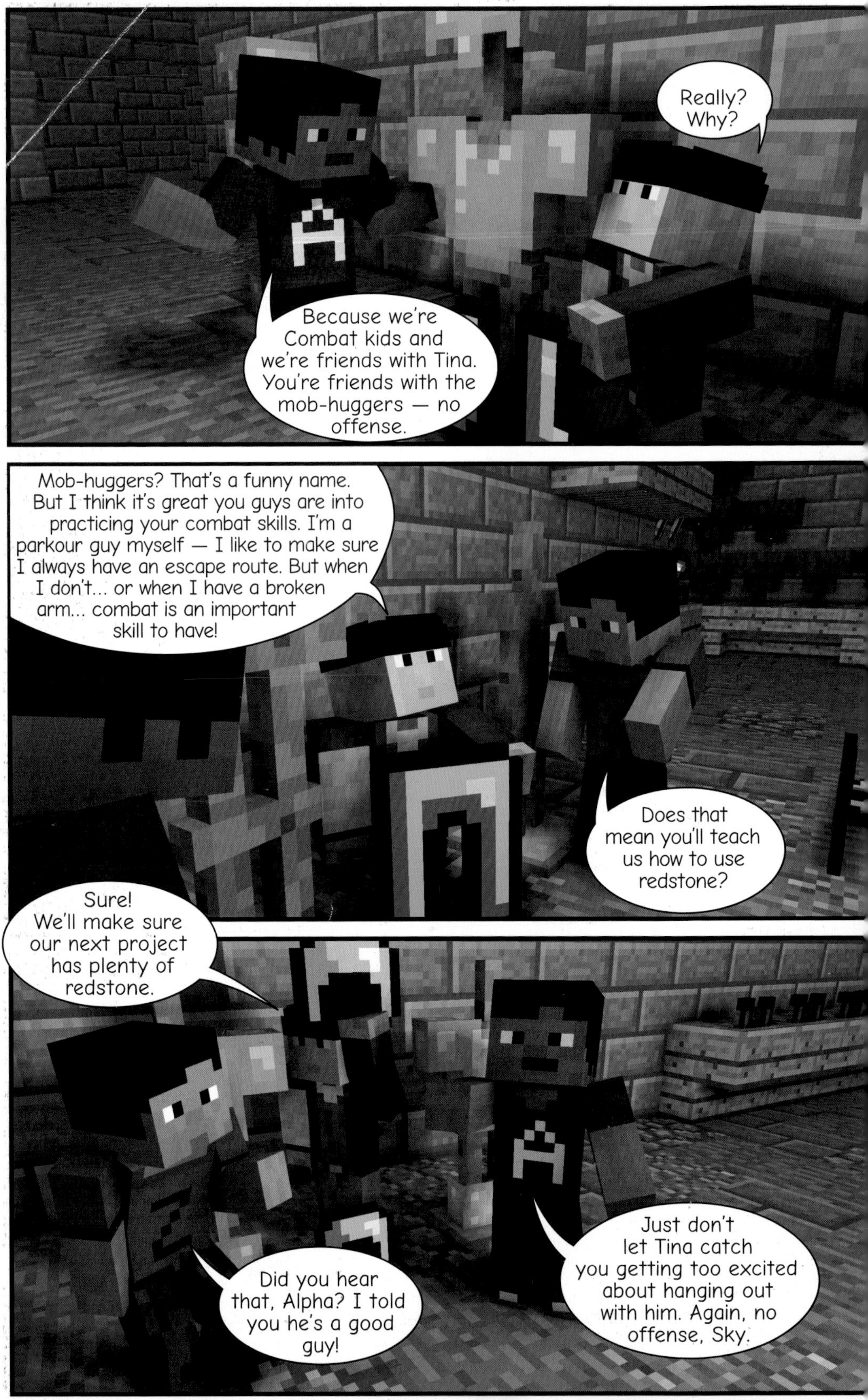
Really? Why?
Because we're Combat kids and we're friends with Tina. You're friends with the mob-huggers — no offense.
Mob-huggers? That's a funny name. But I think it's great you guys are into practicing your combat skills. I'm a parkour guy myself — I like to make sure I always have an escape route. But when I don't... or when I have a broken arm... combat is an important skill to have!
Does that mean you'll teach us how to use redstone?
Sure! We'll make sure our next project has plenty of redstone.
Did you hear that, Alpha? I told you he's a good guy!
Just don't let Tina catch you getting too excited about hanging out with him. Again, no offense, Sky.

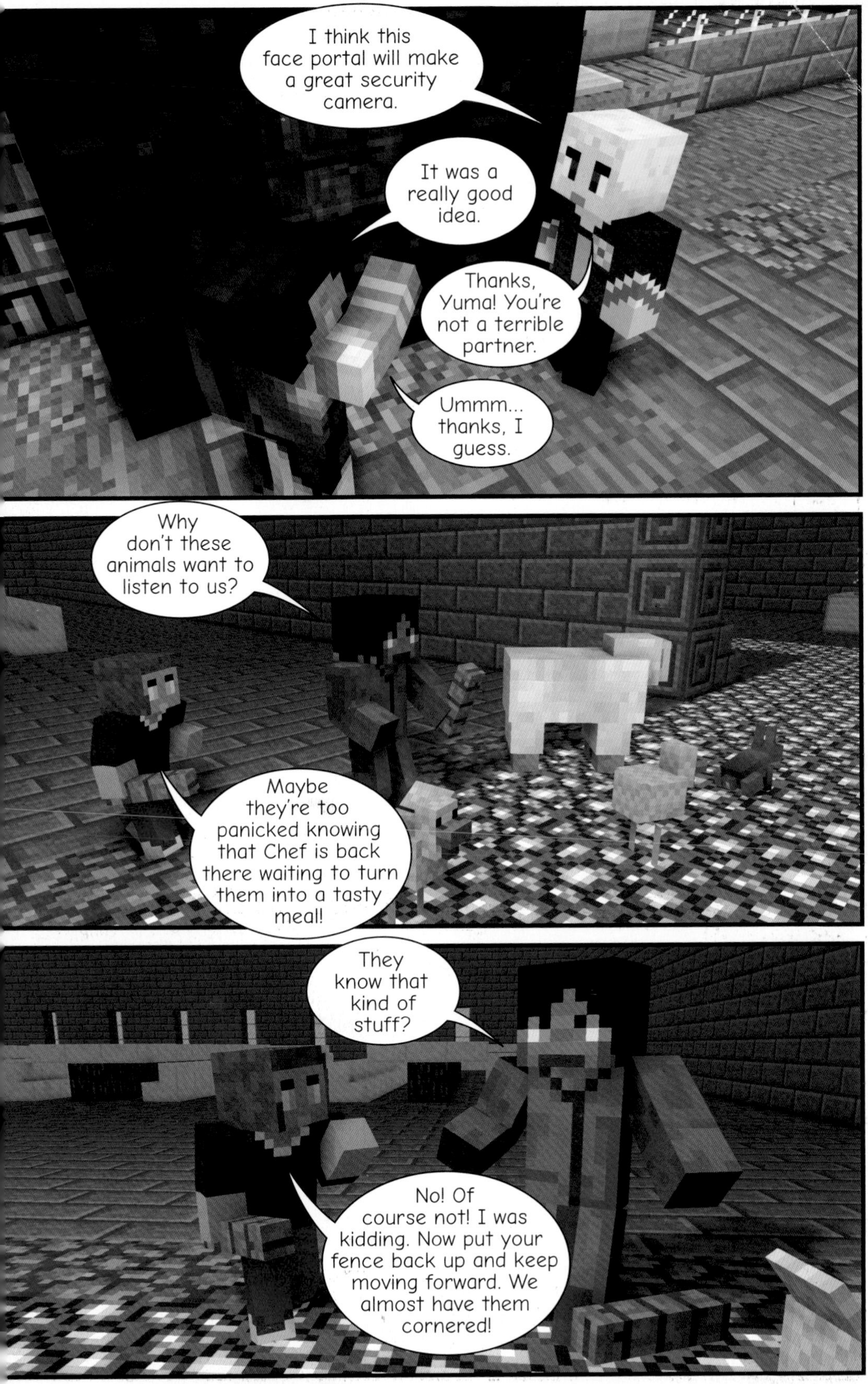
I think this face portal will make a great security camera.
It was a really good idea.
Thanks, Yuma! You're not a terrible partner.
Ummm... thanks, I guess.
Why don't these animals want to listen to us?
Maybe they're too panicked knowing that Chef is back there waiting to turn them into a tasty meal!
They know that kind of stuff?
No! Of course not! I was kidding. Now put your fence back up and keep moving forward. We almost have them cornered!

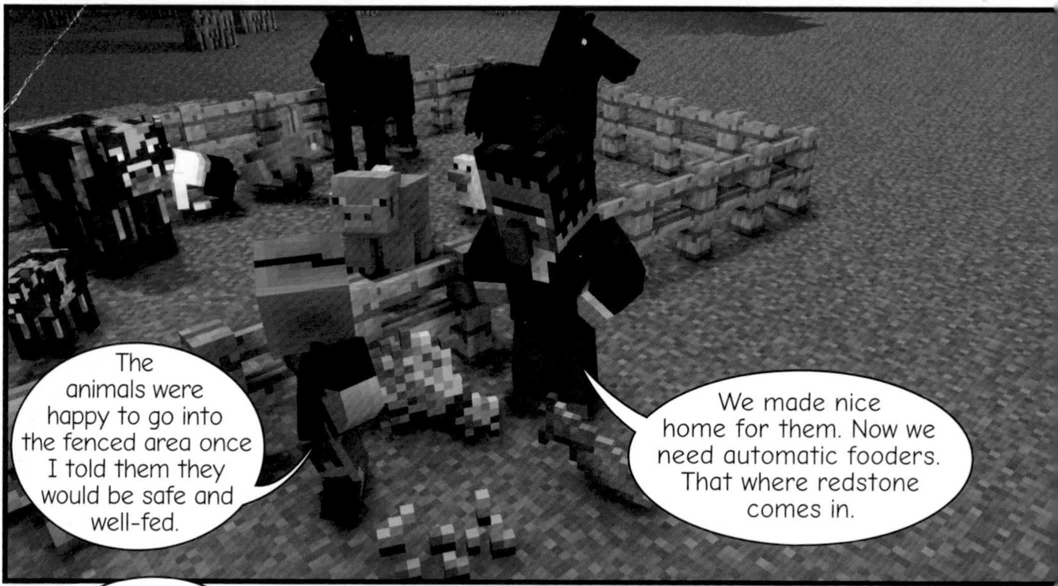
The animals were happy to go into the fenced area once I told them they would be safe and well-fed.
We made nice home for them. Now we need automatic fooders. That where redstone comes in.

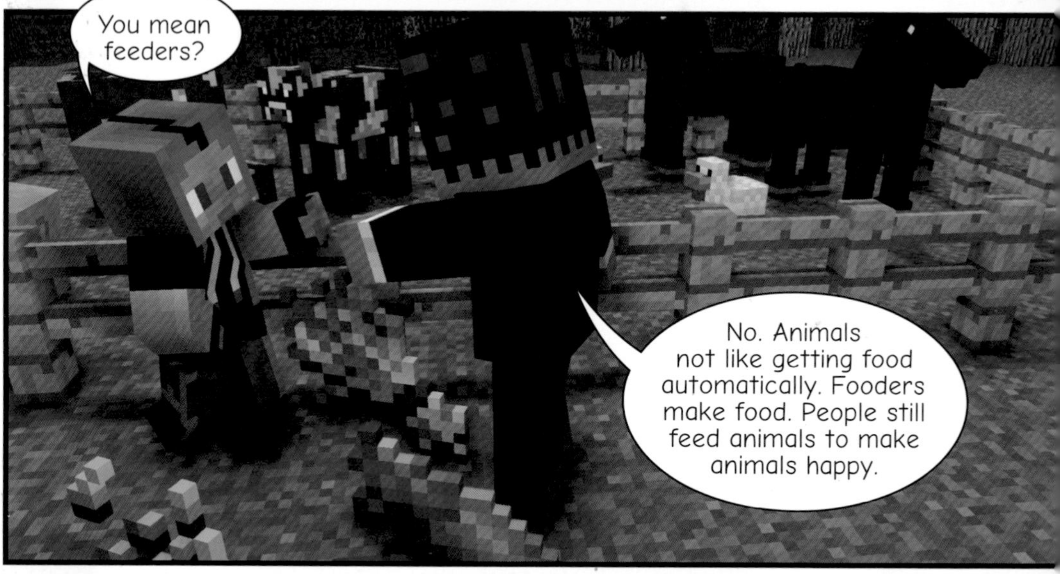
You mean feeders?
No. Animals not like getting food automatically. Fooders make food. People still feed animals to make animals happy.

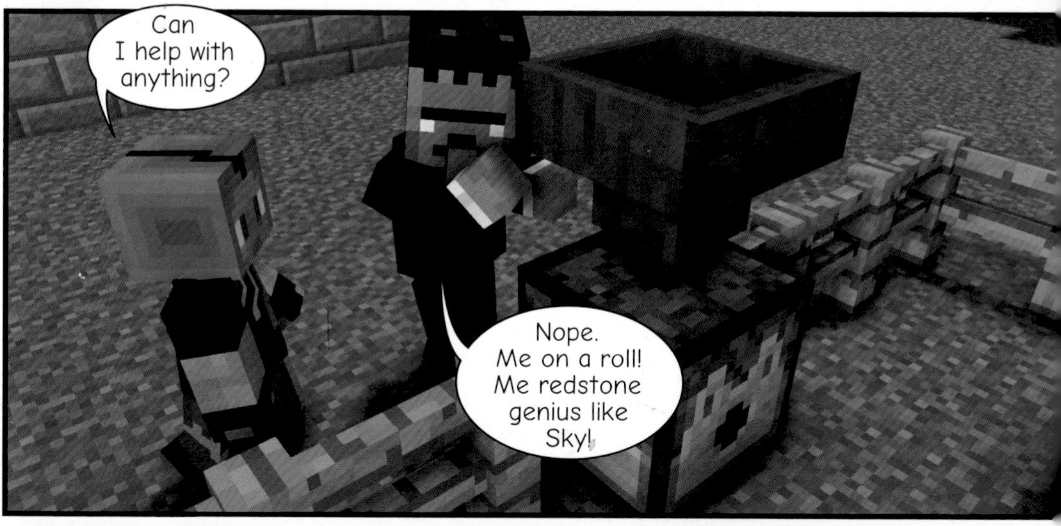
Can I help with anything?
Nope. Me on a roll! Me redstone genius like Sky!

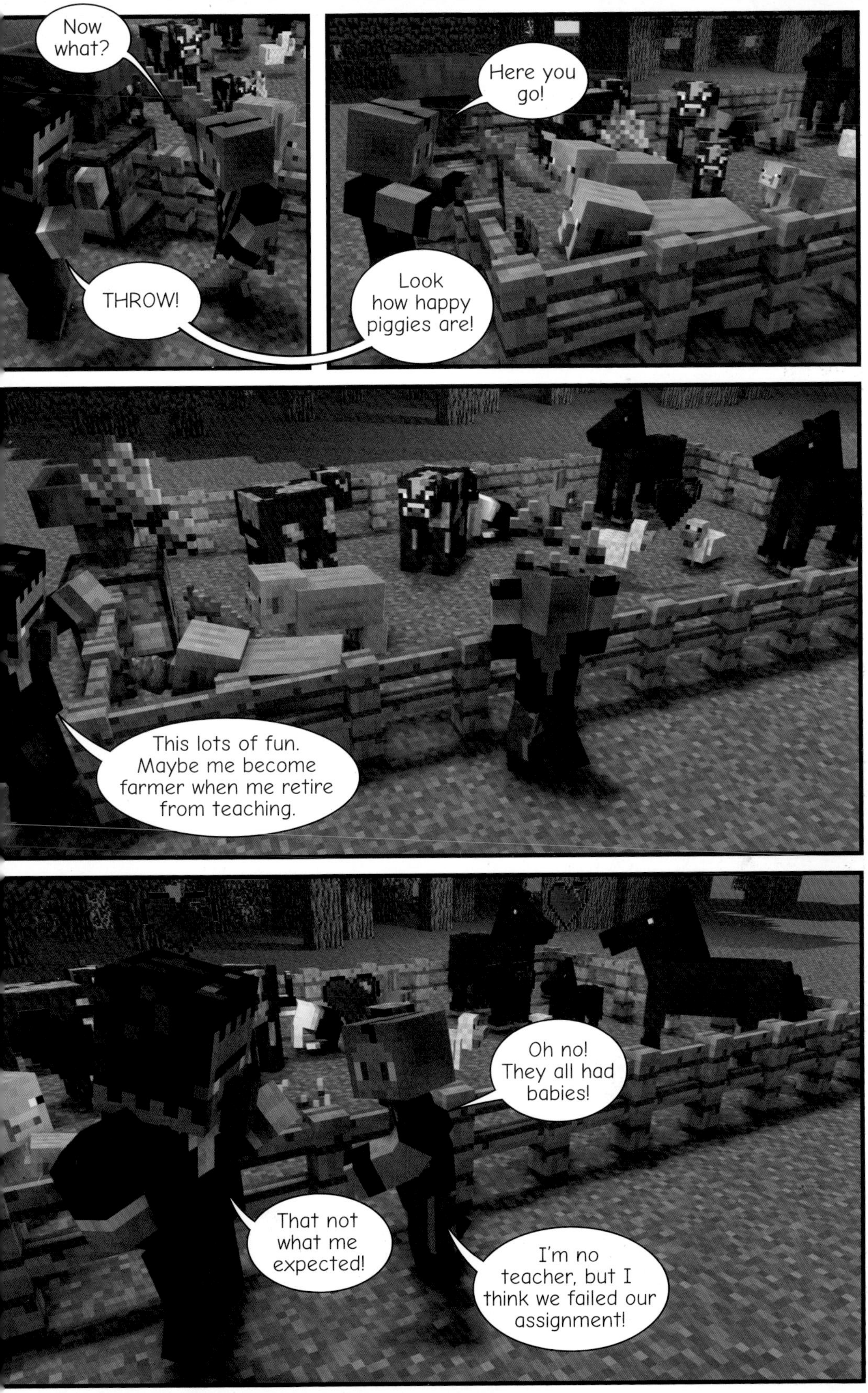
Now what?
THROW!
Here you go!
Look how happy piggies are!
This lots of fun. Maybe me become farmer when me retire from teaching.
Oh no! They all had babies!
That not what me expected!
I'm no teacher, but I think we failed our assignment!

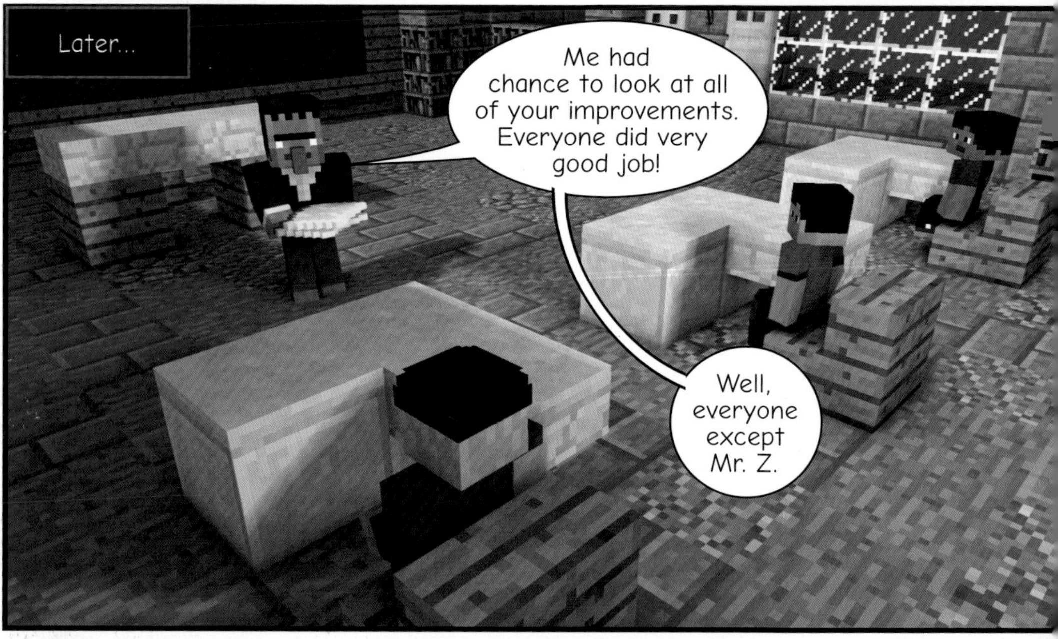
Later...
Me had chance to look at all of your improvements. Everyone did very good job!
Well, everyone except Mr. Z.

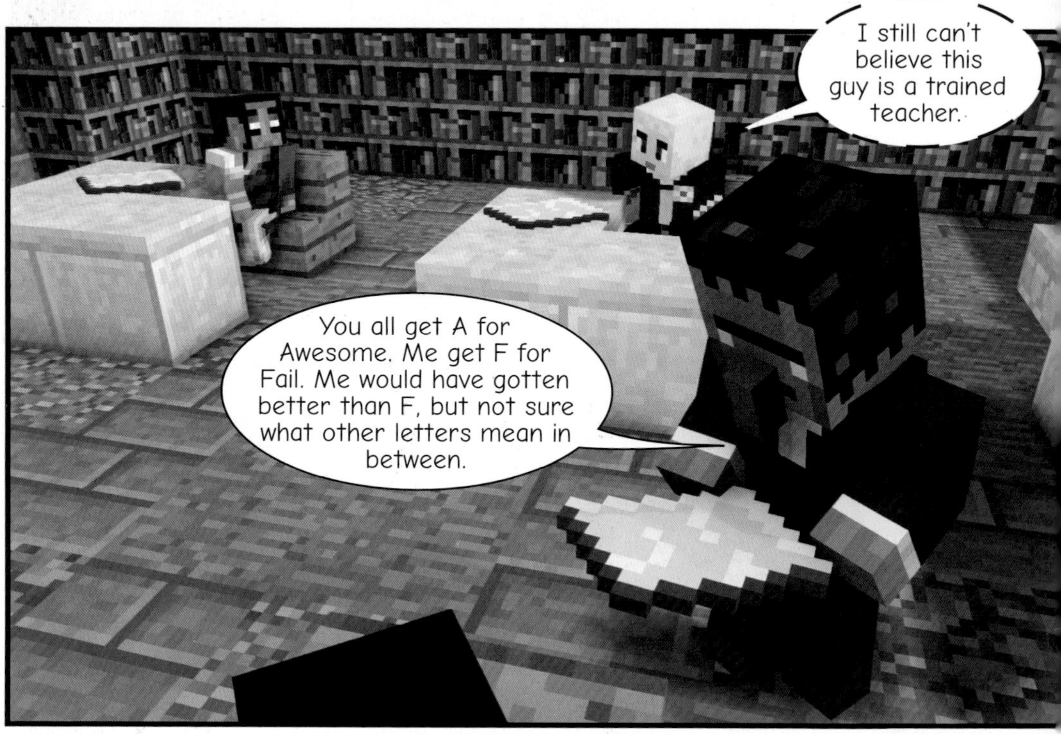
I still can't believe this guy is a trained teacher.
You all get A for Awesome. Me get F for Fail. Me would have gotten better than F, but not sure what other letters mean in between.

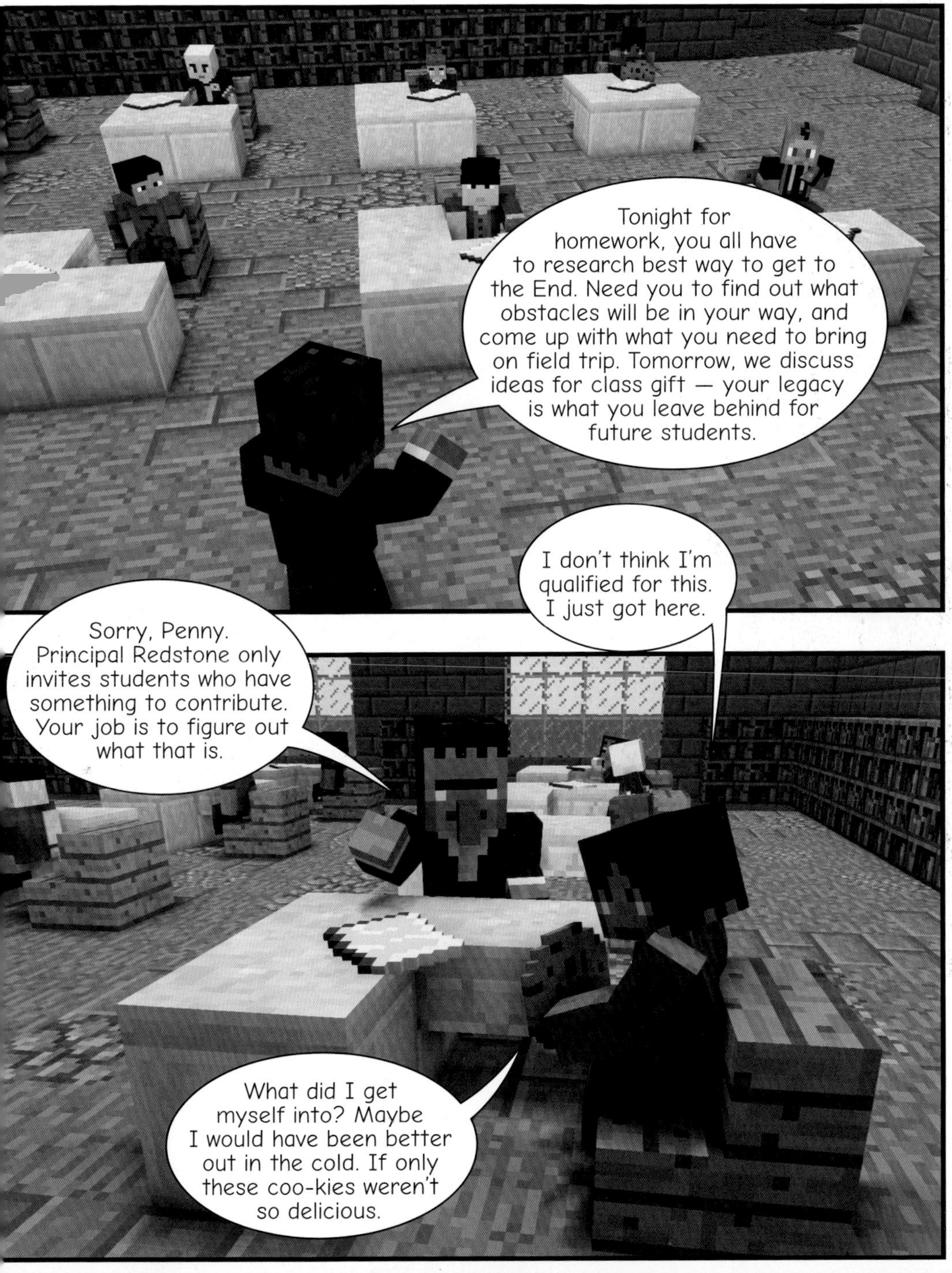
Tonight for homework, you all have to research best way to get to the End. Need you to find out what obstacles will be in your way, and come up with what you need to bring on field trip. Tomorrow, we discuss ideas for class gift — your legacy is what you leave behind for future students.
I don't think I'm qualified for this. I just got here.
Sorry, Penny. Principal Redstone only invites students who have something to contribute. Your job is to figure out what that is.
What did I get myself into? Maybe I would have been better out in the cold. If only these coo-kies weren't so delicious.

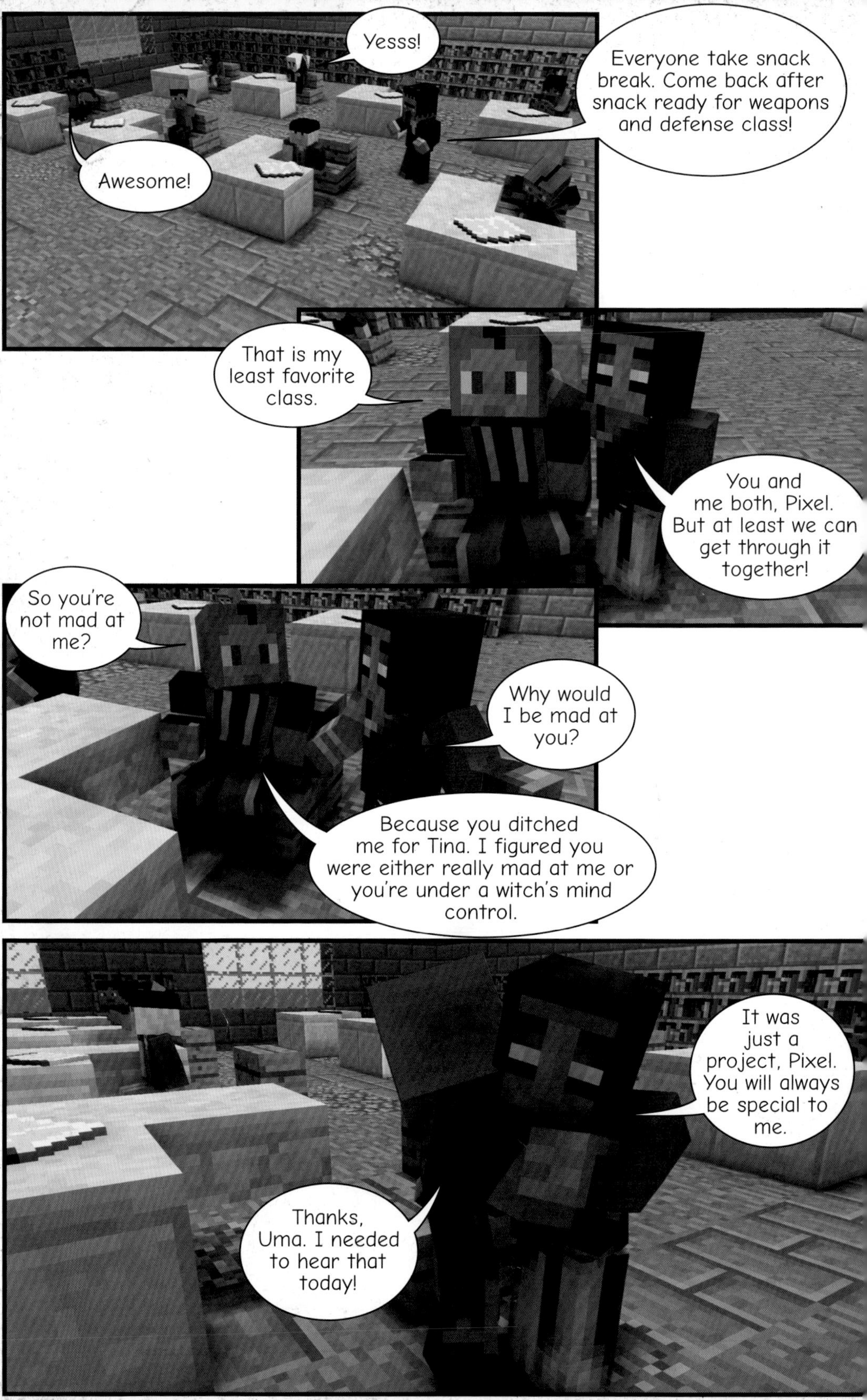
Yesss!
Everyone take snack break. Come back after snack ready for weapons and defense class!
Awesome!
That is my least favorite class.
You and me both, Pixel. But at least we can get through it together!
So you're not mad at me?
Why would I be mad at you?
Because you ditched me for Tina. I figured you were either really mad at me or you're under a witch's mind control.
It was just a project, Pixel. You will always be special to me.
Thanks, Uma. I needed to hear that today!

CHAPTER 4

A STORM
BREWS

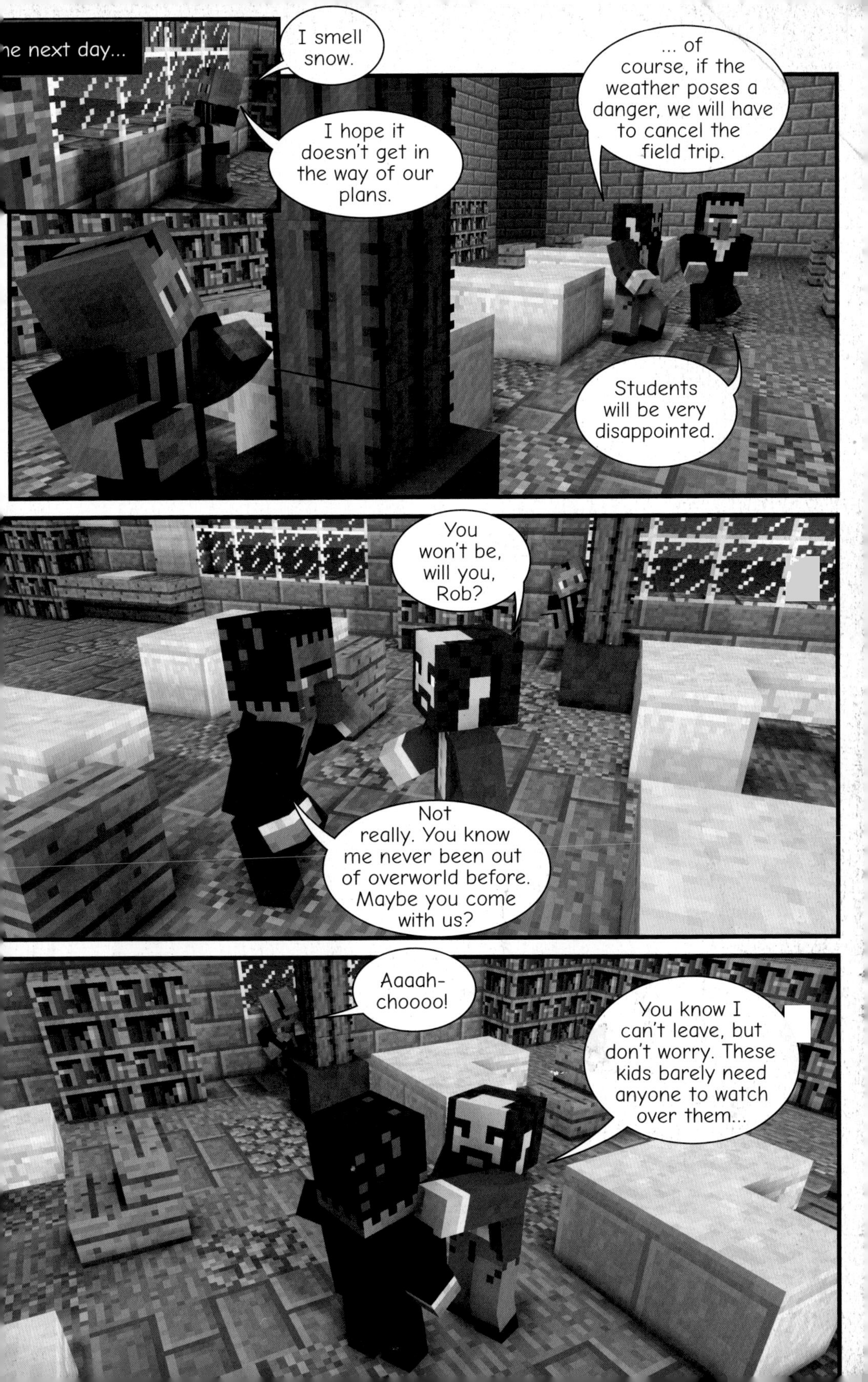

ne next day...
I smell snow.
I hope it doesn't get in the way of our plans.
... of course, if the weather poses a danger, we will have to cancel the field trip.
Students will be very disappointed.
You won't be, will you, Rob?
Not really. You know me never been out of overworld before. Maybe you come with us?
Aaaah-chooooo!
You know I can't leave, but don't worry. These kids barely need anyone to watch over them...

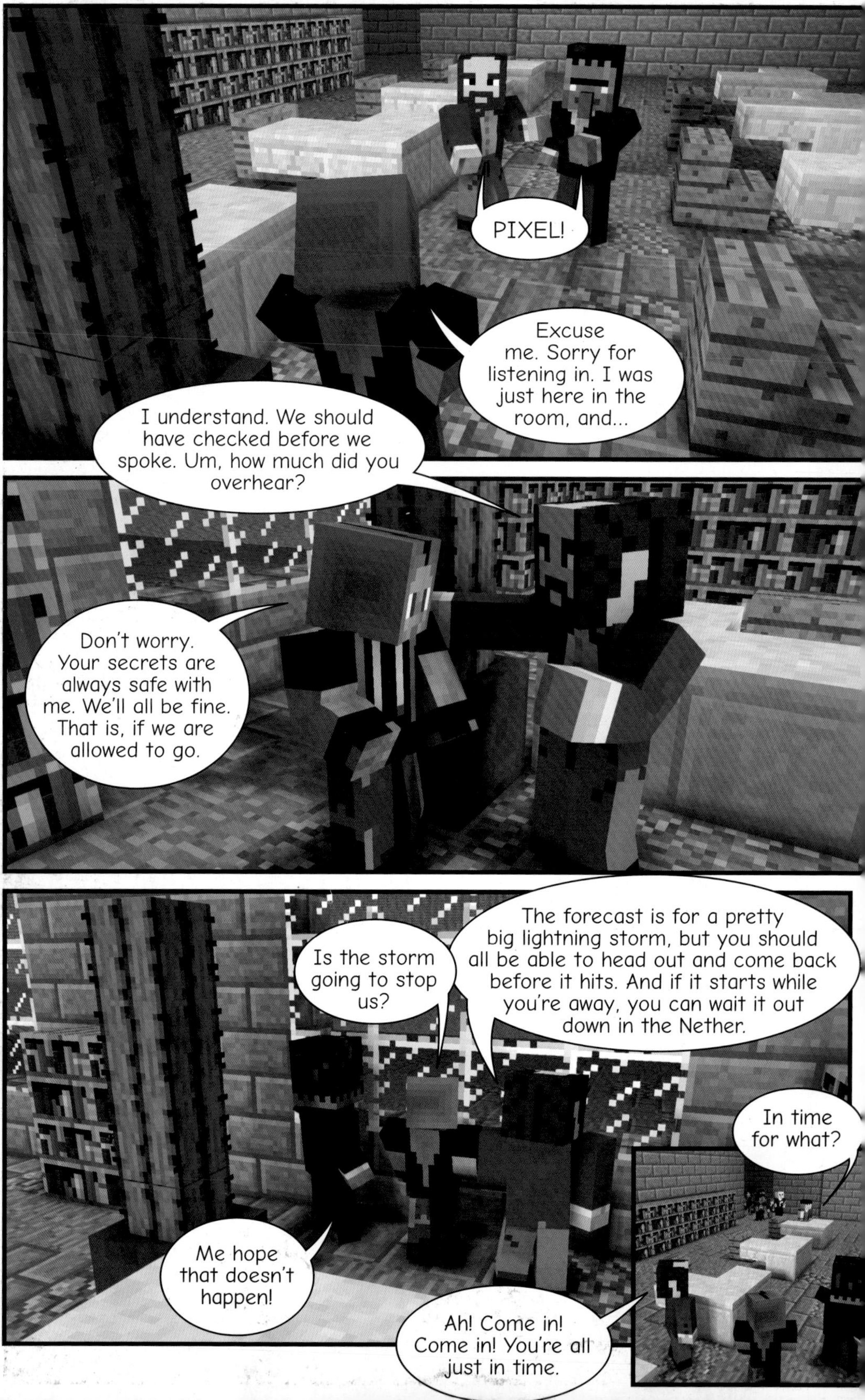
PIXEL!
Excuse me. Sorry for listening in. I was just here in the room, and...
I understand. We should have checked before we spoke. Um, how much did you overhear?
Don't worry. Your secrets are always safe with me. We'll all be fine. That is, if we are allowed to go.
Is the storm going to stop us?
The forecast is for a pretty big lightning storm, but you should all be able to head out and come back before it hits. And if it starts while you're away, you can wait it out down in the Nether.
Me hope that doesn't happen!
In time for what?
Ah! Come in! Come in! You're all just in time.

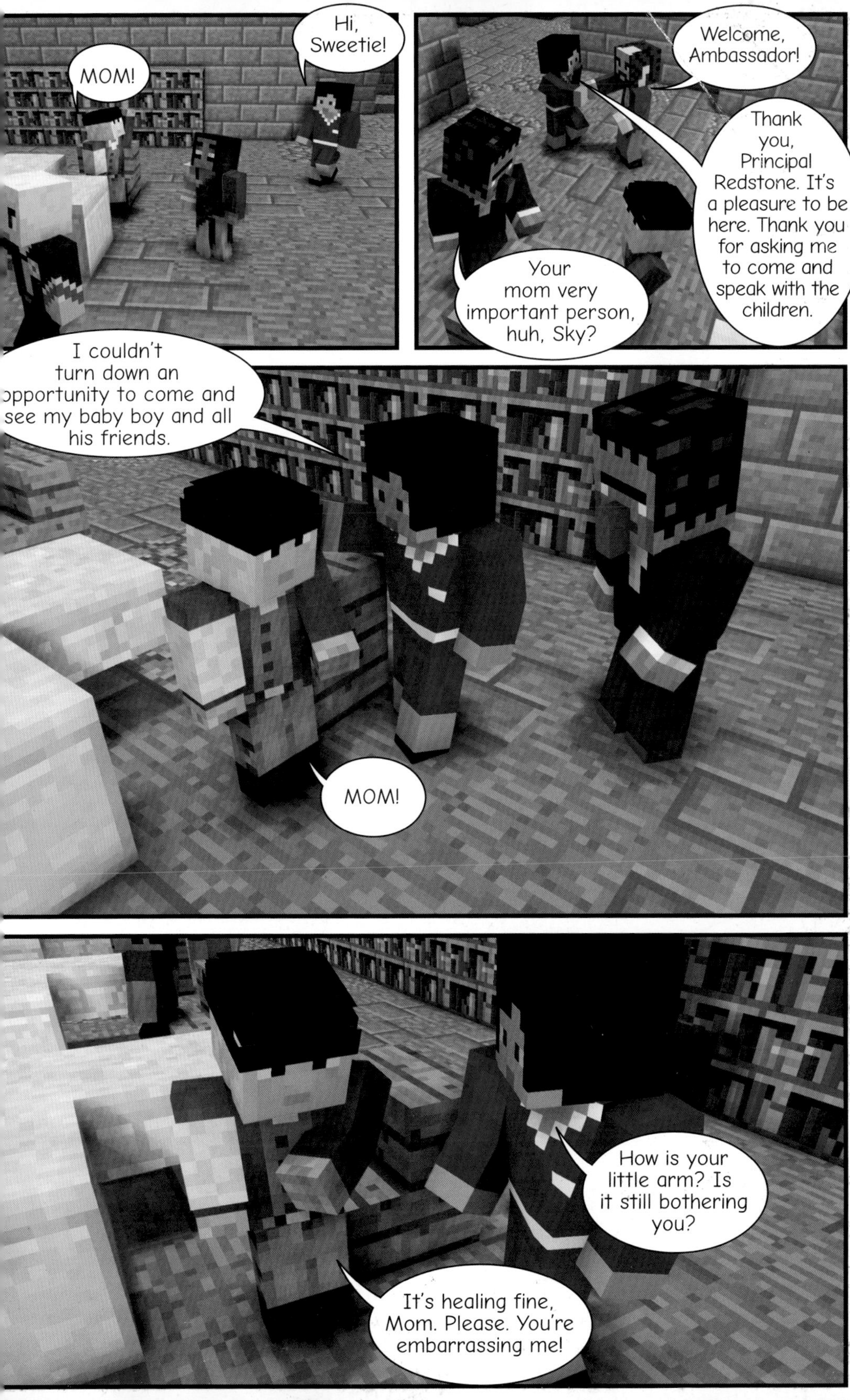
MOM!
Hi, Sweetie!
Welcome, Ambassador!
Thank you, Principal Redstone. It's a pleasure to be here. Thank you for asking me to come and speak with the children.
Your mom very important person, huh, Sky?
I couldn't turn down an opportunity to come and see my baby boy and all his friends.
MOM!
How is your little arm? Is it still bothering you?
It's healing fine, Mom. Please. You're embarrassing me!

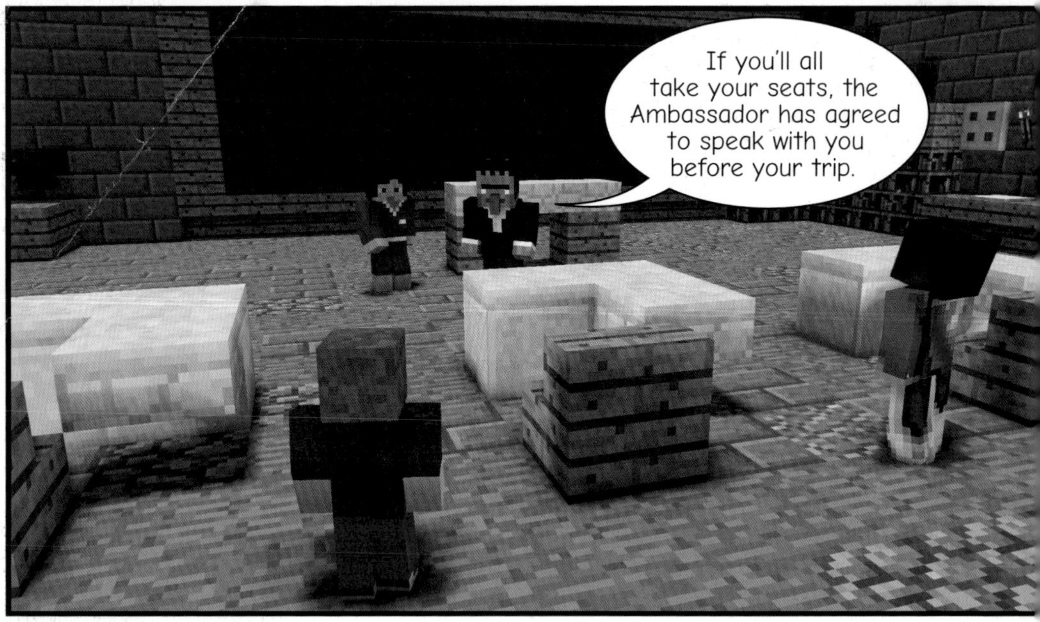
If you'll all take your seats, the Ambassador has agreed to speak with you before your trip.

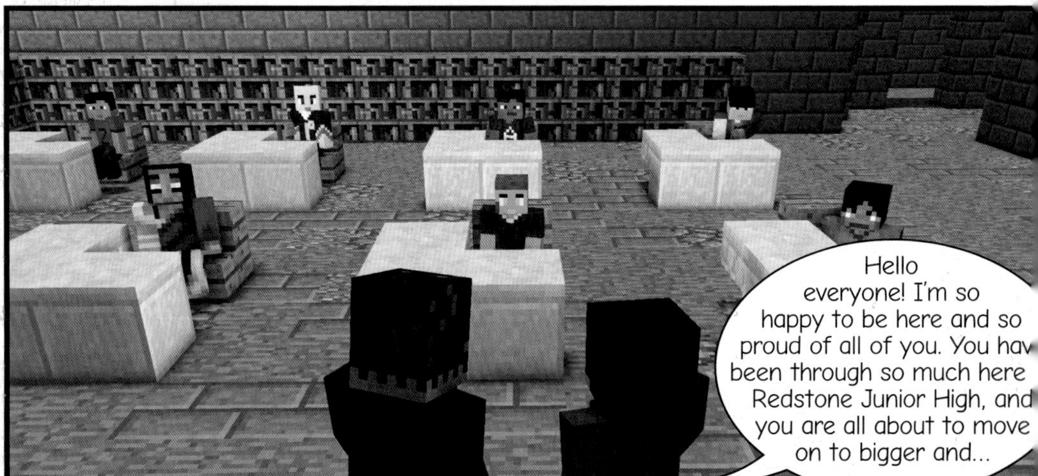
Hello everyone! I'm so happy to be here and so proud of all of you. You hav been through so much here Redstone Junior High, and you are all about to move on to bigger and...
RRRRRUMBLE

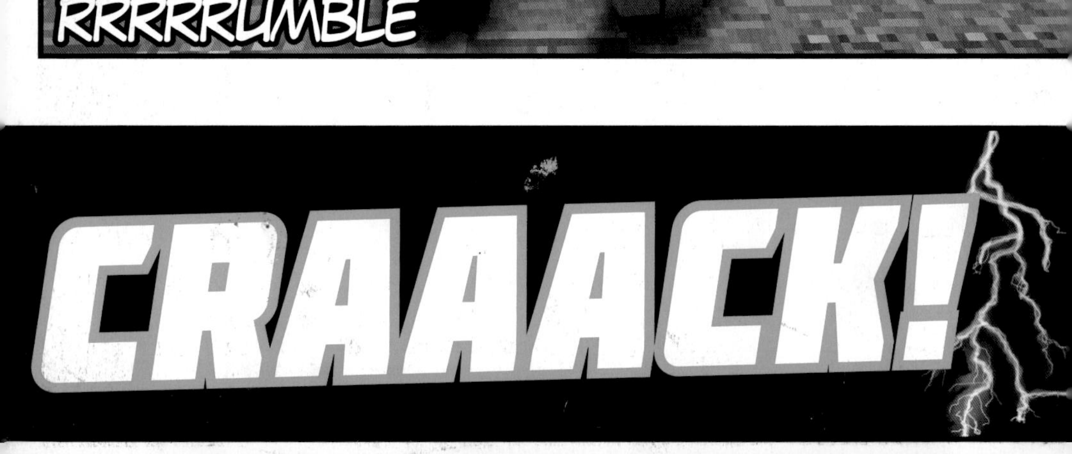
CRAAACK!

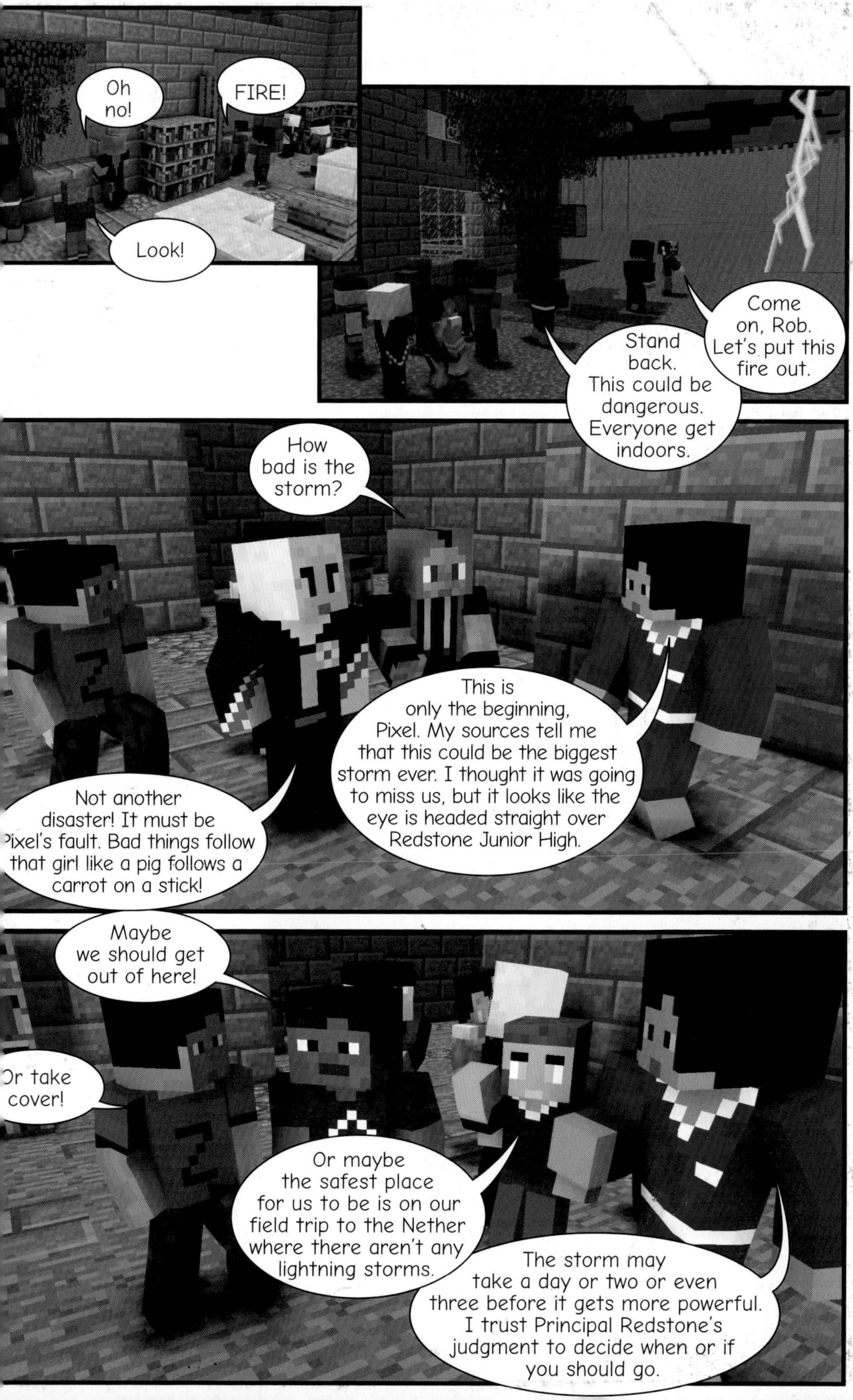
Oh no!
FIRE!
Look!
Stand back. This could be dangerous. Everyone get indoors.
Come on, Rob. Let's put this fire out.
How bad is the storm?
This is only the beginning, Pixel. My sources tell me that this could be the biggest storm ever. I thought it was going to miss us, but it looks like the eye is headed straight over Redstone Junior High.
Not another disaster! It must be Pixel's fault. Bad things follow that girl like a pig follows a carrot on a stick!
Maybe we should get out of here!
Or take cover!
Or maybe the safest place for us to be is on our field trip to the Nether where there aren't any lightning storms.
The storm may take a day or two or even three before it gets more powerful. I trust Principal Redstone's judgment to decide when or if you should go.

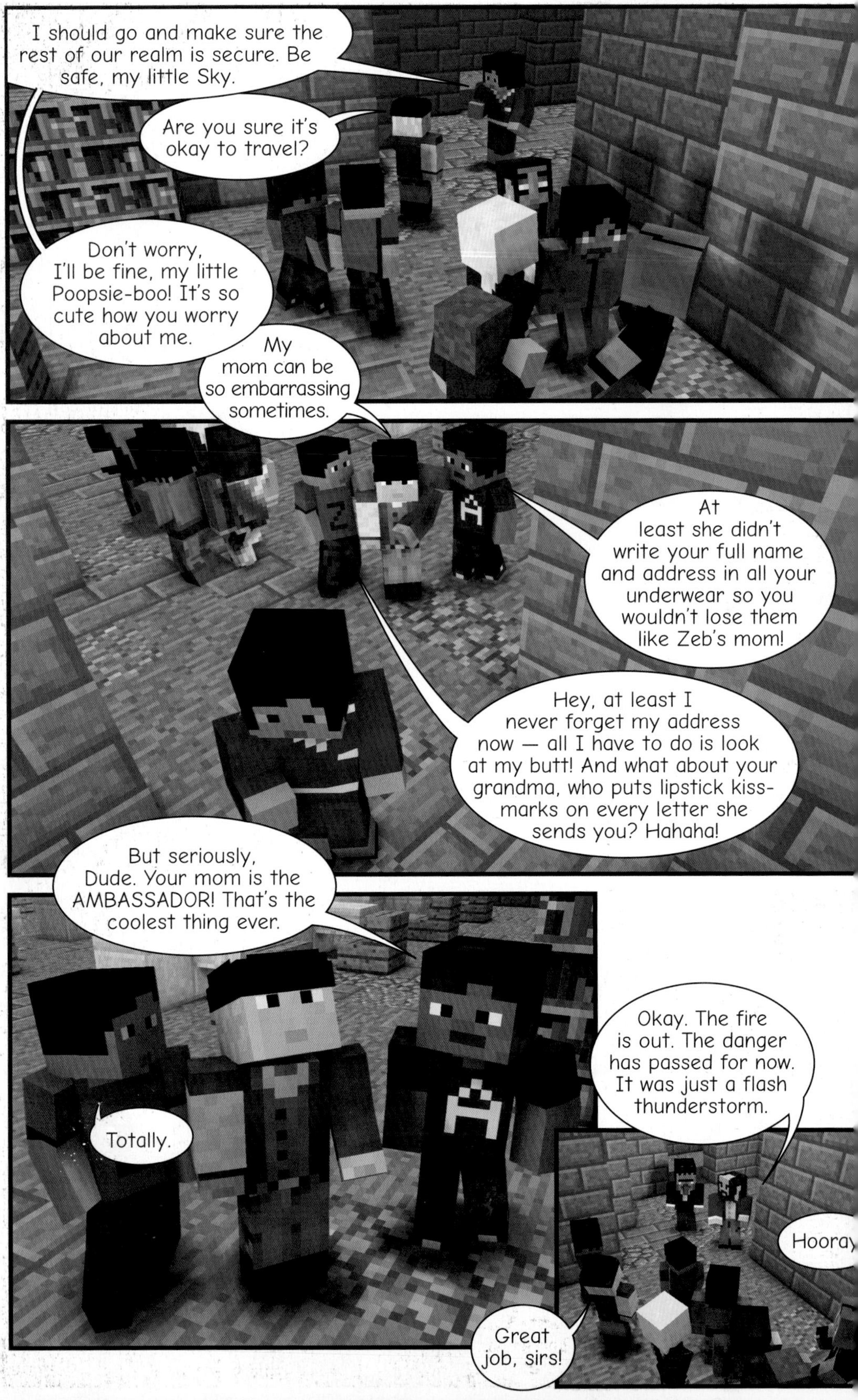
I should go and make sure the rest of our realm is secure. Be safe, my little Sky.
Are you sure it's okay to travel?
Don't worry, I'll be fine, my little Poopsie-boo! It's so cute how you worry about me.
My mom can be so embarrassing sometimes.
At least she didn't write your full name and address in all your underwear so you wouldn't lose them like Zeb's mom!
Hey, at least I never forget my address now — all I have to do is look at my butt! And what about your grandma, who puts lipstick kiss-marks on every letter she sends you? Hahaha!
But seriously, Dude. Your mom is the AMBASSADOR! That's the coolest thing ever.
Totally.
Okay. The fire is out. The danger has passed for now. It was just a flash thunderstorm.
Hooray
Great job, sirs!

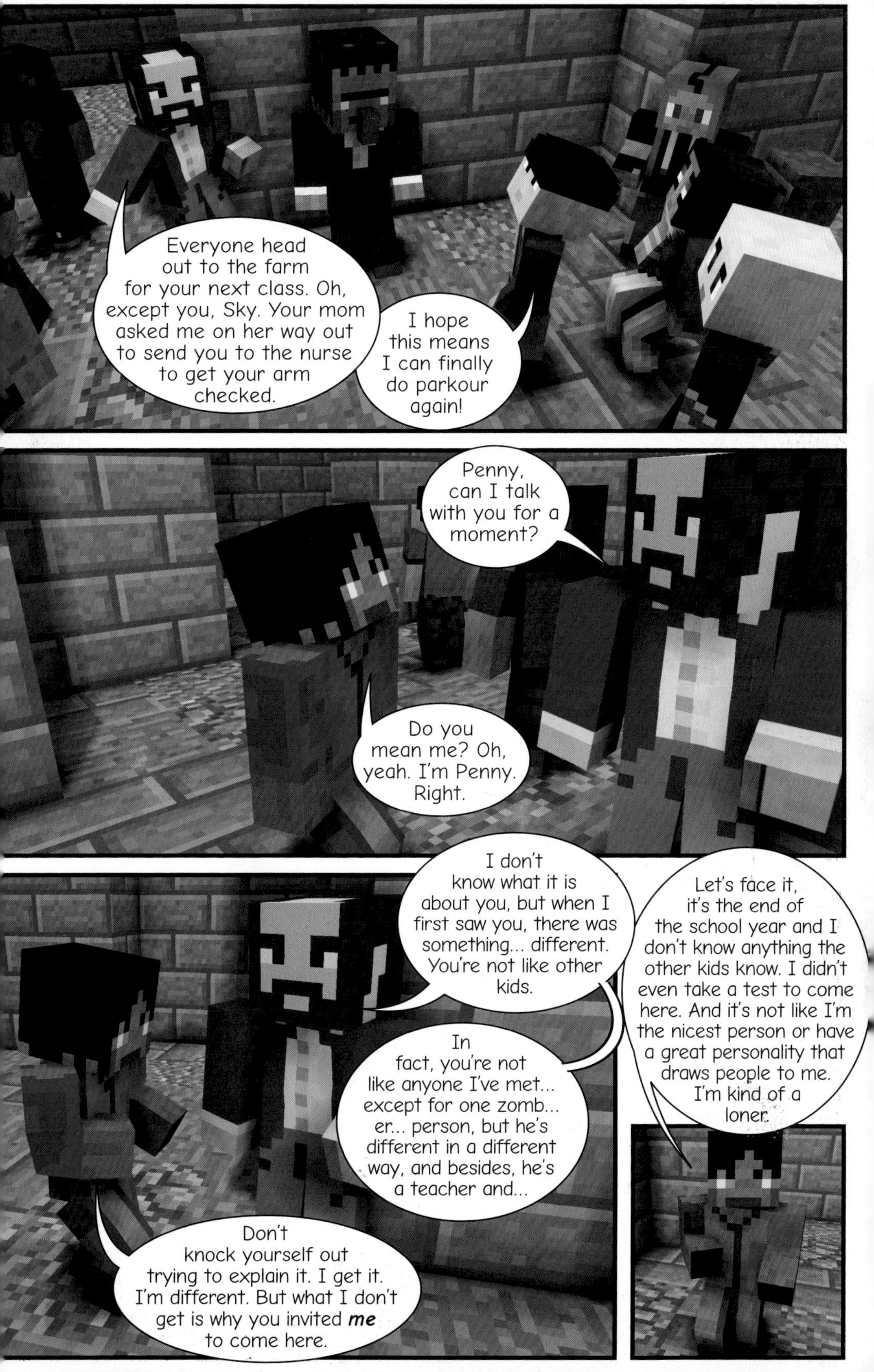
Everyone head out to the farm for your next class. Oh, except you, Sky. Your mom asked me on her way out to send you to the nurse to get your arm checked.
I hope this means I can finally do parkour again!
Penny, can I talk with you for a moment?
Do you mean me? Oh, yeah. I'm Penny. Right.
I don't know what it is about you, but when I first saw you, there was something... different. You're not like other kids.
In fact, you're not like anyone I've met... except for one zomb... er... person, but he's different in a different way, and besides, he's a teacher and...
Don't knock yourself out trying to explain it. I get it. I'm different. But what I don't get is why you invited *me* to come here.
Let's face it, it's the end of the school year and I don't know anything the other kids know. I didn't even take a test to come here. And it's not like I'm the nicest person or have a great personality that draws people to me. I'm kind of a loner.

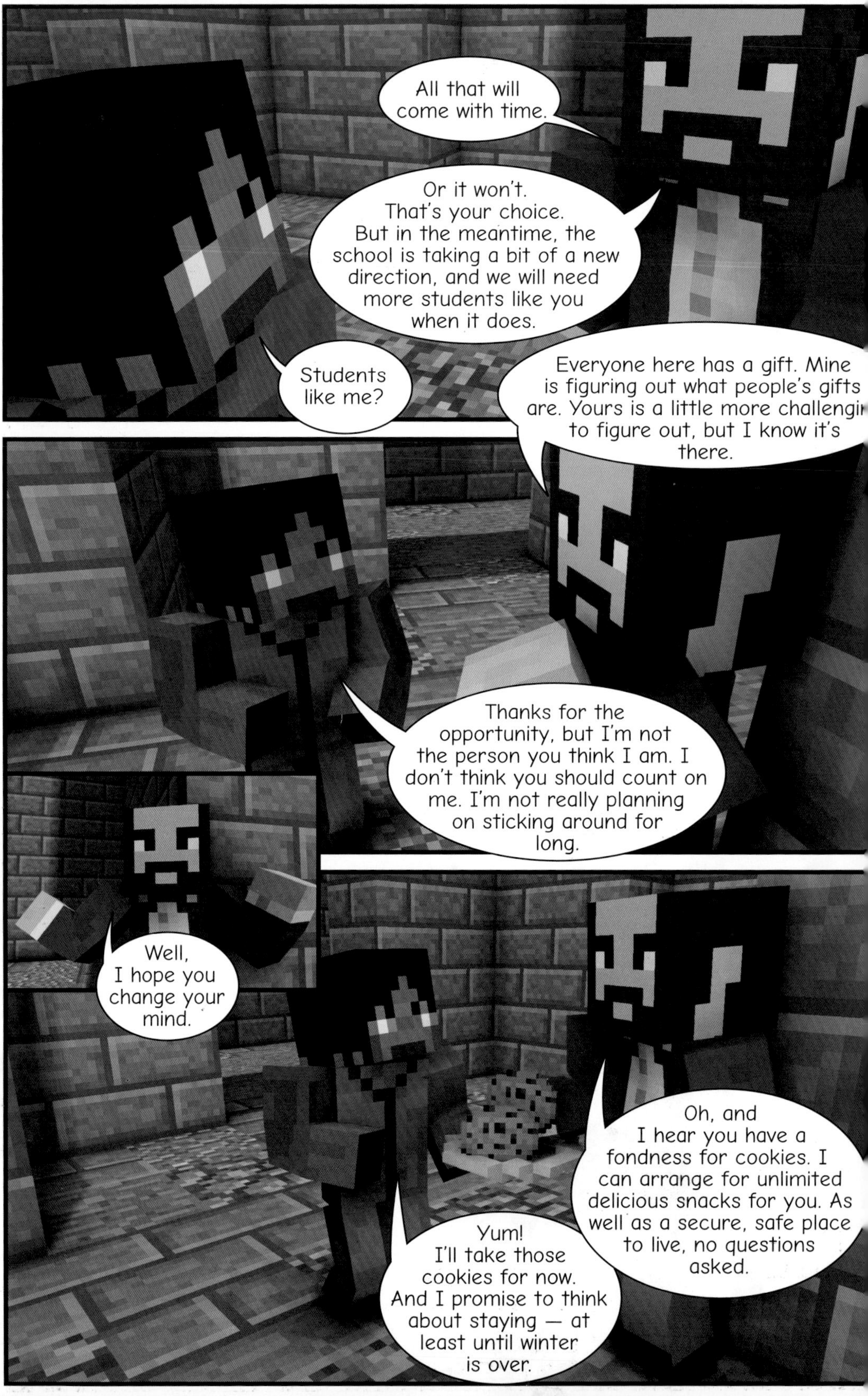
All that will come with time.
Or it won't. That's your choice. But in the meantime, the school is taking a bit of a new direction, and we will need more students like you when it does.
Students like me?
Everyone here has a gift. Mine is figuring out what people's gifts are. Yours is a little more challengi to figure out, but I know it's there.
Thanks for the opportunity, but I'm not the person you think I am. I don't think you should count on me. I'm not really planning on sticking around for long.
Well, I hope you change your mind.
Oh, and I hear you have a fondness for cookies. I can arrange for unlimited delicious snacks for you. As well as a secure, safe place to live, no questions asked.
Yum! I'll take those cookies for now. And I promise to think about staying — at least until winter is over.

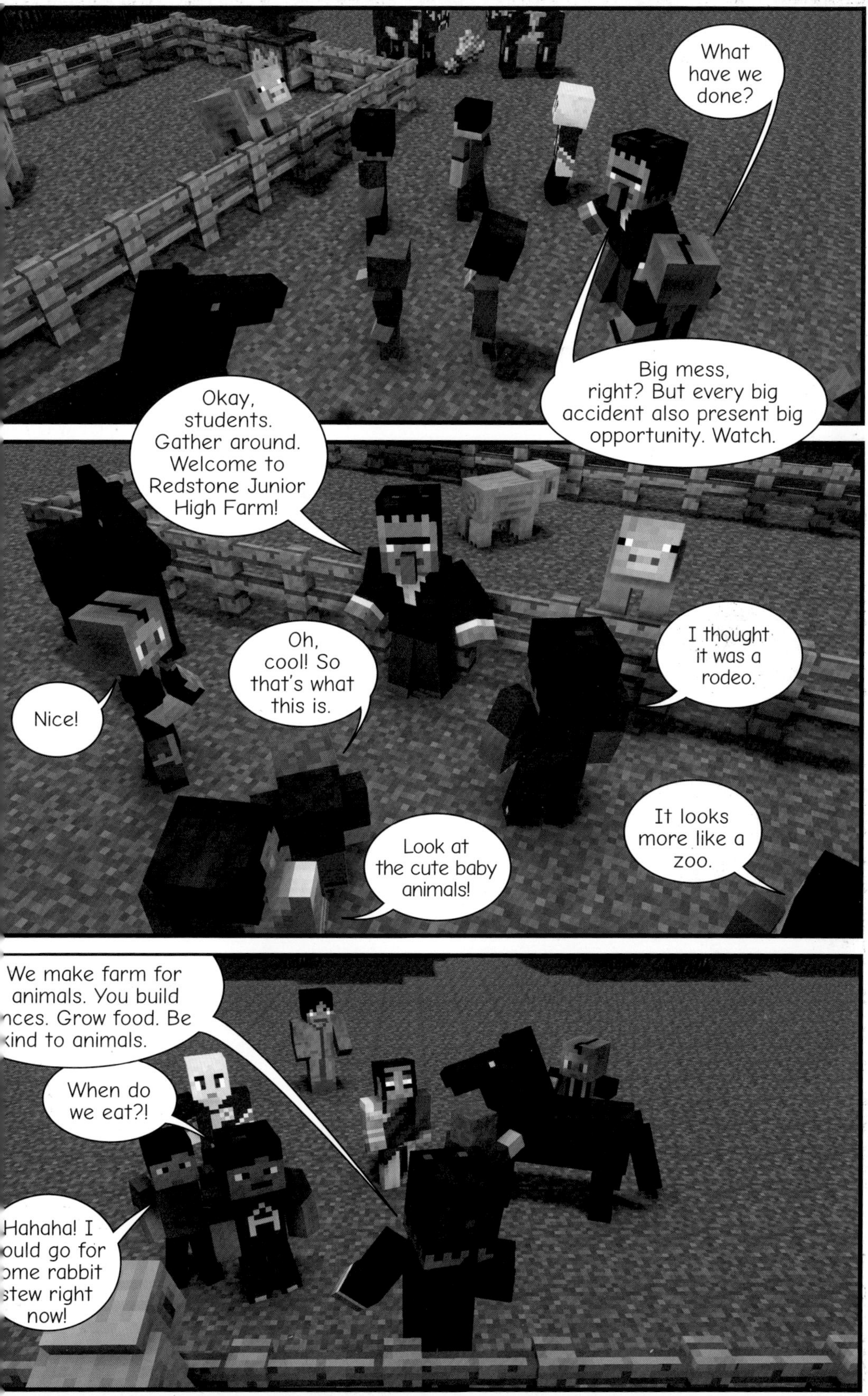

What have we done?
Big mess, right? But every big accident also present big opportunity. Watch.
Okay, students. Gather around. Welcome to Redstone Junior High Farm!
Nice!
Oh, cool! So that's what this is.
I thought it was a rodeo.
Look at the cute baby animals!
It looks more like a zoo.
We make farm for animals. You build nces. Grow food. Be kind to animals.
When do we eat?!
Hahaha! I ould go for ome rabbit stew right now!

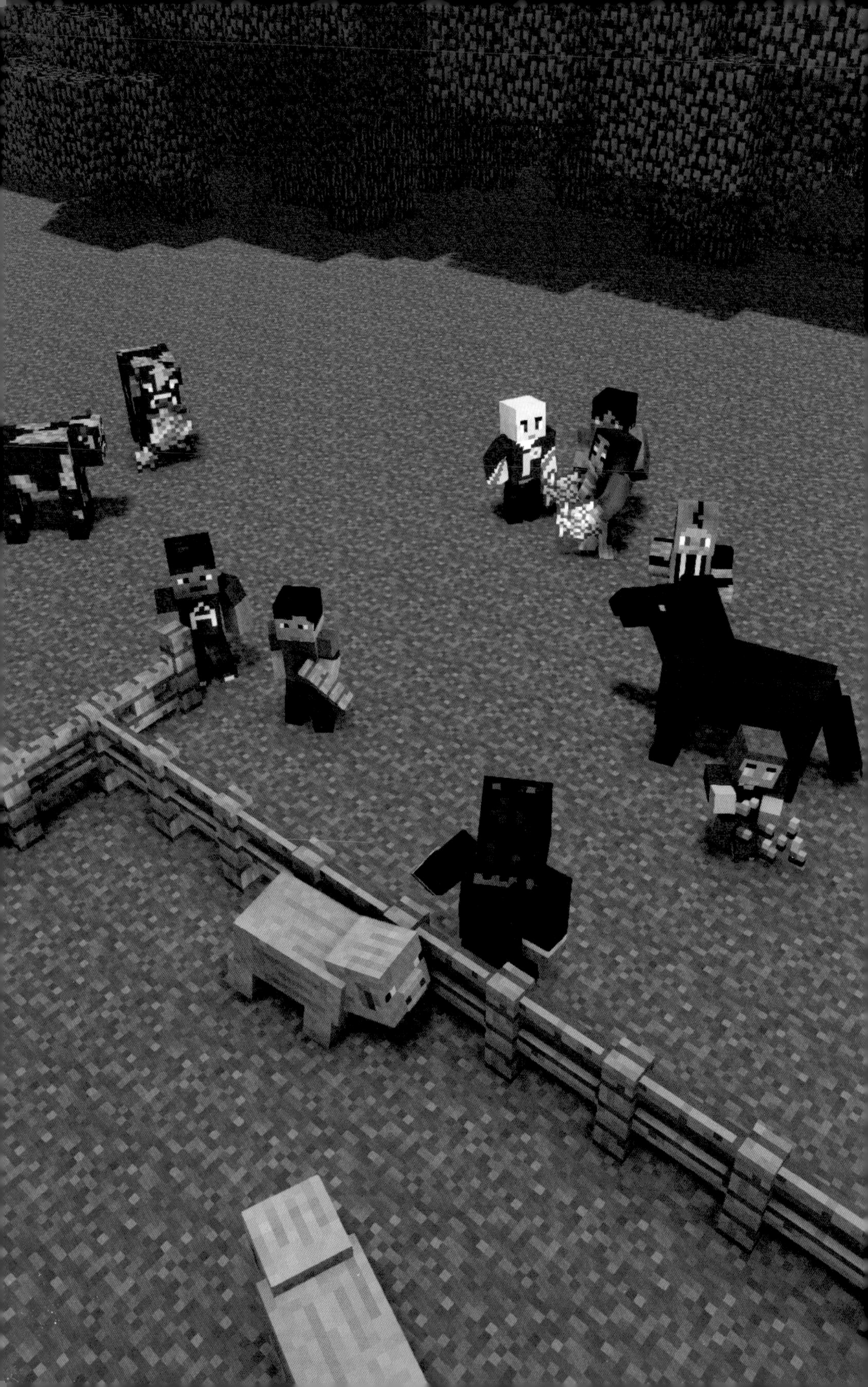

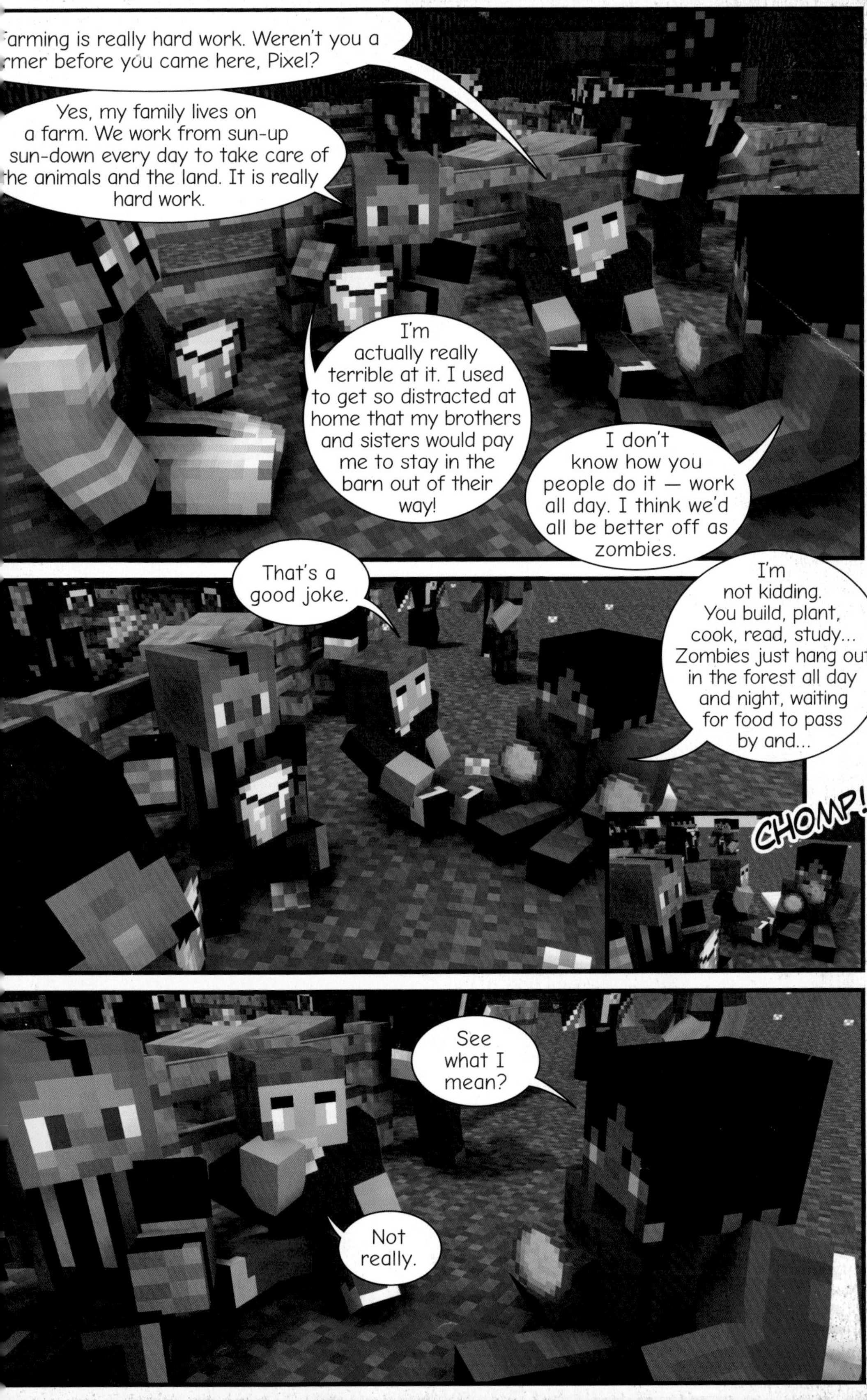

Farming is really hard work. Weren't you a farmer before you came here, Pixel?
Yes, my family lives on a farm. We work from sun-up sun-down every day to take care of the animals and the land. It is really hard work.
I'm actually really terrible at it. I used to get so distracted at home that my brothers and sisters would pay me to stay in the barn out of their way!
I don't know how you people do it — work all day. I think we'd all be better off as zombies.
That's a good joke.
I'm not kidding. You build, plant, cook, read, study... Zombies just hang out in the forest all day and night, waiting for food to pass by and...
CHOMP!
See what I mean?
Not really.

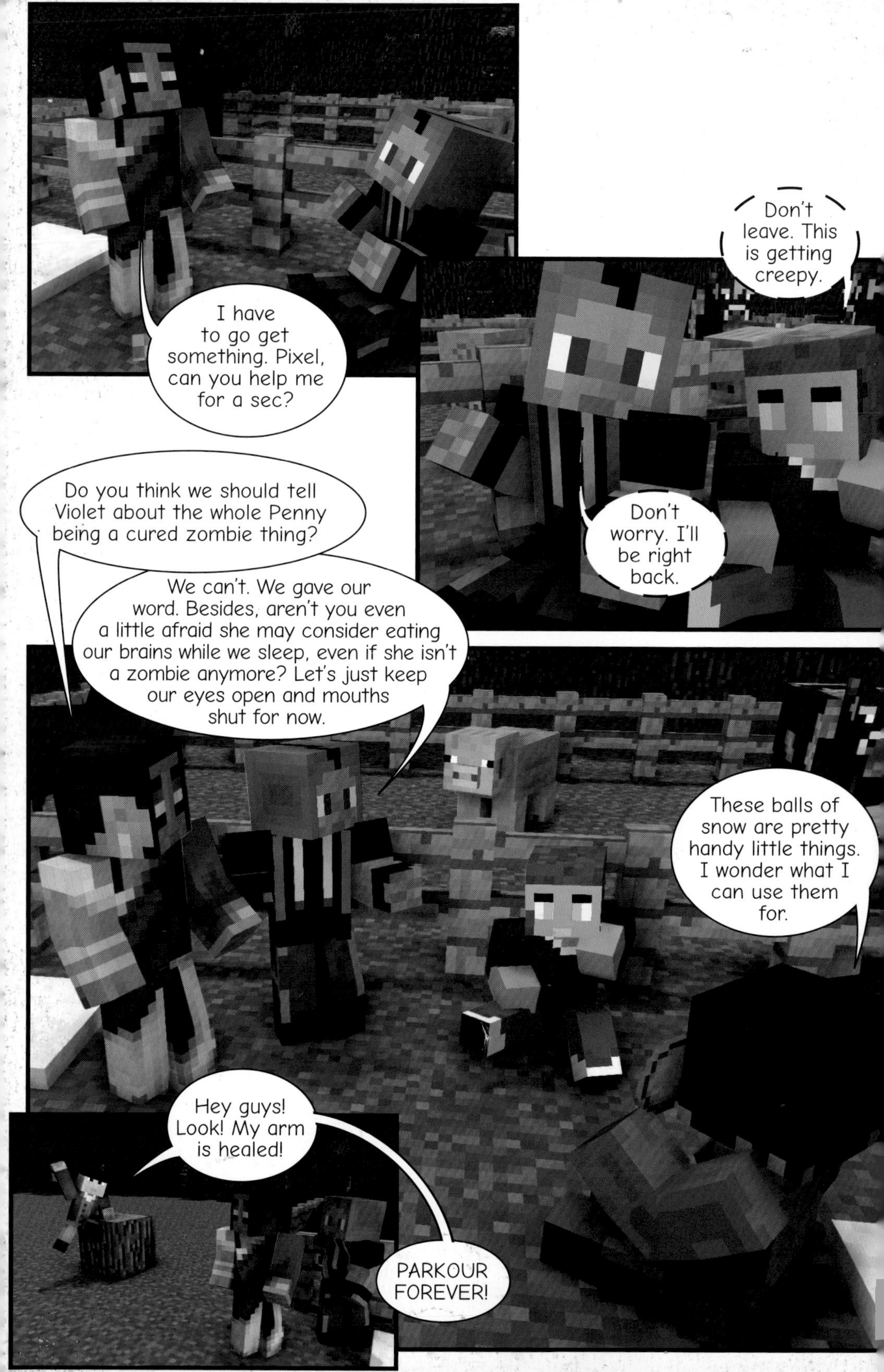
I have to go get something. Pixel, can you help me for a sec?
Don't leave. This is getting creepy.
Don't worry. I'll be right back.
Do you think we should tell Violet about the whole Penny being a cured zombie thing?
We can't. We gave our word. Besides, aren't you even a little afraid she may consider eating our brains while we sleep, even if she isn't a zombie anymore? Let's just keep our eyes open and mouths shut for now.
These balls of snow are pretty handy little things. I wonder what I can use them for.
Hey guys! Look! My arm is healed!
PARKOUR FOREVER!

CHAPTER 5

THE VILLAGE

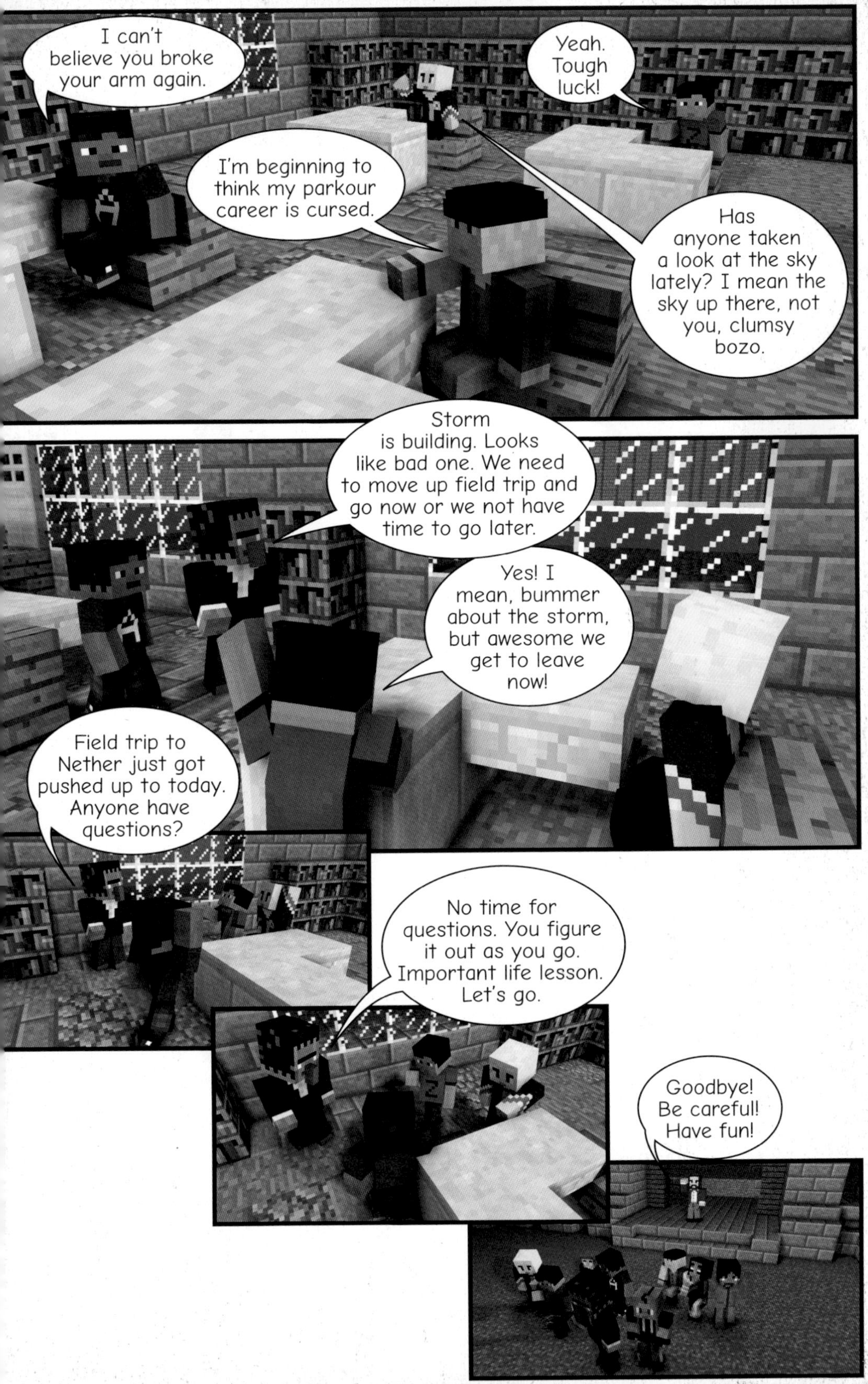
I can't believe you broke your arm again.
Yeah. Tough luck!
I'm beginning to think my parkour career is cursed.
Has anyone taken a look at the sky lately? I mean the sky up there, not you, clumsy bozo.
Storm is building. Looks like bad one. We need to move up field trip and go now or we not have time to go later.
Yes! I mean, bummer about the storm, but awesome we get to leave now!
Field trip to Nether just got pushed up to today. Anyone have questions?
No time for questions. You figure it out as you go. Important life lesson. Let's go.
Goodbye! Be careful! Have fun!

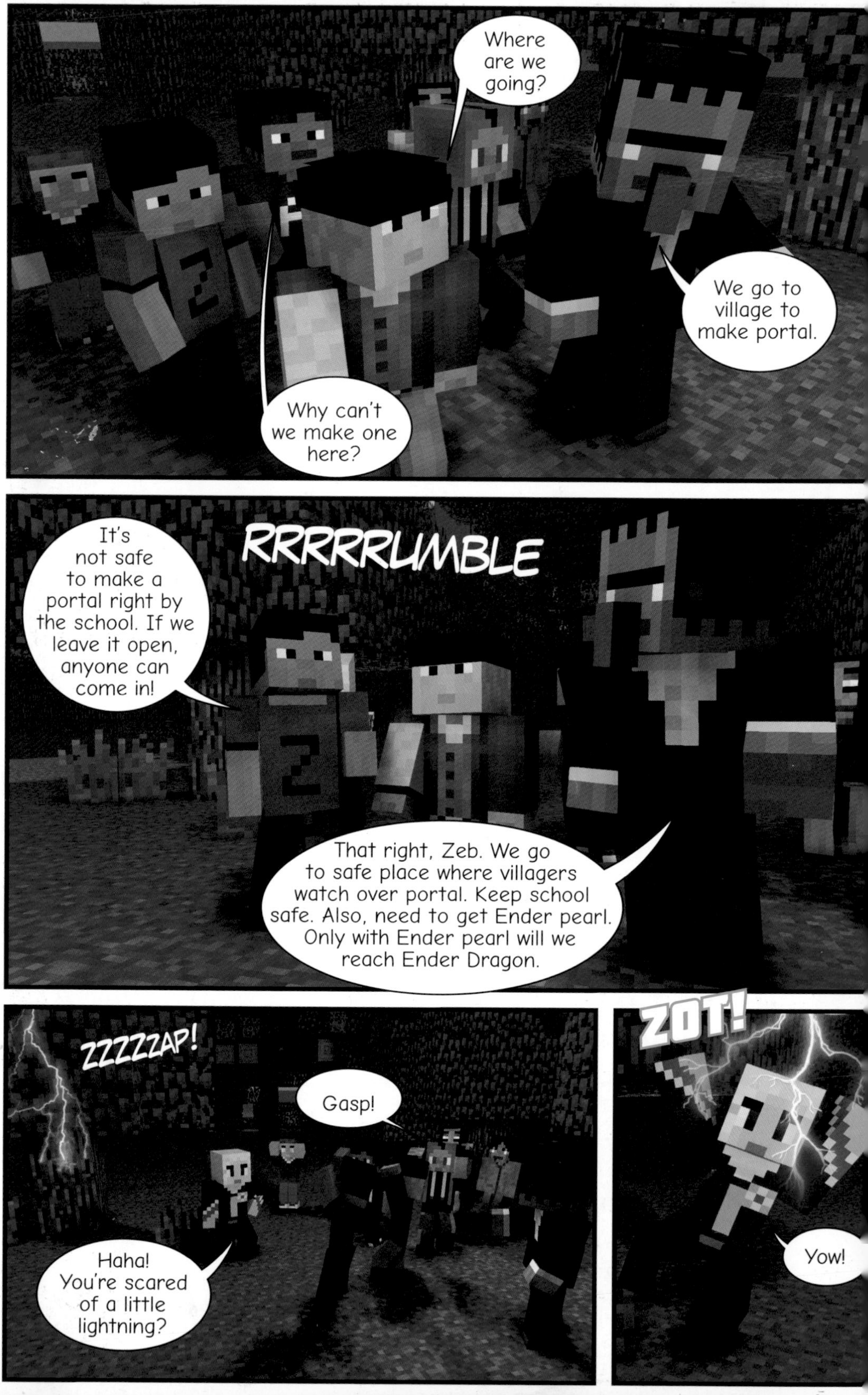
Where are we going?
We go to village to make portal.
Why can't we make one here?
RRRRRUMBLE
It's not safe to make a portal right by the school. If we leave it open, anyone can come in!
That right, Zeb. We go to safe place where villagers watch over portal. Keep school safe. Also, need to get Ender pearl. Only with Ender pearl will we reach Ender Dragon.
ZZZZZAP!
Gasp!
Haha! You're scared of a little lightning?
ZOT!
Yow!

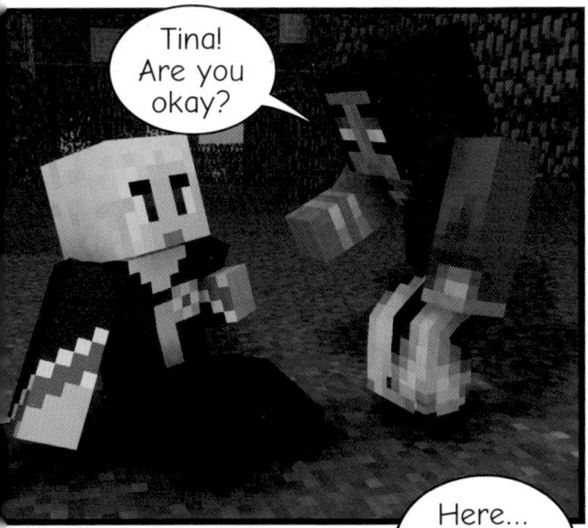
Tina!
Are you
okay?

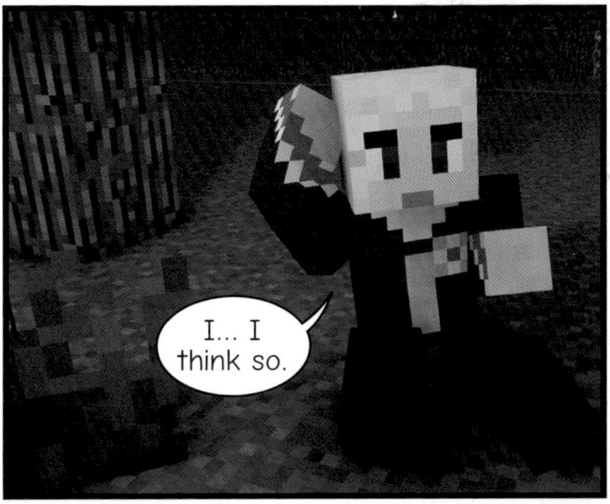
I... I
think so.

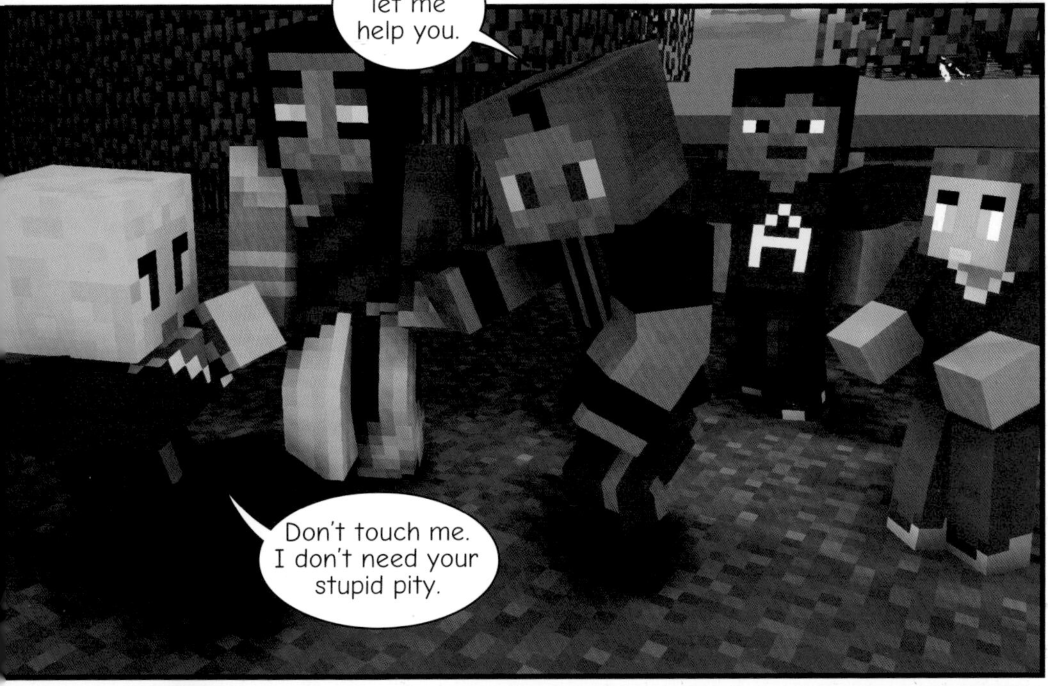
Here...
let me
help you.
Don't touch me.
I don't need your
stupid pity.

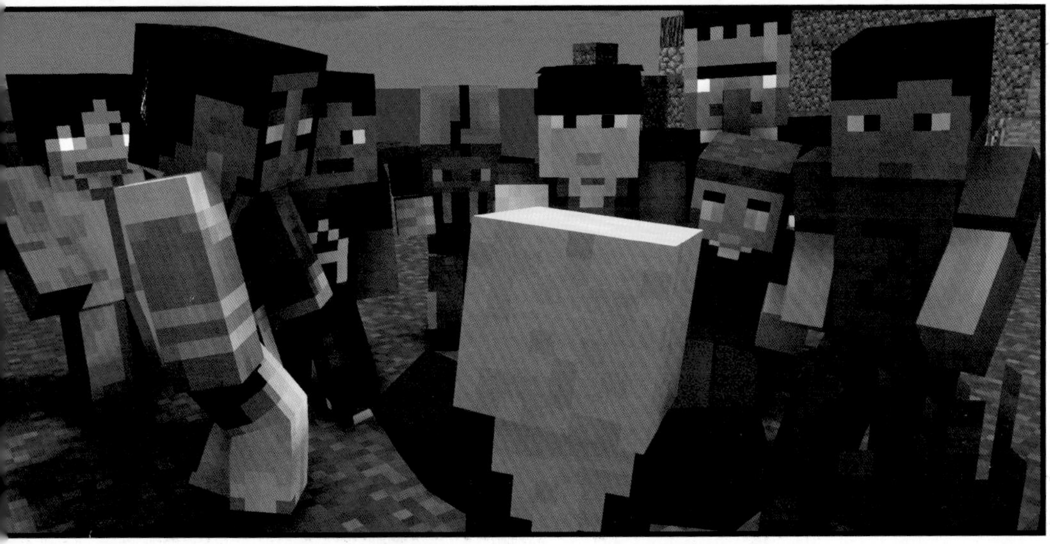

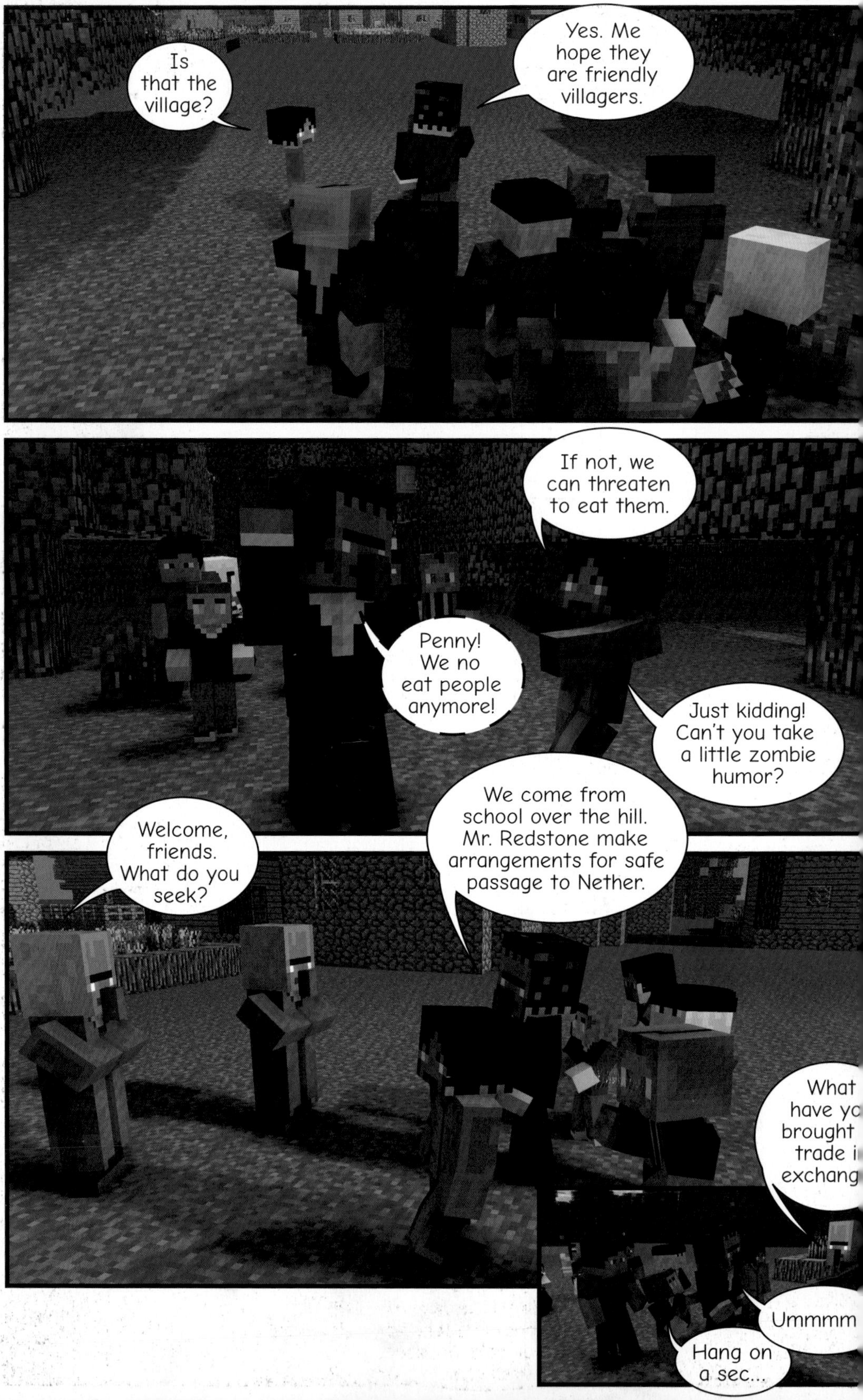
Is that the village?
Yes. Me hope they are friendly villagers.
If not, we can threaten to eat them.
Penny! We no eat people anymore!
Just kidding! Can't you take a little zombie humor?
Welcome, friends. What do you seek?
We come from school over the hill. Mr. Redstone make arrangements for safe passage to Nether.
What have yo brought trade i exchang
Ummmm
Hang on a sec...

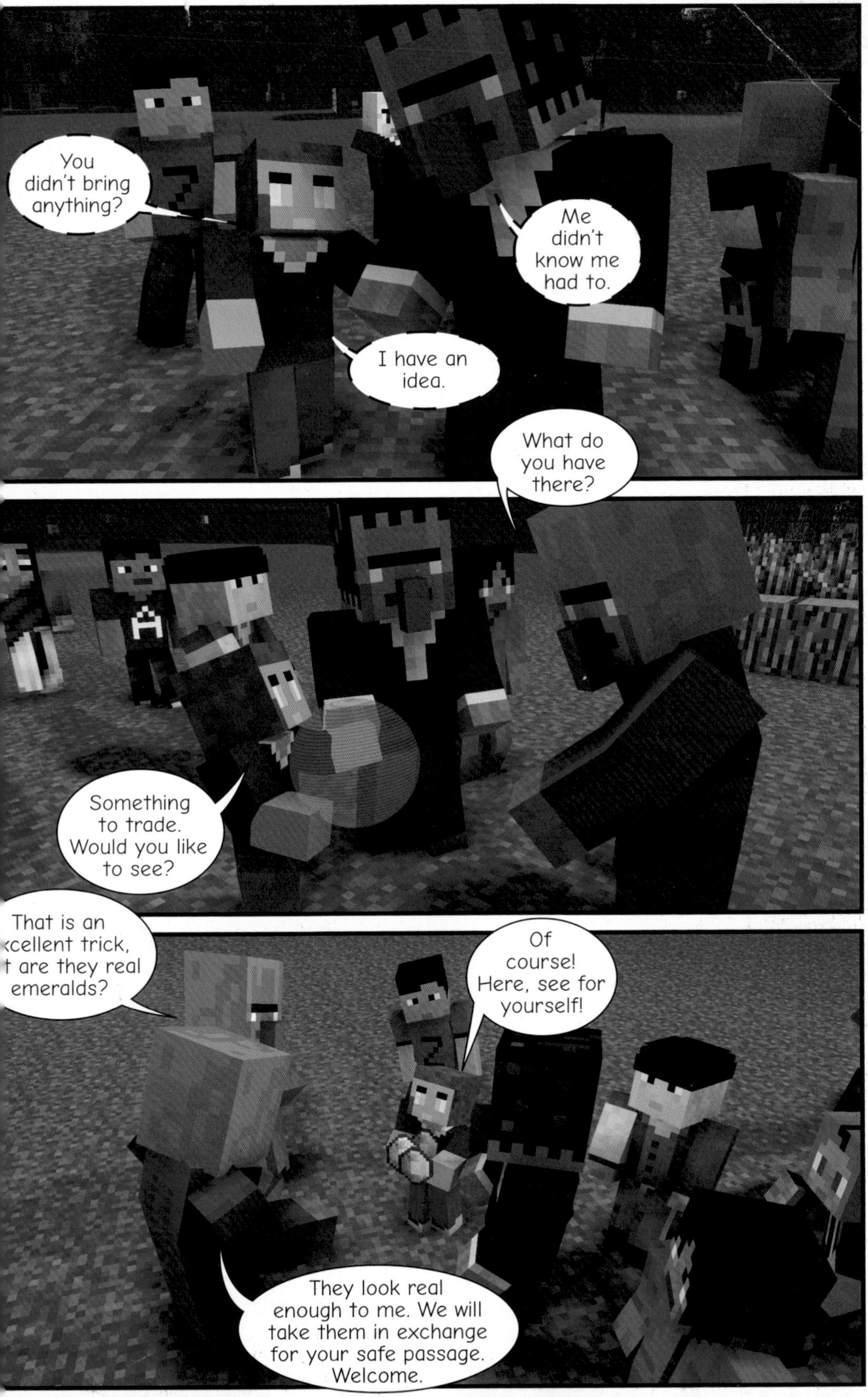
You didn't bring anything?
Me didn't know me had to.
I have an idea.
What do you have there?
Something to trade. Would you like to see?
That is an xcellent trick, t are they real emeralds?
Of course! Here, see for yourself!
They look real enough to me. We will take them in exchange for your safe passage. Welcome.

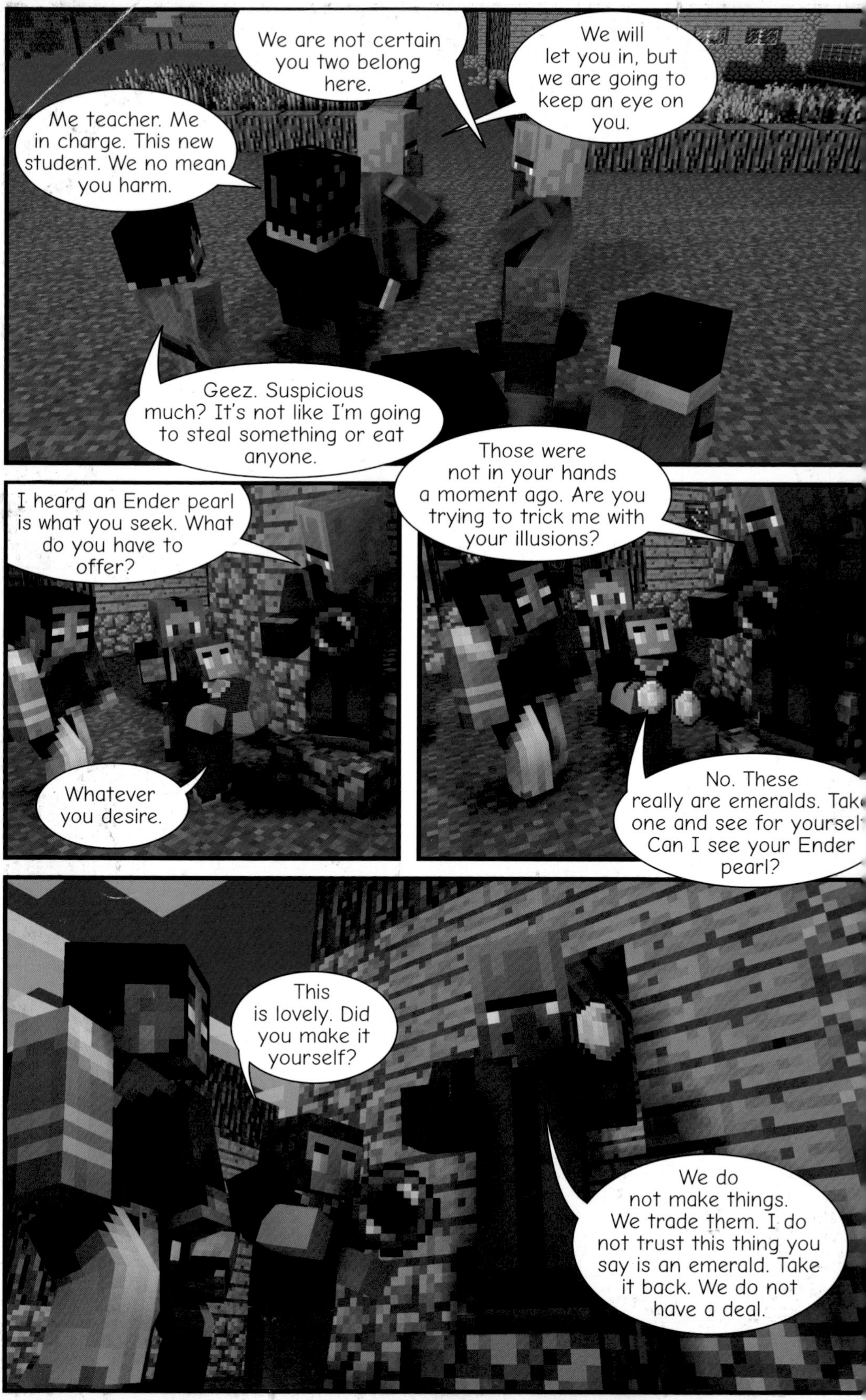
Me teacher. Me in charge. This new student. We no mean you harm.
We are not certain you two belong here.
We will let you in, but we are going to keep an eye on you.
Geez. Suspicious much? It's not like I'm going to steal something or eat anyone.
I heard an Ender pearl is what you seek. What do you have to offer?
Whatever you desire.
Those were not in your hands a moment ago. Are you trying to trick me with your illusions?
No. These really are emeralds. Tak one and see for yoursel Can I see your Ender pearl?
This is lovely. Did you make it yourself?
We do not make things. We trade them. I do not trust this thing you say is an emerald. Take it back. We do not have a deal.

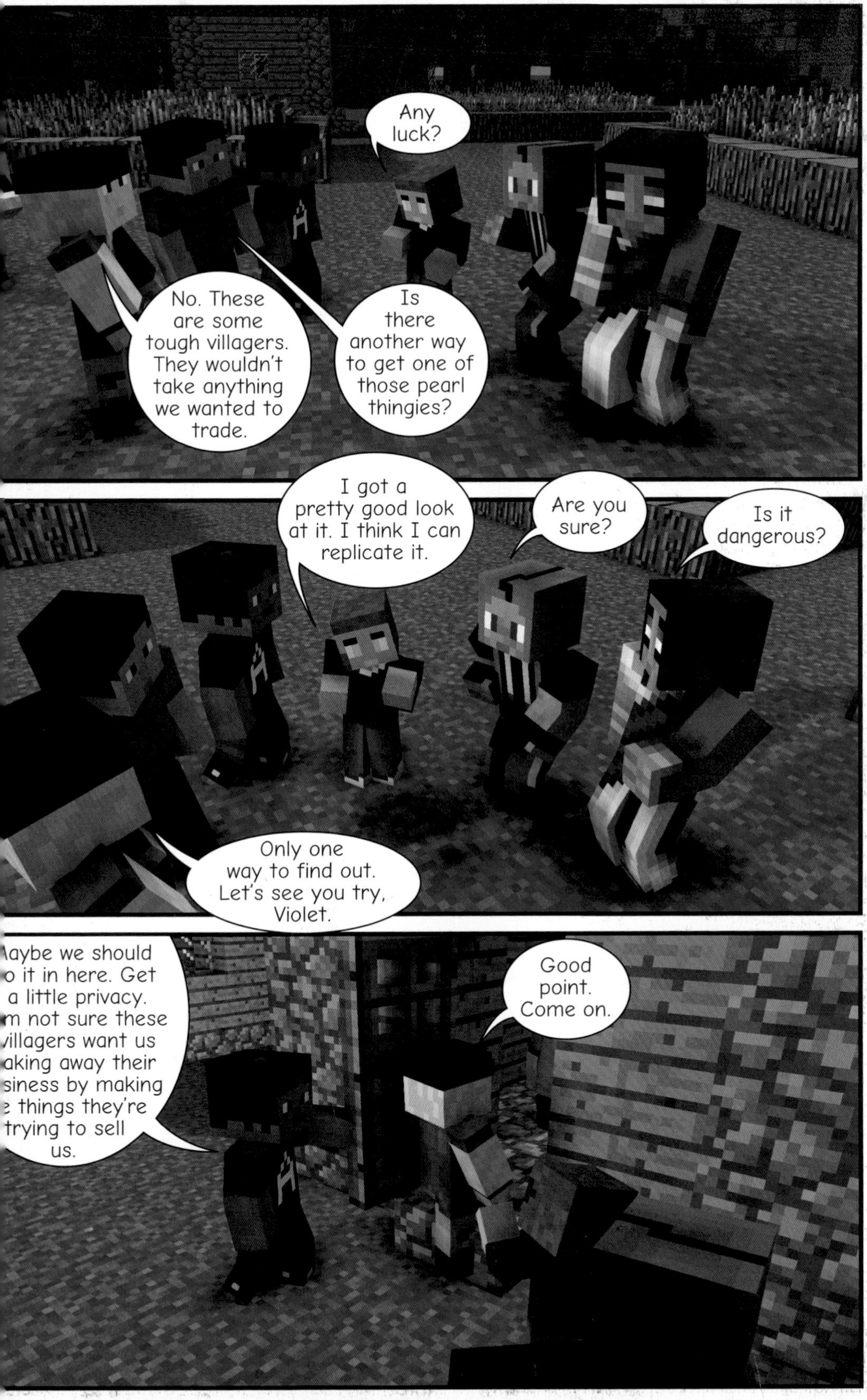
Any luck?
No. These are some tough villagers. They wouldn't take anything we wanted to trade.
Is there another way to get one of those pearl thingies?
I got a pretty good look at it. I think I can replicate it.
Are you sure?
Is it dangerous?
Only one way to find out. Let's see you try, Violet.
aybe we should o it in here. Get a little privacy. m not sure these villagers want us aking away their siness by making things they're trying to sell us.
Good point. Come on.

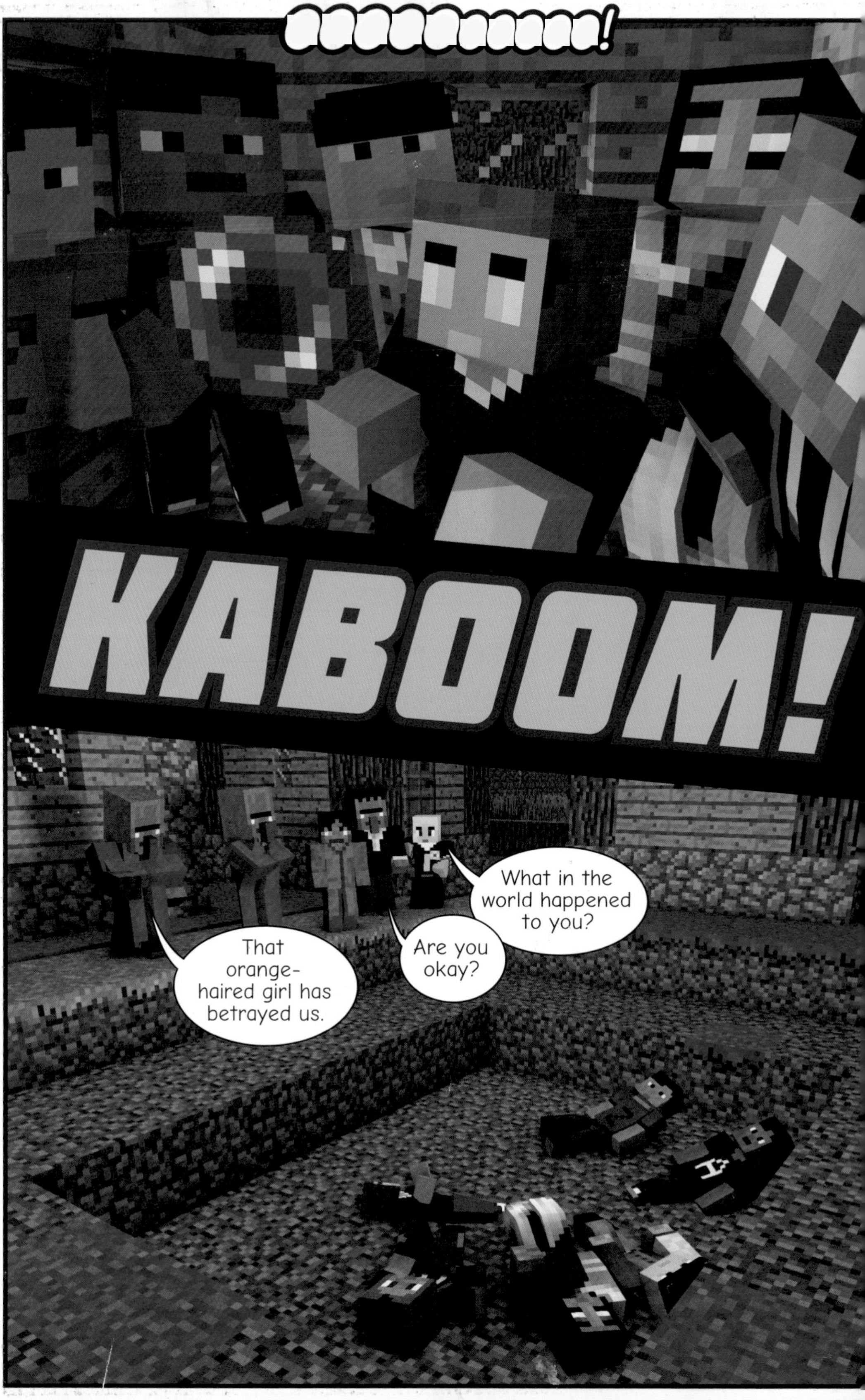
KABOOM!
That orange-haired girl has betrayed us.
Are you okay?
What in the world happened to you?

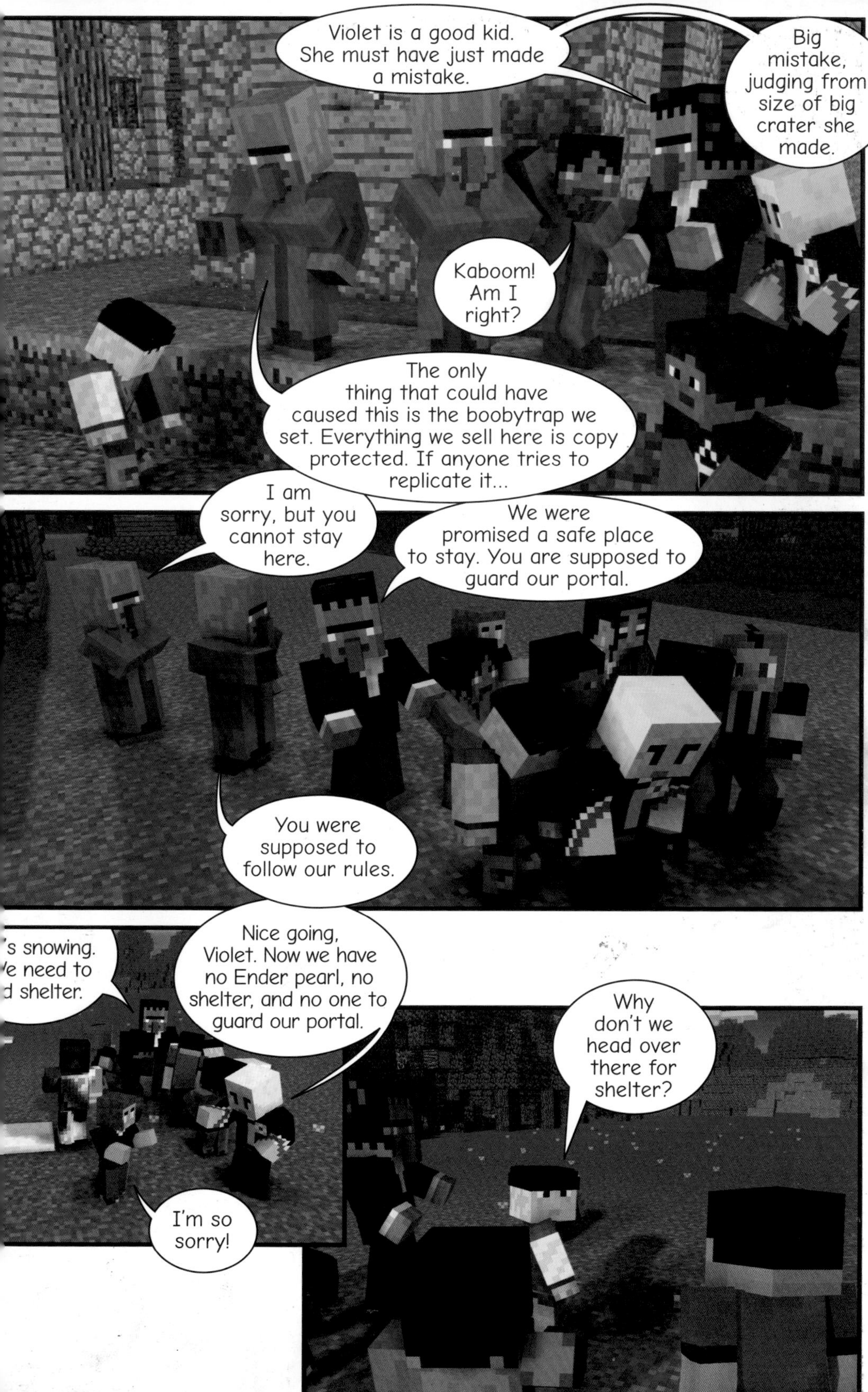
Violet is a good kid. She must have just made a mistake.
Big mistake, judging from size of big crater she made.
Kaboom! Am I right?
The only thing that could have caused this is the boobytrap we set. Everything we sell here is copy protected. If anyone tries to replicate it...
I am sorry, but you cannot stay here.
We were promised a safe place to stay. You are supposed to guard our portal.
You were supposed to follow our rules.
’s snowing. ’e need to d shelter.
Nice going, Violet. Now we have no Ender pearl, no shelter, and no one to guard our portal.
I’m so sorry!
Why don’t we head over there for shelter?

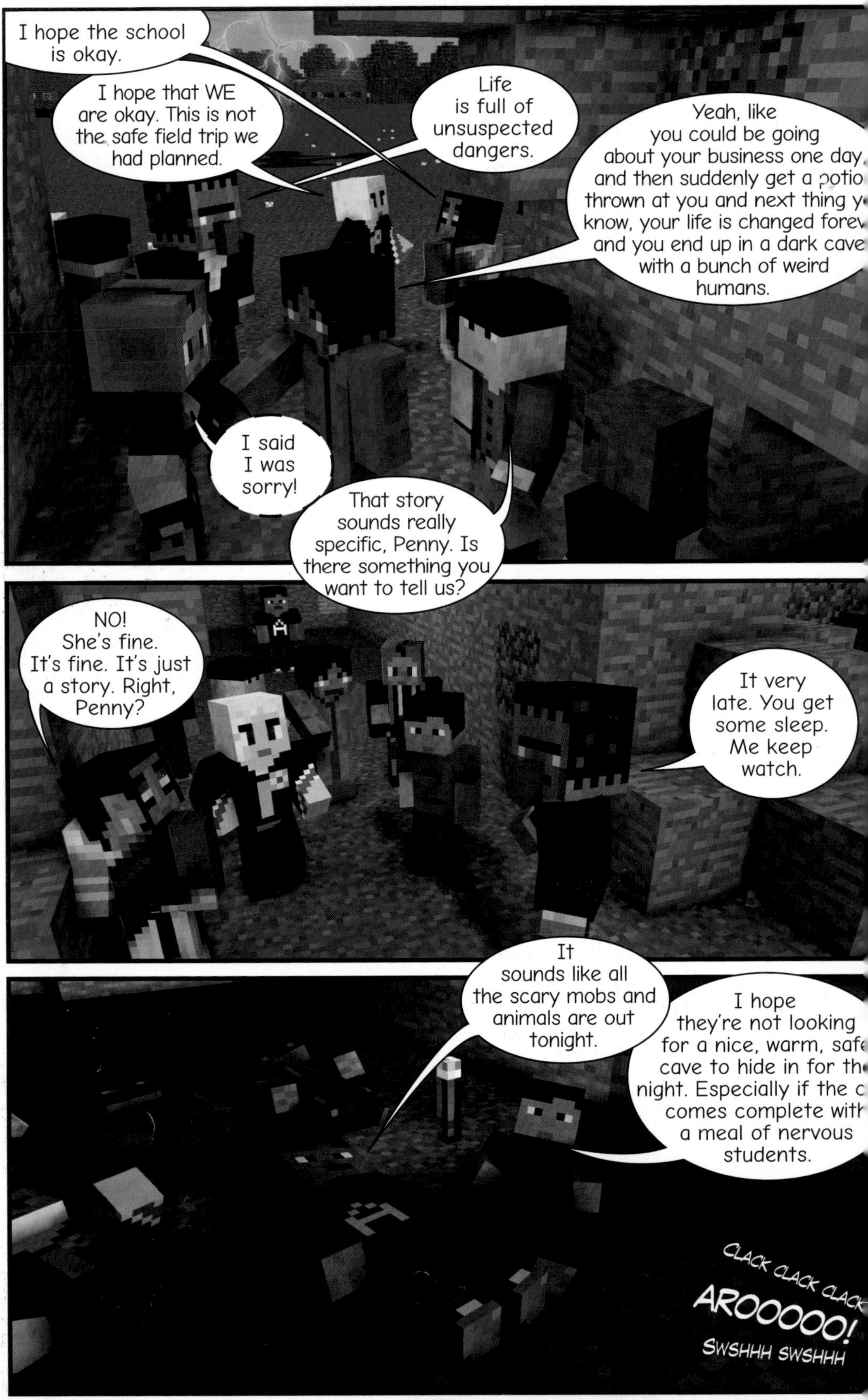

I hope the school is okay.
I hope that WE are okay. This is not the safe field trip we had planned.
Life is full of unsuspected dangers.
Yeah, like you could be going about your business one day, and then suddenly get a potio thrown at you and next thing y know, your life is changed forev and you end up in a dark cave with a bunch of weird humans.
I said I was sorry!
That story sounds really specific, Penny. Is there something you want to tell us?
NO! She's fine. It's fine. It's just a story. Right, Penny?
It very late. You get some sleep. Me keep watch.
It sounds like all the scary mobs and animals are out tonight.
I hope they're not looking for a nice, warm, saf cave to hide in for th night. Especially if the c comes complete wit a meal of nervous students.
CLACK CLACK CLACK
AROOOOO!
SWSHHH SWSHHH

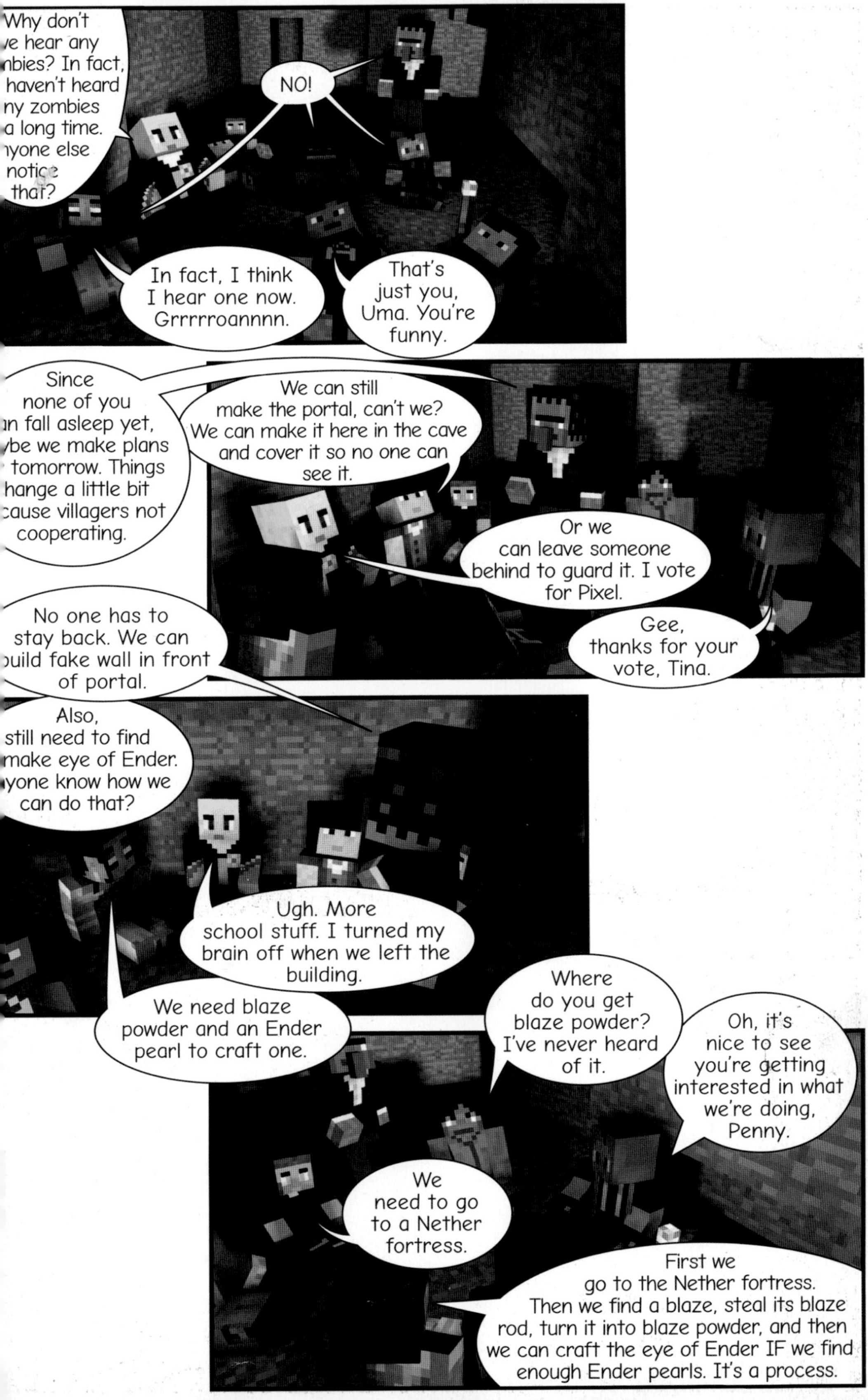
Why don't ve hear any nbies? In fact, haven't heard ny zombies a long time. nyone else notice that?
NO!
In fact, I think I hear one now. Grrrrroannnn.
That's just you, Uma. You're funny.
Since none of you an fall asleep yet, ybe we make plans tomorrow. Things hange a little bit cause villagers not cooperating.
We can still make the portal, can't we? We can make it here in the cave and cover it so no one can see it.
Or we can leave someone behind to guard it. I vote for Pixel.
Gee, thanks for your vote, Tina.
No one has to stay back. We can ouild fake wall in front of portal.
Also, still need to find make eye of Ender. yone know how we can do that?
Ugh. More school stuff. I turned my brain off when we left the building.
We need blaze powder and an Ender pearl to craft one.
Where do you get blaze powder? I've never heard of it.
Oh, it's nice to see you're getting interested in what we're doing, Penny.
We need to go to a Nether fortress.
First we go to the Nether fortress. Then we find a blaze, steal its blaze rod, turn it into blaze powder, and then we can craft the eye of Ender IF we find enough Ender pearls. It's a process.

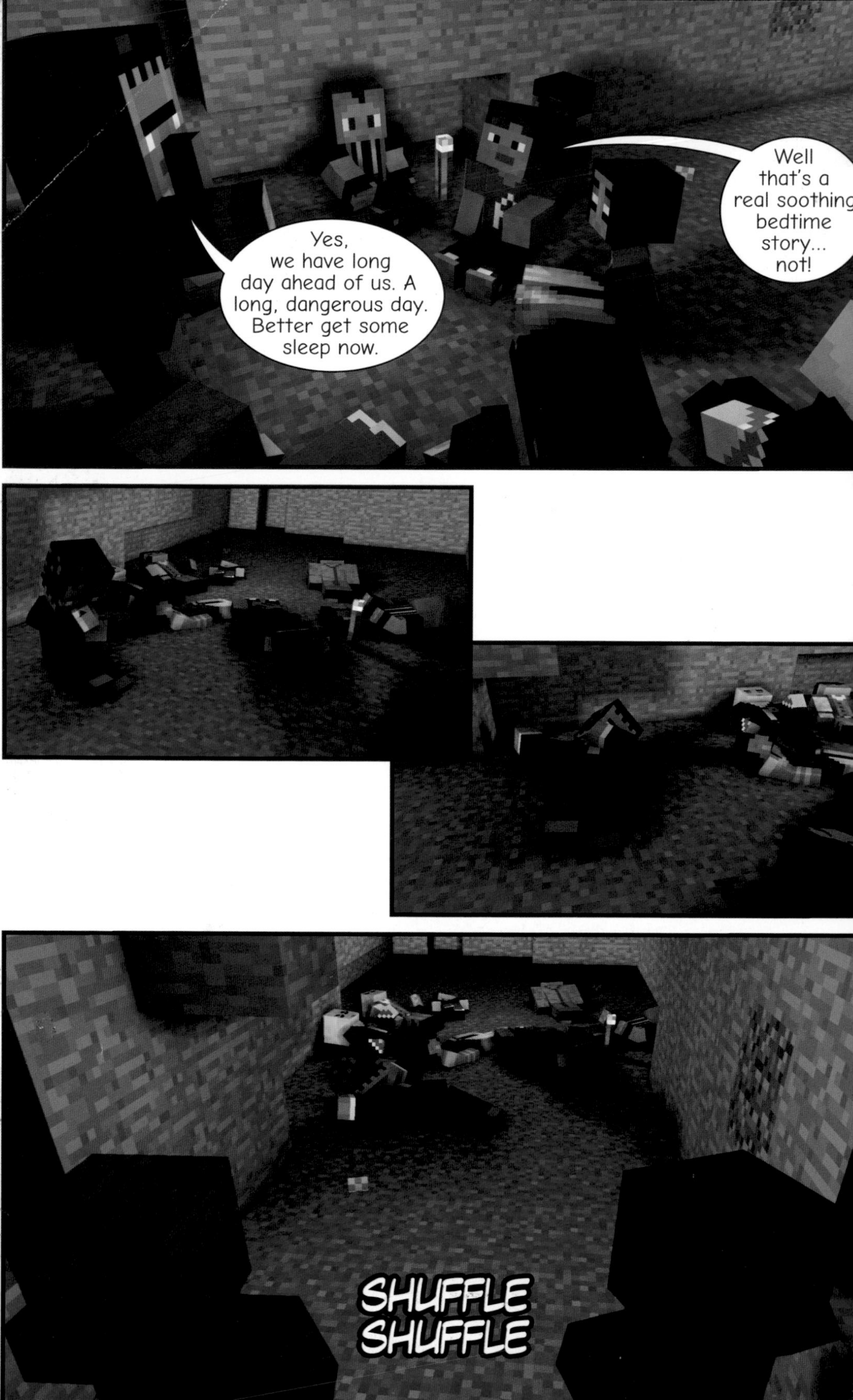
Yes, we have long day ahead of us. A long, dangerous day. Better get some sleep now.
Well that's a real soothing bedtime story... not!
SHUFFLE SHUFFLE

CHAPTER 6

TEACHER-NAPPED

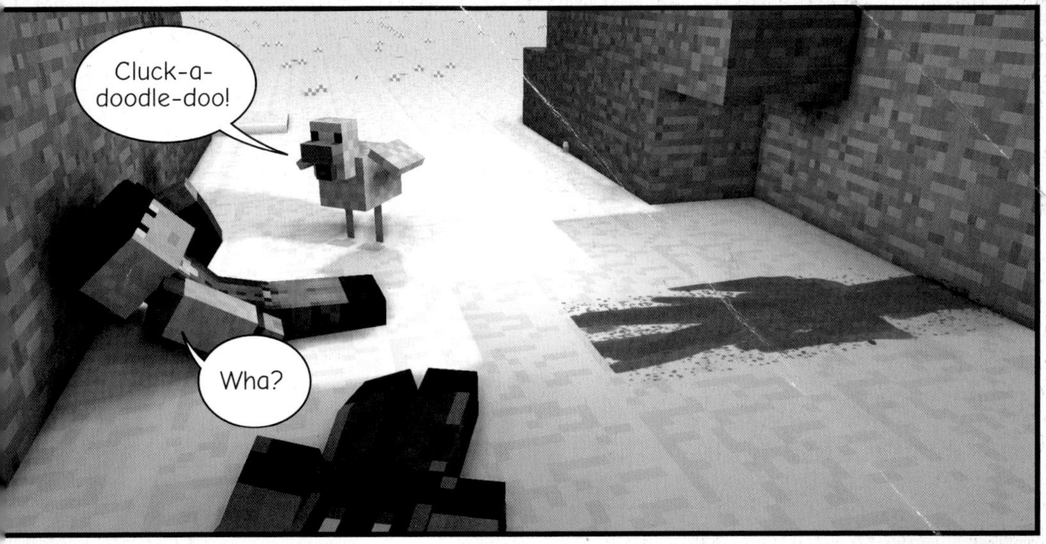
Cluck-a-doodle-doo!
Wha?

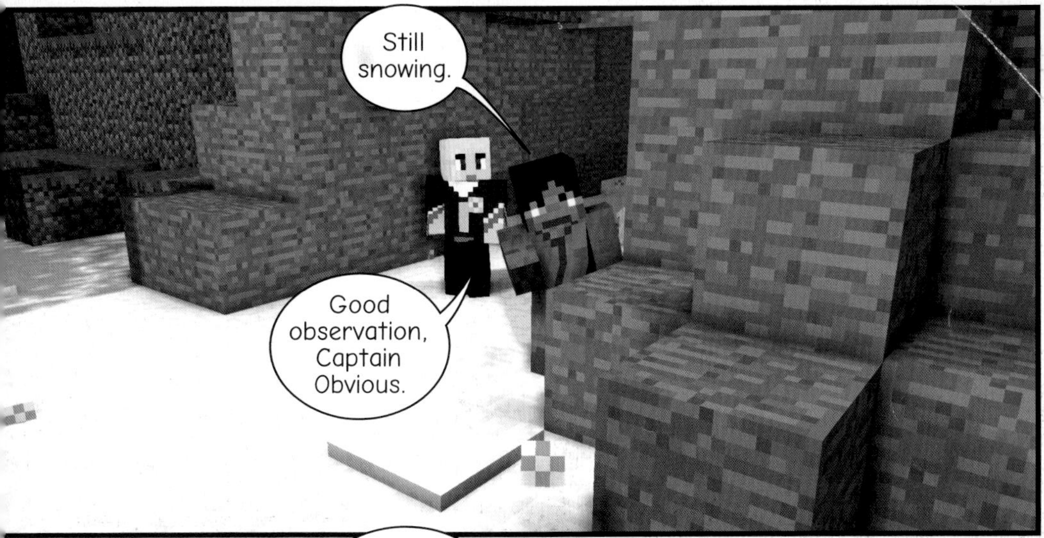
Still snowing.
Good observation, Captain Obvious.

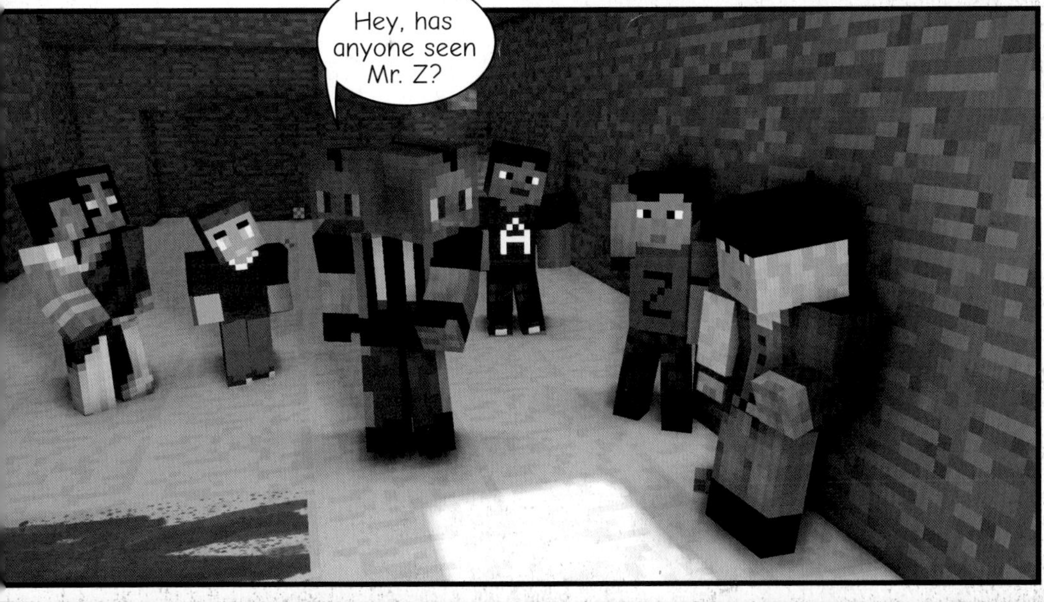
Hey, has anyone seen Mr. Z?

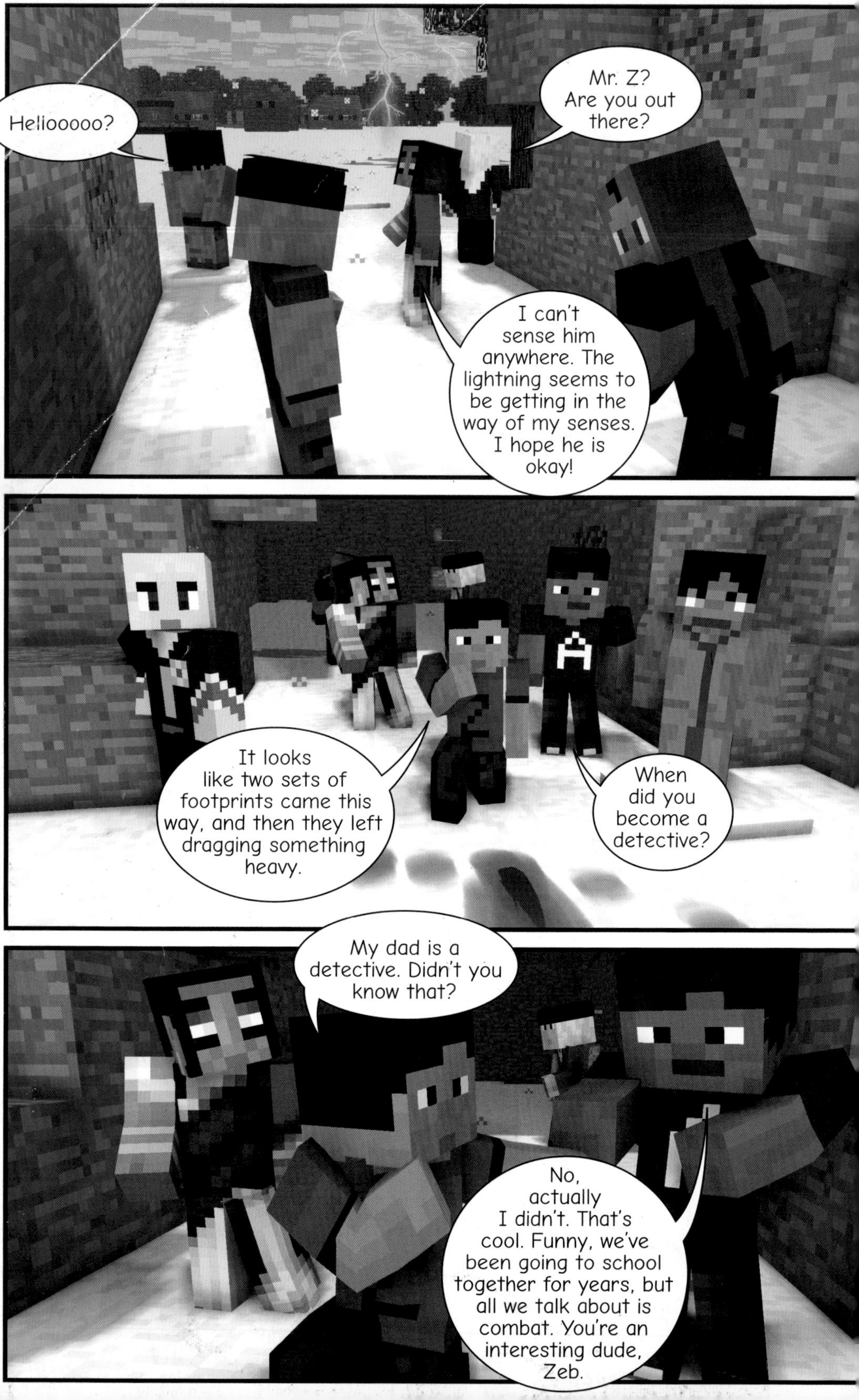
Helloooo?
Mr. Z? Are you out there?
I can't sense him anywhere. The lightning seems to be getting in the way of my senses. I hope he is okay!
It looks like two sets of footprints came this way, and then they left dragging something heavy.
When did you become a detective?
My dad is a detective. Didn't you know that?
No, actually I didn't. That's cool. Funny, we've been going to school together for years, but all we talk about is combat. You're an interesting dude, Zeb.

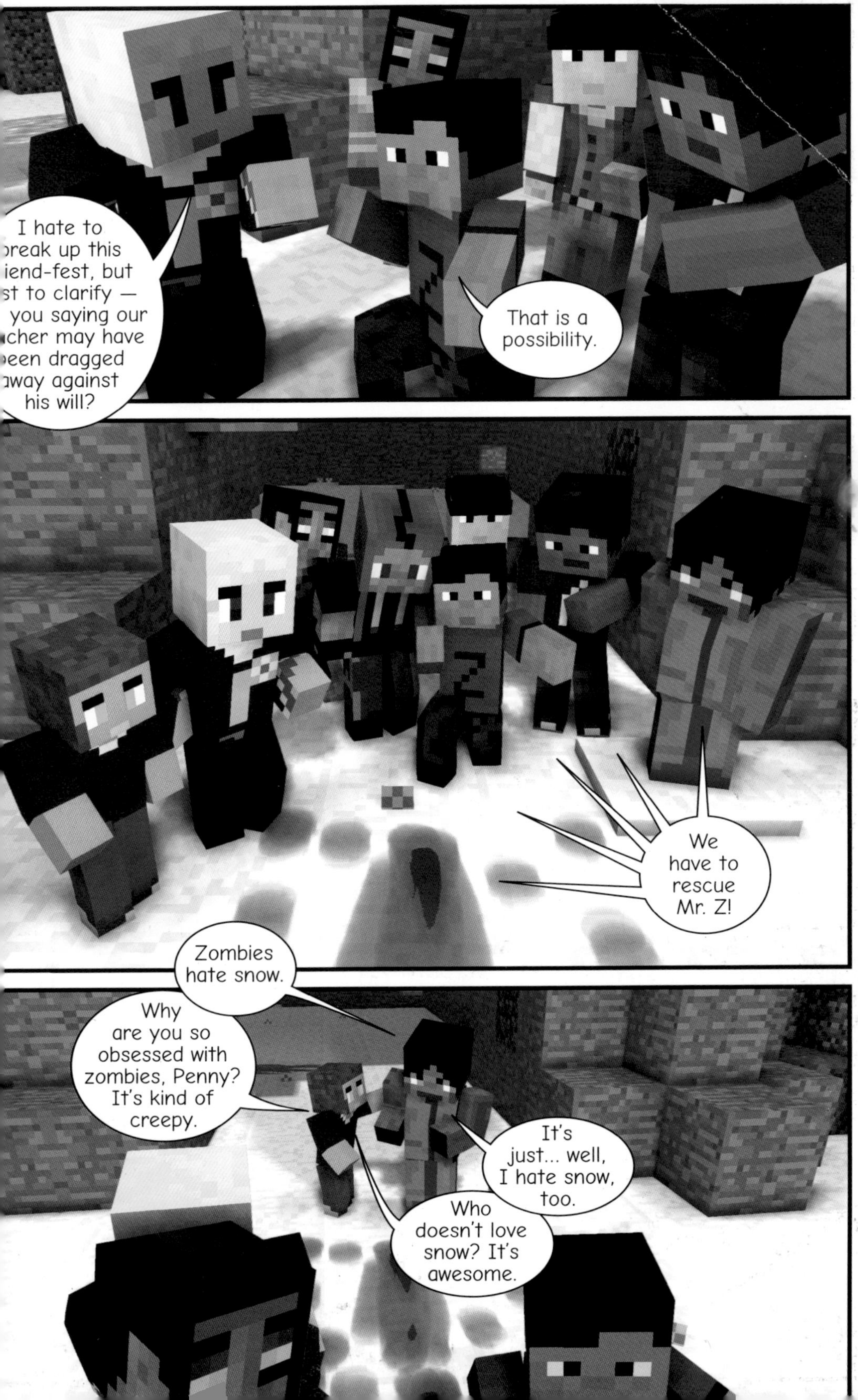

I hate to reak up this iend-fest, but st to clarify — you saying our cher may have een dragged way against his will?
That is a possibility.
We have to rescue Mr. Z!
Zombies hate snow.
Why are you so obsessed with zombies, Penny? It's kind of creepy.
It's just... well, I hate snow, too.
Who doesn't love snow? It's awesome.

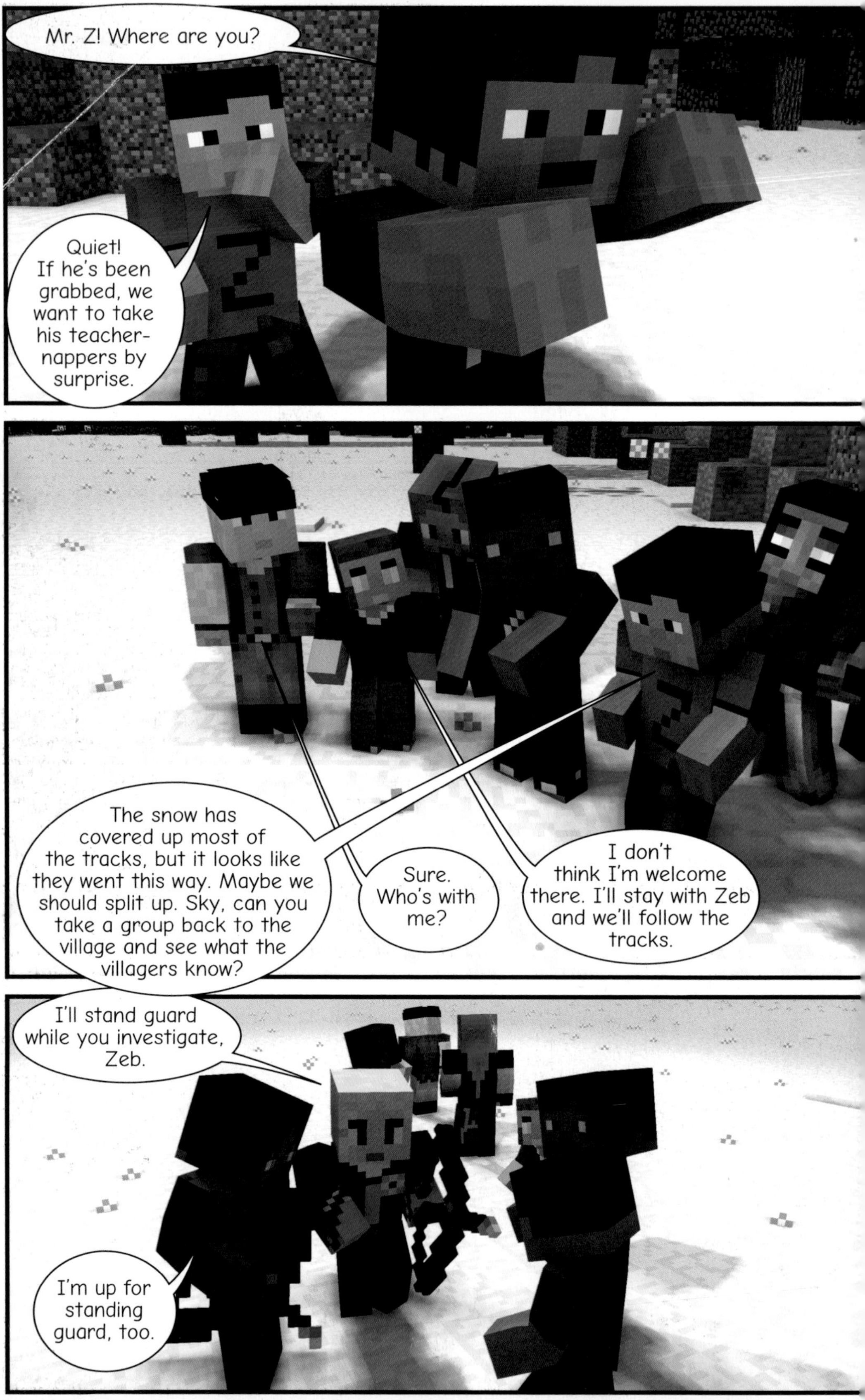

Mr. Z! Where are you?
Quiet! If he's been grabbed, we want to take his teacher-nappers by surprise.
The snow has covered up most of the tracks, but it looks like they went this way. Maybe we should split up. Sky, can you take a group back to the village and see what the villagers know?
Sure. Who's with me?
I don't think I'm welcome there. I'll stay with Zeb and we'll follow the tracks.
I'll stand guard while you investigate, Zeb.
I'm up for standing guard, too.

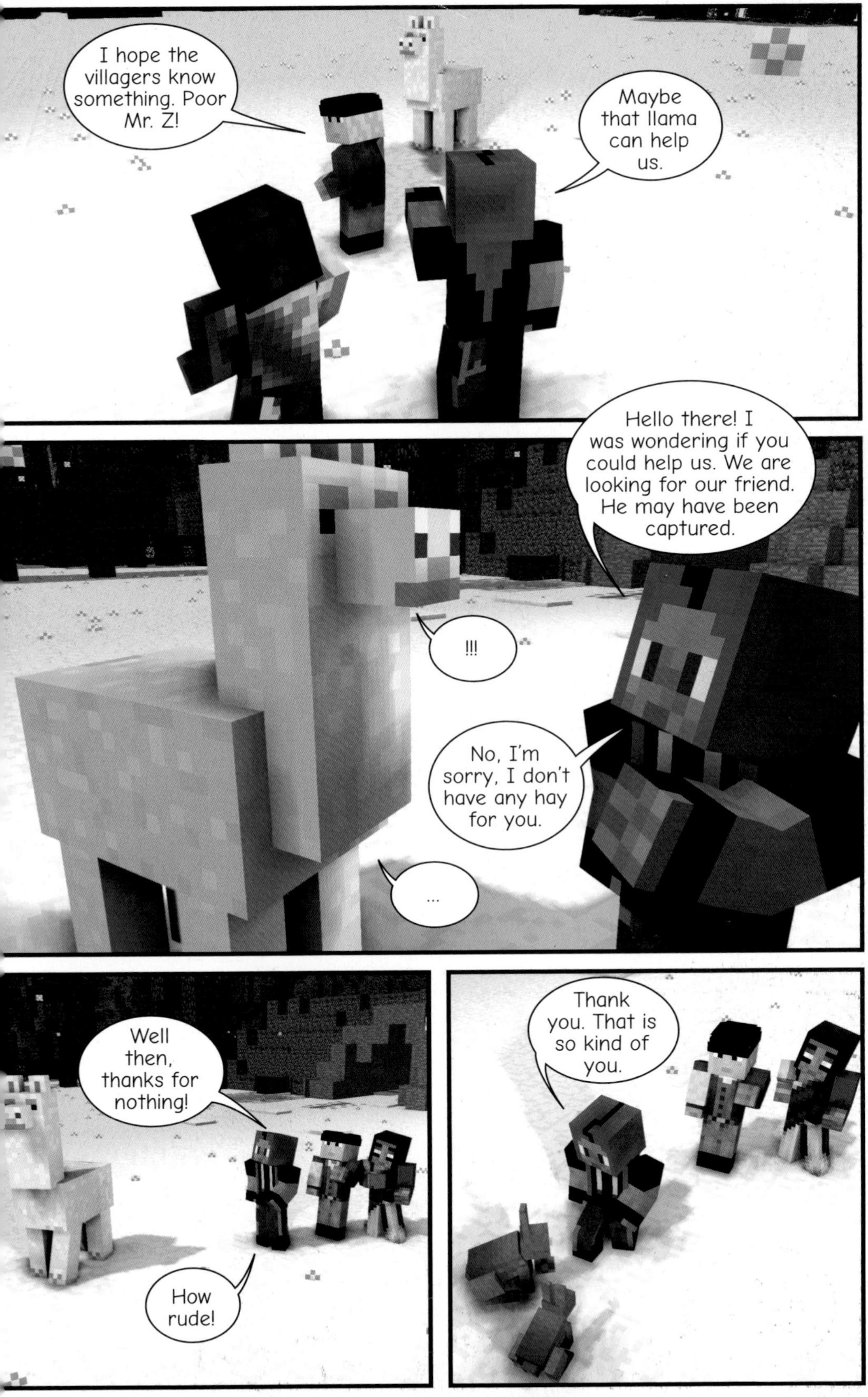
I hope the villagers know something. Poor Mr. Z!
Maybe that llama can help us.
Hello there! I was wondering if you could help us. We are looking for our friend. He may have been captured.
!!!
No, I'm sorry, I don't have any hay for you.
...
Well then, thanks for nothing!
How rude!
Thank you. That is so kind of you.

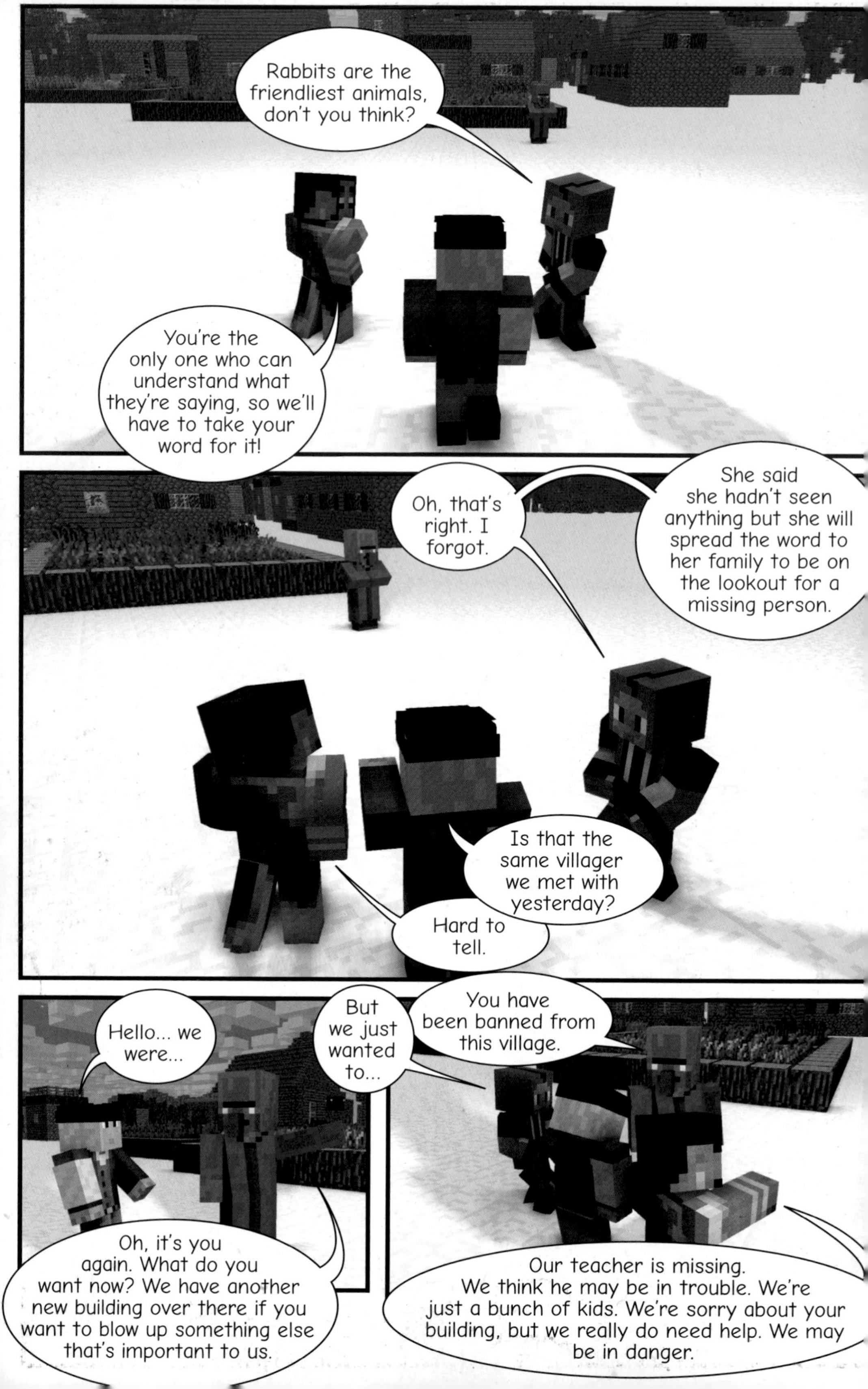
Rabbits are the friendliest animals, don't you think?
You're the only one who can understand what they're saying, so we'll have to take your word for it!
Oh, that's right. I forgot.
She said she hadn't seen anything but she will spread the word to her family to be on the lookout for a missing person.
Is that the same villager we met with yesterday?
Hard to tell.
Hello... we were...
Oh, it's you again. What do you want now? We have another new building over there if you want to blow up something else that's important to us.
But we just wanted to...
You have been banned from this village.
Our teacher is missing. We think he may be in trouble. We're just a bunch of kids. We're sorry about your building, but we really do need help. We may be in danger.

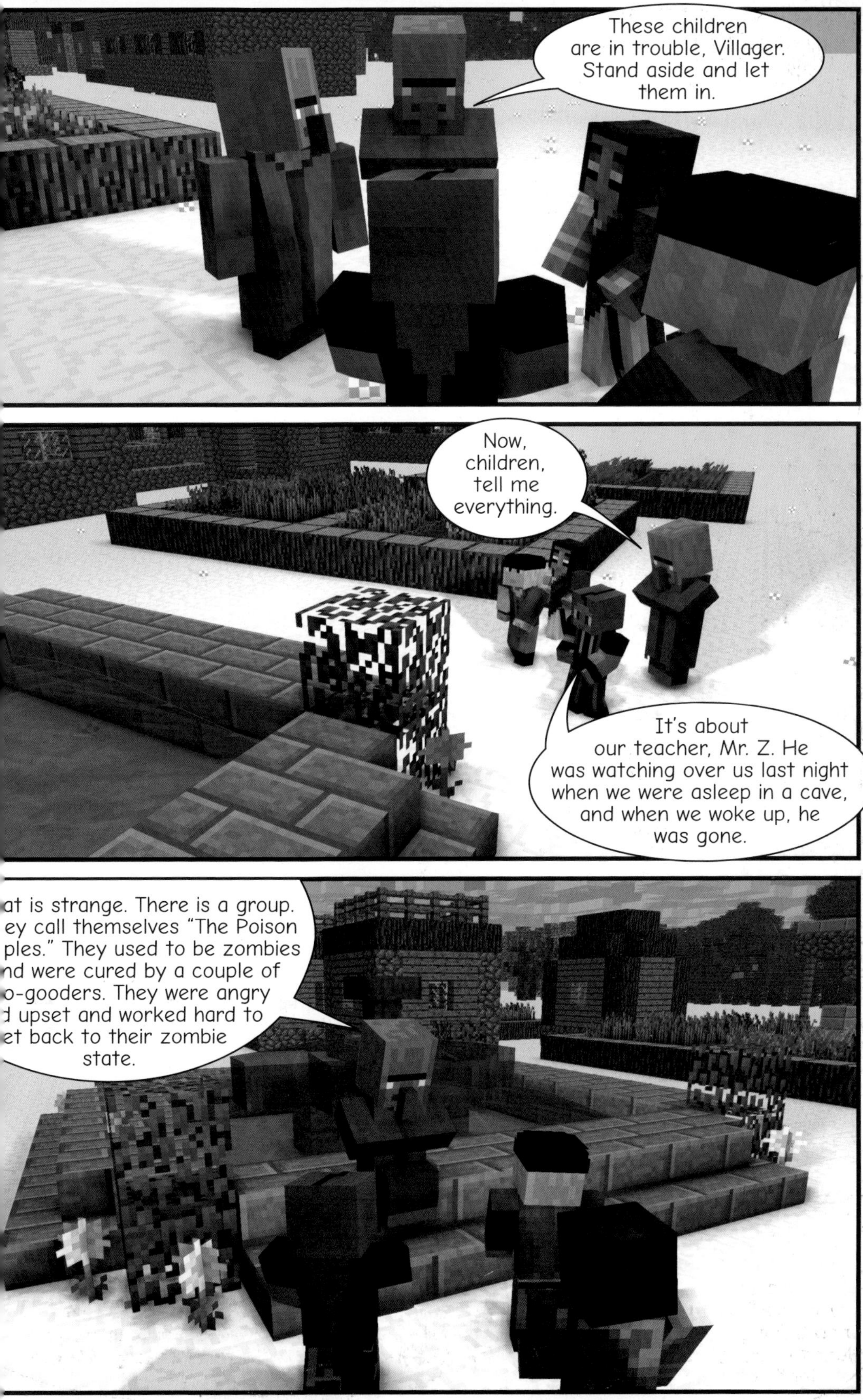
These children are in trouble, Villager. Stand aside and let them in.
Now, children, tell me everything.
It's about our teacher, Mr. Z. He was watching over us last night when we were asleep in a cave, and when we woke up, he was gone.
at is strange. There is a group. ey call themselves "The Poison ples." They used to be zombies nd were cured by a couple of o-gooders. They were angry d upset and worked hard to et back to their zombie state.

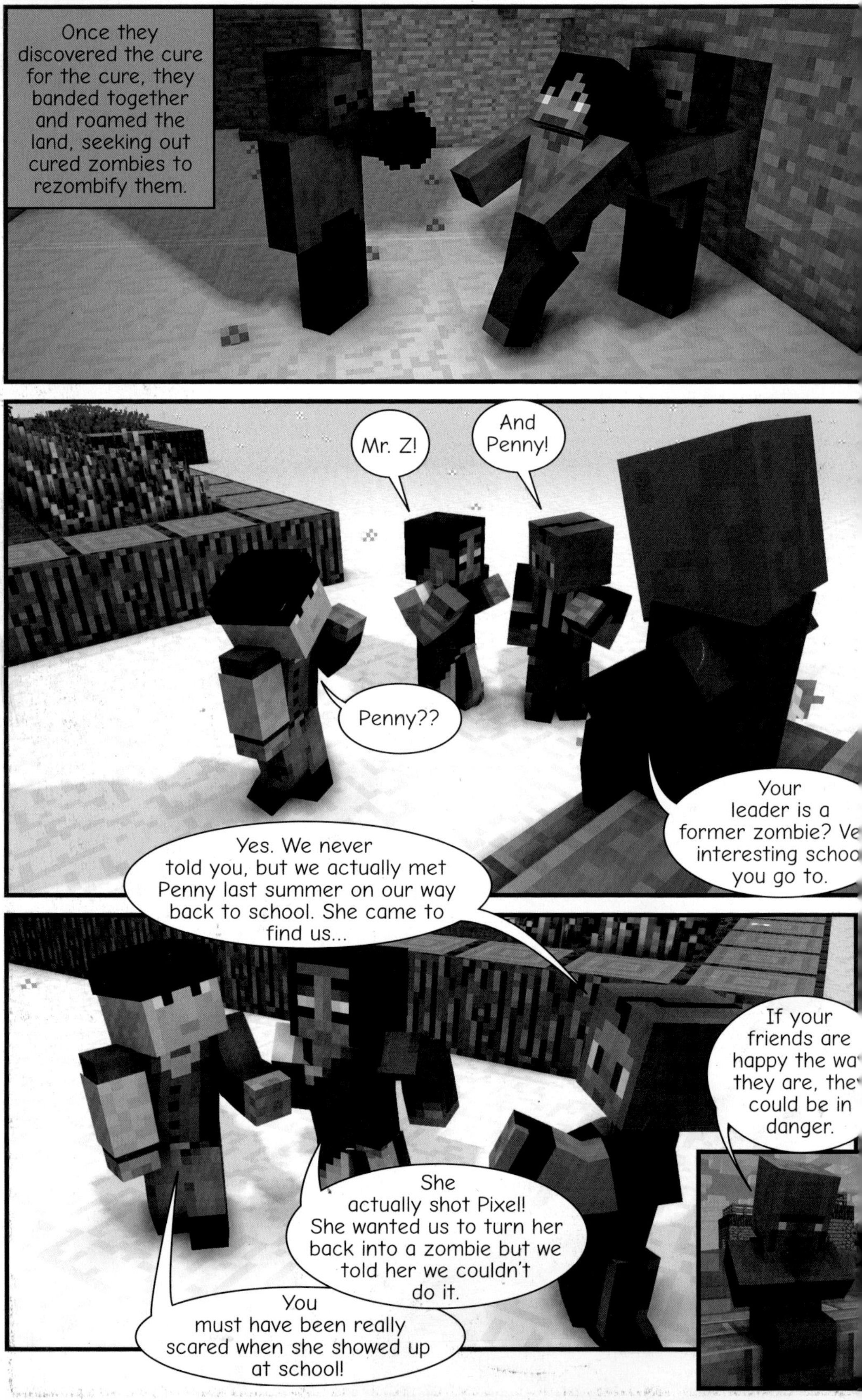

Once they discovered the cure for the cure, they banded together and roamed the land, seeking out cured zombies to rezombify them.
Mr. Z!
And Penny!
Penny??
Your leader is a former zombie? Ve interesting schoo you go to.
Yes. We never told you, but we actually met Penny last summer on our way back to school. She came to find us...
If your friends are happy the wa they are, the could be in danger.
She actually shot Pixel! She wanted us to turn her back into a zombie but we told her we couldn't do it.
You must have been really scared when she showed up at school!

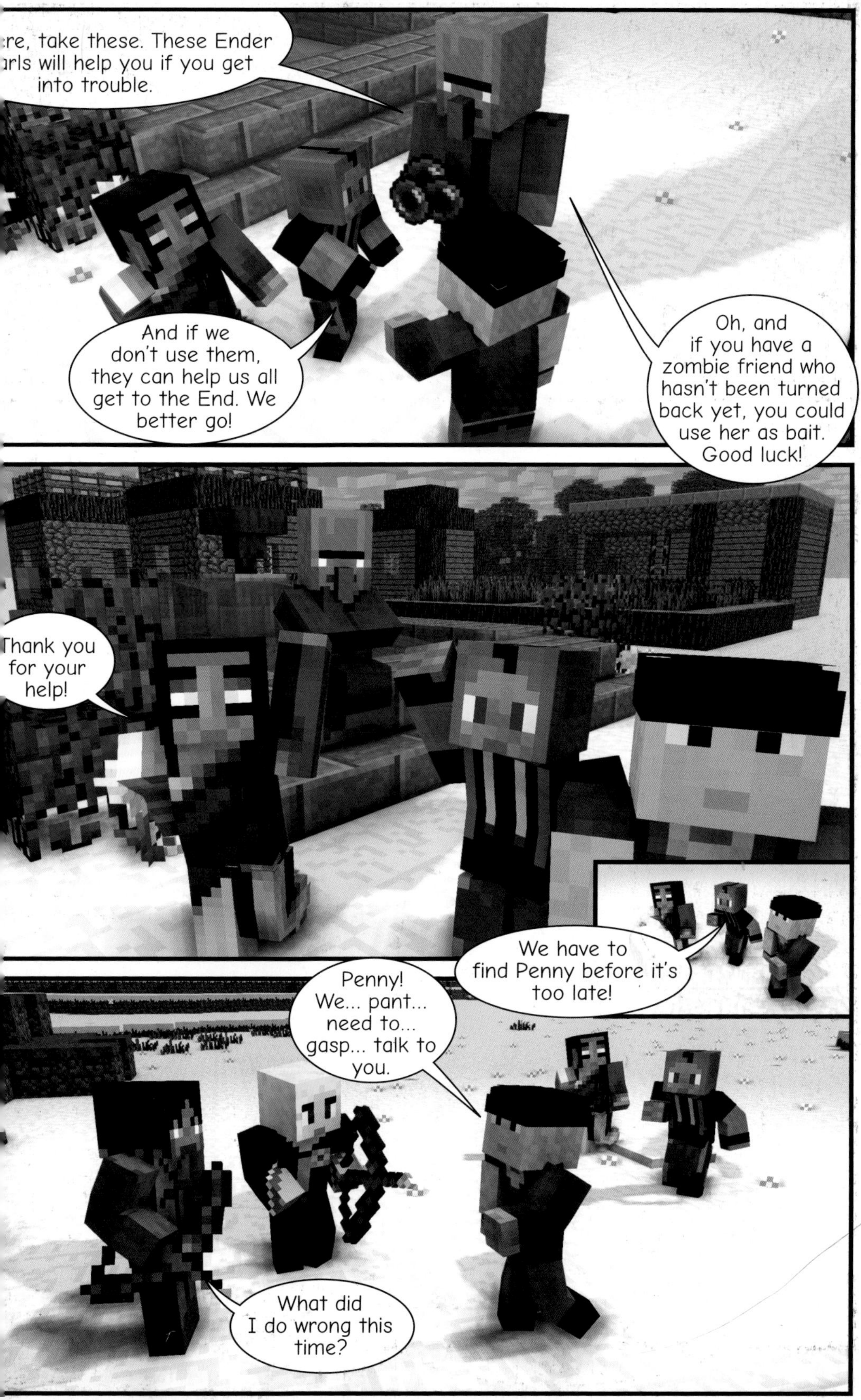
re, take these. These Ender rls will help you if you get into trouble.
And if we don't use them, they can help us all get to the End. We better go!
Oh, and if you have a zombie friend who hasn't been turned back yet, you could use her as bait. Good luck!
hank you for your help!
We have to find Penny before it's too late!
Penny! We... pant... need to... gasp... talk to you.
What did I do wrong this time?

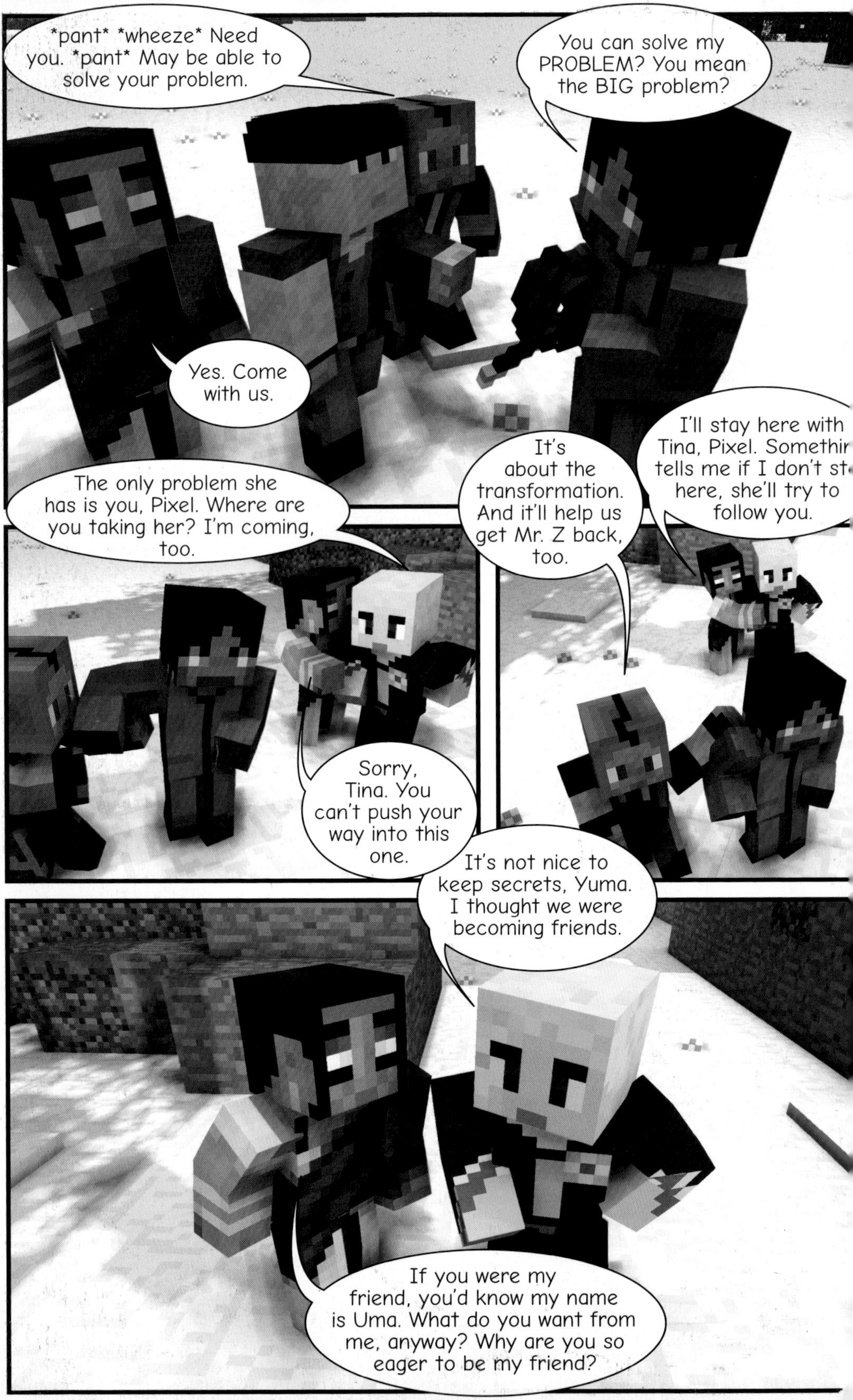
pant *wheeze* Need you. *pant* May be able to solve your problem.
You can solve my PROBLEM? You mean the BIG problem?
Yes. Come with us.
The only problem she has is you, Pixel. Where are you taking her? I'm coming, too.
Sorry, Tina. You can't push your way into this one.
It's about the transformation. And it'll help us get Mr. Z back, too.
I'll stay here with Tina, Pixel. Somethi tells me if I don't st here, she'll try to follow you.
It's not nice to keep secrets, Yuma. I thought we were becoming friends.
If you were my friend, you'd know my name is Uma. What do you want from me, anyway? Why are you so eager to be my friend?

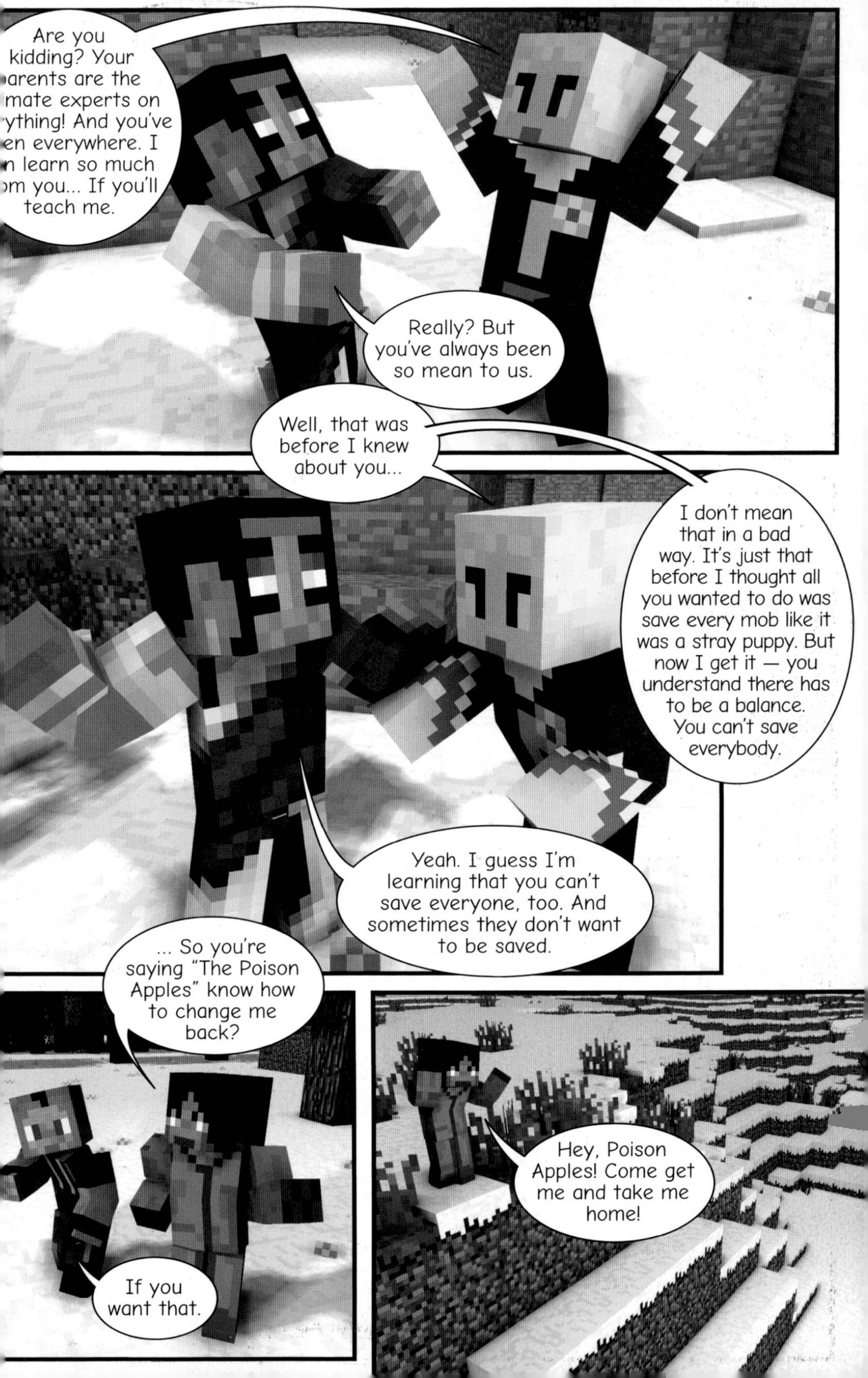
Are you kidding? Your arents are the mate experts on ything! And you've en everywhere. I n learn so much m you... If you'll teach me.
Really? But you've always been so mean to us.
Well, that was before I knew about you...
I don't mean that in a bad way. It's just that before I thought all you wanted to do was save every mob like it was a stray puppy. But now I get it — you understand there has to be a balance. You can't save everybody.
Yeah. I guess I'm learning that you can't save everyone, too. And sometimes they don't want to be saved.
... So you're saying "The Poison Apples" know how to change me back?
If you want that.
Hey, Poison Apples! Come get me and take me home!

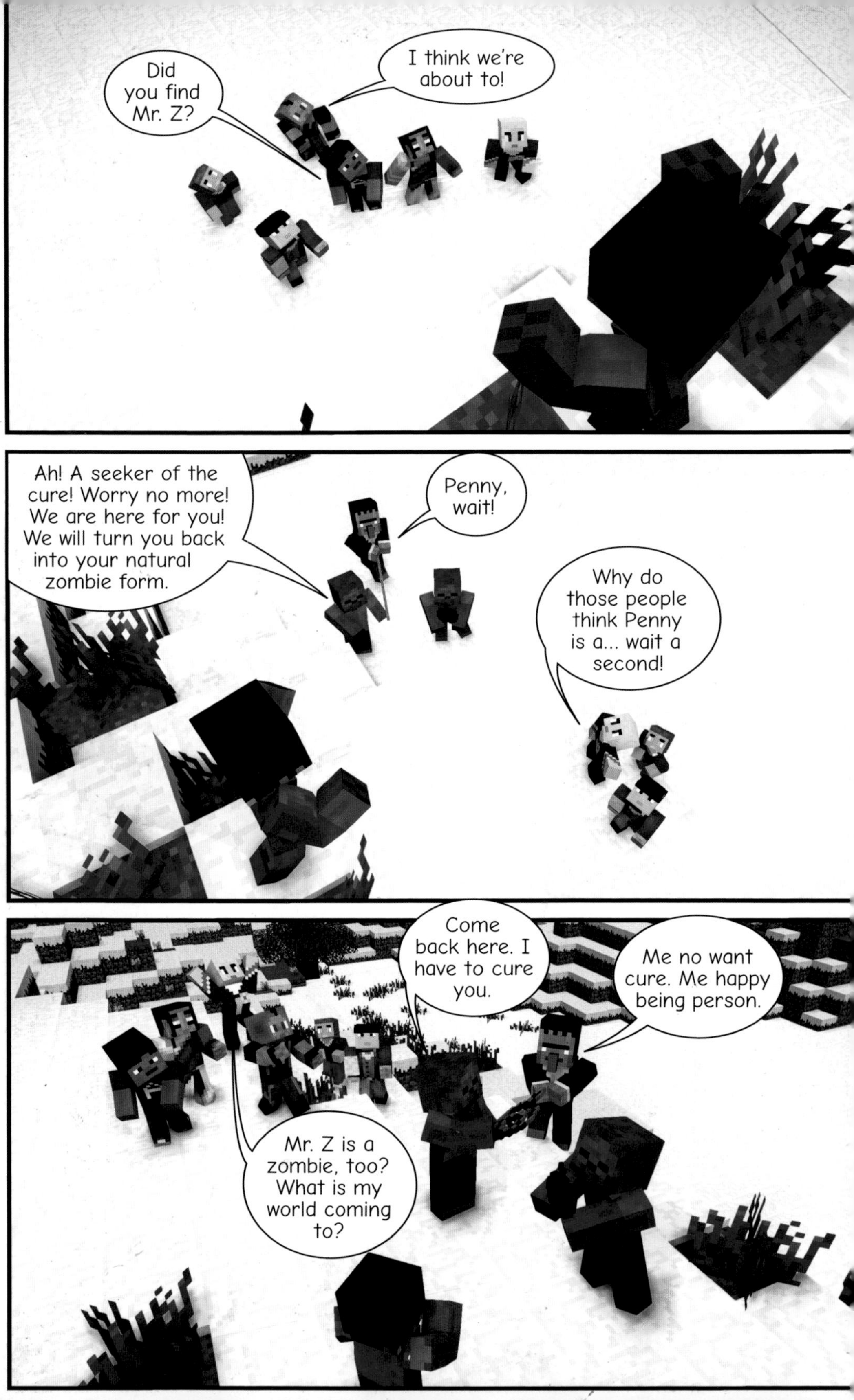
Did you find Mr. Z?
I think we're about to!
Ah! A seeker of the cure! Worry no more! We are here for you! We will turn you back into your natural zombie form.
Penny, wait!
Why do those people think Penny is a... wait a second!
Come back here. I have to cure you.
Me no want cure. Me happy being person.
Mr. Z is a zombie, too? What is my world coming to?

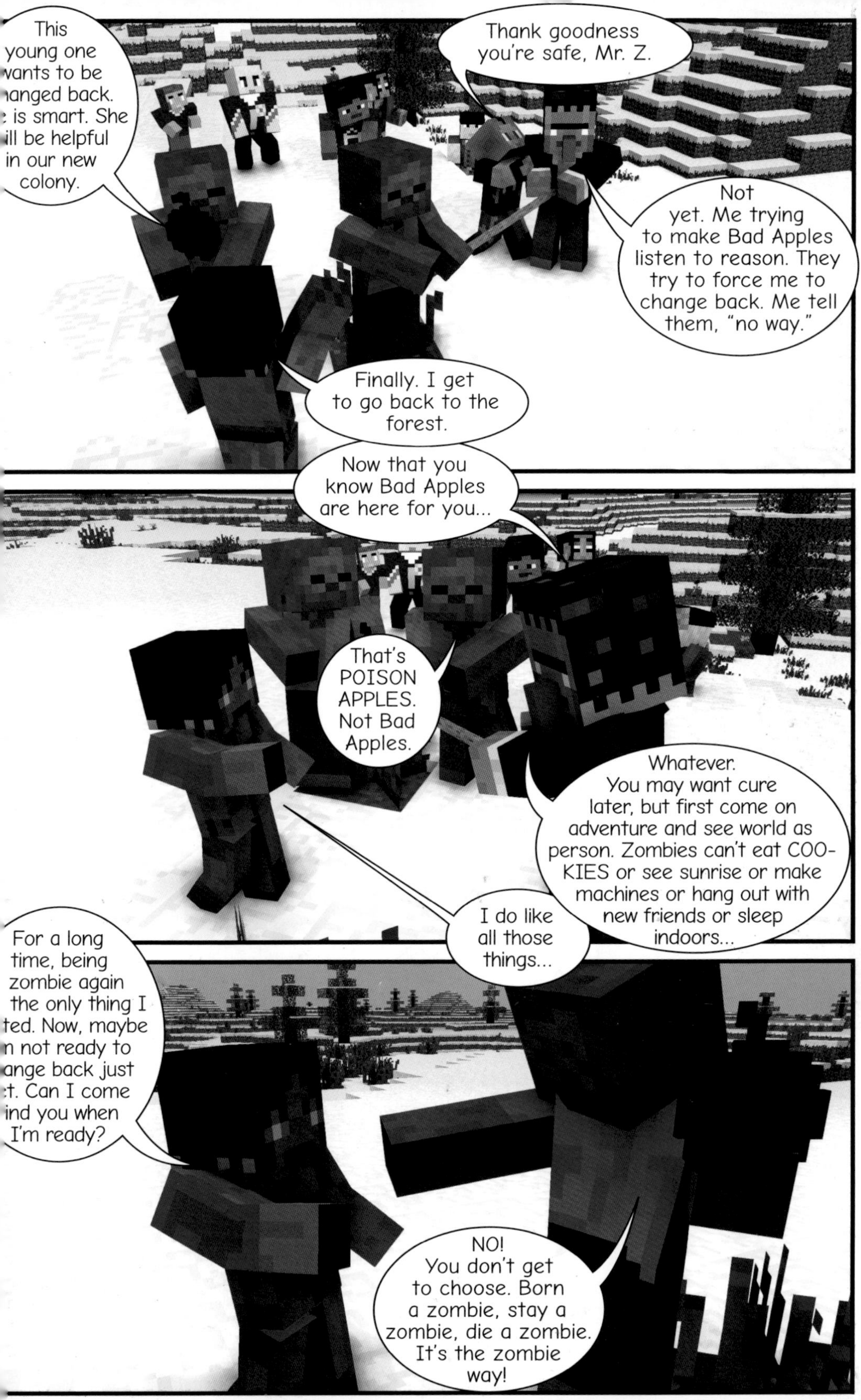
This young one vants to be ıanged back. : is smart. She ill be helpful in our new colony.
Thank goodness you're safe, Mr. Z.
Not yet. Me trying to make Bad Apples listen to reason. They try to force me to change back. Me tell them, "no way."
Finally. I get to go back to the forest.
Now that you know Bad Apples are here for you...
That's POISON APPLES. Not Bad Apples.
Whatever. You may want cure later, but first come on adventure and see world as person. Zombies can't eat COO-KIES or see sunrise or make machines or hang out with new friends or sleep indoors...
I do like all those things...
For a long time, being zombie again the only thing I ted. Now, maybe n not ready to ange back just t. Can I come ind you when I'm ready?
NO! You don't get to choose. Born a zombie, stay a zombie, die a zombie. It's the zombie way!

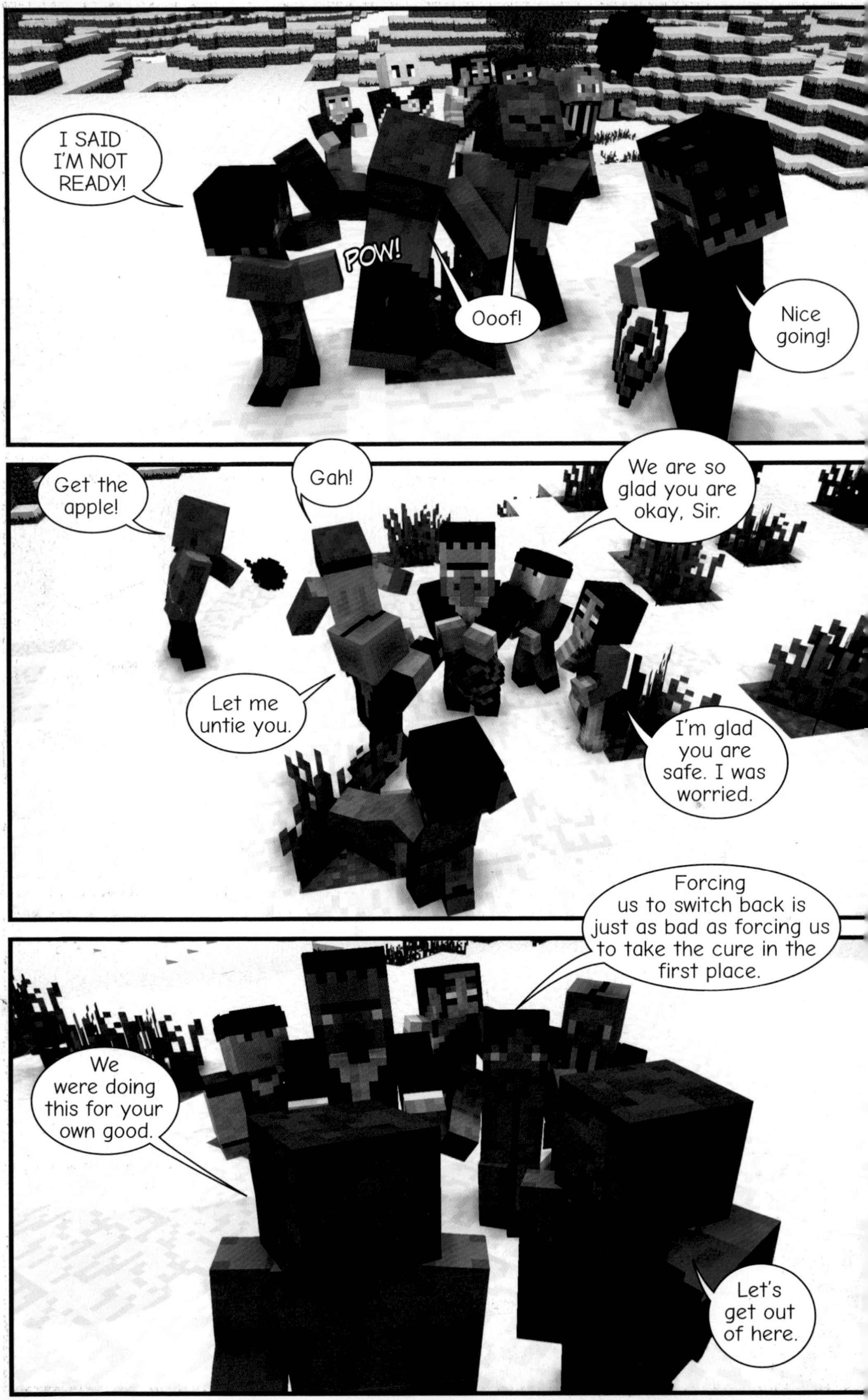
I SAID I'M NOT READY!
POW!
Ooof!
Nice going!
Get the apple!
Gah!
We are so glad you are okay, Sir.
Let me untie you.
I'm glad you are safe. I was worried.
Forcing us to switch back is just as bad as forcing us to take the cure in the first place.
We were doing this for your own good.
Let's get out of here.

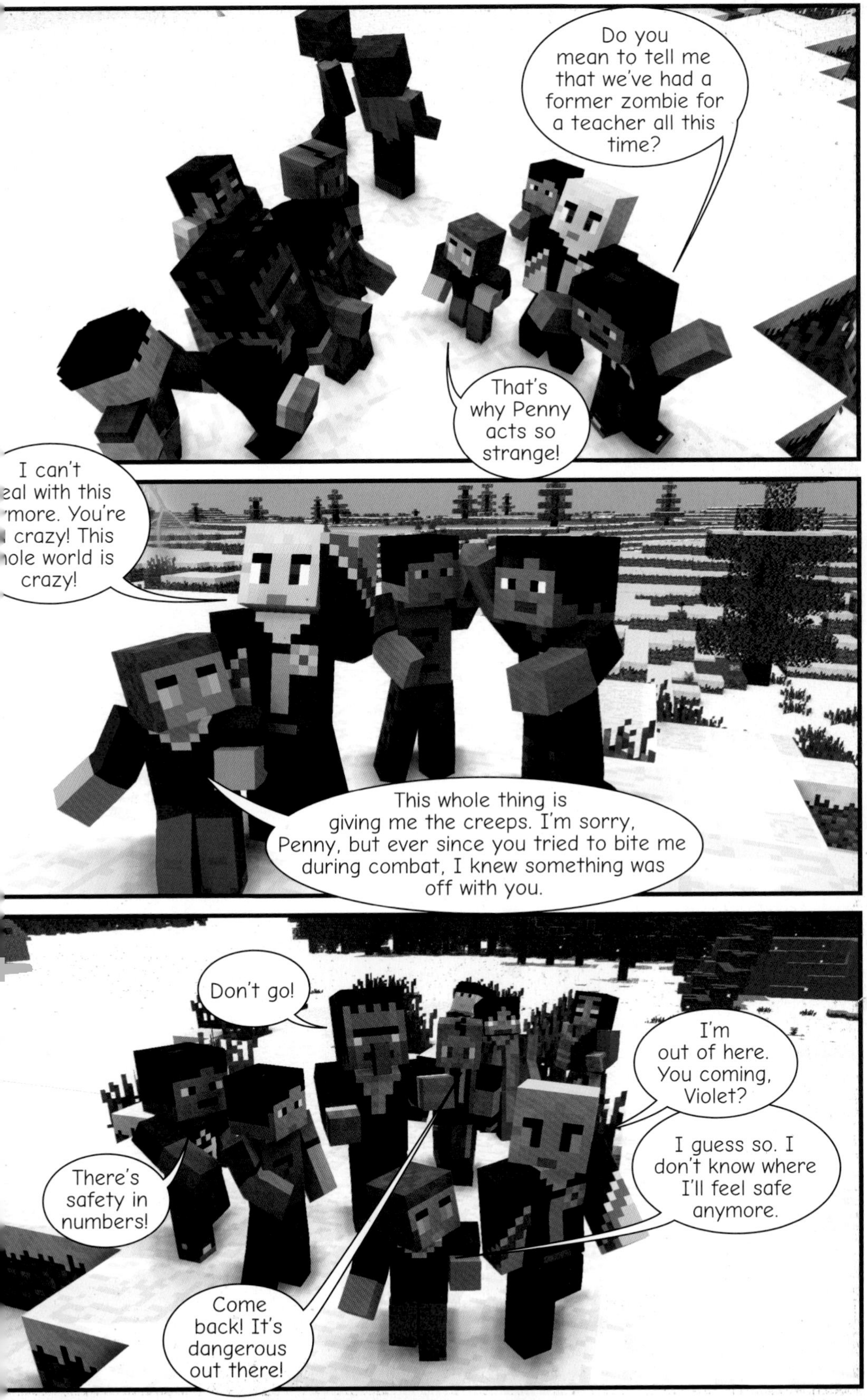
Do you mean to tell me that we've had a former zombie for a teacher all this time?
That's why Penny acts so strange!
I can't eal with this more. You're crazy! This ole world is crazy!
This whole thing is giving me the creeps. I'm sorry, Penny, but ever since you tried to bite me during combat, I knew something was off with you.
Don't go!
I'm out of here. You coming, Violet?
I guess so. I don't know where I'll feel safe anymore.
There's safety in numbers!
Come back! It's dangerous out there!

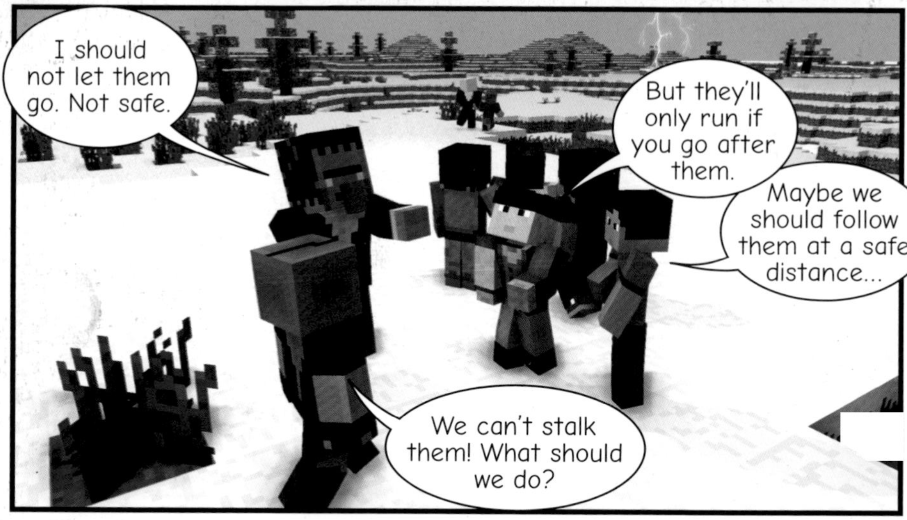
I should not let them go. Not safe.
But they'll only run if you go after them.
Maybe we should follow them at a safe distance...
We can't stalk them! What should we do?

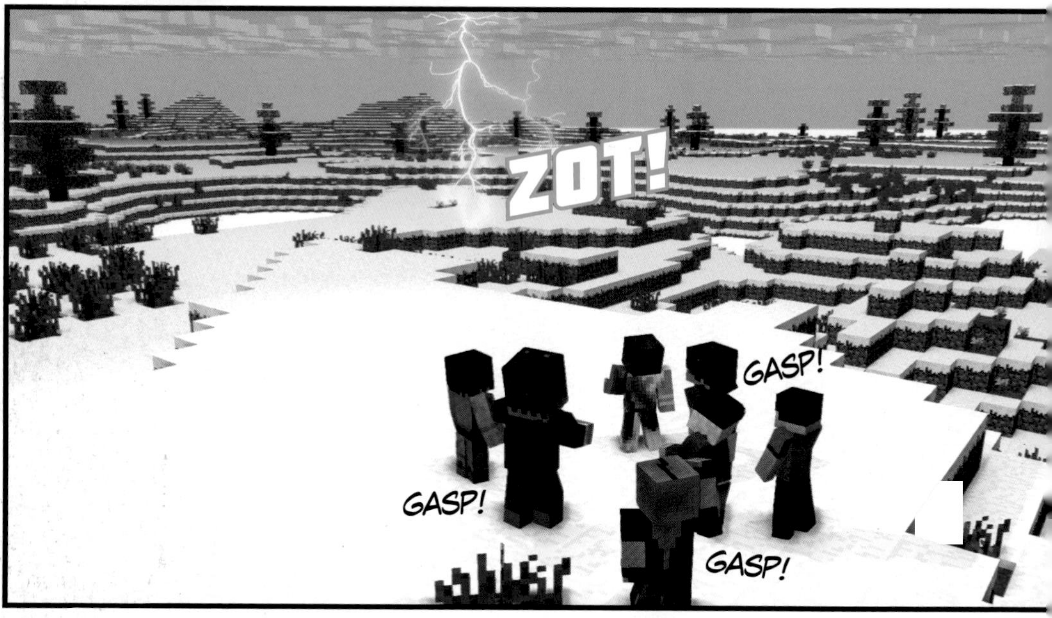
ZOT!
GASP!
GASP!
GASP!

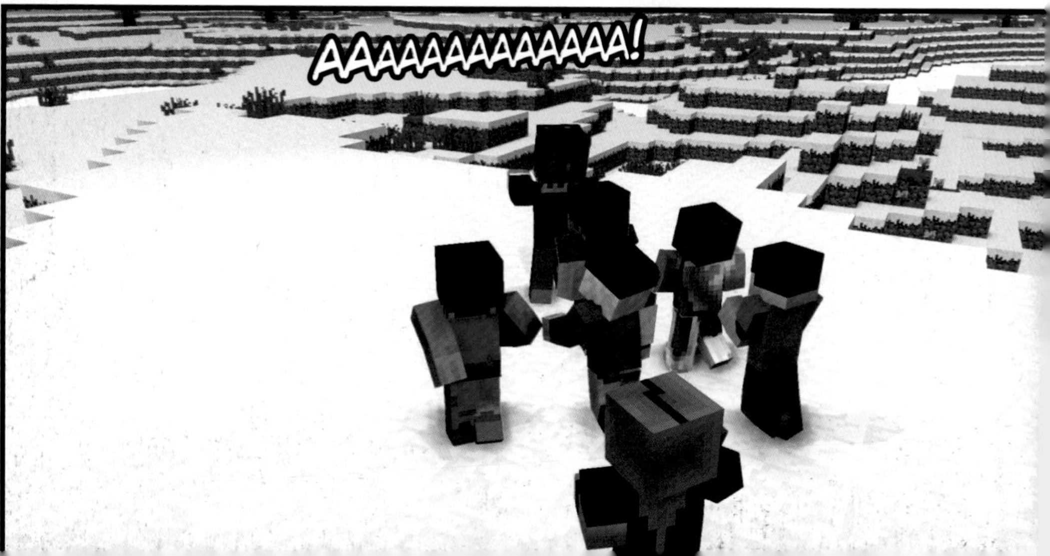
AAAAAAAAAAAAA!

CHAPTER 7

TATTLES AND
CONFESSIONS

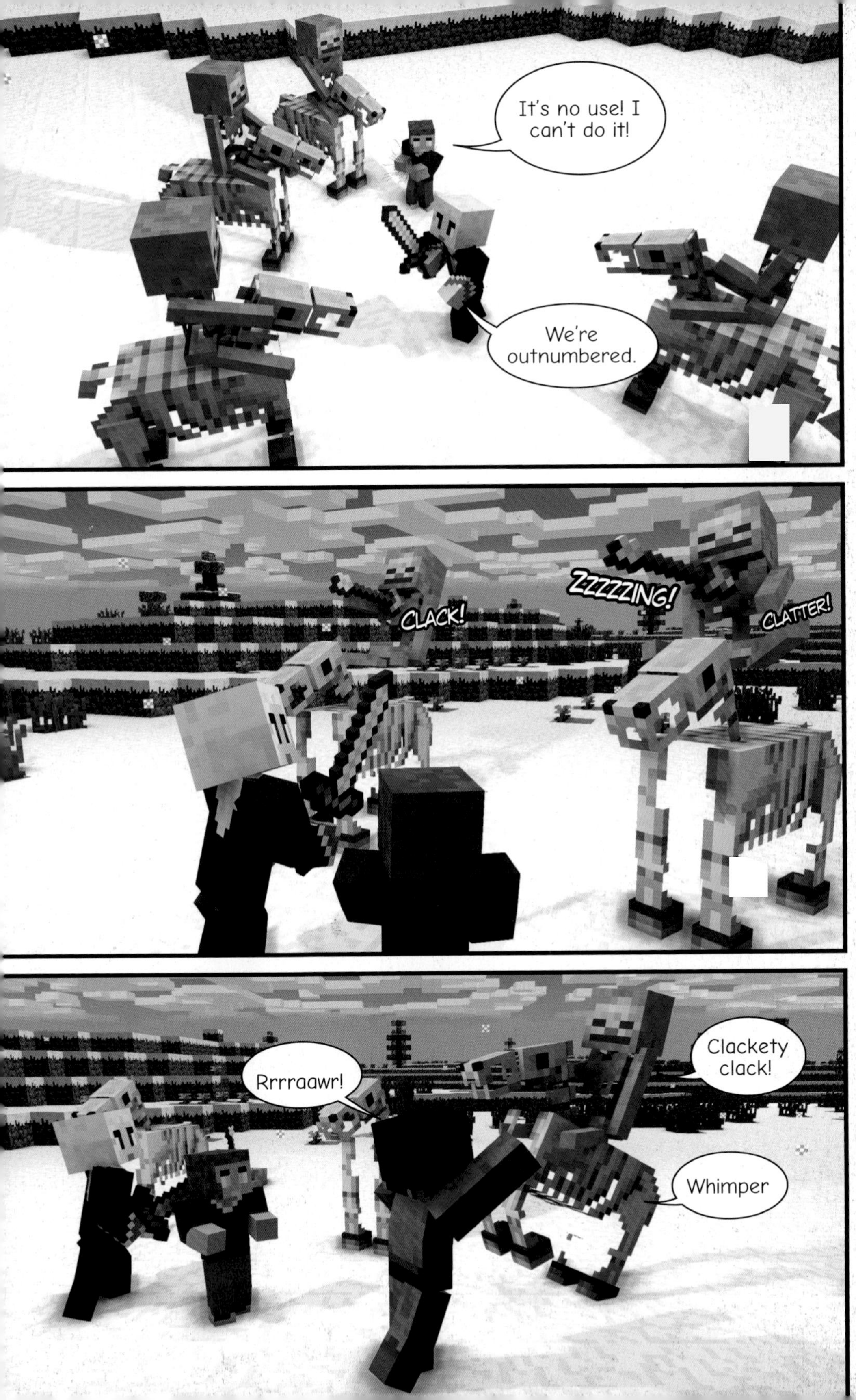
It's no use! I can't do it!
We're outnumbered.
CLACK!
ZZZZZING!
CLATTER!
Rrrraawr!
Clackety clack!
Whimper

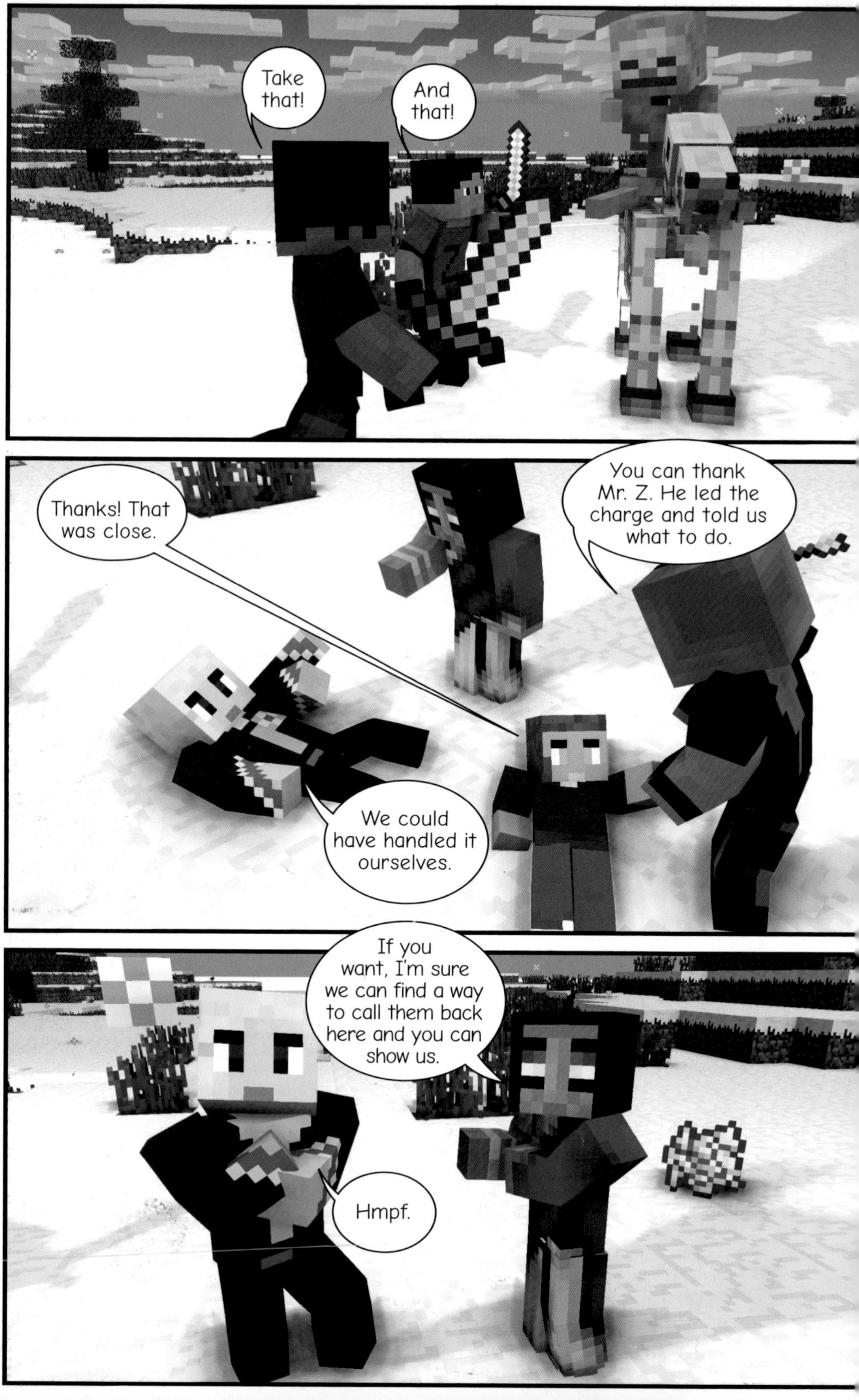
Take that!
And that!
Thanks! That was close.
You can thank Mr. Z. He led the charge and told us what to do.
We could have handled it ourselves.
If you want, I'm sure we can find a way to call them back here and you can show us.
Hmpf.

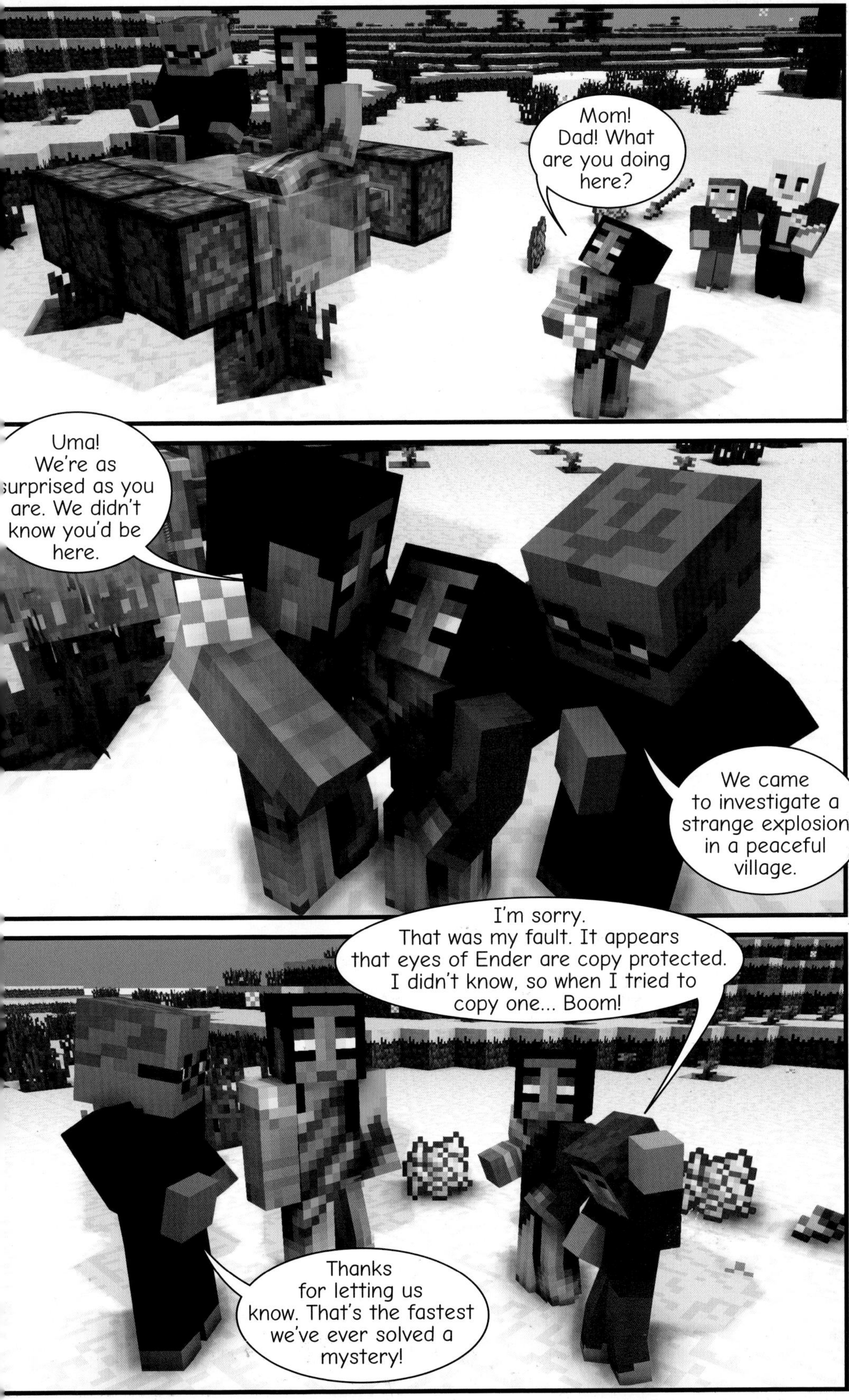
Mom! Dad! What are you doing here?
Uma! We're as surprised as you are. We didn't know you'd be here.
We came to investigate a strange explosion in a peaceful village.
I'm sorry. That was my fault. It appears that eyes of Ender are copy protected. I didn't know, so when I tried to copy one... Boom!
Thanks for letting us know. That's the fastest we've ever solved a mystery!

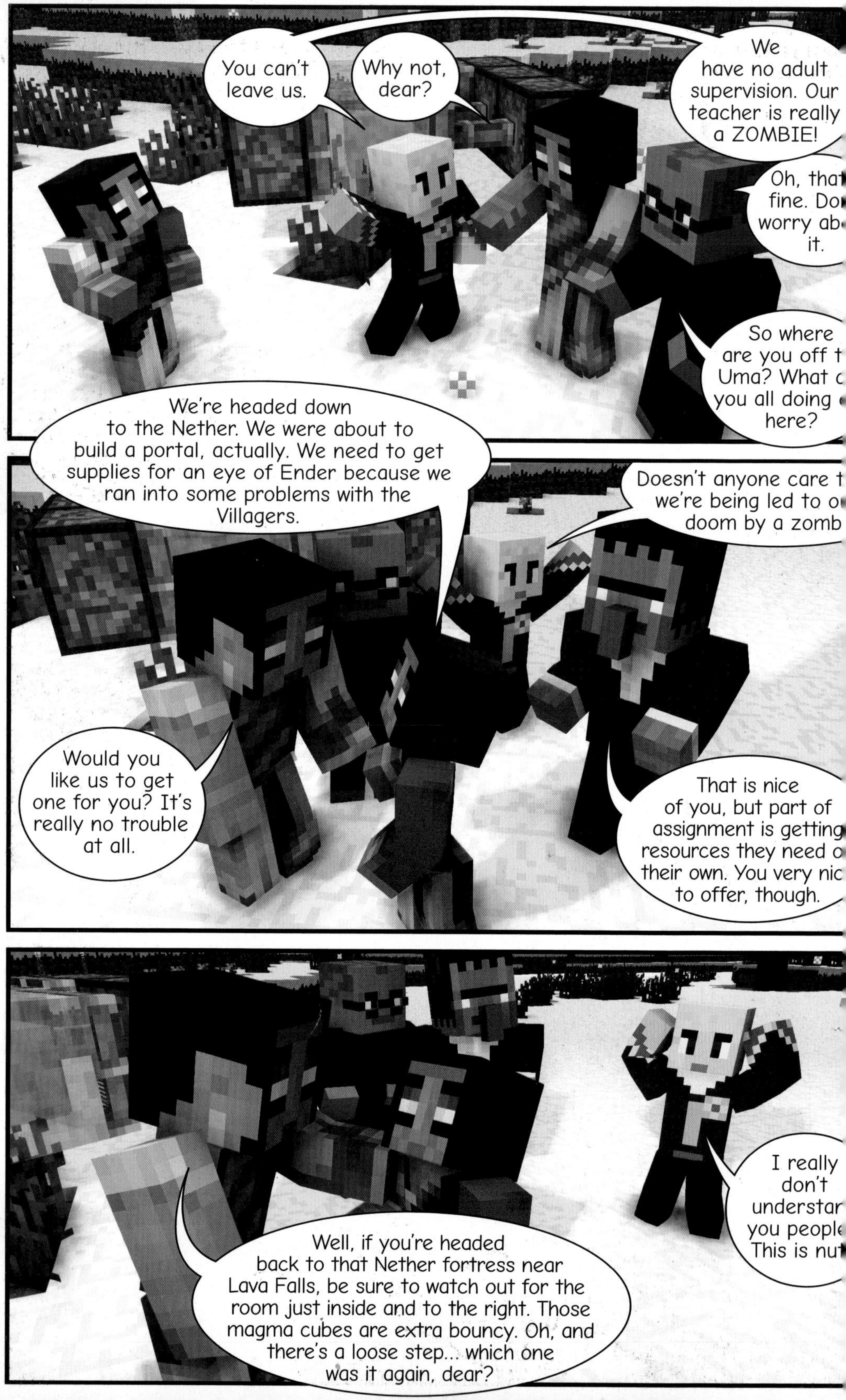

You can't leave us.
Why not, dear?
We have no adult supervision. Our teacher is really a ZOMBIE!
Oh, tha fine. Do worry ab it.
So where are you off Uma? What you all doing here?
We're headed down to the Nether. We were about to build a portal, actually. We need to get supplies for an eye of Ender because we ran into some problems with the Villagers.
Doesn't anyone care we're being led to doom by a zomb
Would you like us to get one for you? It's really no trouble at all.
That is nice of you, but part of assignment is getting resources they need their own. You very nic to offer, though.
Well, if you're headed back to that Nether fortress near Lava Falls, be sure to watch out for the room just inside and to the right. Those magma cubes are extra bouncy. Oh, and there's a loose step... which one was it again, dear?
I really don't understa you peopl This is nu

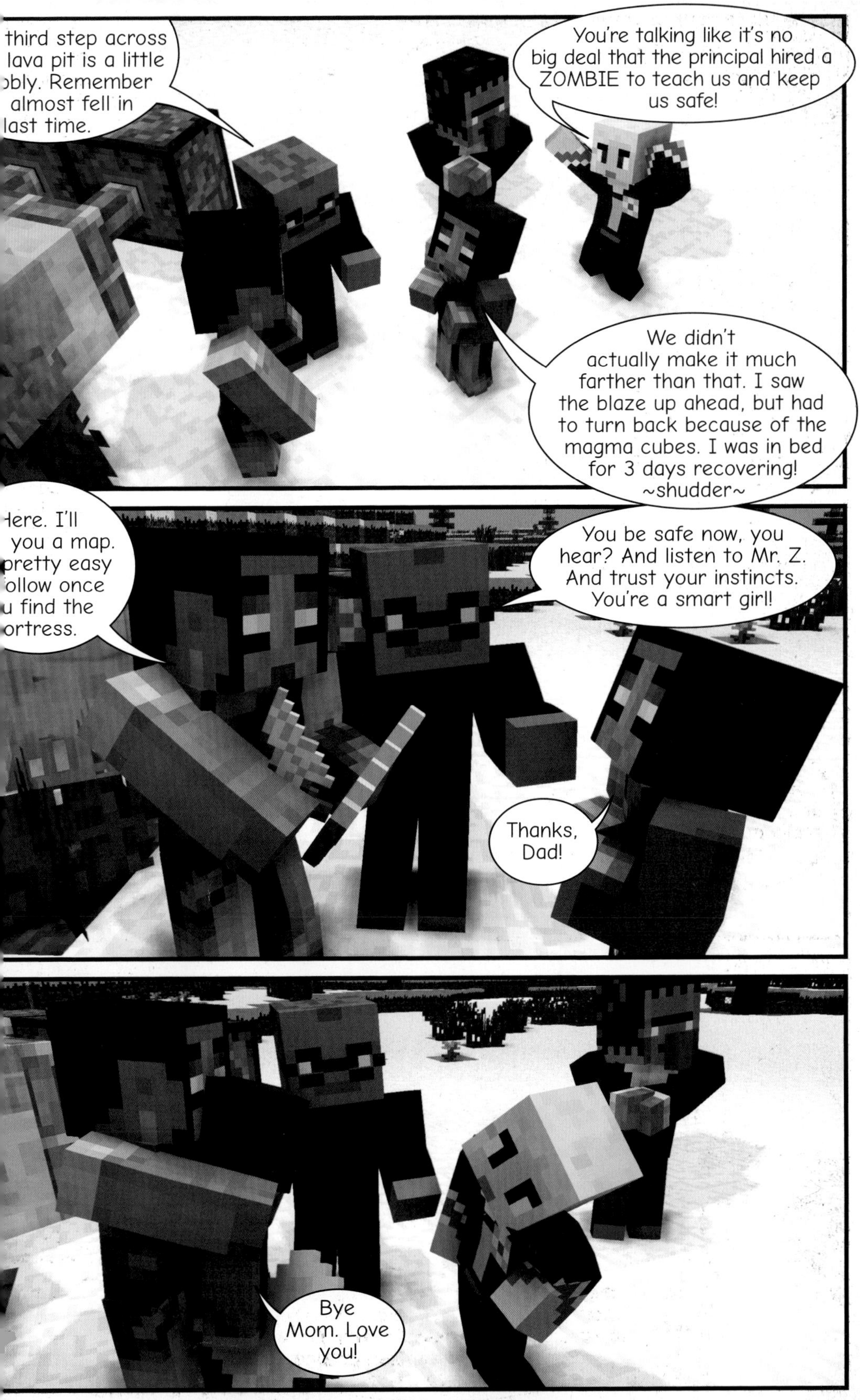
third step across
lava pit is a little
obly. Remember
almost fell in
last time.
You're talking like it's no big deal that the principal hired a ZOMBIE to teach us and keep us safe!
We didn't actually make it much farther than that. I saw the blaze up ahead, but had to turn back because of the magma cubes. I was in bed for 3 days recovering! ~shudder~
Here. I'll
you a map.
pretty easy
follow once
u find the
ortress.
You be safe now, you hear? And listen to Mr. Z. And trust your instincts. You're a smart girl!
Thanks, Dad!
Bye Mom. Love you!

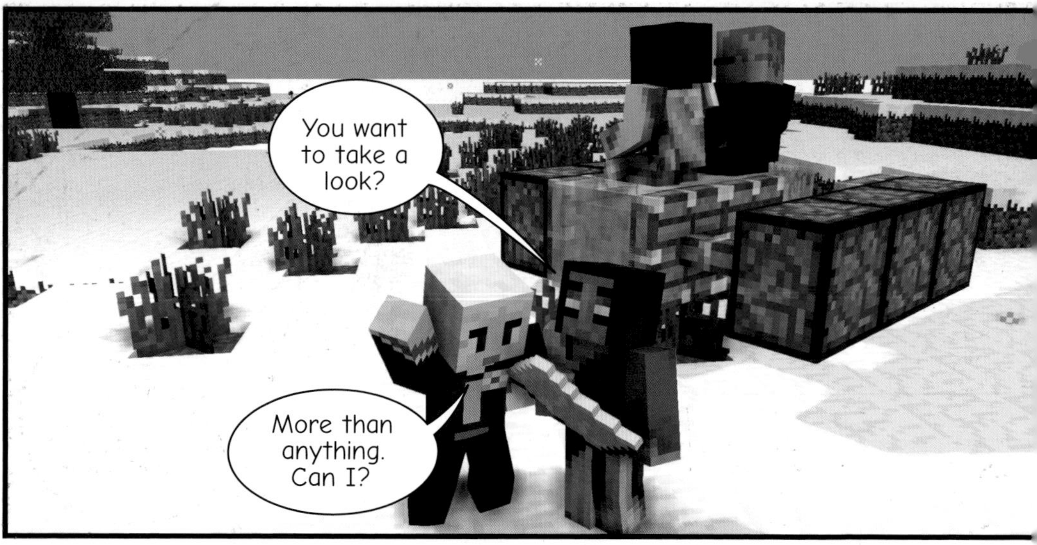
You want to take a look?
More than anything. Can I?

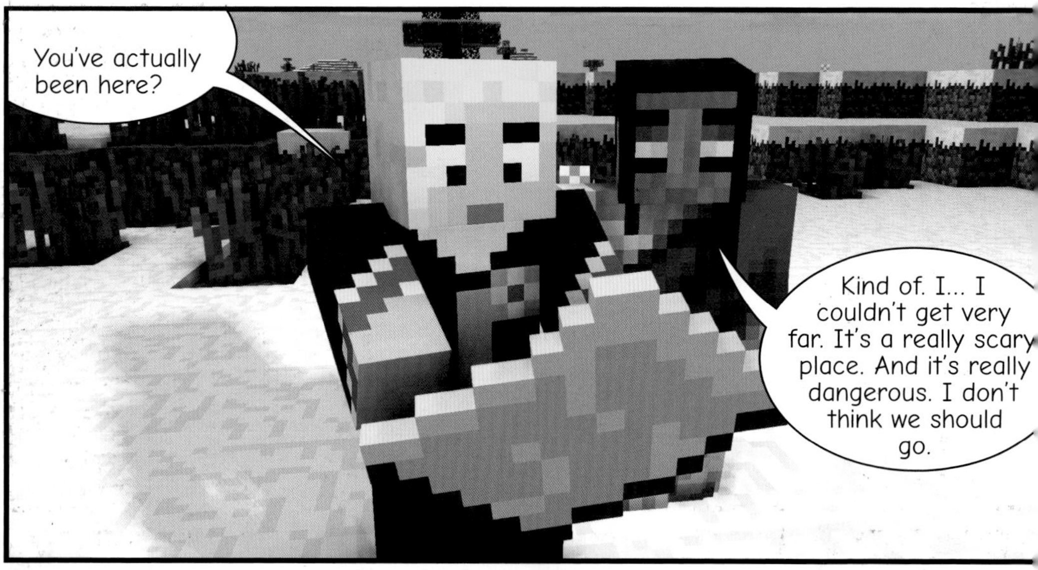
You've actually been here?
Kind of. I... I couldn't get very far. It's a really scary place. And it's really dangerous. I don't think we should go.

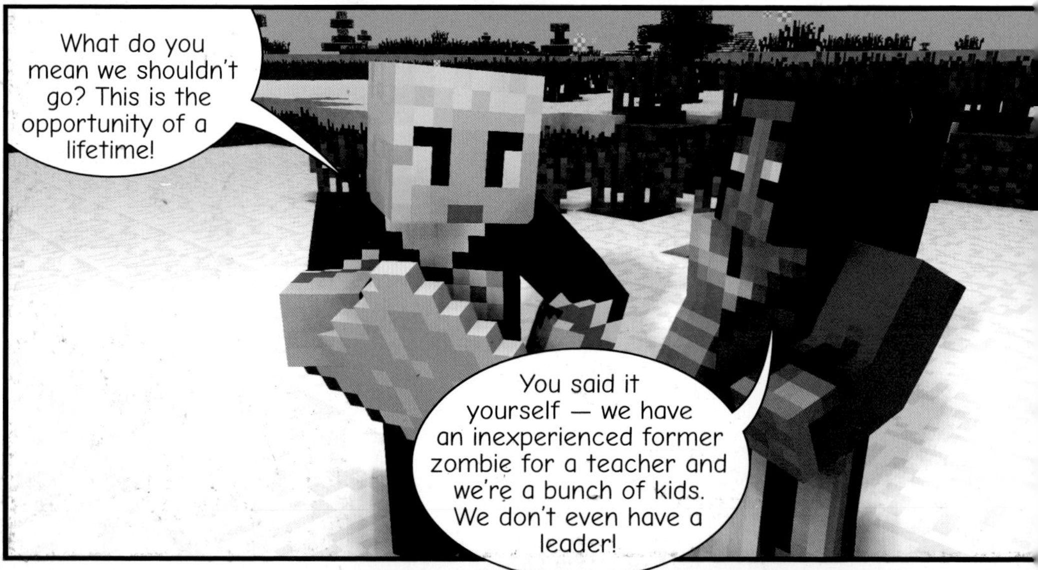
What do you mean we shouldn't go? This is the opportunity of a lifetime!
You said it yourself — we have an inexperienced former zombie for a teacher and we're a bunch of kids. We don't even have a leader!

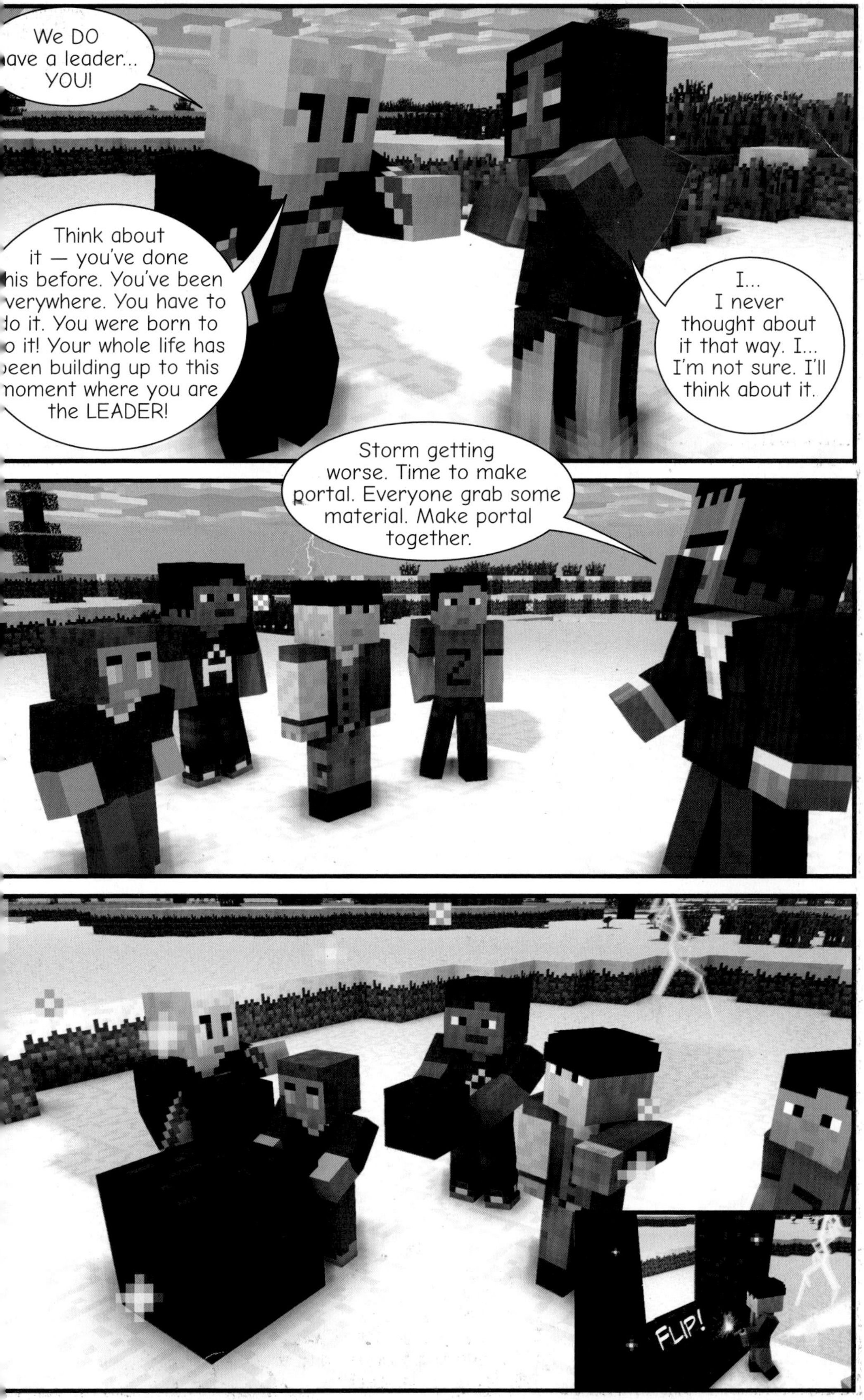
We DO
ave a leader...
YOU!
Think about
it — you've done
his before. You've been
verywhere. You have to
lo it. You were born to
o it! Your whole life has
een building up to this
moment where you are
the LEADER!
I...
I never
thought about
it that way. I...
I'm not sure. I'll
think about it.
Storm getting
worse. Time to make
portal. Everyone grab some
material. Make portal
together.
FLIP!

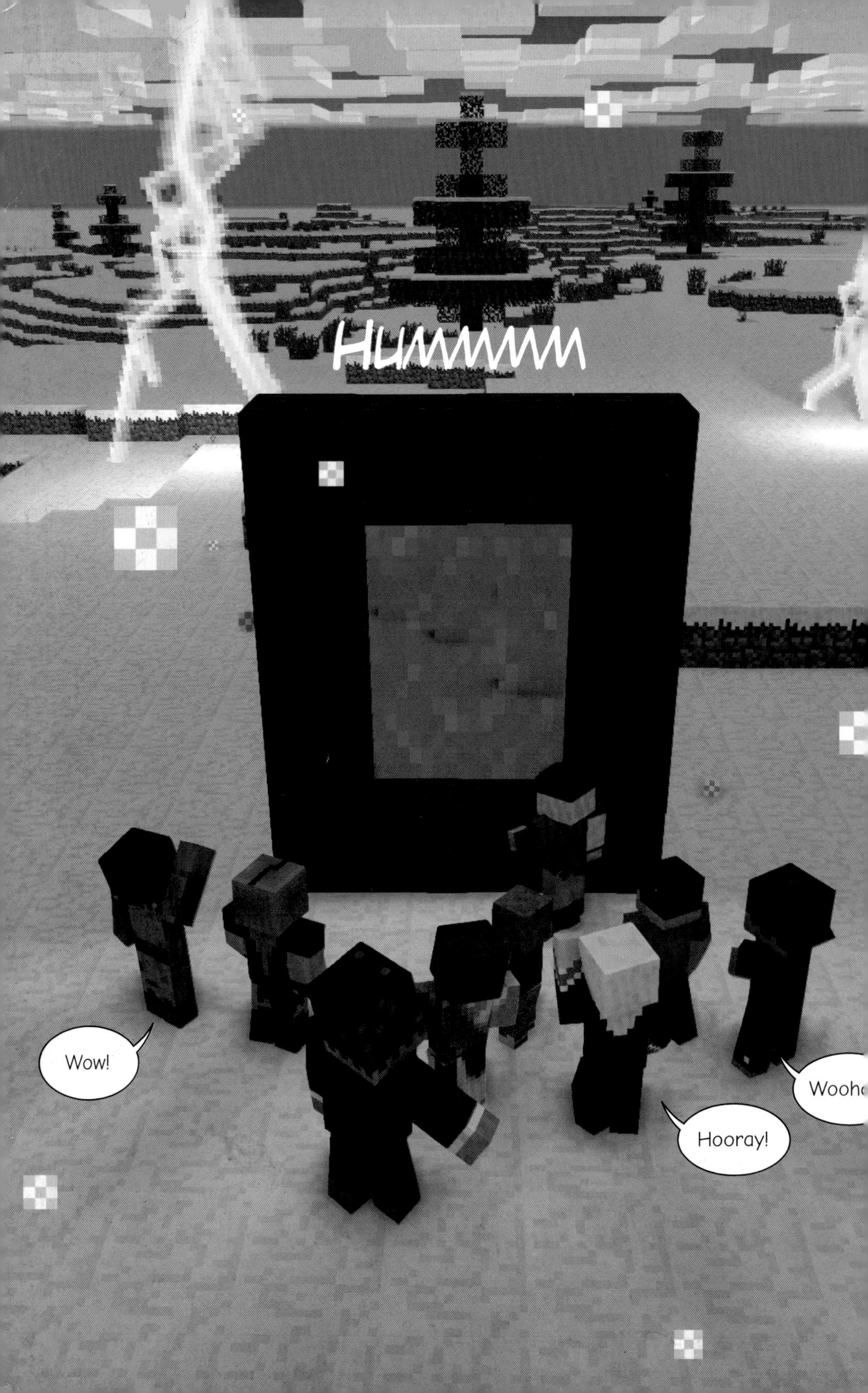

HUMMMM
Wow!
Hooray!

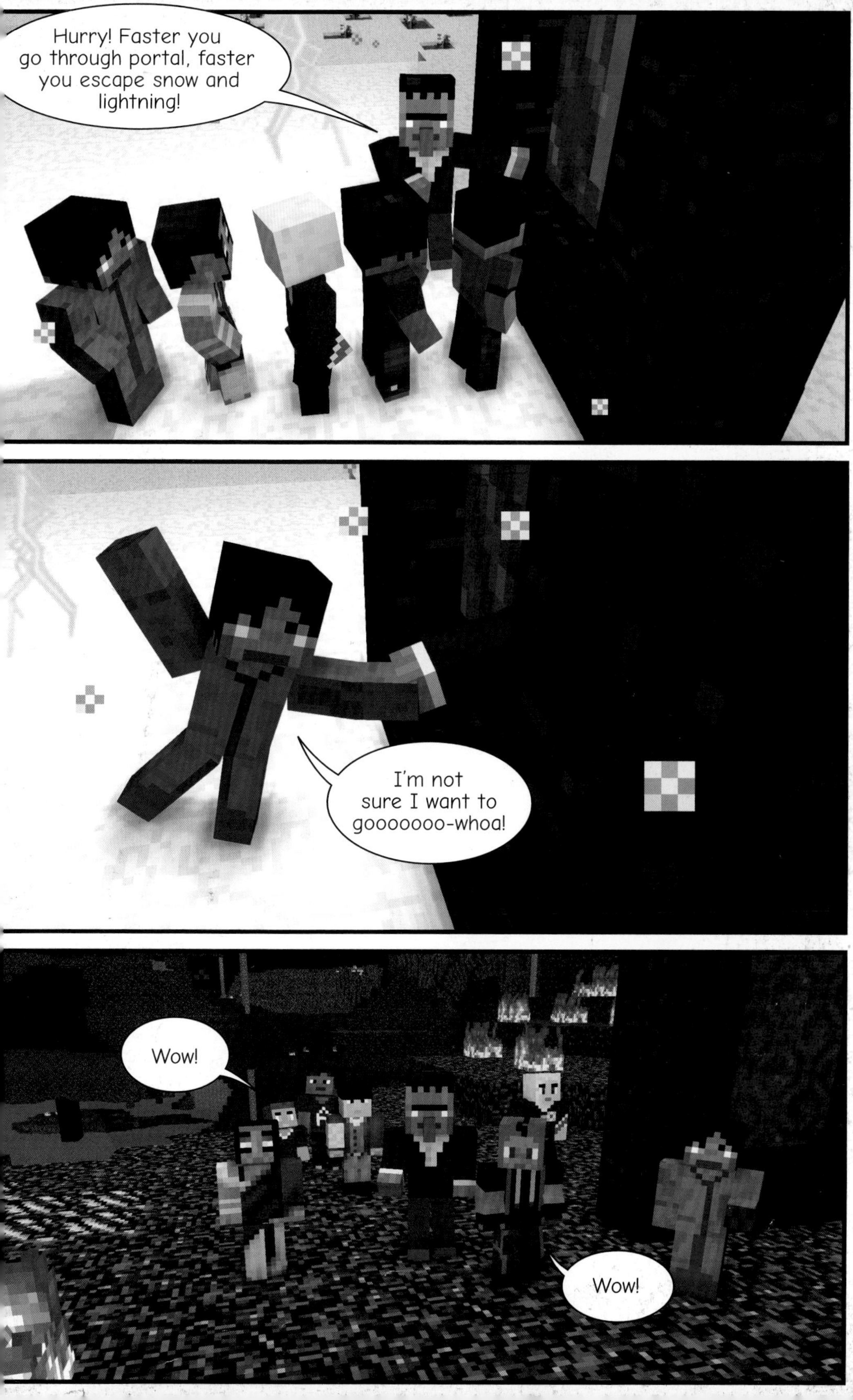
Hurry! Faster you go through portal, faster you escape snow and lightning!
I'm not sure I want to goooooo-whoa!
Wow!
Wow!

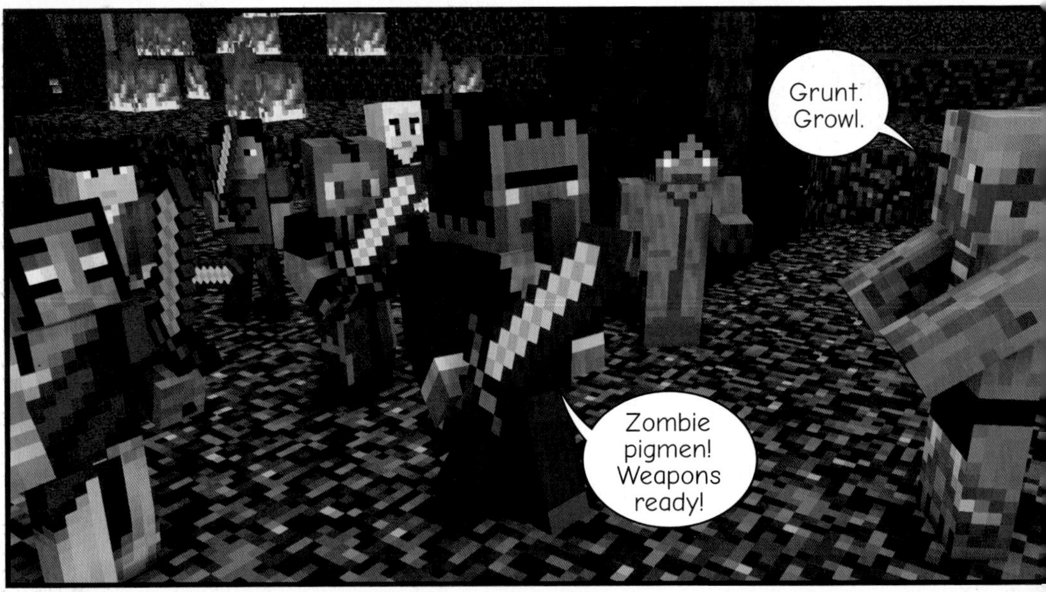
Grunt. Growl.
Zombie pigmen! Weapons ready!

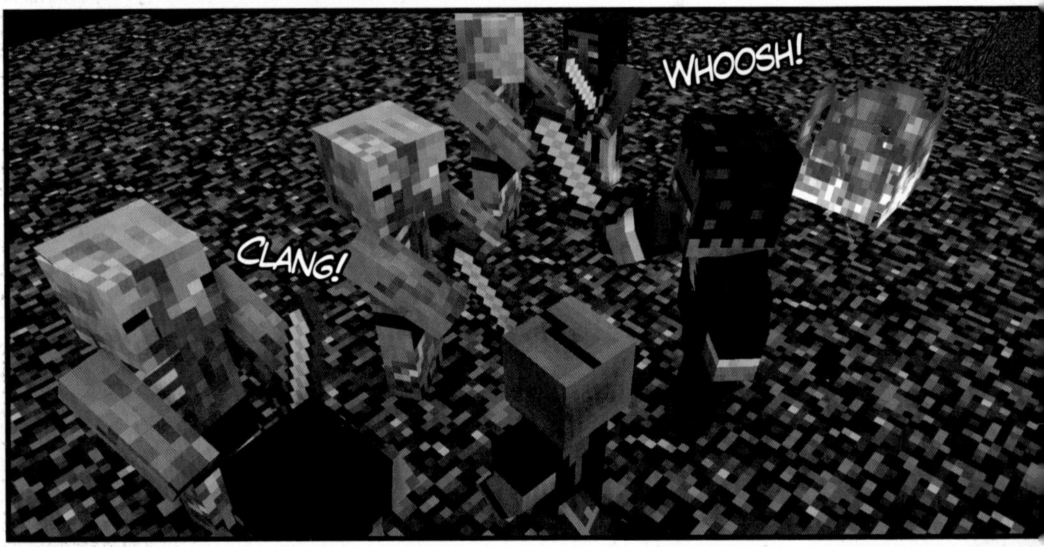
WHOOSH!
CLANG!

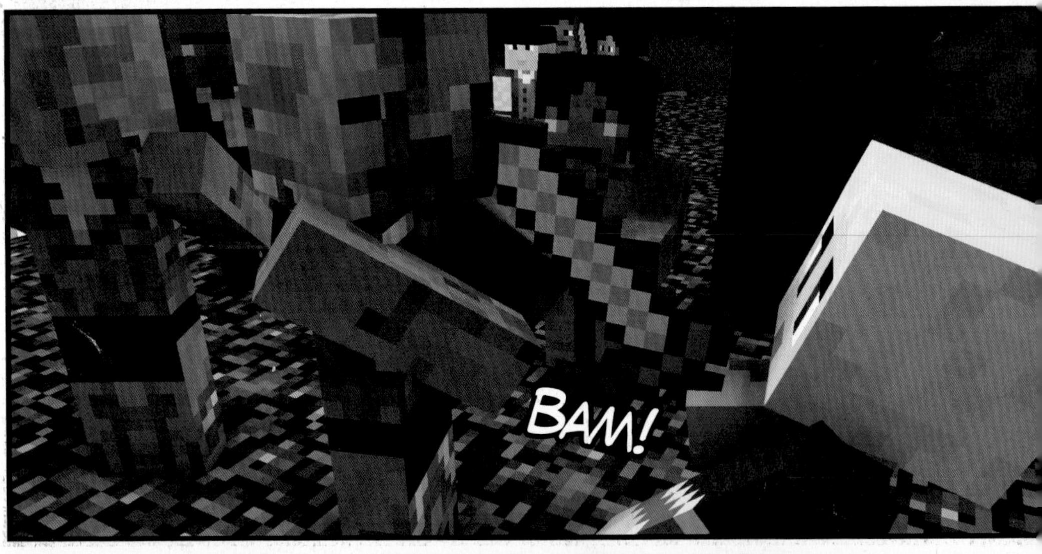
BAM!

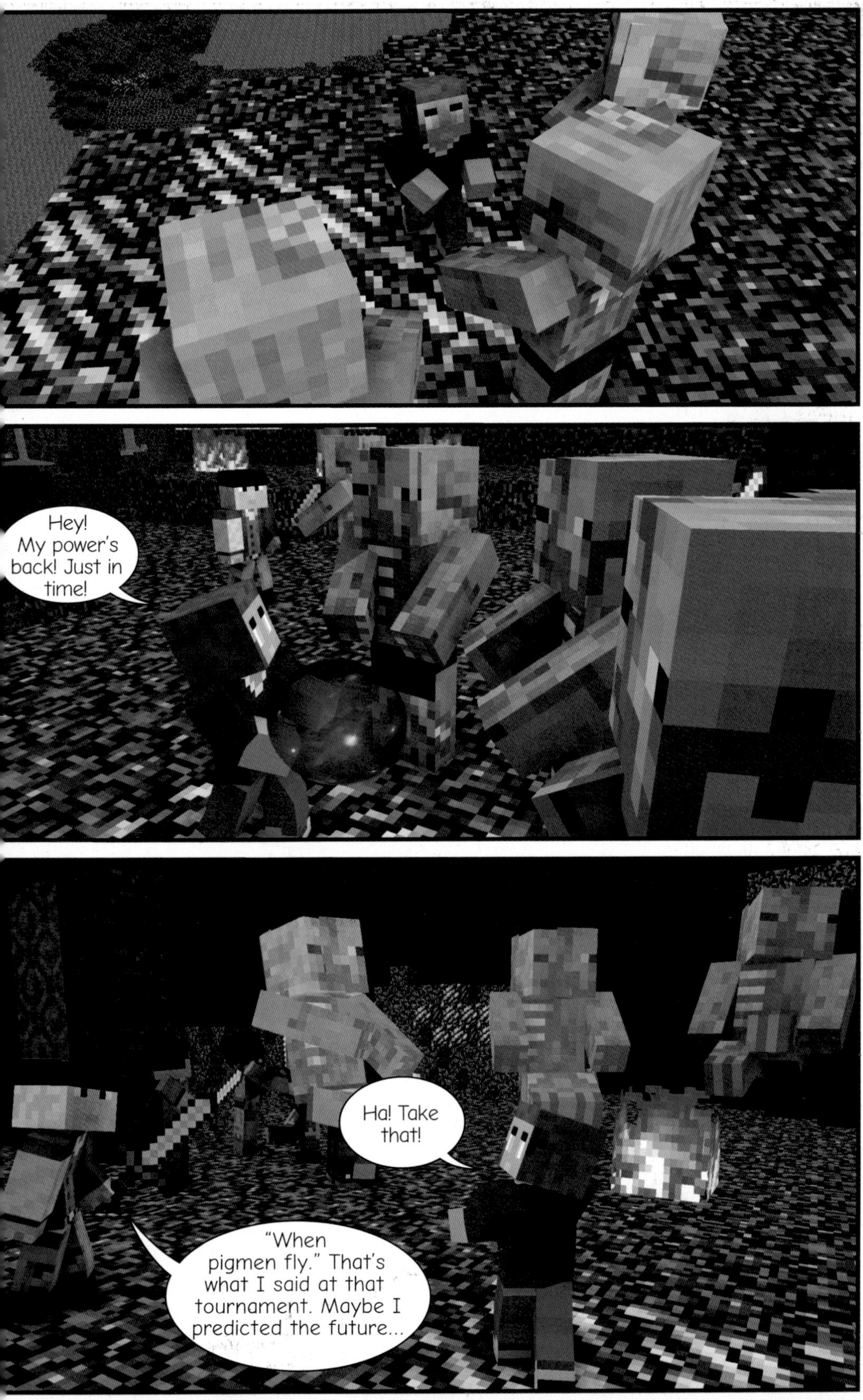
Hey! My power's back! Just in time!
Ha! Take that!
"When pigmen fly." That's what I said at that tournament. Maybe I predicted the future...

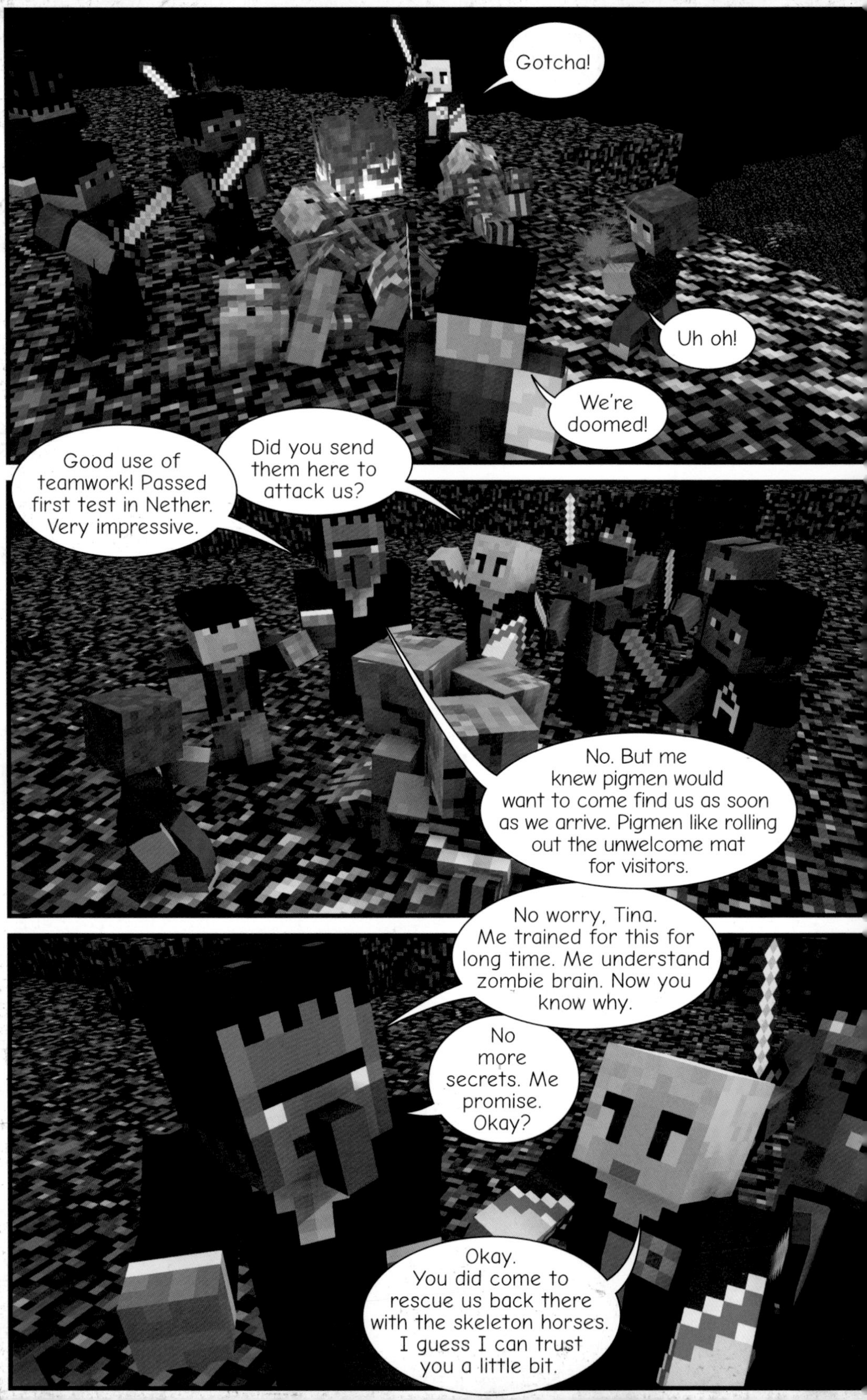
Gotcha!
Uh oh!
We're doomed!
Good use of teamwork! Passed first test in Nether. Very impressive.
Did you send them here to attack us?
No. But me knew pigmen would want to come find us as soon as we arrive. Pigmen like rolling out the unwelcome mat for visitors.
No worry, Tina. Me trained for this for long time. Me understand zombie brain. Now you know why.
No more secrets. Me promise. Okay?
Okay. You did come to rescue us back there with the skeleton horses. I guess I can trust you a little bit.

CHAPTER 8

INTO THE

FORTRESS

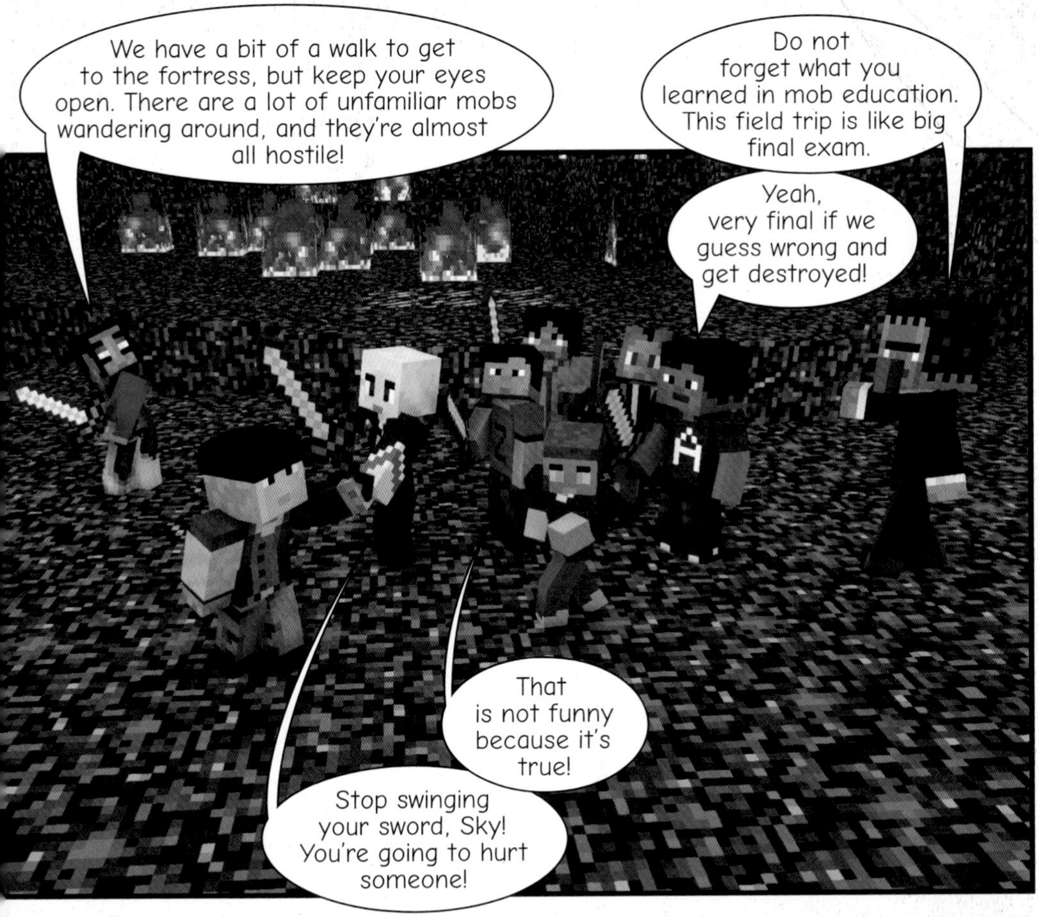
We have a bit of a walk to get to the fortress, but keep your eyes open. There are a lot of unfamiliar mobs wandering around, and they're almost all hostile!
Do not forget what you learned in mob education. This field trip is like big final exam.
Yeah, very final if we guess wrong and get destroyed!
That is not funny because it's true!
Stop swinging your sword, Sky! You're going to hurt someone!

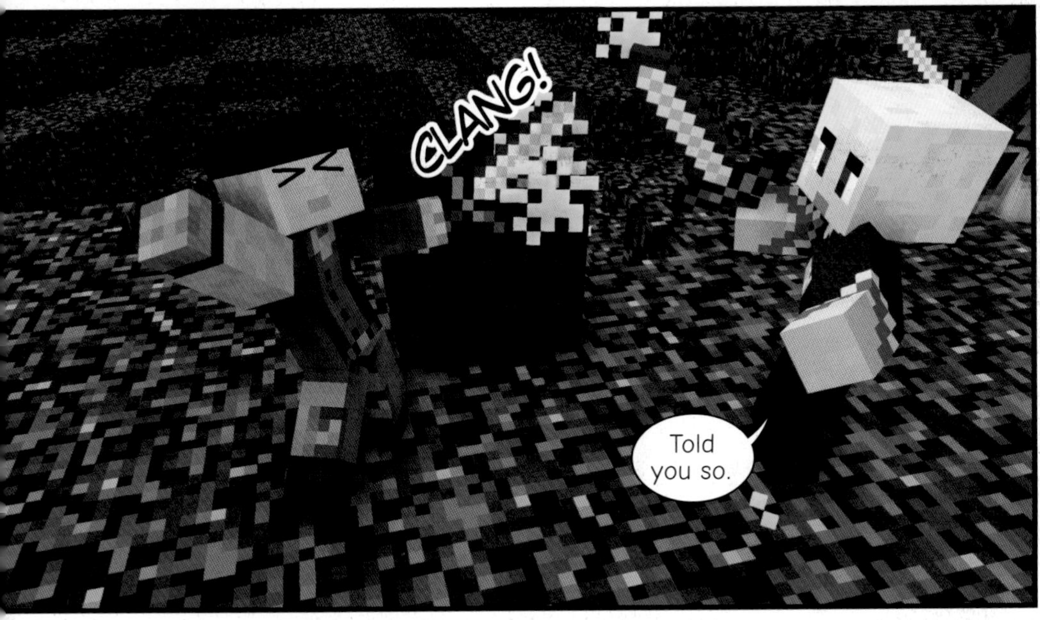
CLANG!
Told you so.

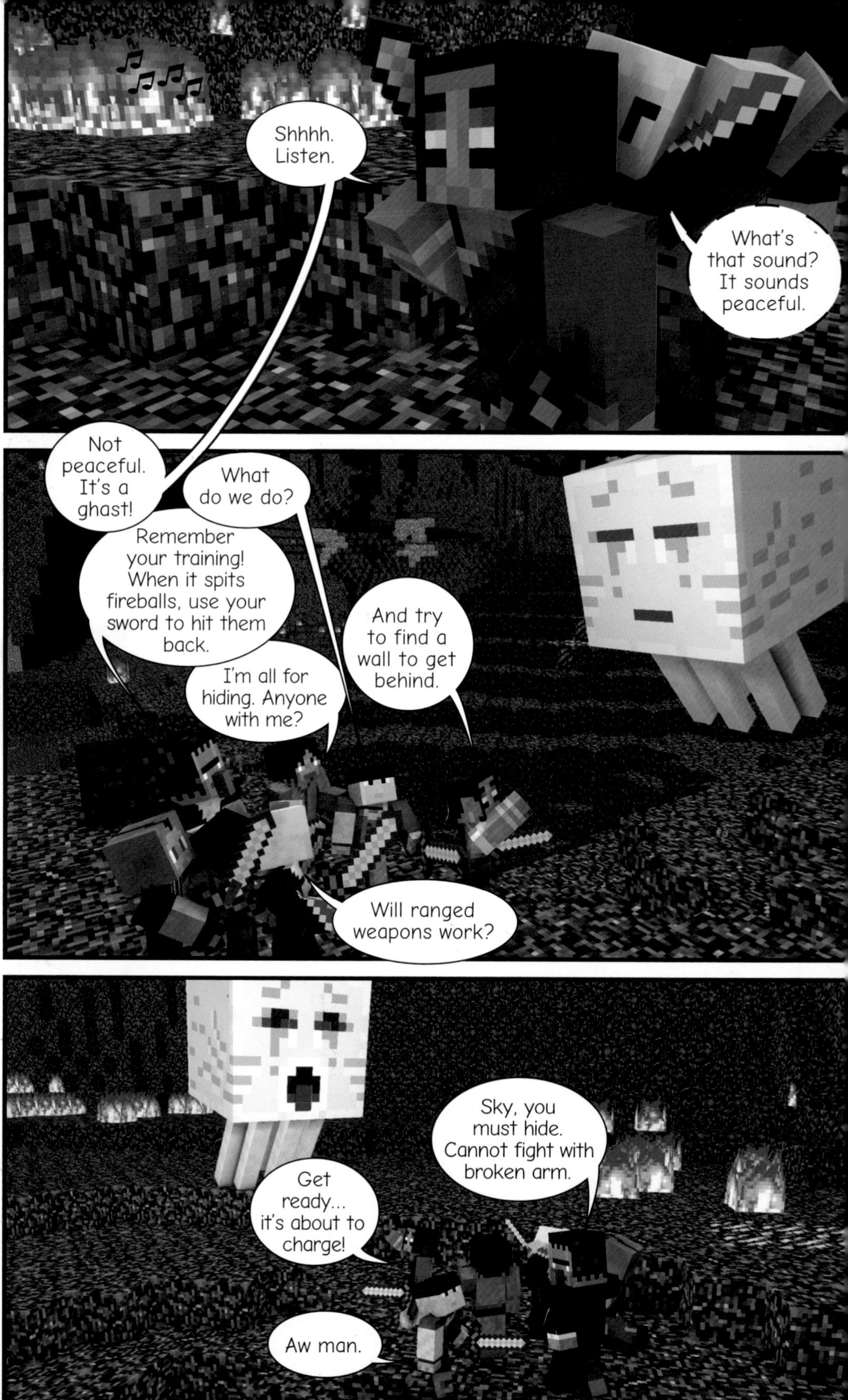
Shhhh. Listen.
What's that sound? It sounds peaceful.
Not peaceful. It's a ghast!
What do we do?
Remember your training! When it spits fireballs, use your sword to hit them back.
And try to find a wall to get behind.
I'm all for hiding. Anyone with me?
Will ranged weapons work?
Sky, you must hide. Cannot fight with broken arm.
Get ready... it's about to charge!
Aw man.

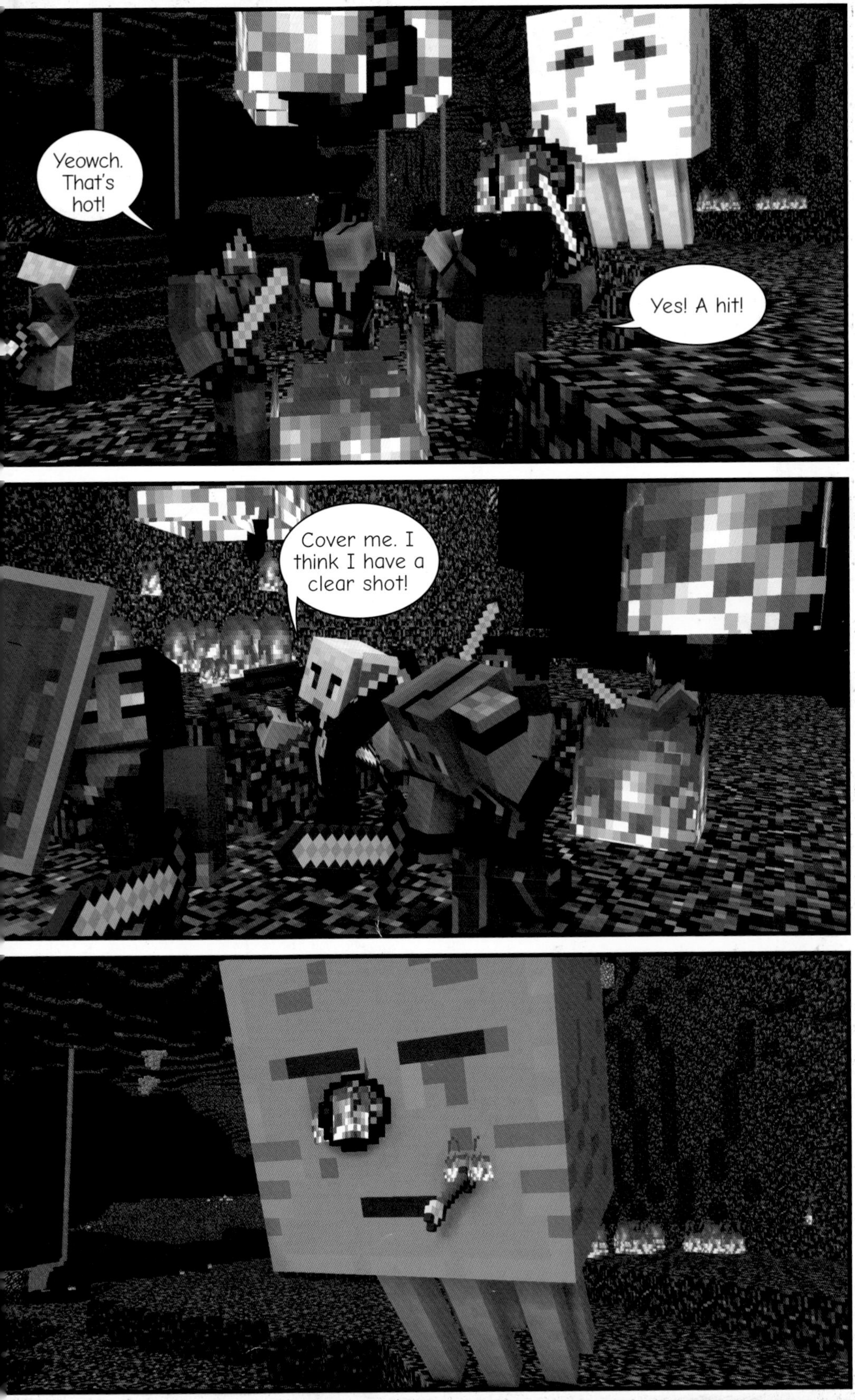
Yeowch. That's hot!
Yes! A hit!
Cover me. I think I have a clear shot!

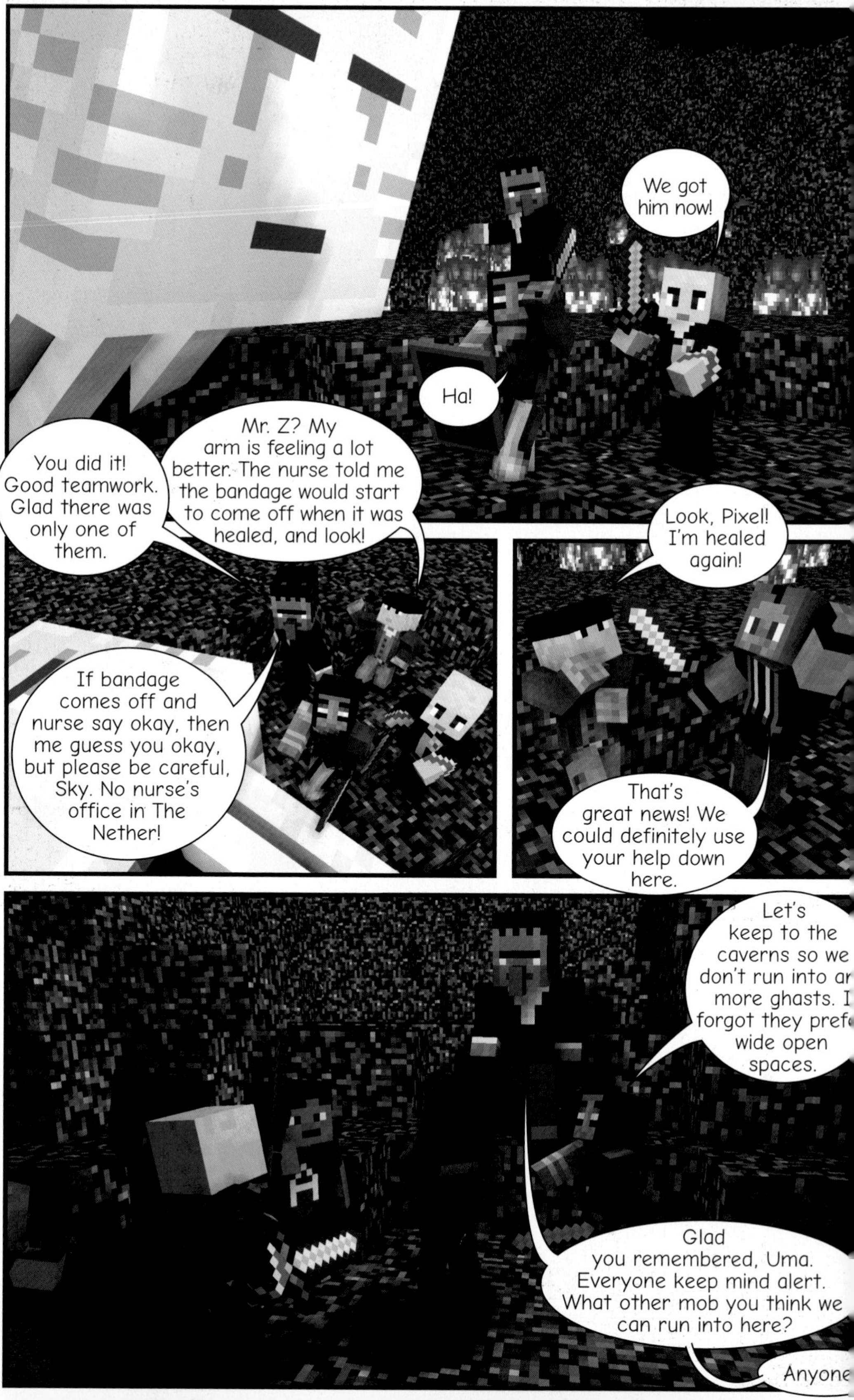
We got him now!
Ha!
You did it! Good teamwork. Glad there was only one of them.
Mr. Z? My arm is feeling a lot better. The nurse told me the bandage would start to come off when it was healed, and look!
If bandage comes off and nurse say okay, then me guess you okay, but please be careful, Sky. No nurse's office in The Nether!
Look, Pixel! I'm healed again!
That's great news! We could definitely use your help down here.
Let's keep to the caverns so we don't run into ar more ghasts. I forgot they pref wide open spaces.
Glad you remembered, Uma. Everyone keep mind alert. What other mob you think we can run into here?
Anyone

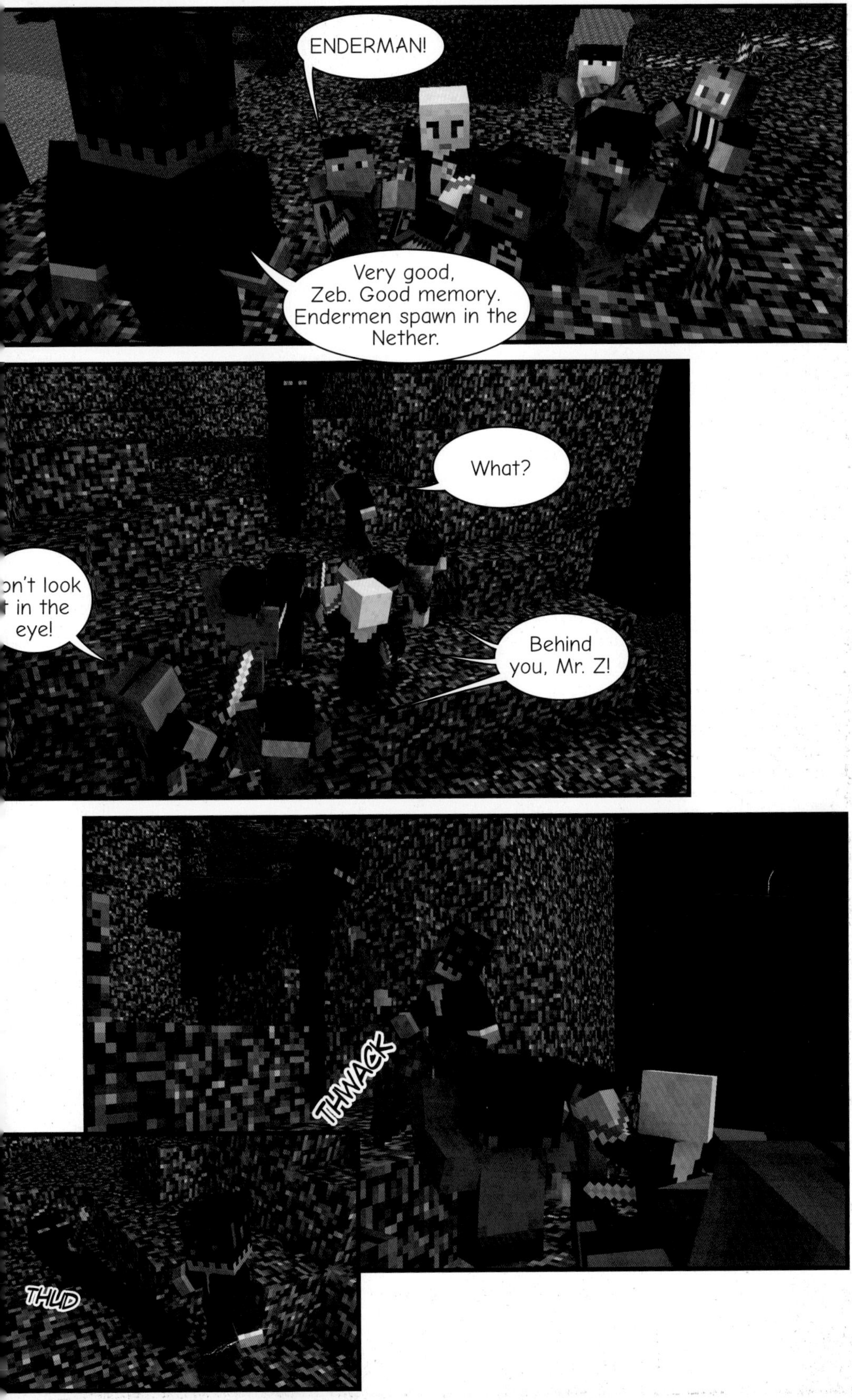
ENDERMAN!
Very good, Zeb. Good memory. Endermen spawn in the Nether.
What?
on't look t in the eye!
Behind you, Mr. Z!
THWACK
THUD

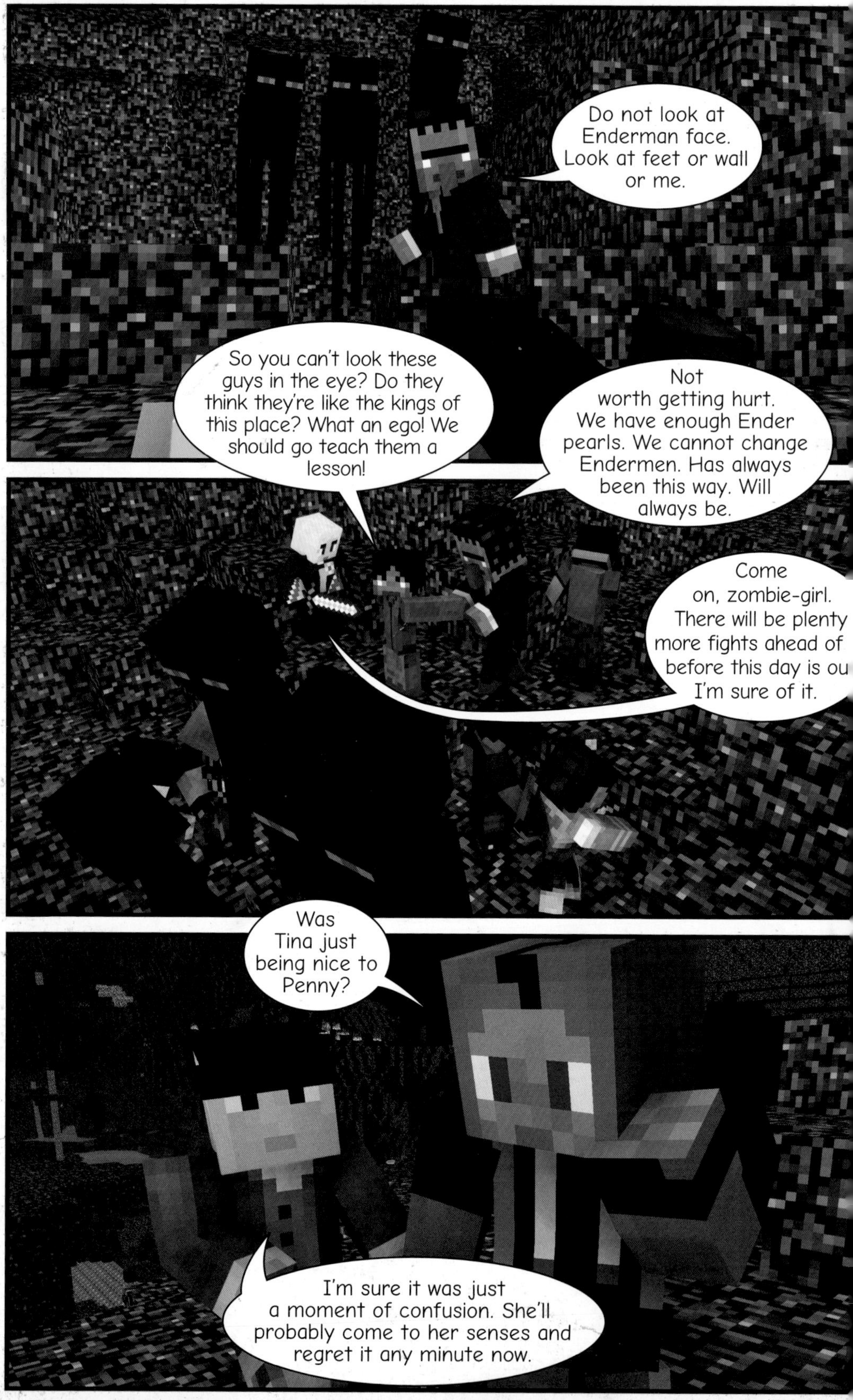
Do not look at Enderman face. Look at feet or wall or me.
So you can't look these guys in the eye? Do they think they're like the kings of this place? What an ego! We should go teach them a lesson!
Not worth getting hurt. We have enough Ender pearls. We cannot change Endermen. Has always been this way. Will always be.
Come on, zombie-girl. There will be plenty more fights ahead of before this day is ou I'm sure of it.
Was Tina just being nice to Penny?
I'm sure it was just a moment of confusion. She'll probably come to her senses and regret it any minute now.

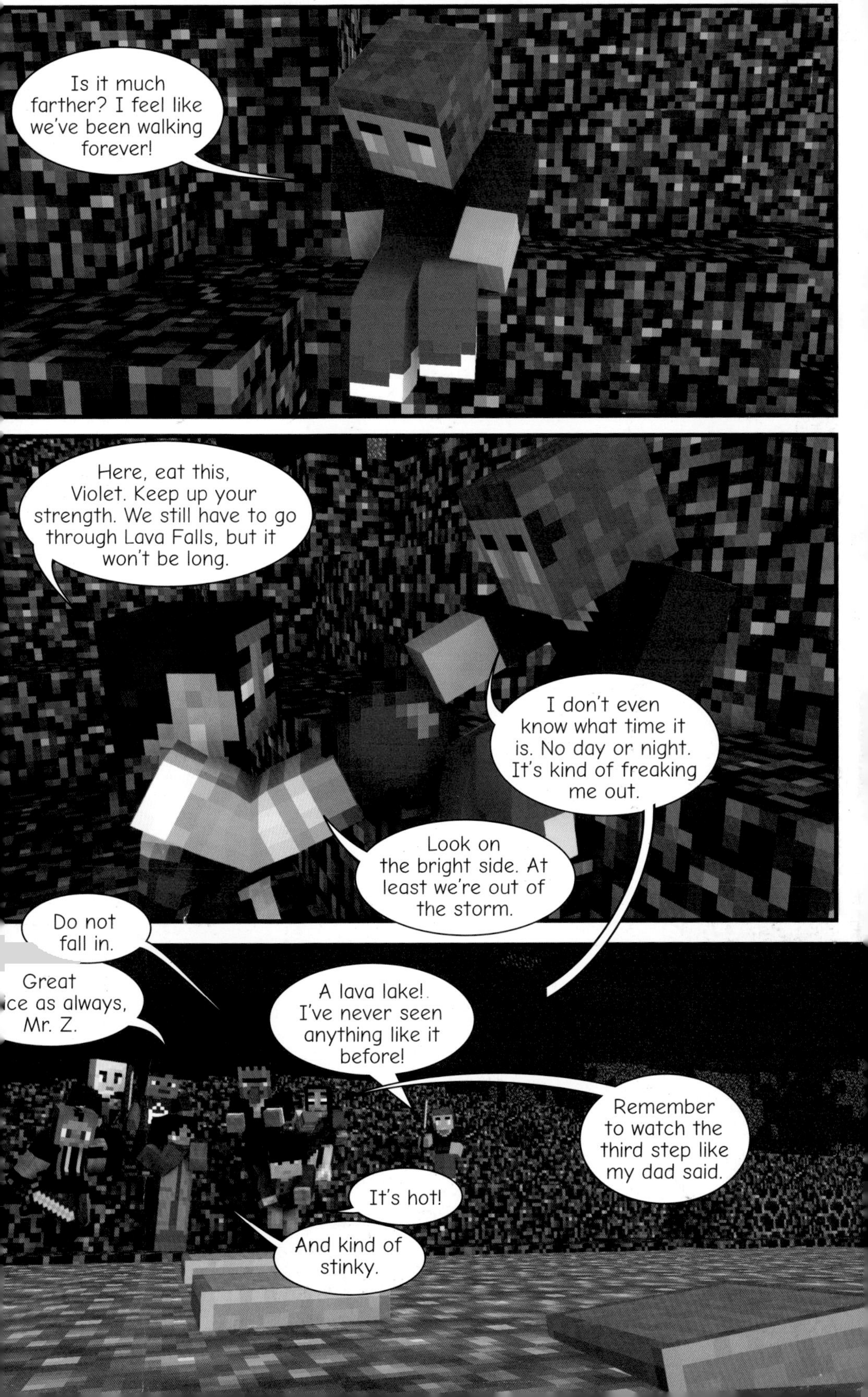

Is it much farther? I feel like we've been walking forever!
Here, eat this, Violet. Keep up your strength. We still have to go through Lava Falls, but it won't be long.
I don't even know what time it is. No day or night. It's kind of freaking me out.
Look on the bright side. At least we're out of the storm.
Do not fall in.
Great ice as always, Mr. Z.
A lava lake! I've never seen anything like it before!
Remember to watch the third step like my dad said.
It's hot!
And kind of stinky.

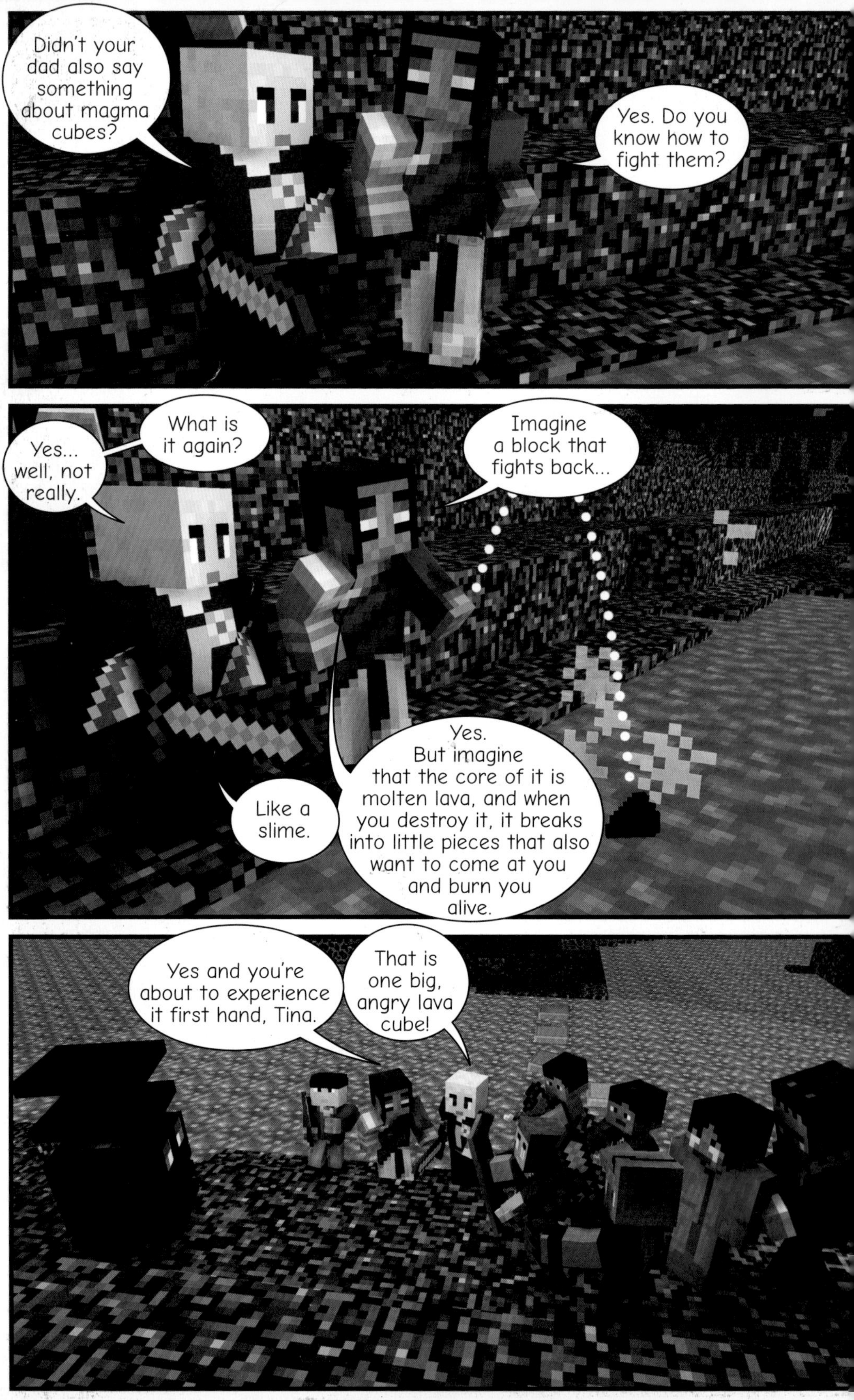
Didn't your dad also say something about magma cubes?
Yes. Do you know how to fight them?
Yes... well, not really.
What is it again?
Imagine a block that fights back...
Like a slime.
Yes. But imagine that the core of it is molten lava, and when you destroy it, it breaks into little pieces that also want to come at you and burn you alive.
Yes and you're about to experience it first hand, Tina.
That is one big, angry lava cube!

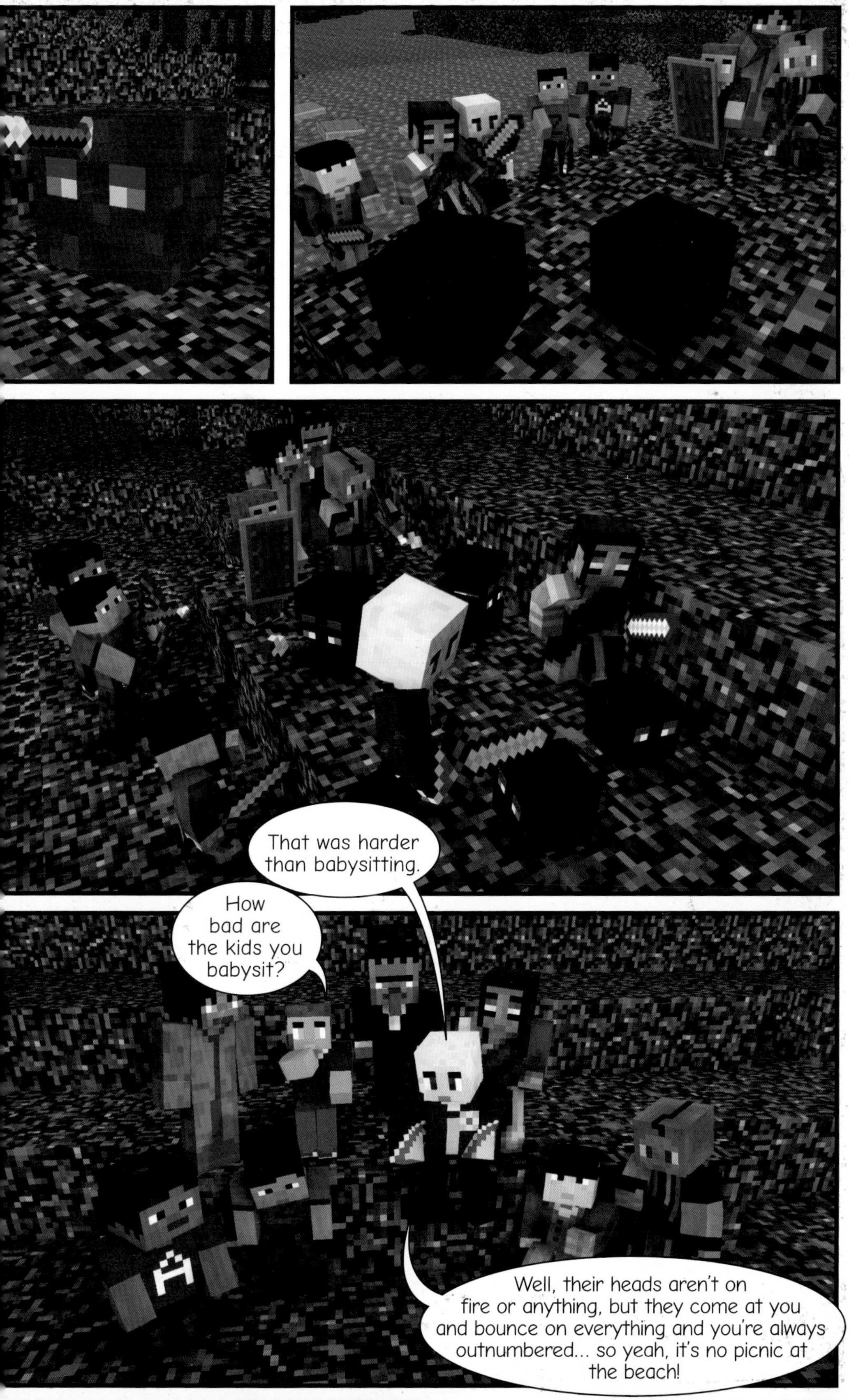

That was harder than babysitting.
How bad are the kids you babysit?
Well, their heads aren't on fire or anything, but they come at you and bounce on everything and you're always outnumbered... so yeah, it's no picnic at the beach!

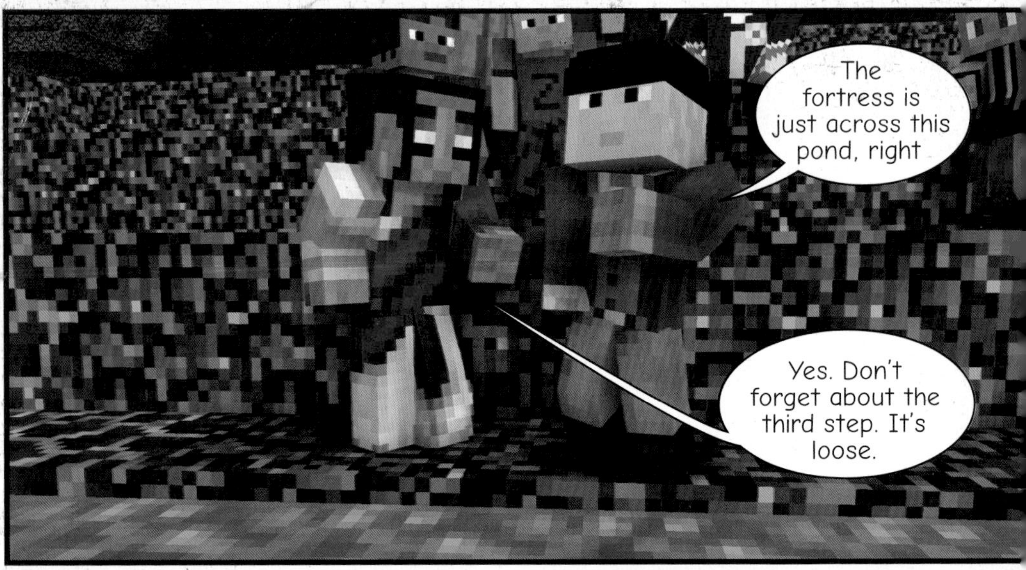
The fortress is just across this pond, right
Yes. Don't forget about the third step. It's loose.

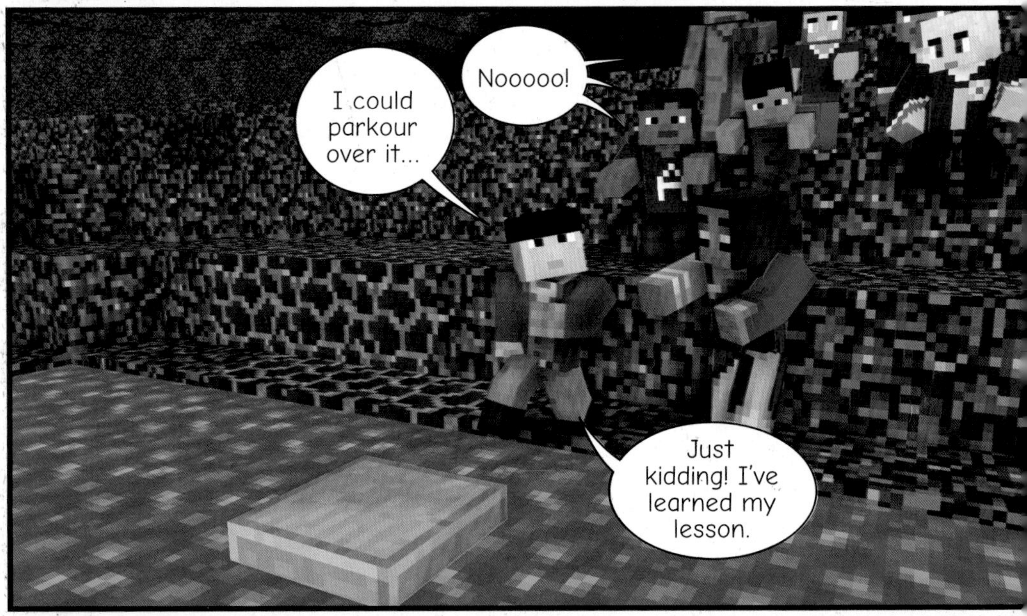
I could parkour over it...
Nooooo!
Just kidding! I've learned my lesson.

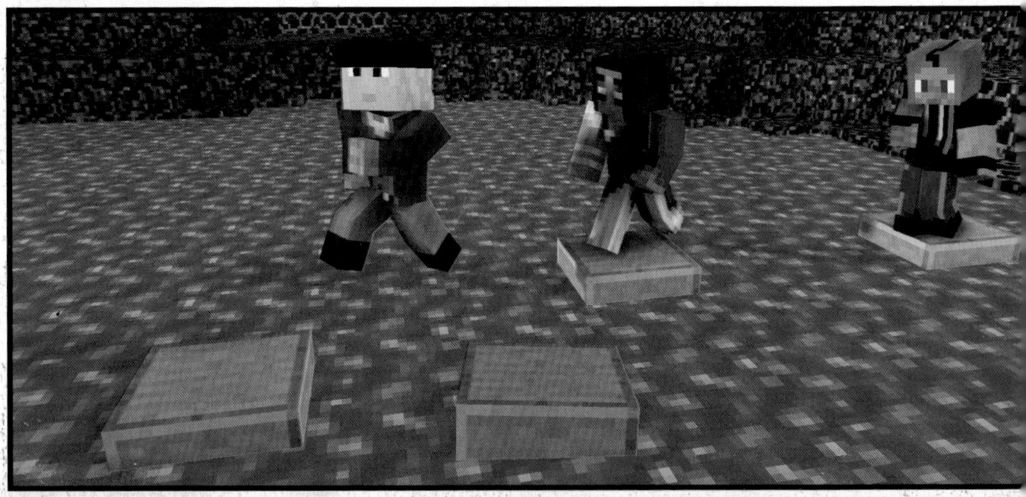

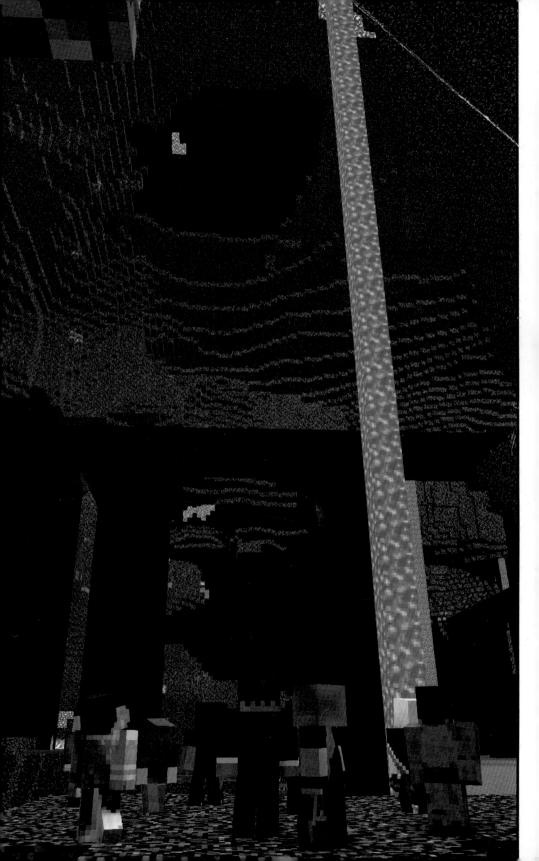

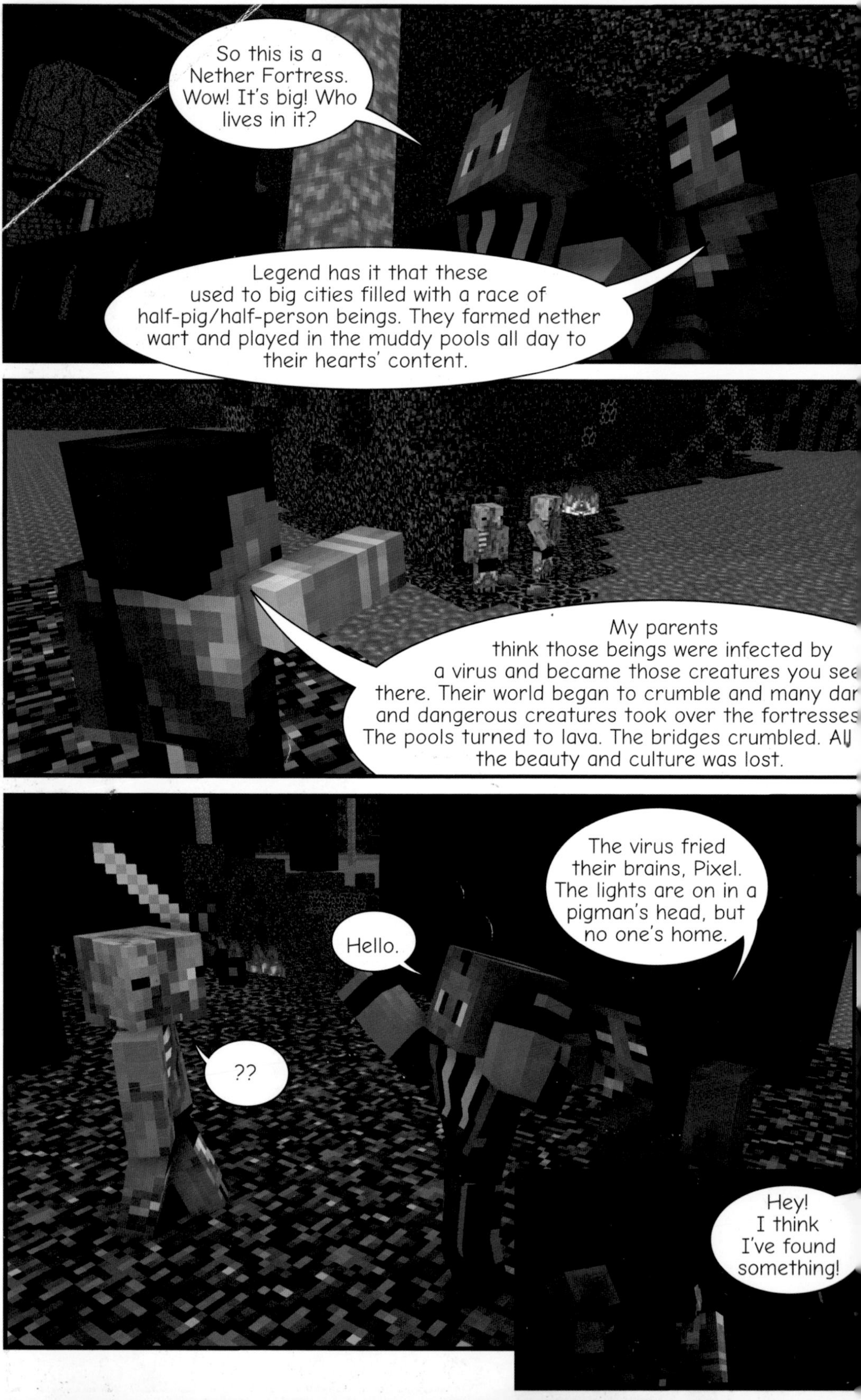
So this is a Nether Fortress. Wow! It's big! Who lives in it?
Legend has it that these used to big cities filled with a race of half-pig/half-person beings. They farmed nether wart and played in the muddy pools all day to their hearts' content.
My parents think those beings were infected by a virus and became those creatures you se there. Their world began to crumble and many dar and dangerous creatures took over the fortresses The pools turned to lava. The bridges crumbled. All the beauty and culture was lost.
Hello.
The virus fried their brains, Pixel. The lights are on in a pigman's head, but no one's home.
??
Hey! I think I've found something!

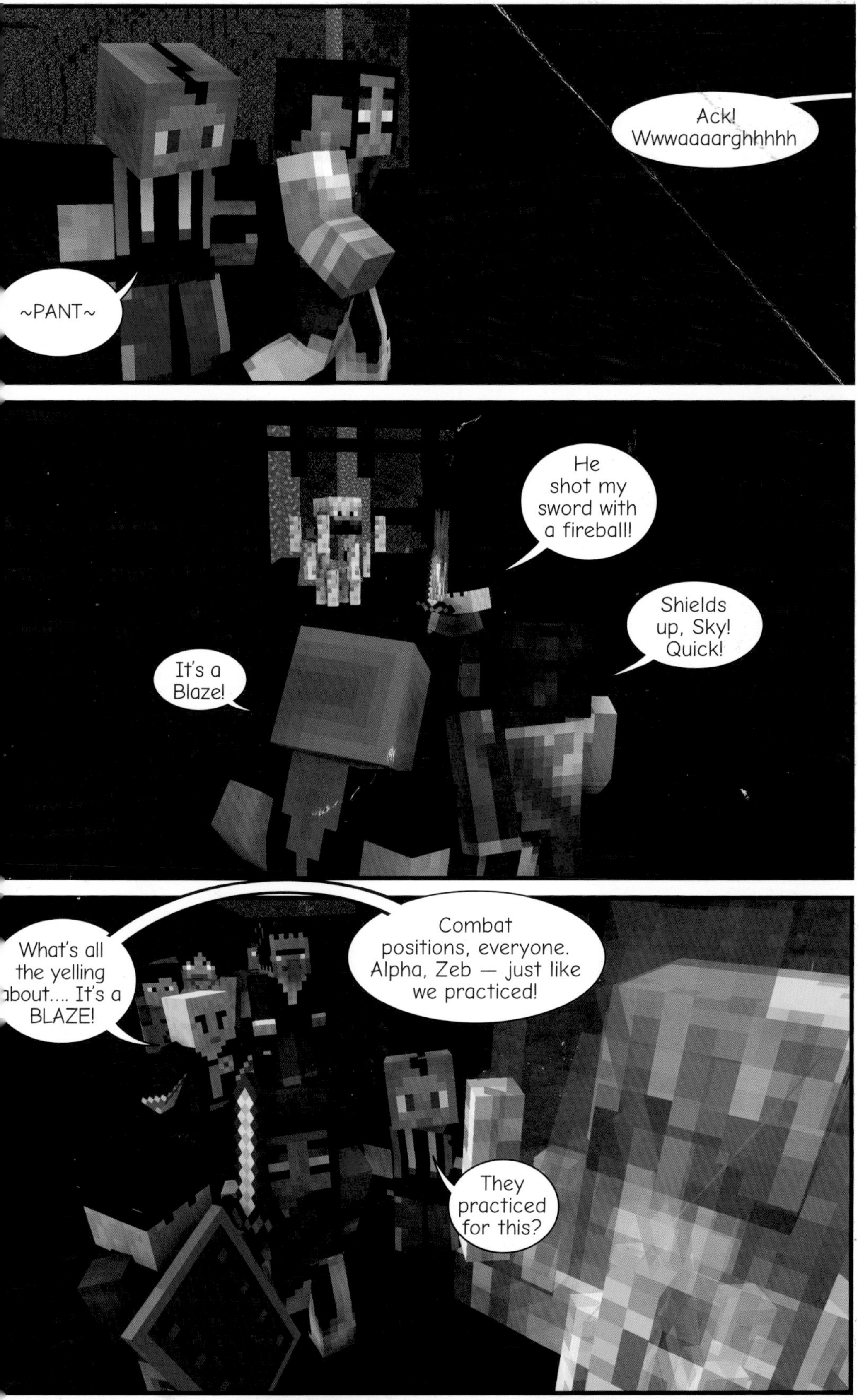
~PANT~
Ack! Wwwaaaarghhhhh
He shot my sword with a fireball!
It's a Blaze!
Shields up, Sky! Quick!
What's all the yelling about.... It's a BLAZE!
Combat positions, everyone. Alpha, Zeb — just like we practiced!
They practiced for this?

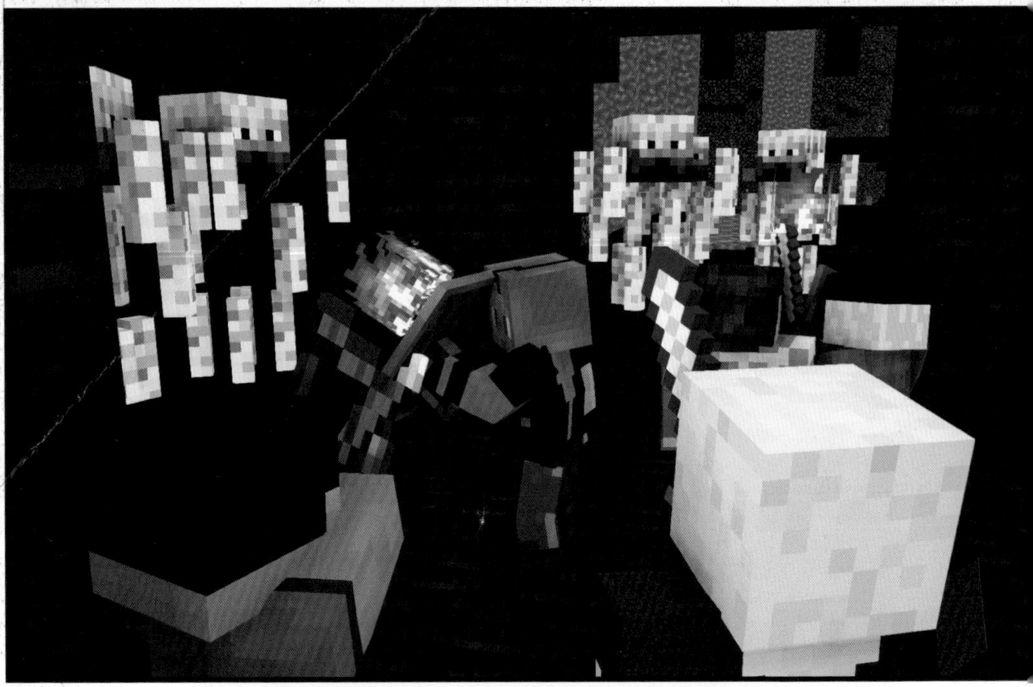
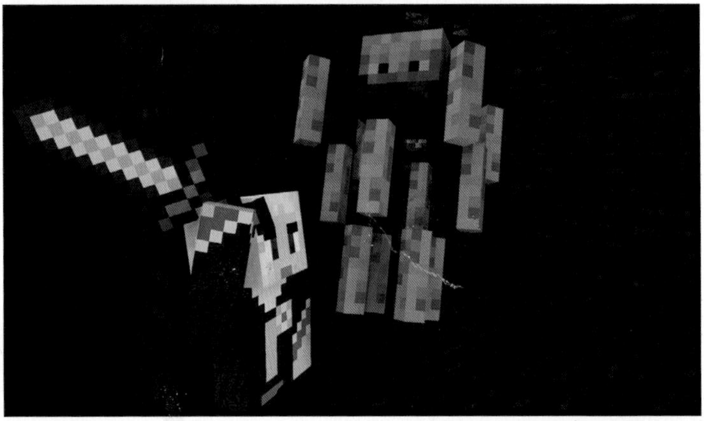
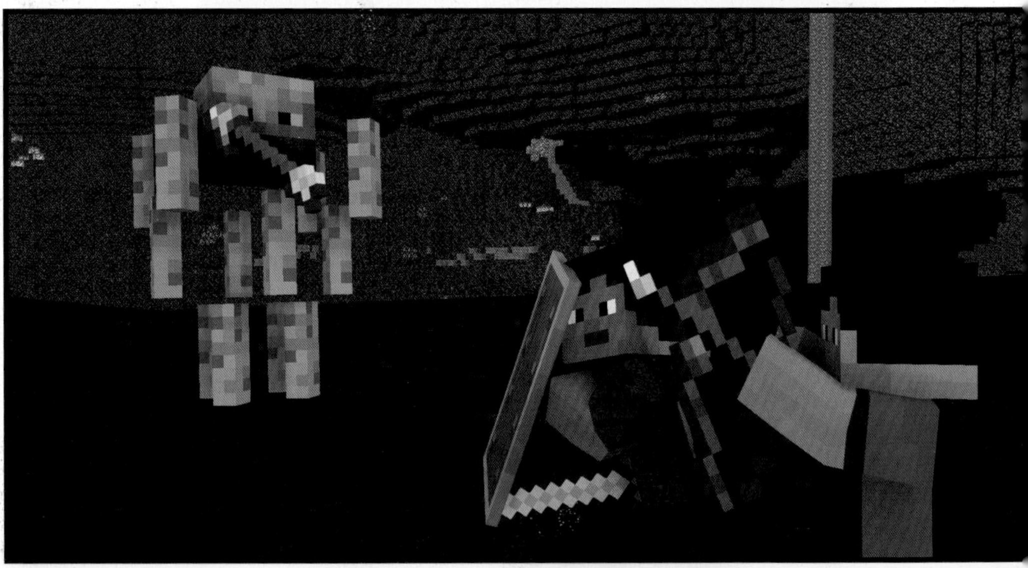

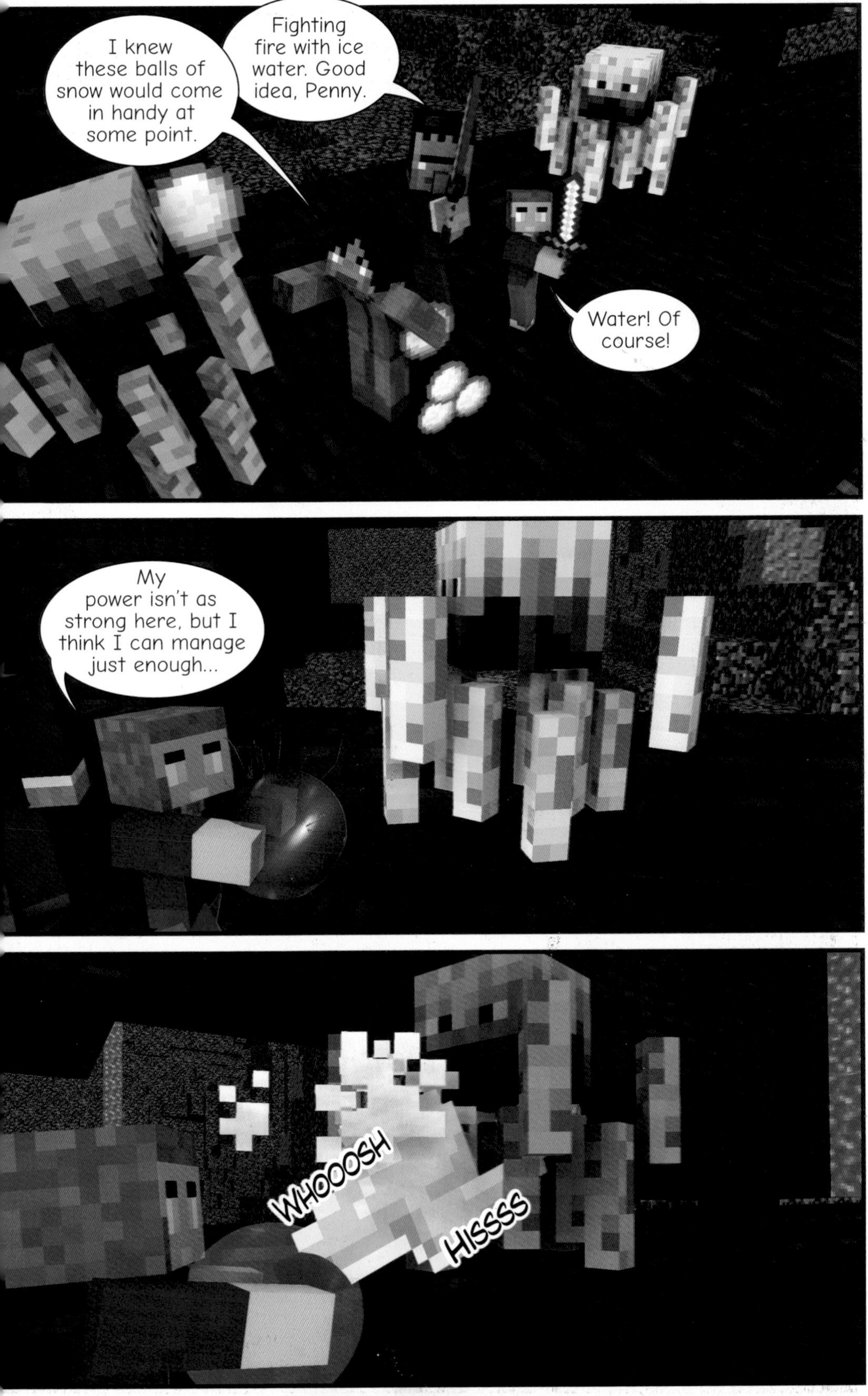
I knew these balls of snow would come in handy at some point.
Fighting fire with ice water. Good idea, Penny.
Water! Of course!
My power isn't as strong here, but I think I can manage just enough...
WHOOOSH
HISSSS

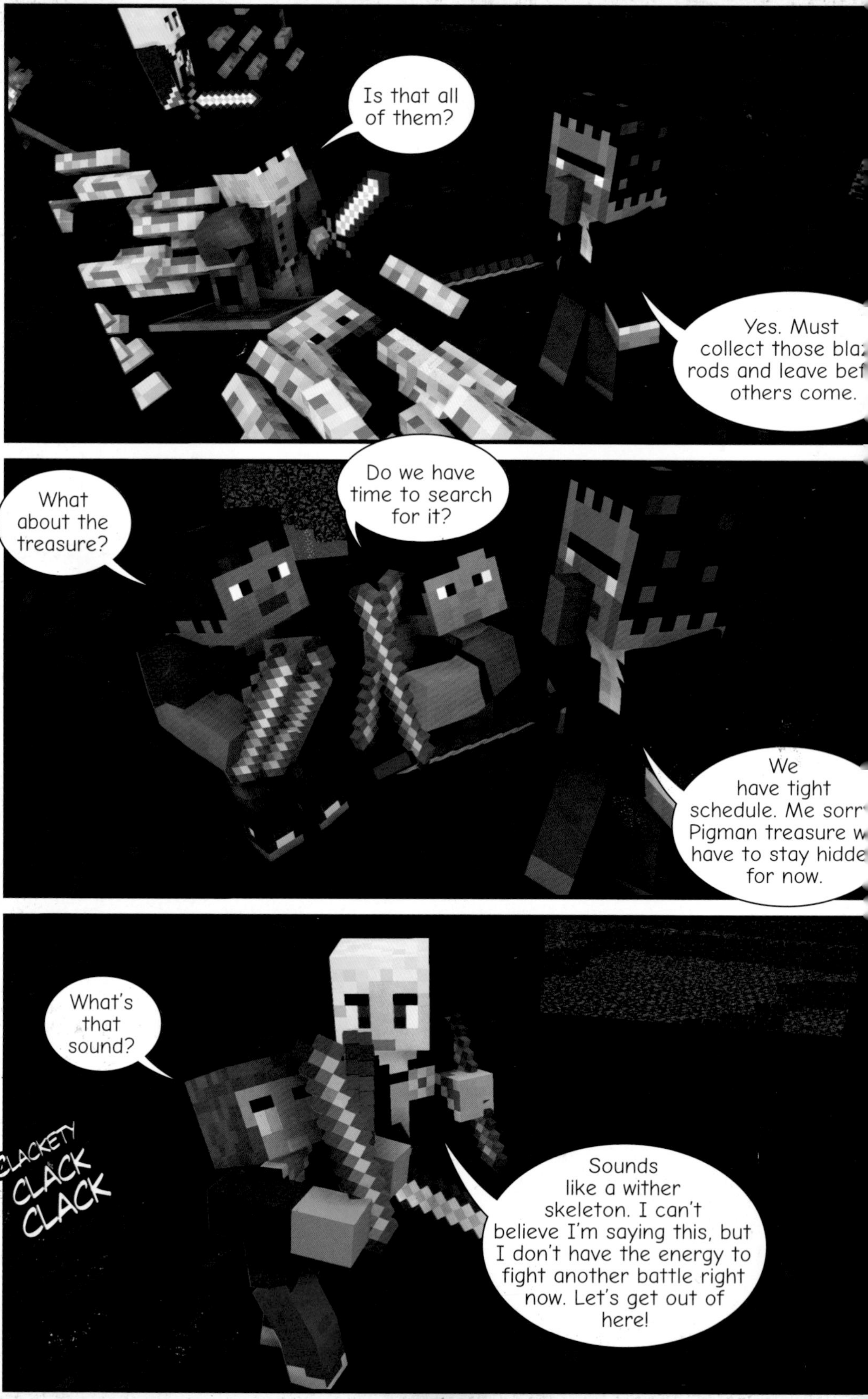
Is that all of them?
Yes. Must collect those bla rods and leave bef others come.
What about the treasure?
Do we have time to search for it?
We have tight schedule. Me sorr Pigman treasure w have to stay hidde for now.
What's that sound?
CLACKETY CLACK CLACK
Sounds like a wither skeleton. I can't believe I'm saying this, but I don't have the energy to fight another battle right now. Let's get out of here!

CHAPTER 9

RIDING THE DRAGON

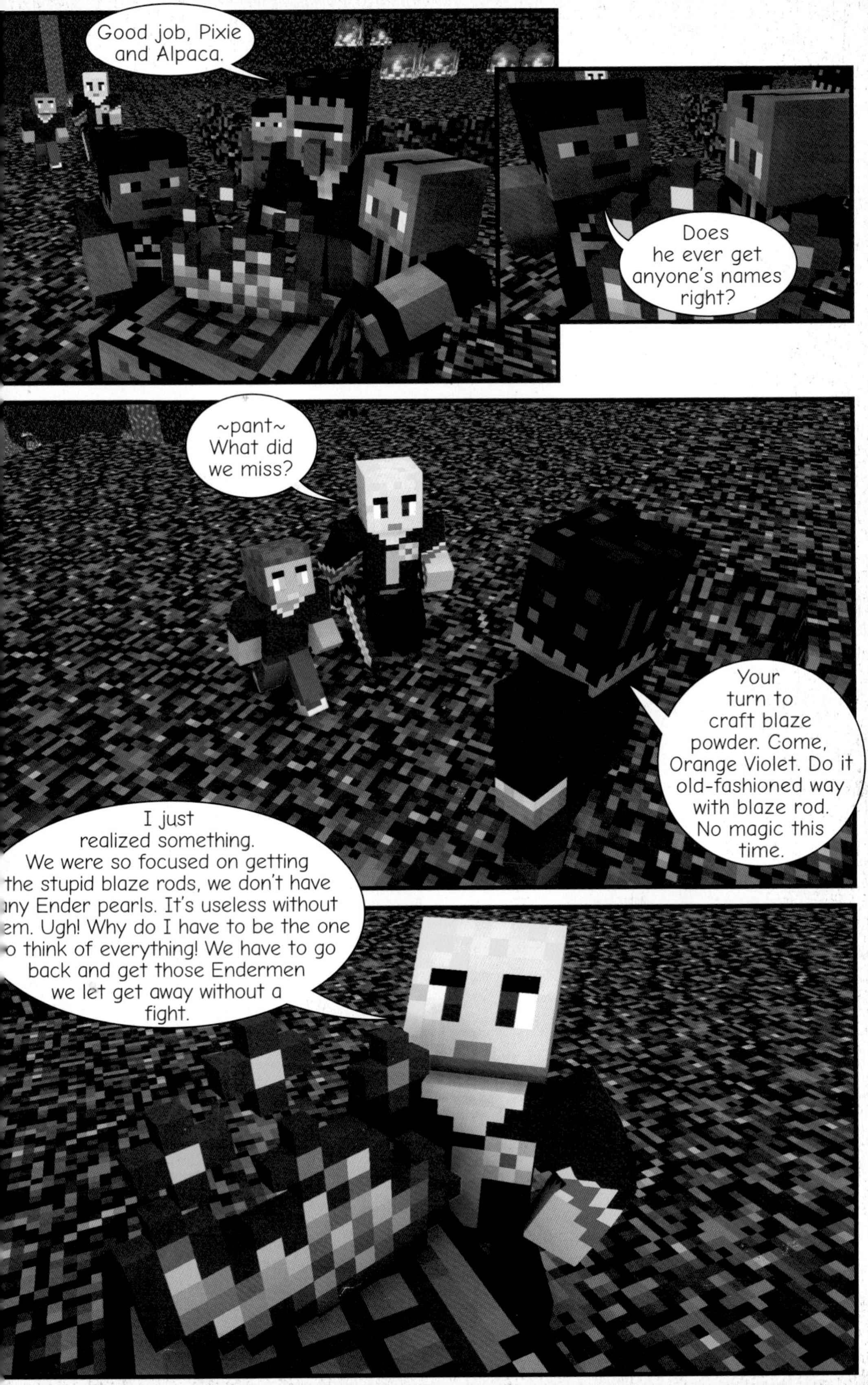

Good job, Pixie and Alpaca.
Does he ever get anyone's names right?
~pant~ What did we miss?
Your turn to craft blaze powder. Come, Orange Violet. Do it old-fashioned way with blaze rod. No magic this time.
I just realized something. We were so focused on getting the stupid blaze rods, we don't have ıny Ender pearls. It's useless without ɛm. Ugh! Why do I have to be the one o think of everything! We have to go back and get those Endermen we let get away without a fight.

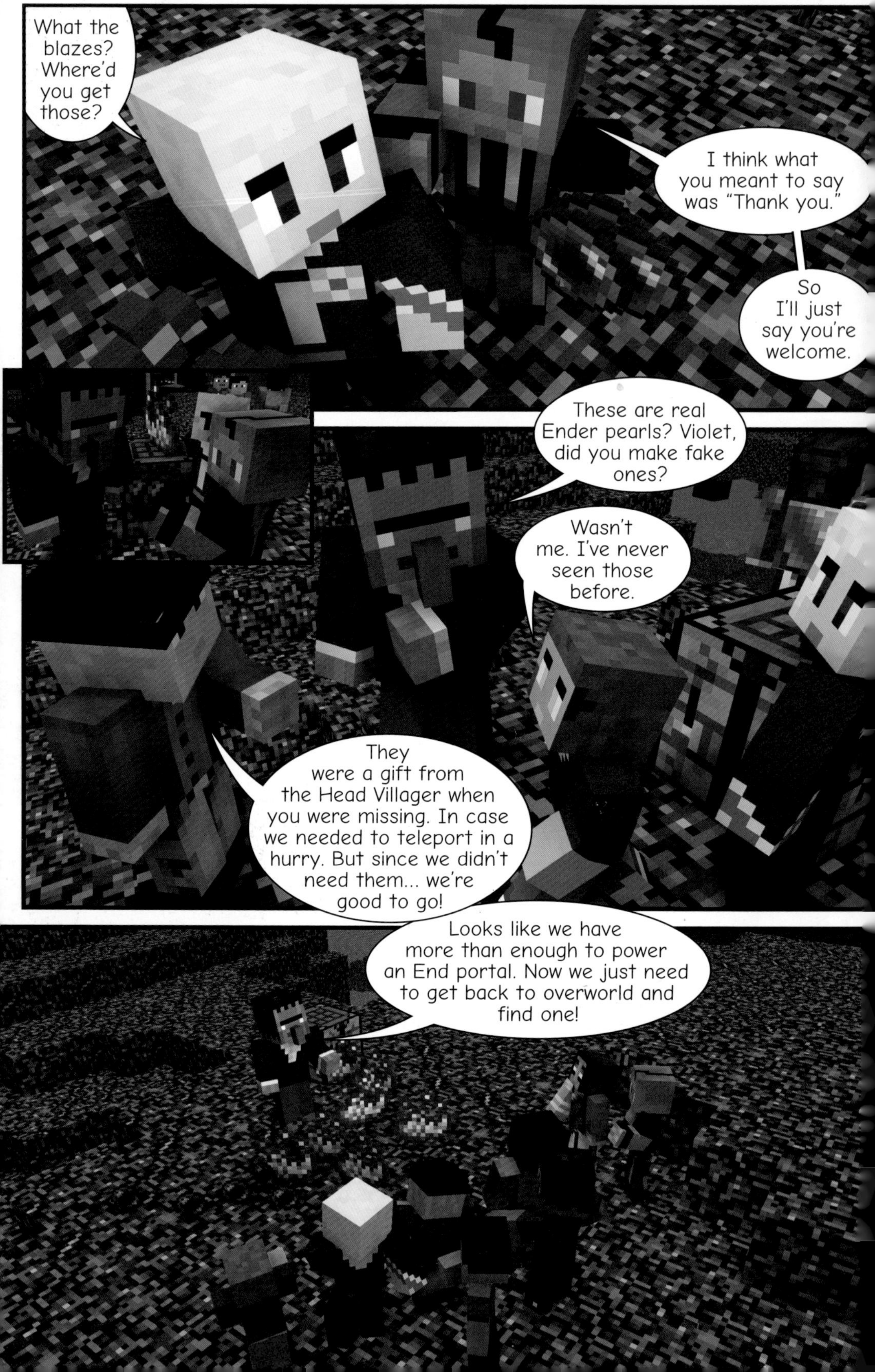
What the blazes? Where'd you get those?
I think what you meant to say was "Thank you."
So I'll just say you're welcome.
These are real Ender pearls? Violet, did you make fake ones?
Wasn't me. I've never seen those before.
They were a gift from the Head Villager when you were missing. In case we needed to teleport in a hurry. But since we didn't need them... we're good to go!
Looks like we have more than enough to power an End portal. Now we just need to get back to overworld and find one!

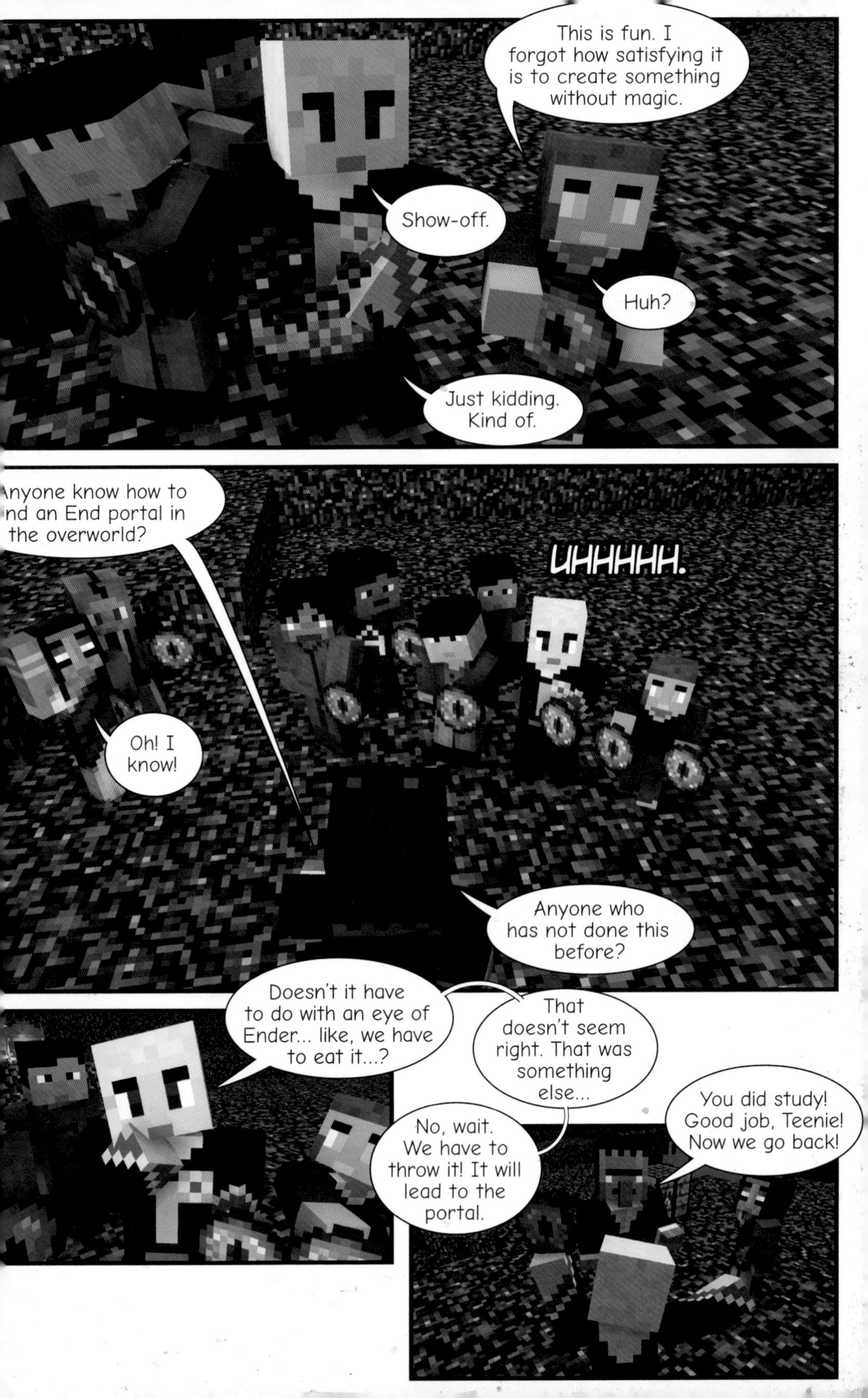
This is fun. I forgot how satisfying it is to create something without magic.
Show-off.
Huh?
Just kidding. Kind of.
nyone know how to nd an End portal in the overworld?
UHHHHH.
Oh! I know!
Anyone who has not done this before?
Doesn't it have to do with an eye of Ender... like, we have to eat it...?
That doesn't seem right. That was something else...
No, wait. We have to throw it! It will lead to the portal.
You did study! Good job, Teenie! Now we go back!

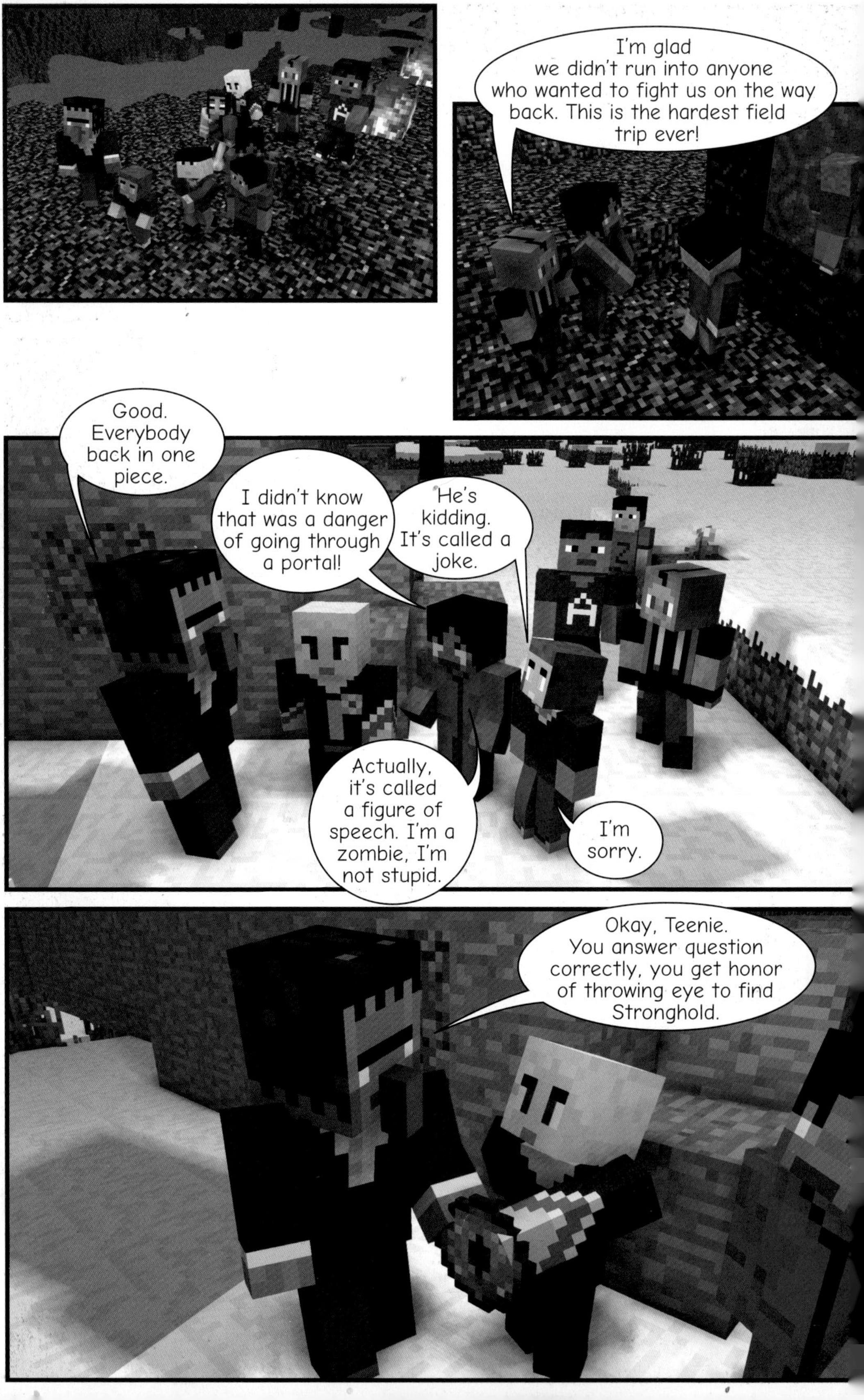
I'm glad we didn't run into anyone who wanted to fight us on the way back. This is the hardest field trip ever!
Good. Everybody back in one piece.
I didn't know that was a danger of going through a portal!
He's kidding. It's called a joke.
Actually, it's called a figure of speech. I'm a zombie, I'm not stupid.
I'm sorry.
Okay, Teenie. You answer question correctly, you get honor of throwing eye to find Stronghold.

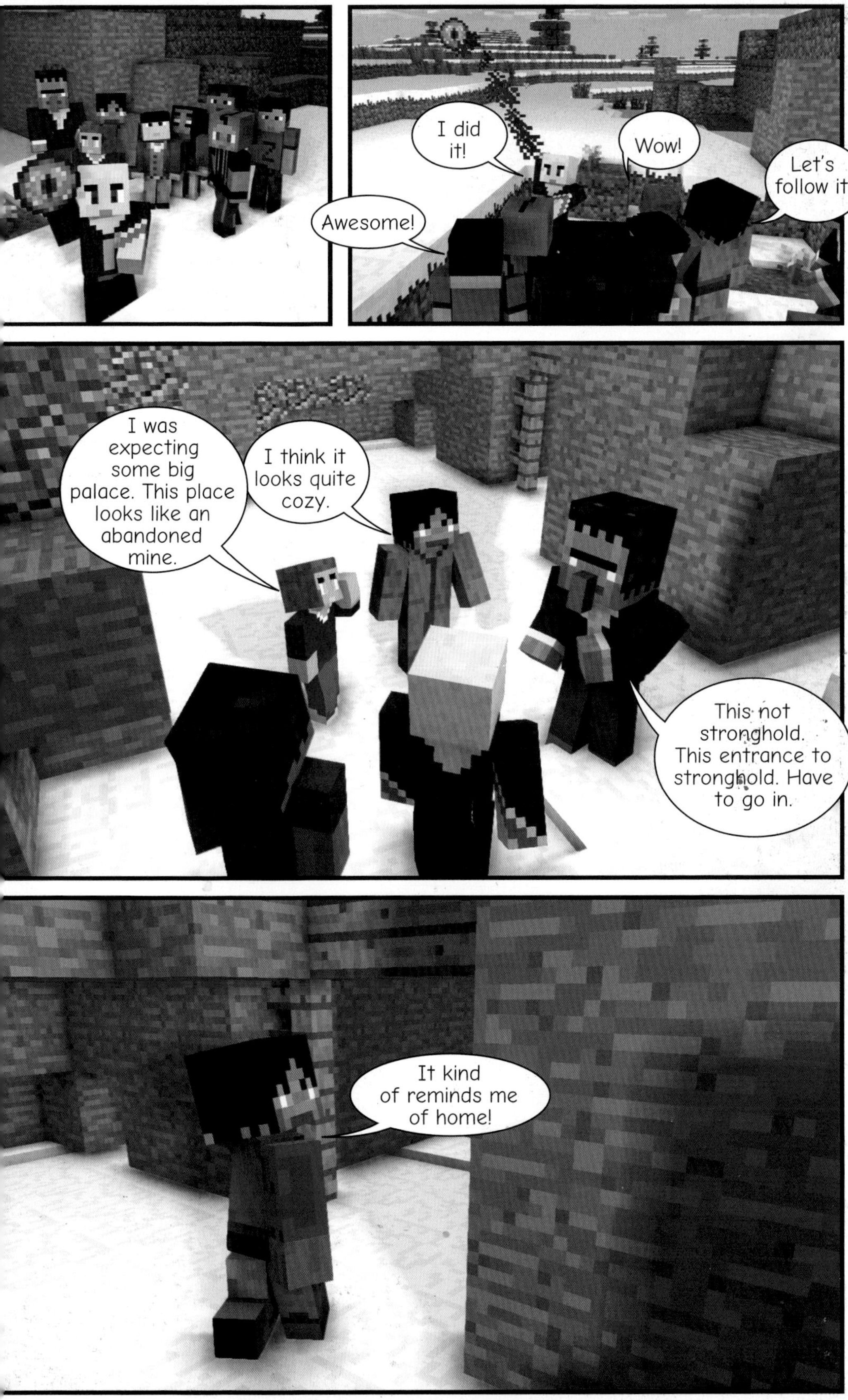
I did it!
Wow!
Let's follow it!
Awesome!
I was expecting some big palace. This place looks like an abandoned mine.
I think it looks quite cozy.
This not stronghold. This entrance to stronghold. Have to go in.
It kind of reminds me of home!

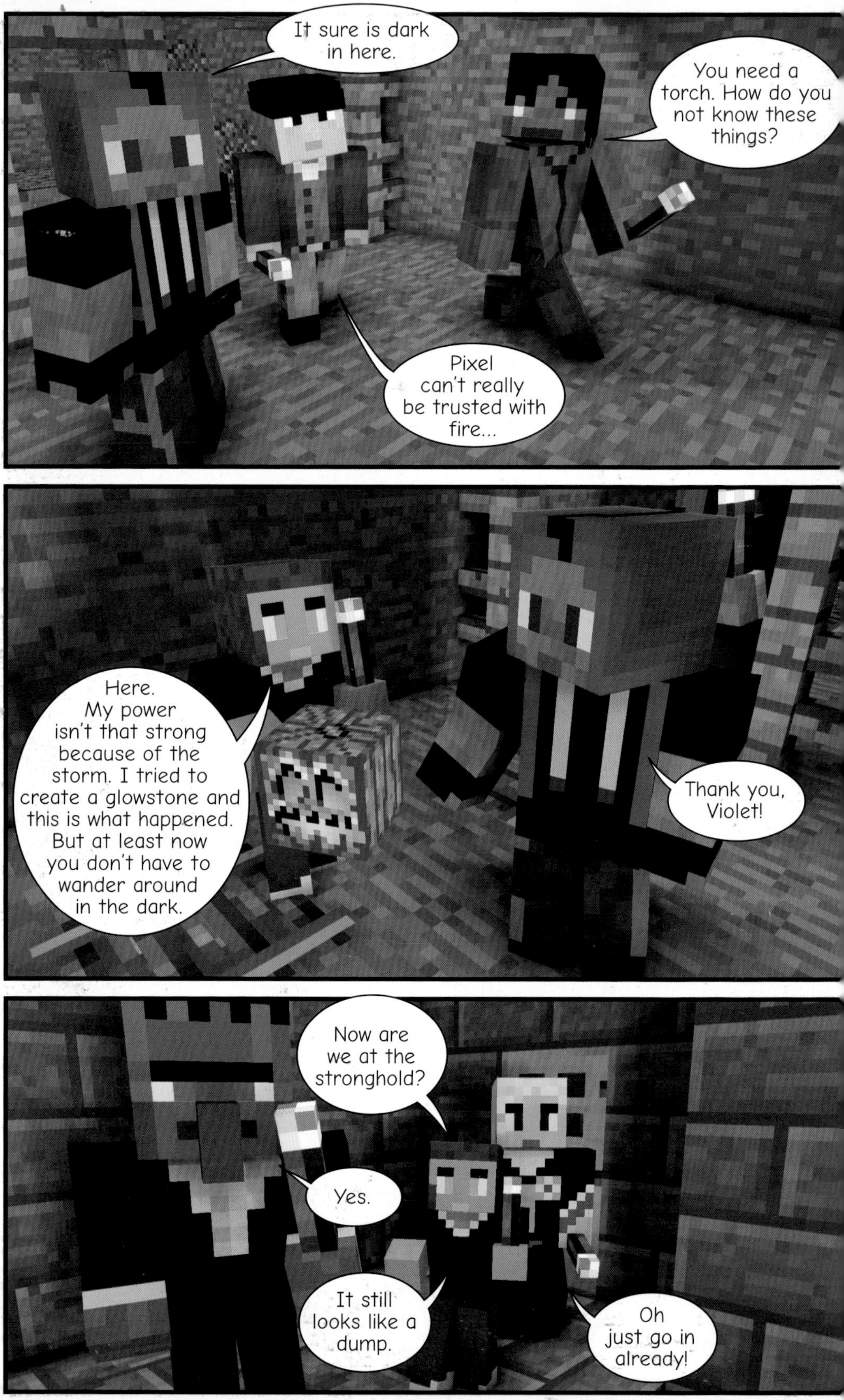
It sure is dark in here.
You need a torch. How do you not know these things?
Pixel can't really be trusted with fire...
Here. My power isn't that strong because of the storm. I tried to create a glowstone and this is what happened. But at least now you don't have to wander around in the dark.
Thank you, Violet!
Now are we at the stronghold?
Yes.
It still looks like a dump.
Oh just go in already!

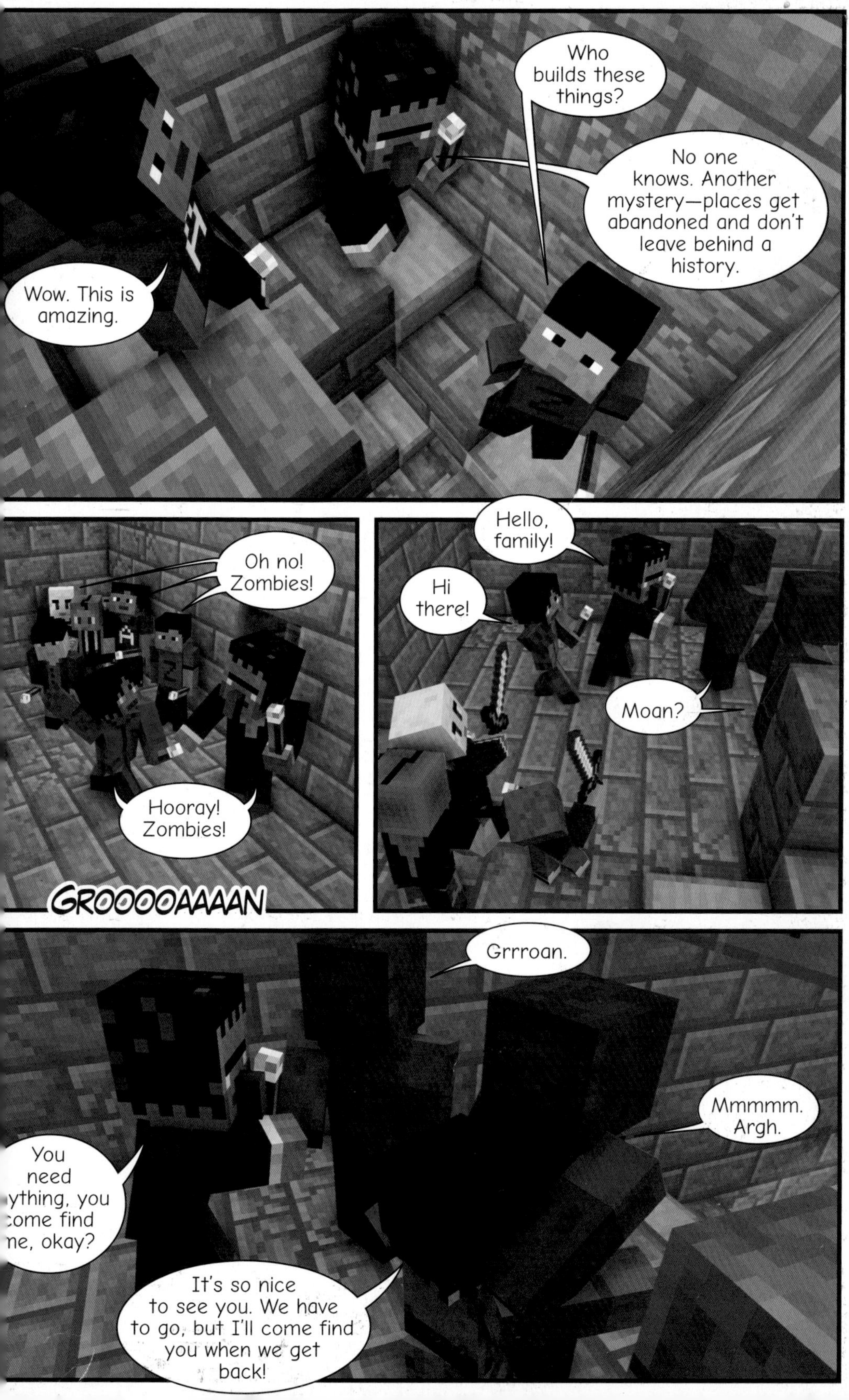
Who builds these things?
No one knows. Another mystery—places get abandoned and don't leave behind a history.
Wow. This is amazing.
Oh no! Zombies!
Hooray! Zombies!
GROOOOAAAAN
Hello, family!
Hi there!
Moan?
Grrroan.
Mmmmm. Argh.
You need ything, you ome find ne, okay?
It's so nice to see you. We have to go, but I'll come find you when we get back!

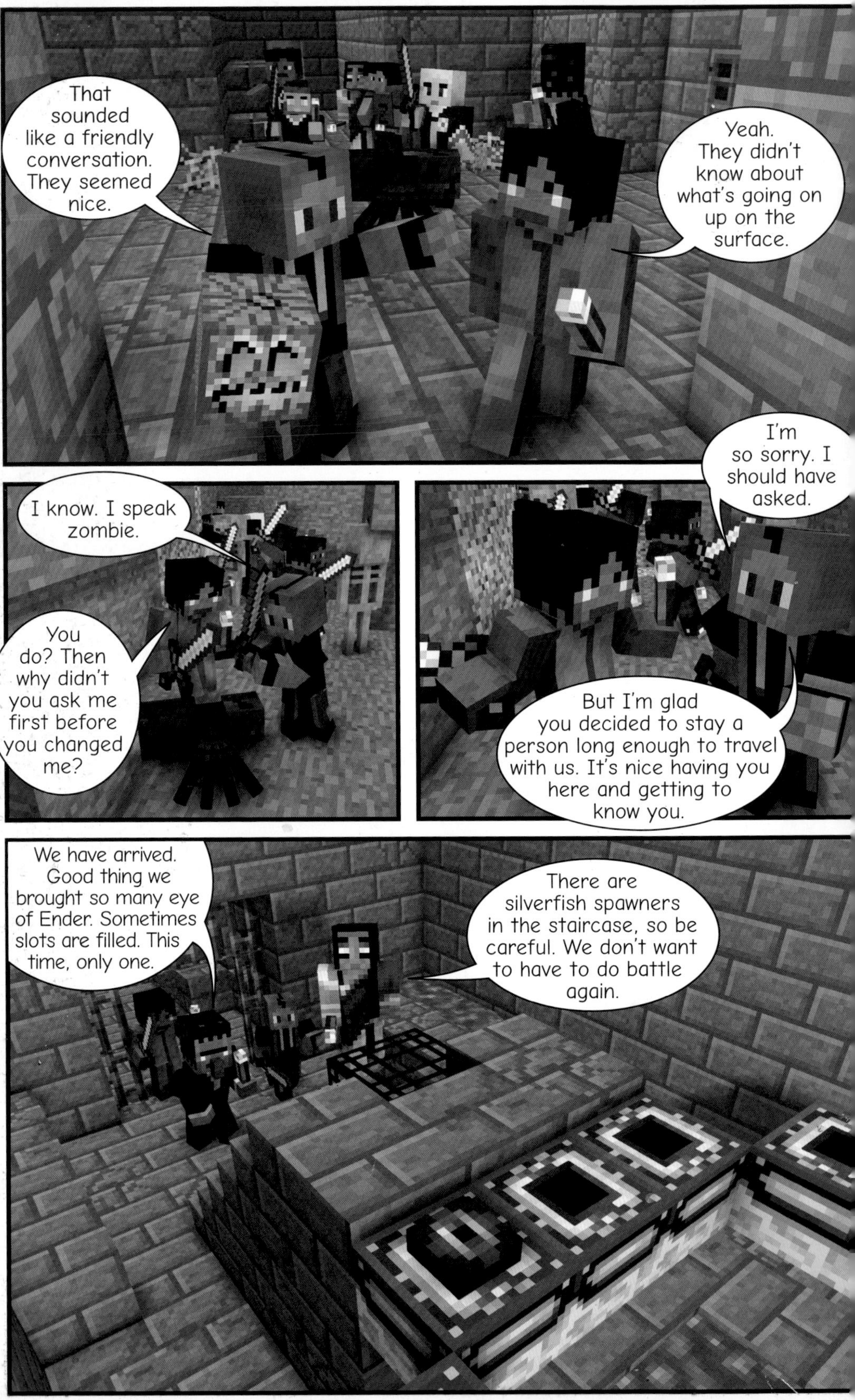
That sounded like a friendly conversation. They seemed nice.
Yeah. They didn't know about what's going on up on the surface.
I know. I speak zombie.
You do? Then why didn't you ask me first before you changed me?
I'm so sorry. I should have asked.
But I'm glad you decided to stay a person long enough to travel with us. It's nice having you here and getting to know you.
We have arrived. Good thing we brought so many eye of Ender. Sometimes slots are filled. This time, only one.
There are silverfish spawners in the staircase, so be careful. We don't want to have to do battle again.

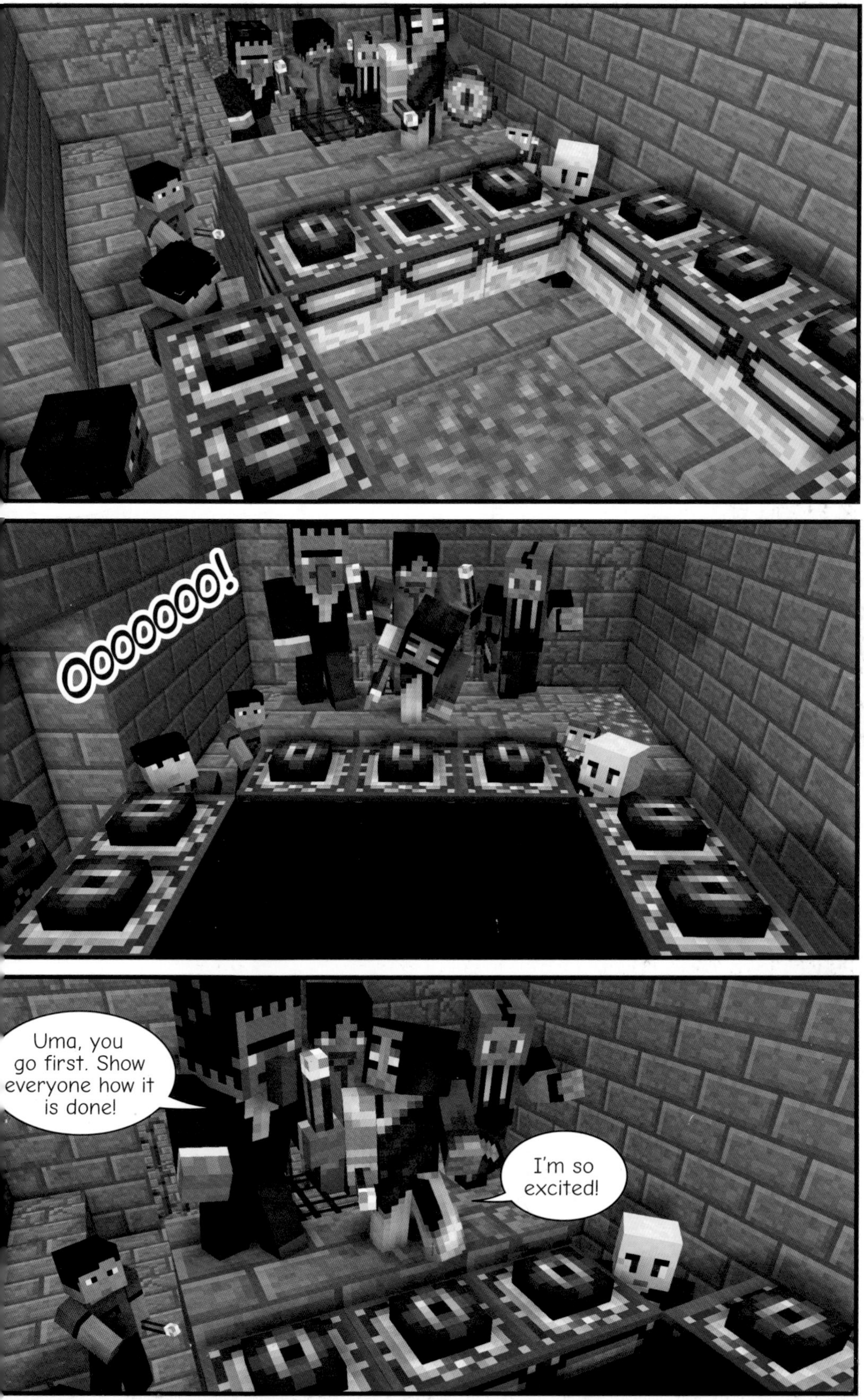
Oooooooo!
Uma, you go first. Show everyone how it is done!
I'm so excited!

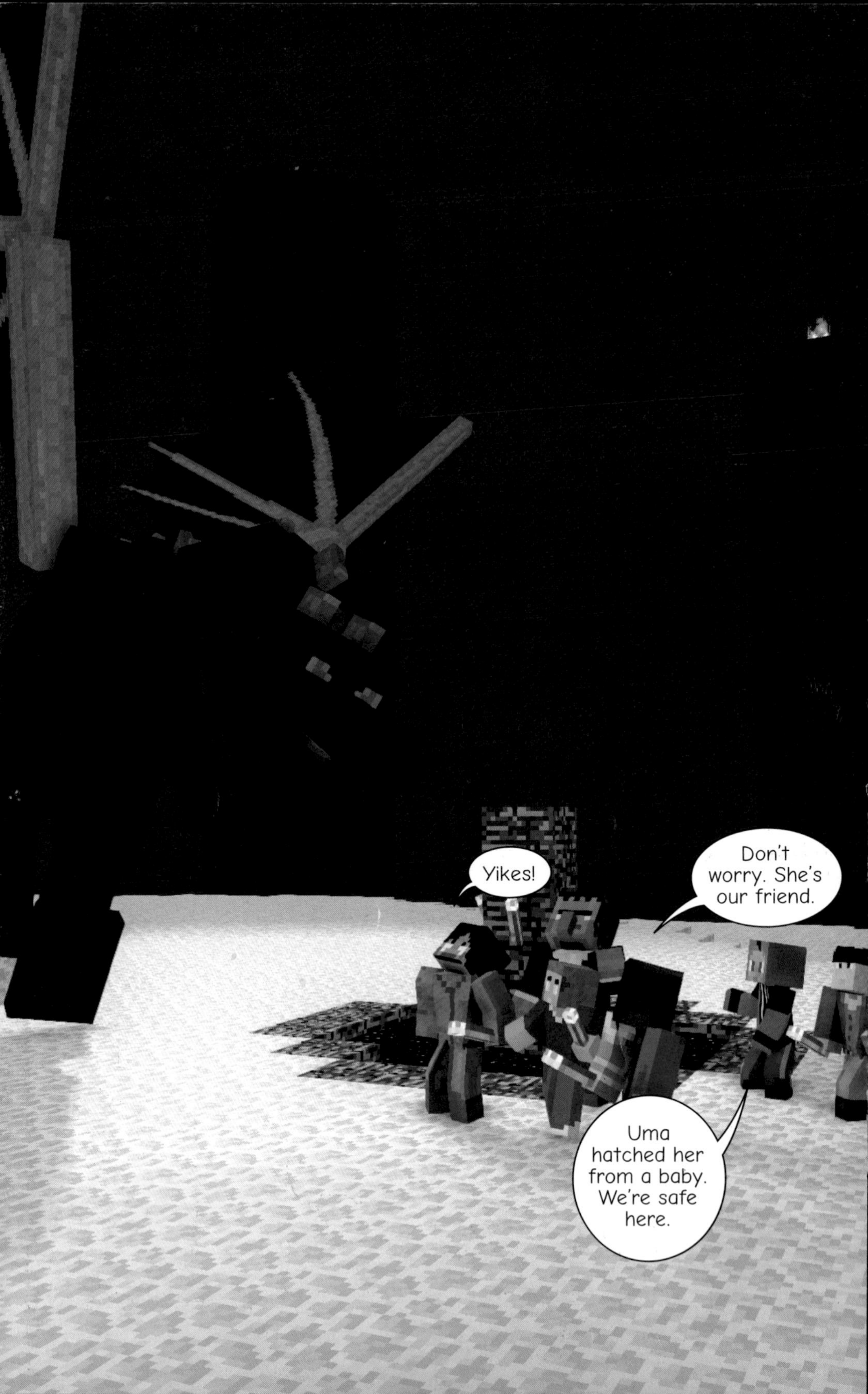
Yikes!
Don't worry. She's our friend.
Uma hatched her from a baby. We're safe here.

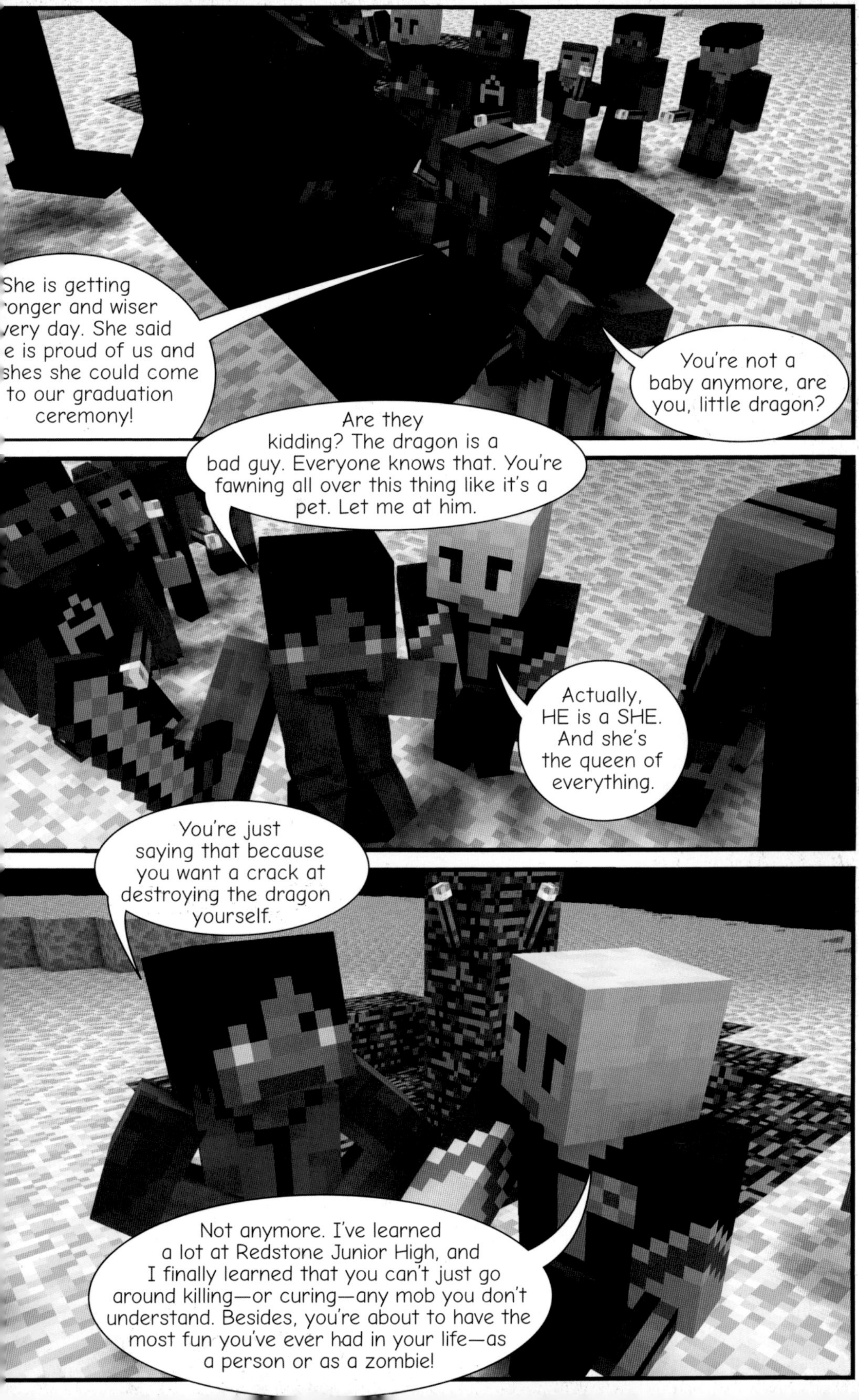
She is getting ronger and wiser very day. She said e is proud of us and shes she could come to our graduation ceremony!
You're not a baby anymore, are you, little dragon?
Are they kidding? The dragon is a bad guy. Everyone knows that. You're fawning all over this thing like it's a pet. Let me at him.
Actually, HE is a SHE. And she's the queen of everything.
You're just saying that because you want a crack at destroying the dragon yourself.
Not anymore. I've learned a lot at Redstone Junior High, and I finally learned that you can't just go around killing—or curing—any mob you don't understand. Besides, you're about to have the most fun you've ever had in your life—as a person or as a zombie!

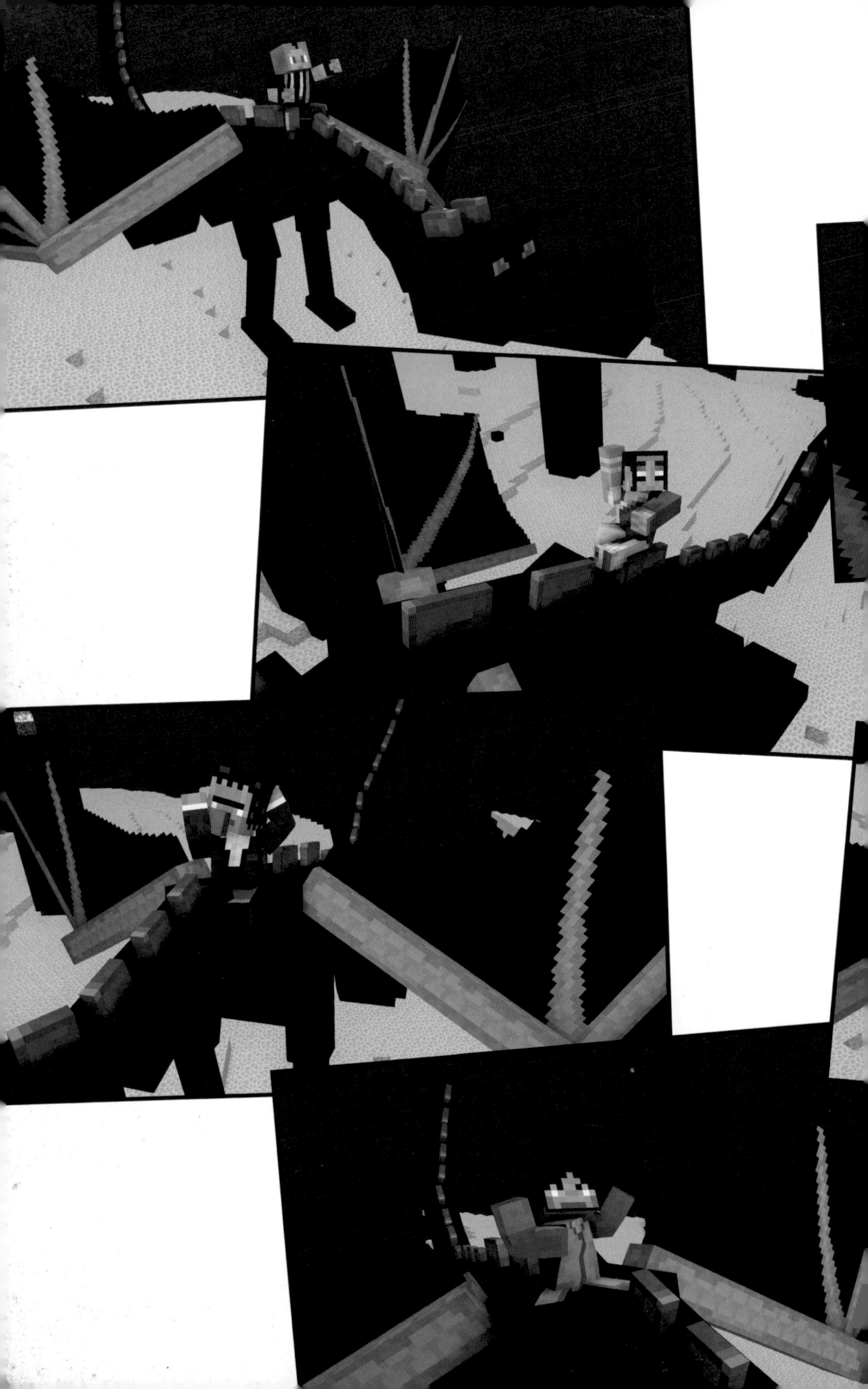

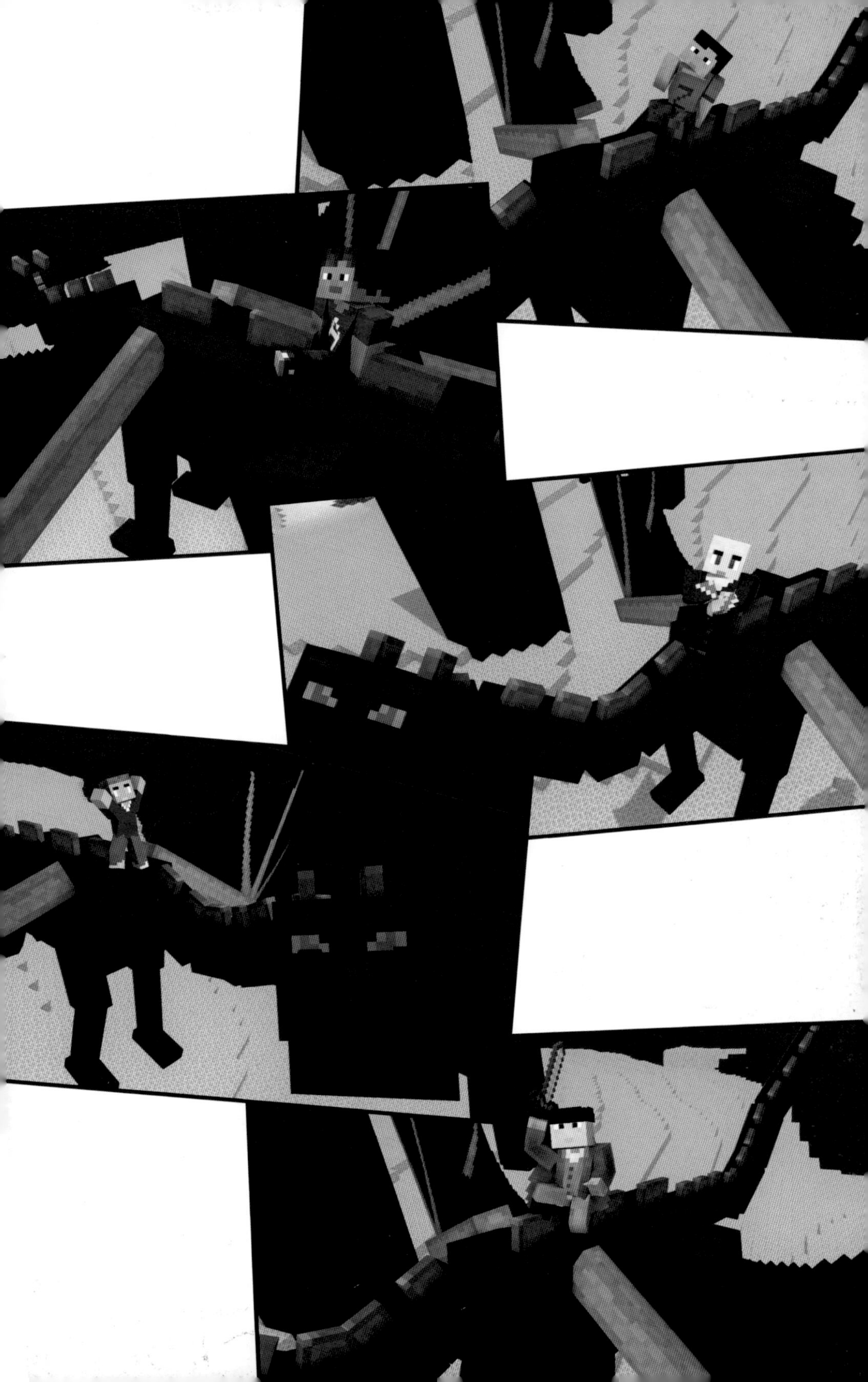

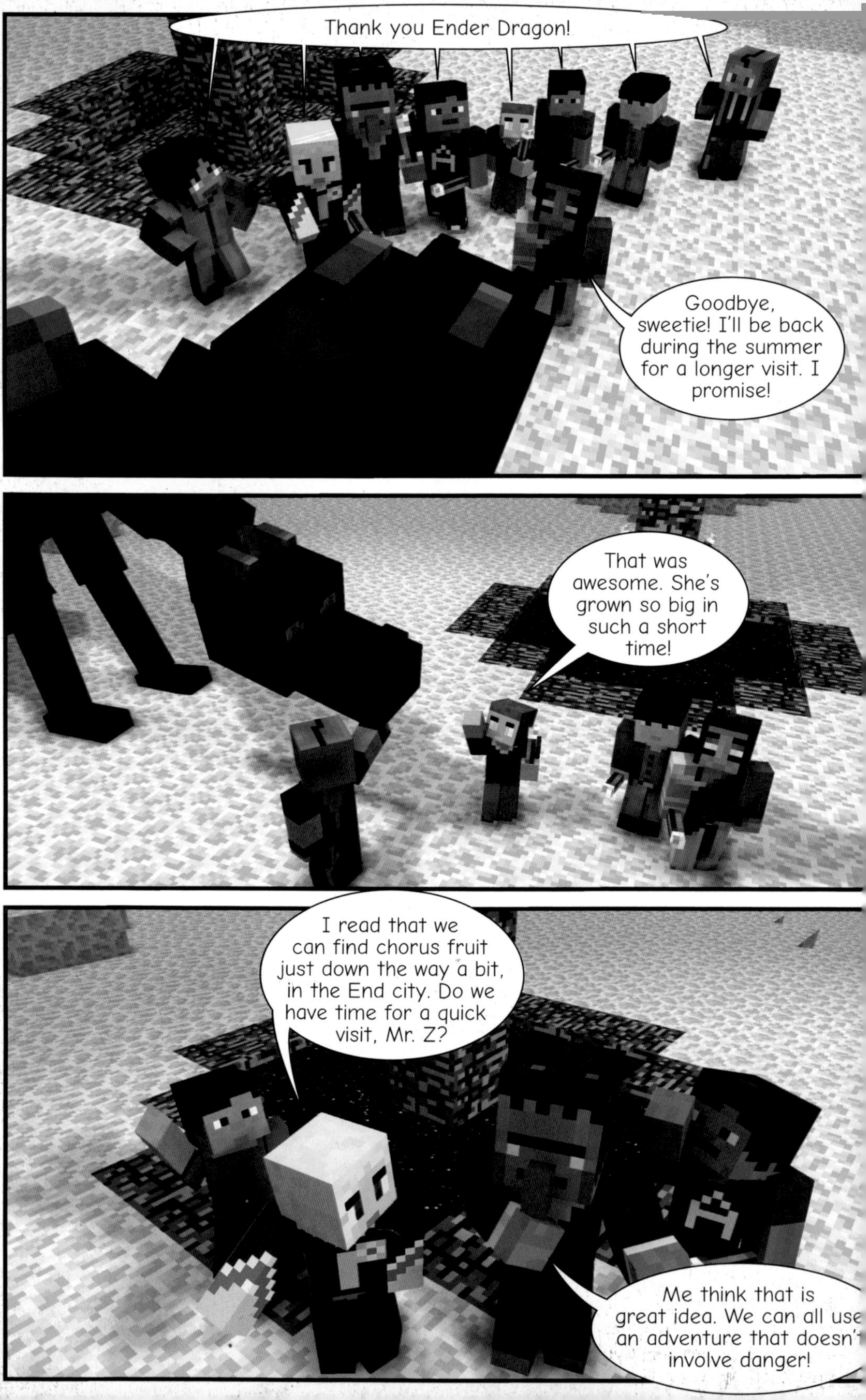
Thank you Ender Dragon!
Goodbye, sweetie! I'll be back during the summer for a longer visit. I promise!
That was awesome. She's grown so big in such a short time!
I read that we can find chorus fruit just down the way a bit, in the End city. Do we have time for a quick visit, Mr. Z?
Me think that is great idea. We can all use an adventure that doesn't involve danger!

CHAPTER 10

LIGHTNING STRIKES

What's that? It wasn't here before.

That would be the gateway portal. That's where we have to go to get to the End cities, right?

Yes. All we need is elytra or more Ender pearls.

I can make elytra for everyone!

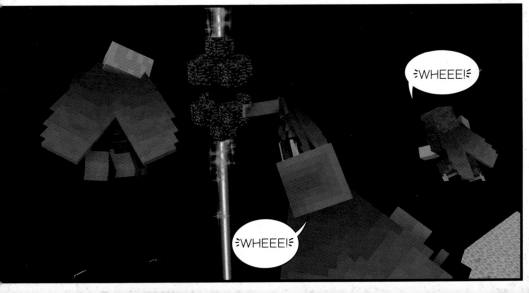

≥WHEEE!≤

≥WHEEE!≤

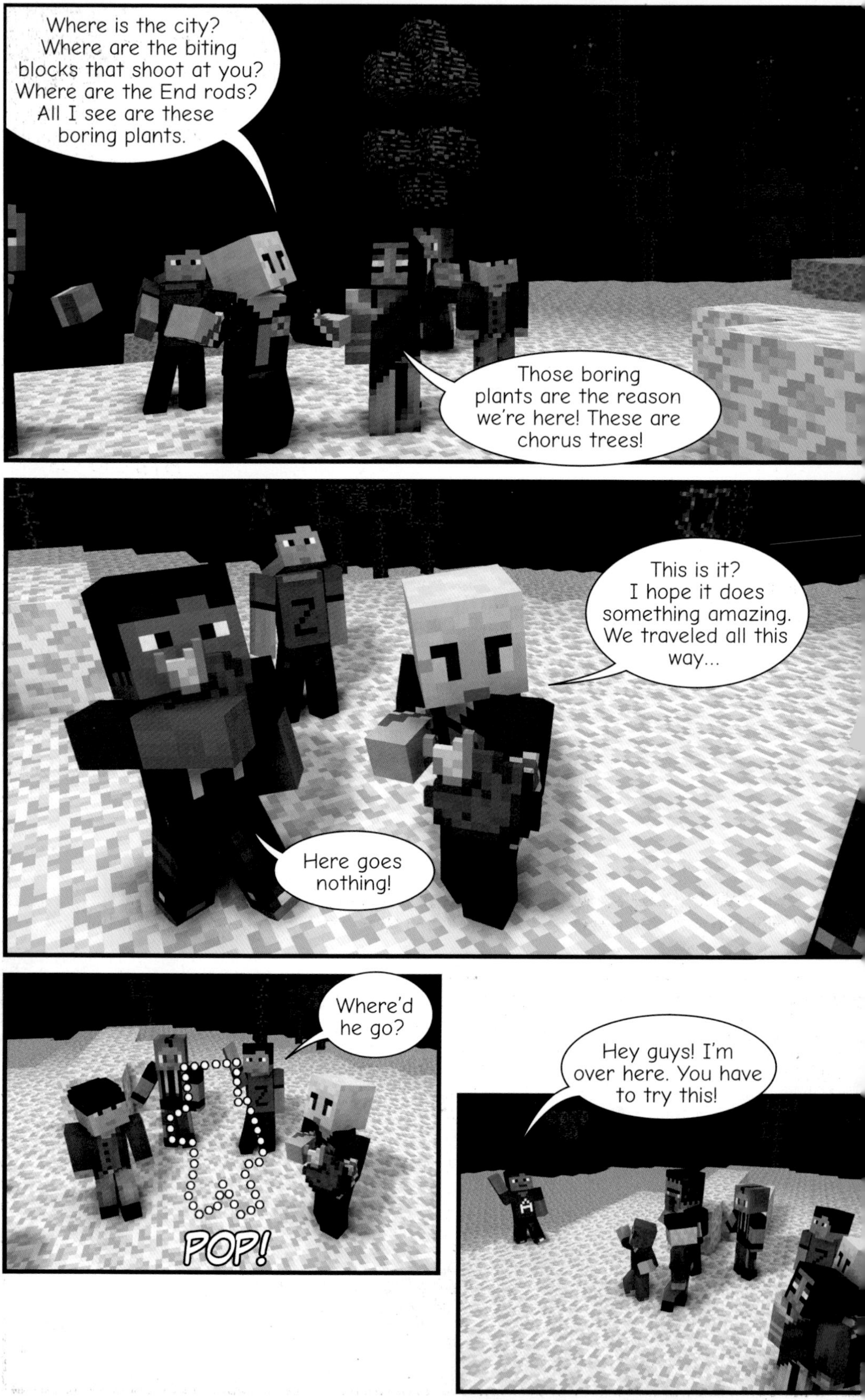
Where is the city? Where are the biting blocks that shoot at you? Where are the End rods? All I see are these boring plants.
Those boring plants are the reason we're here! These are chorus trees!
This is it? I hope it does something amazing. We traveled all this way...
Here goes nothing!
Where'd he go?
POP!
Hey guys! I'm over here. You have to try this!

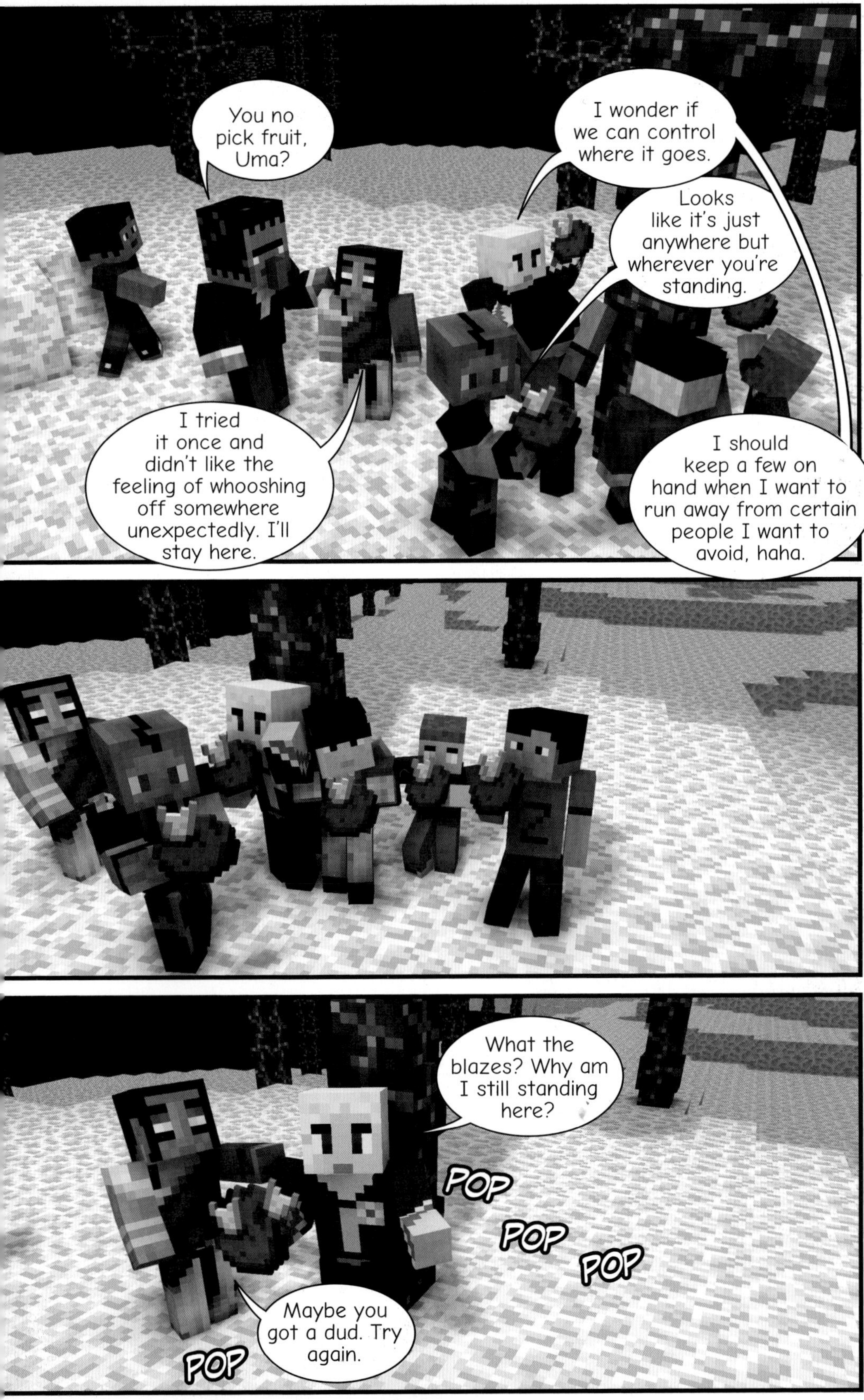
You no pick fruit, Uma?
I wonder if we can control where it goes.
Looks like it's just anywhere but wherever you're standing.
I tried it once and didn't like the feeling of whooshing off somewhere unexpectedly. I'll stay here.
I should keep a few on hand when I want to run away from certain people I want to avoid, haha.
What the blazes? Why am I still standing here?
POP
POP
POP
Maybe you got a dud. Try again.
POP

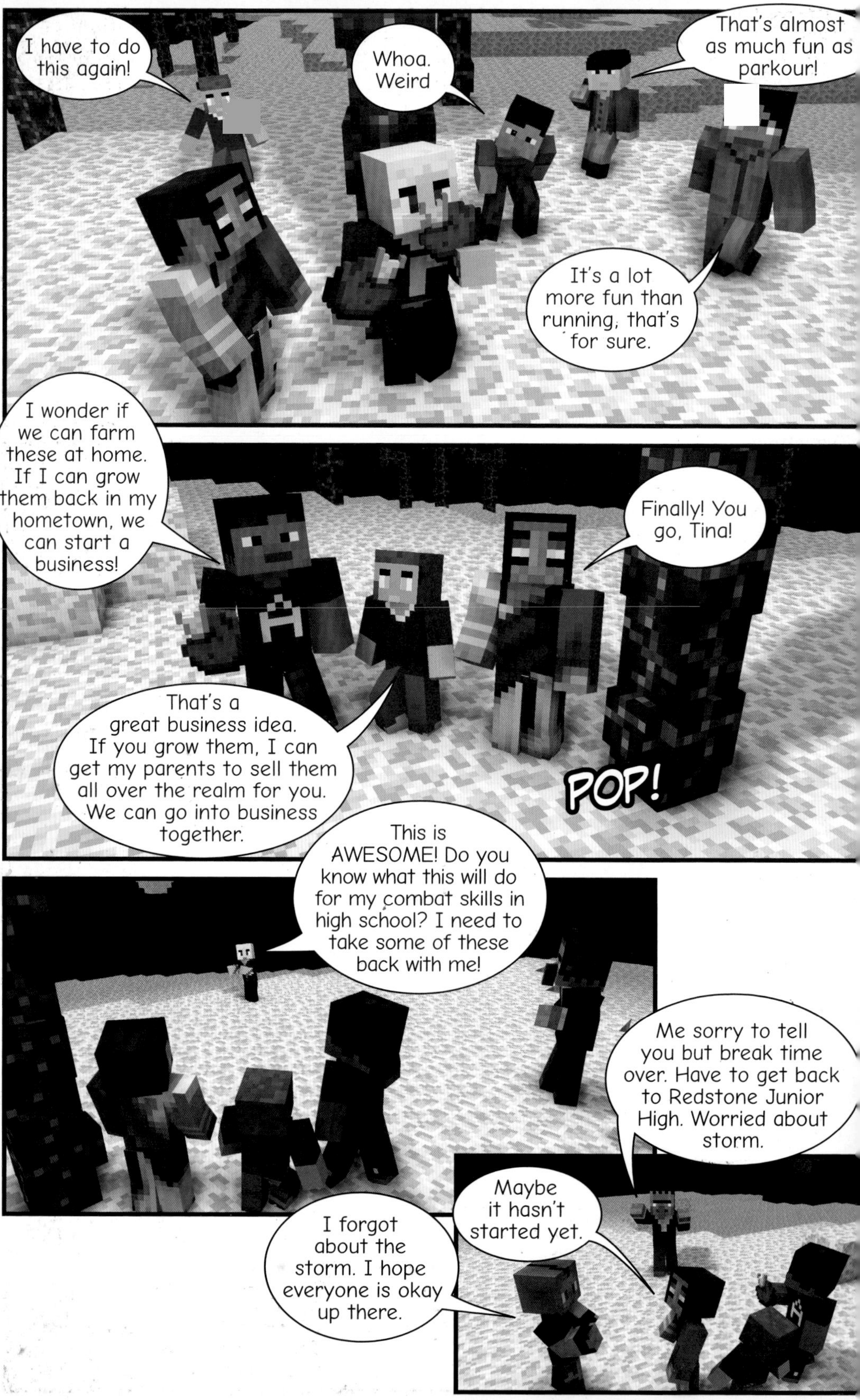
I have to do this again!
Whoa. Weird
That's almost as much fun as parkour!
It's a lot more fun than running, that's for sure.
I wonder if we can farm these at home. If I can grow them back in my hometown, we can start a business!
Finally! You go, Tina!
That's a great business idea. If you grow them, I can get my parents to sell them all over the realm for you. We can go into business together.
POP!
This is AWESOME! Do you know what this will do for my combat skills in high school? I need to take some of these back with me!
Me sorry to tell you but break time over. Have to get back to Redstone Junior High. Worried about storm.
Maybe it hasn't started yet.
I forgot about the storm. I hope everyone is okay up there.

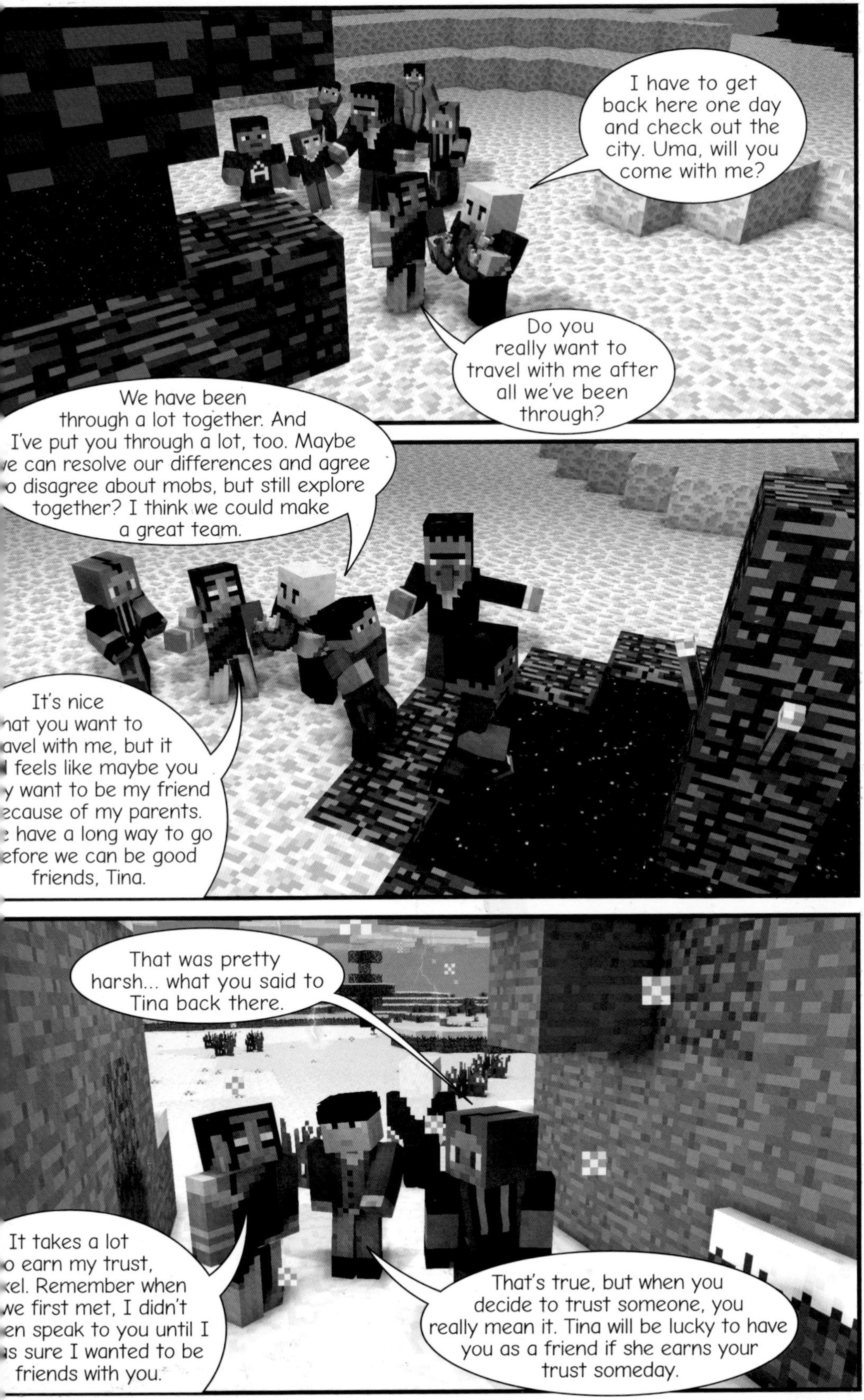
I have to get back here one day and check out the city. Uma, will you come with me?
Do you really want to travel with me after all we've been through?
We have been through a lot together. And I've put you through a lot, too. Maybe /e can resolve our differences and agree o disagree about mobs, but still explore together? I think we could make a great team.
It's nice nat you want to avel with me, but it feels like maybe you y want to be my friend ecause of my parents. have a long way to go efore we can be good friends, Tina.
That was pretty harsh... what you said to Tina back there.
It takes a lot o earn my trust, el. Remember when we first met, I didn't en speak to you until I s sure I wanted to be friends with you.
That's true, but when you decide to trust someone, you really mean it. Tina will be lucky to have you as a friend if she earns your trust someday.

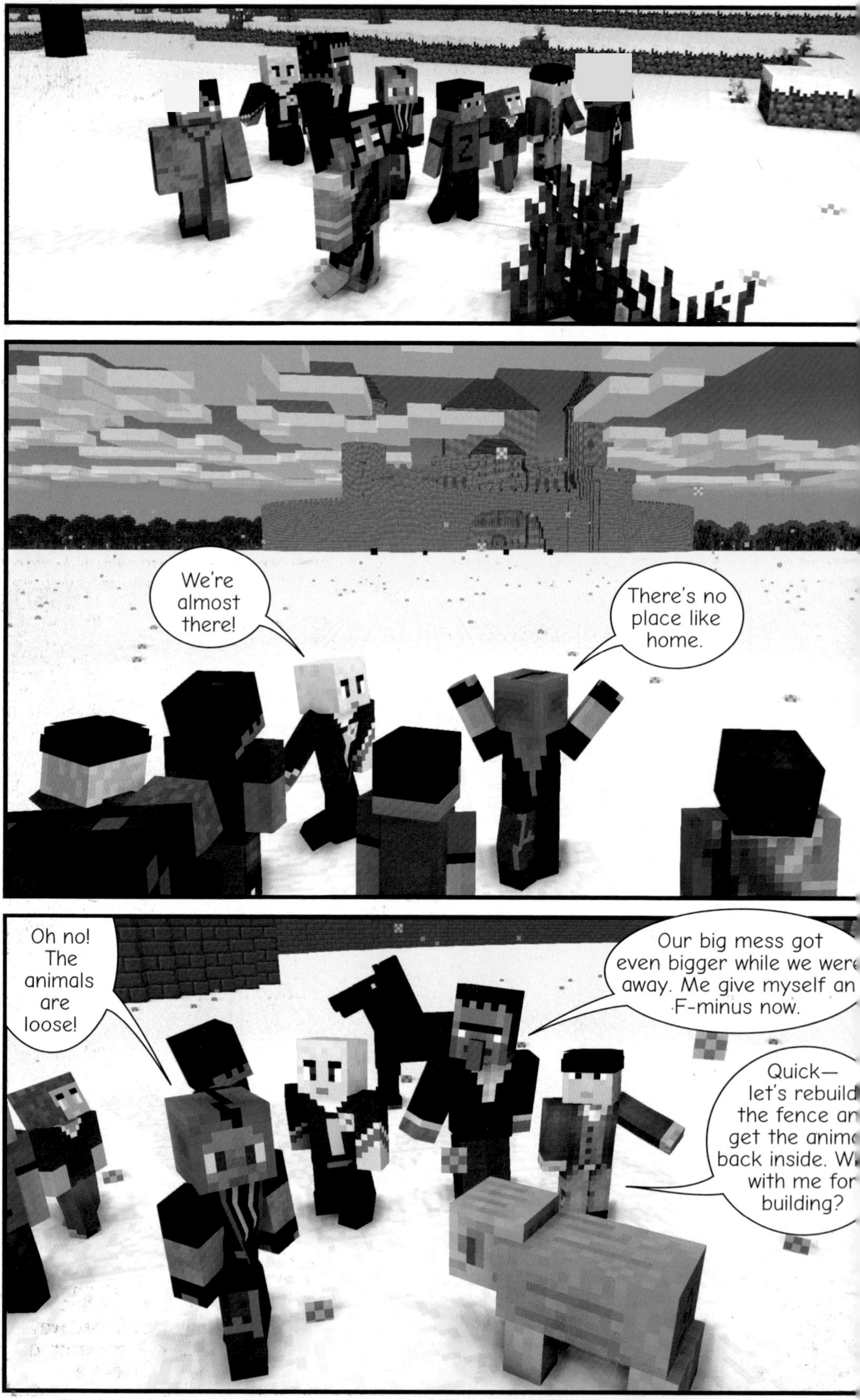
We're almost there!
There's no place like home.
Oh no! The animals are loose!
Our big mess got even bigger while we wer away. Me give myself an F-minus now.
Quick— let's rebuild the fence an get the anim back inside. W with me for building?

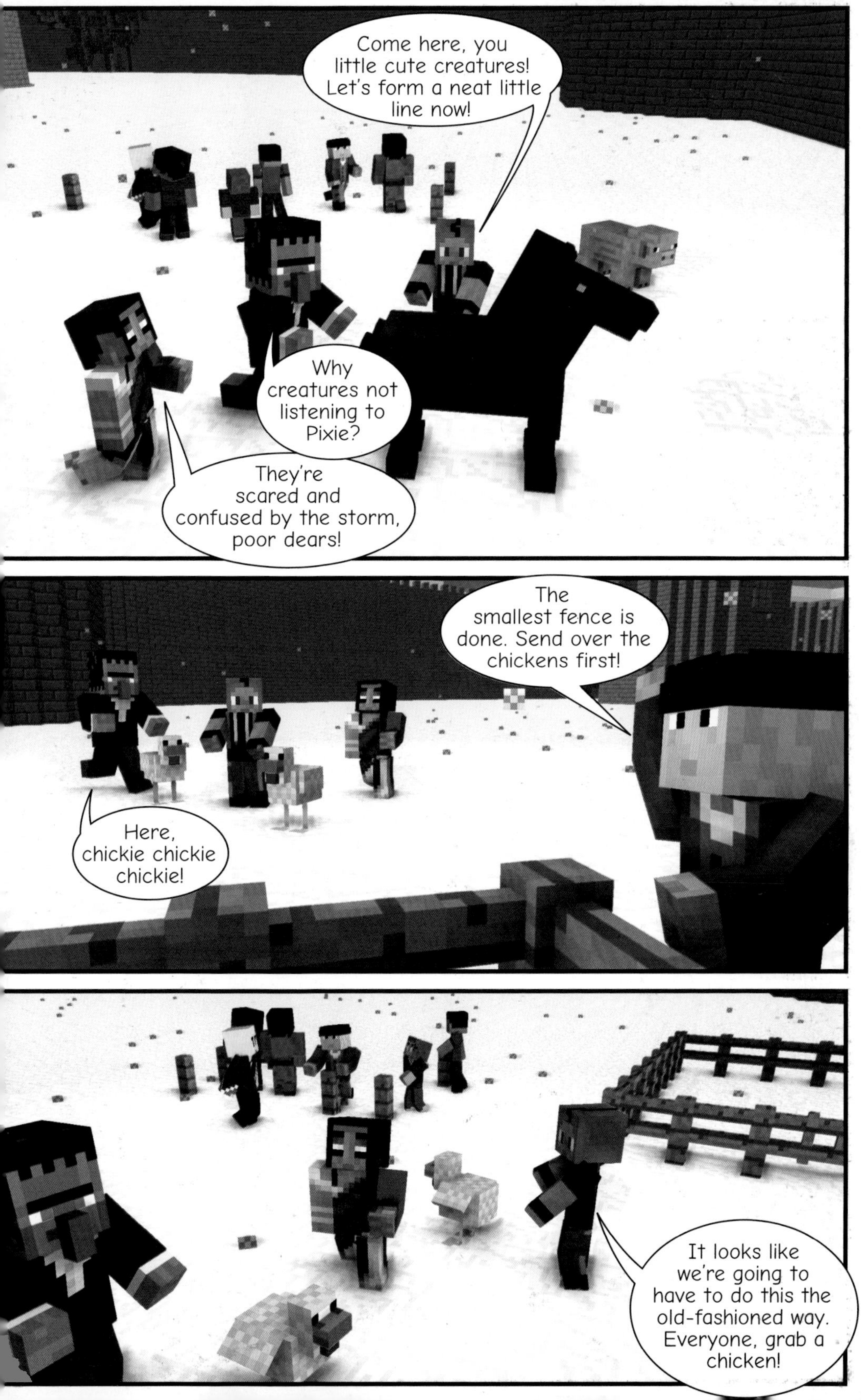
Come here, you little cute creatures! Let's form a neat little line now!
Why creatures not listening to Pixie?
They're scared and confused by the storm, poor dears!
The smallest fence is done. Send over the chickens first!
Here, chickie chickie chickie!
It looks like we're going to have to do this the old-fashioned way. Everyone, grab a chicken!

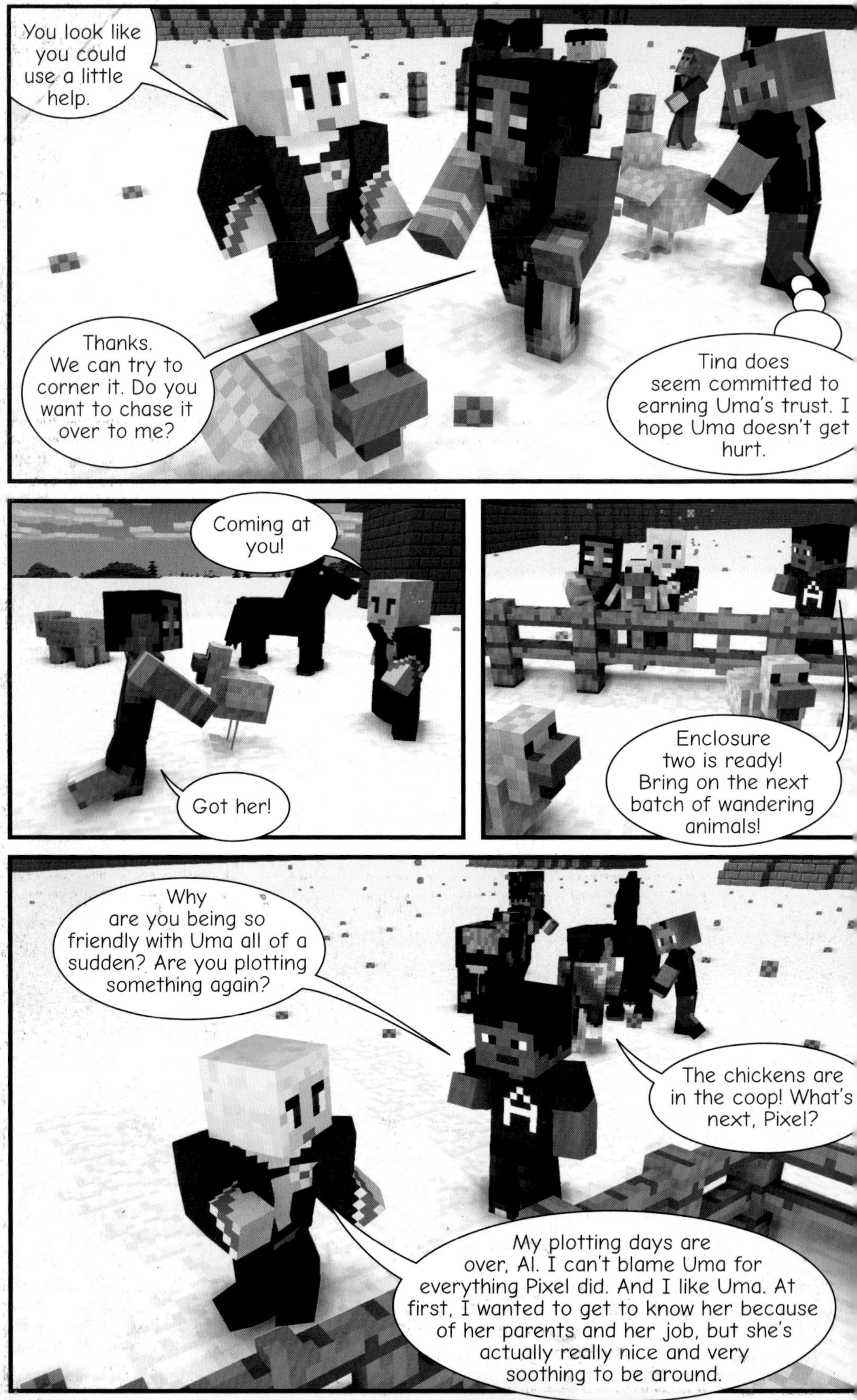
You look like you could use a little help.
Thanks. We can try to corner it. Do you want to chase it over to me?
Tina does seem committed to earning Uma's trust. I hope Uma doesn't get hurt.
Coming at you!
Got her!
Enclosure two is ready! Bring on the next batch of wandering animals!
Why are you being so friendly with Uma all of a sudden? Are you plotting something again?
The chickens are in the coop! What's next, Pixel?
My plotting days are over, Al. I can't blame Uma for everything Pixel did. And I like Uma. At first, I wanted to get to know her because of her parents and her job, but she's actually really nice and very soothing to be around.

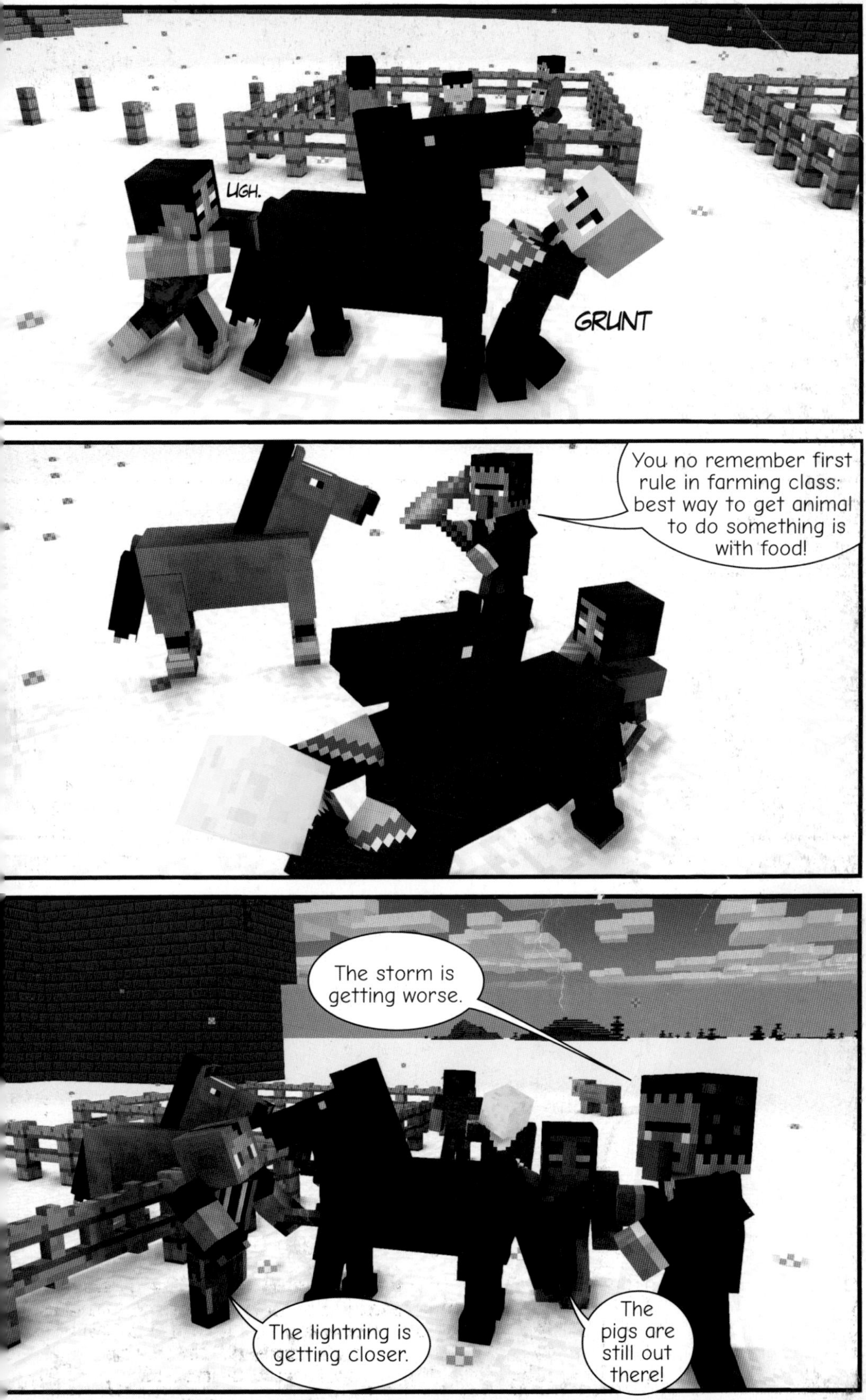
UGH.
GRUNT
You no remember first rule in farming class: best way to get animal to do something is with food!
The storm is getting worse.
The lightning is getting closer.
The pigs are still out there!

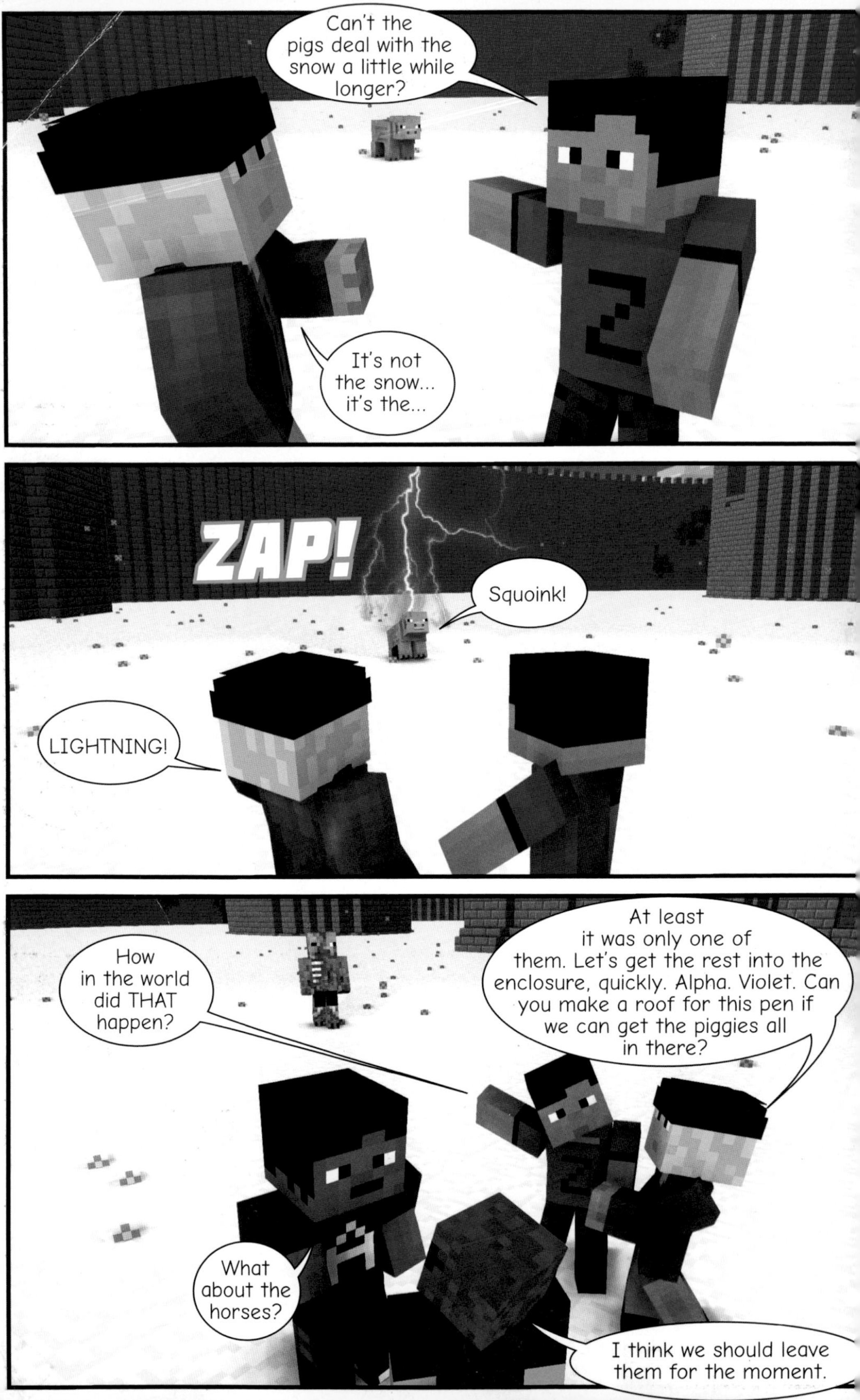
Can't the pigs deal with the snow a little while longer?
It's not the snow... it's the...
ZAP!
Squoink!
LIGHTNING!
How in the world did THAT happen?
At least it was only one of them. Let's get the rest into the enclosure, quickly. Alpha. Violet. Can you make a roof for this pen if we can get the piggies all in there?
What about the horses?
I think we should leave them for the moment.

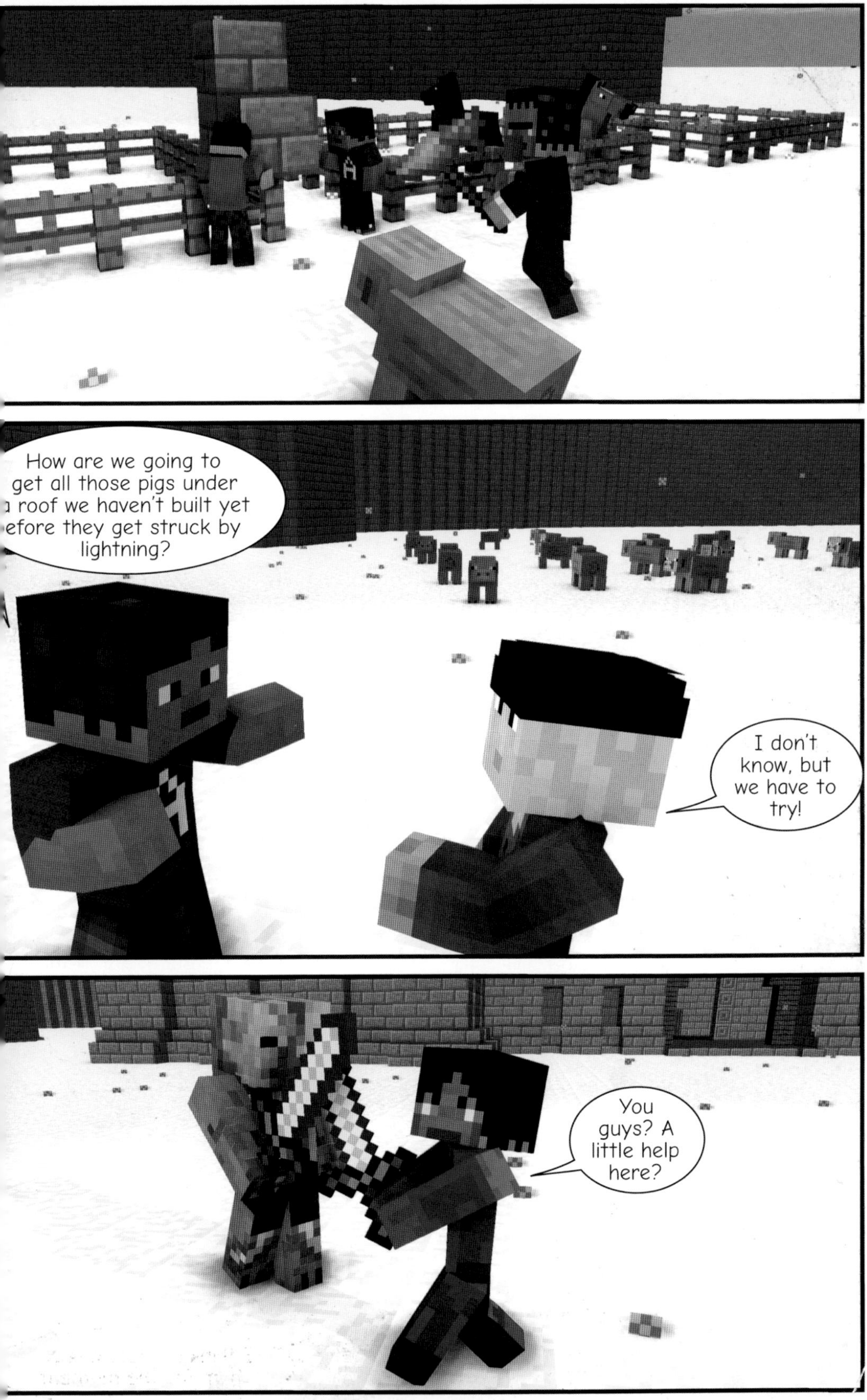
How are we going to get all those pigs under roof we haven't built yet efore they get struck by lightning?
I don't know, but we have to try!
You guys? A little help here?

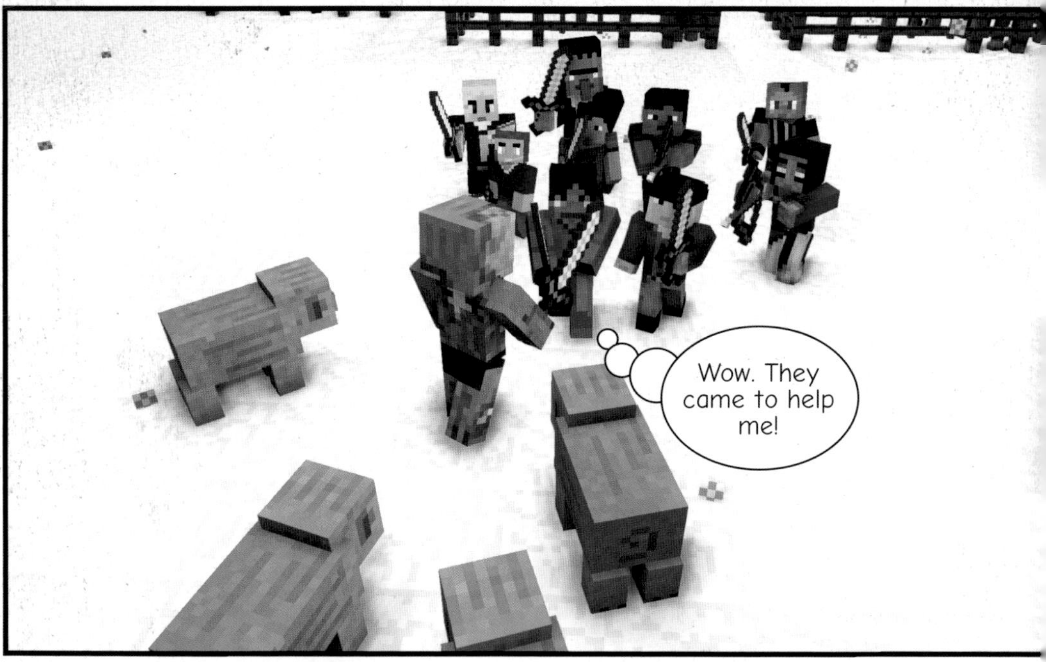
Wow. They came to help me!

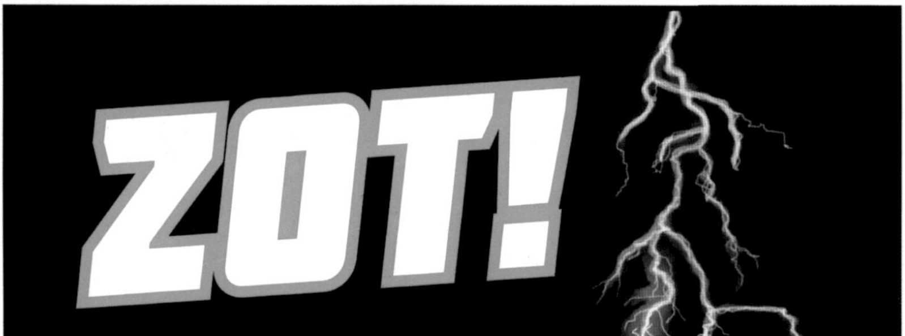
ZOT!

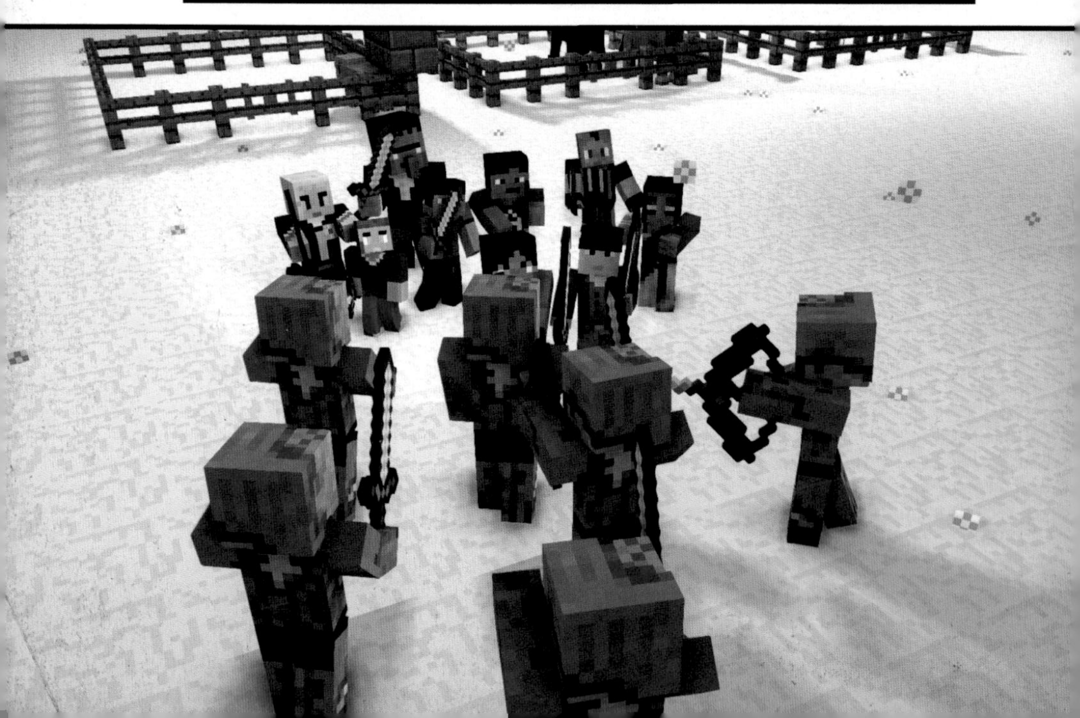

CHAPTER 11

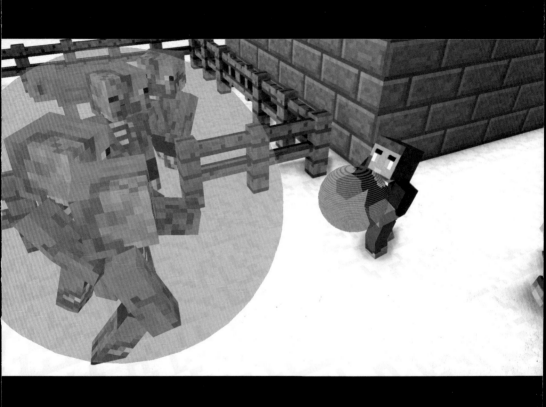

WHEN
PIGMEN FLY

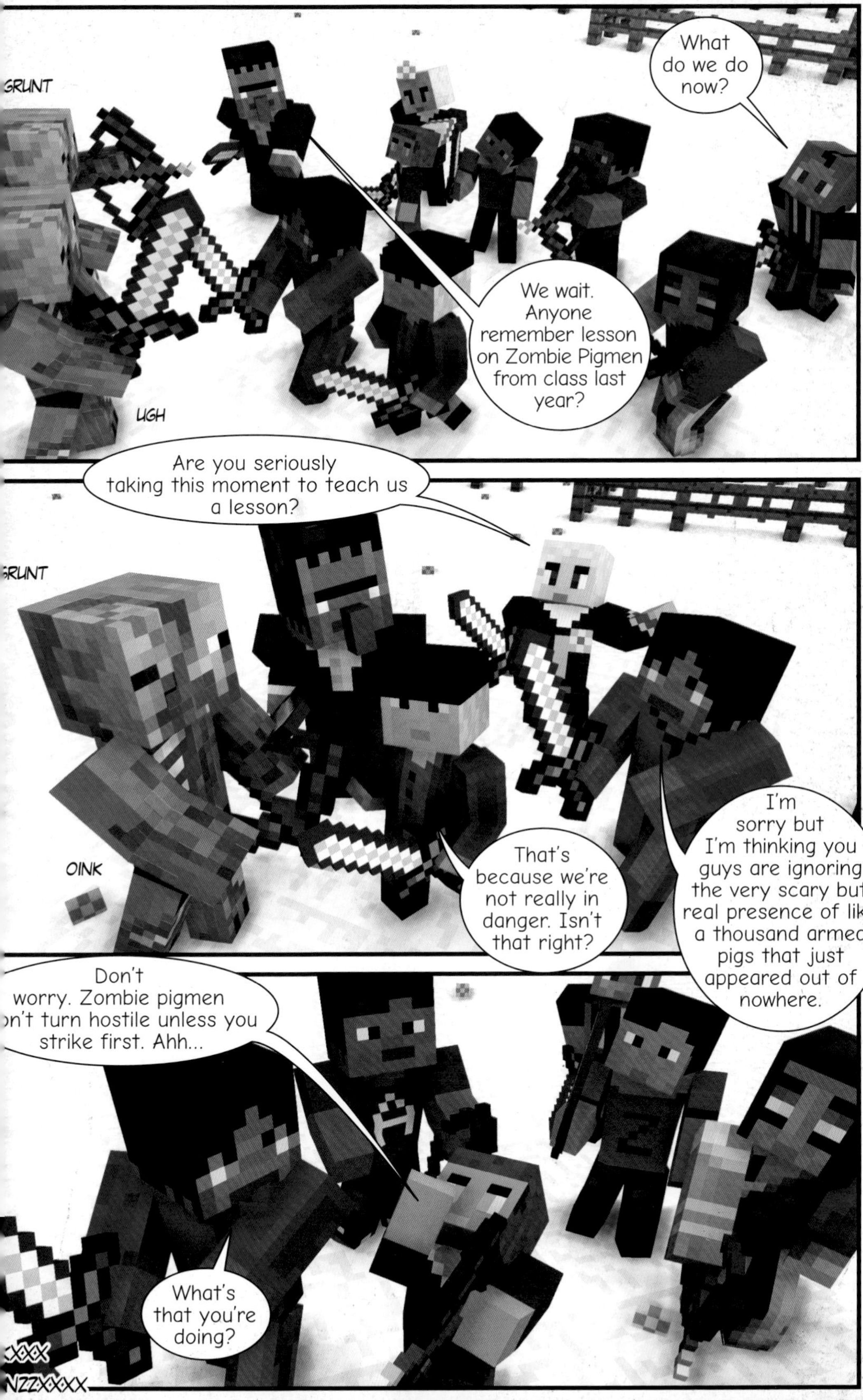
GRUNT
What do we do now?
We wait. Anyone remember lesson on Zombie Pigmen from class last year?
UGH
Are you seriously taking this moment to teach us a lesson?
RUNT
OINK
That's because we're not really in danger. Isn't that right?
I'm sorry but I'm thinking you guys are ignoring the very scary but real presence of like a thousand armed pigs that just appeared out of nowhere.
Don't worry. Zombie pigmen on't turn hostile unless you strike first. Ahh...
What's that you're doing?
XXXX
NZZXXXX

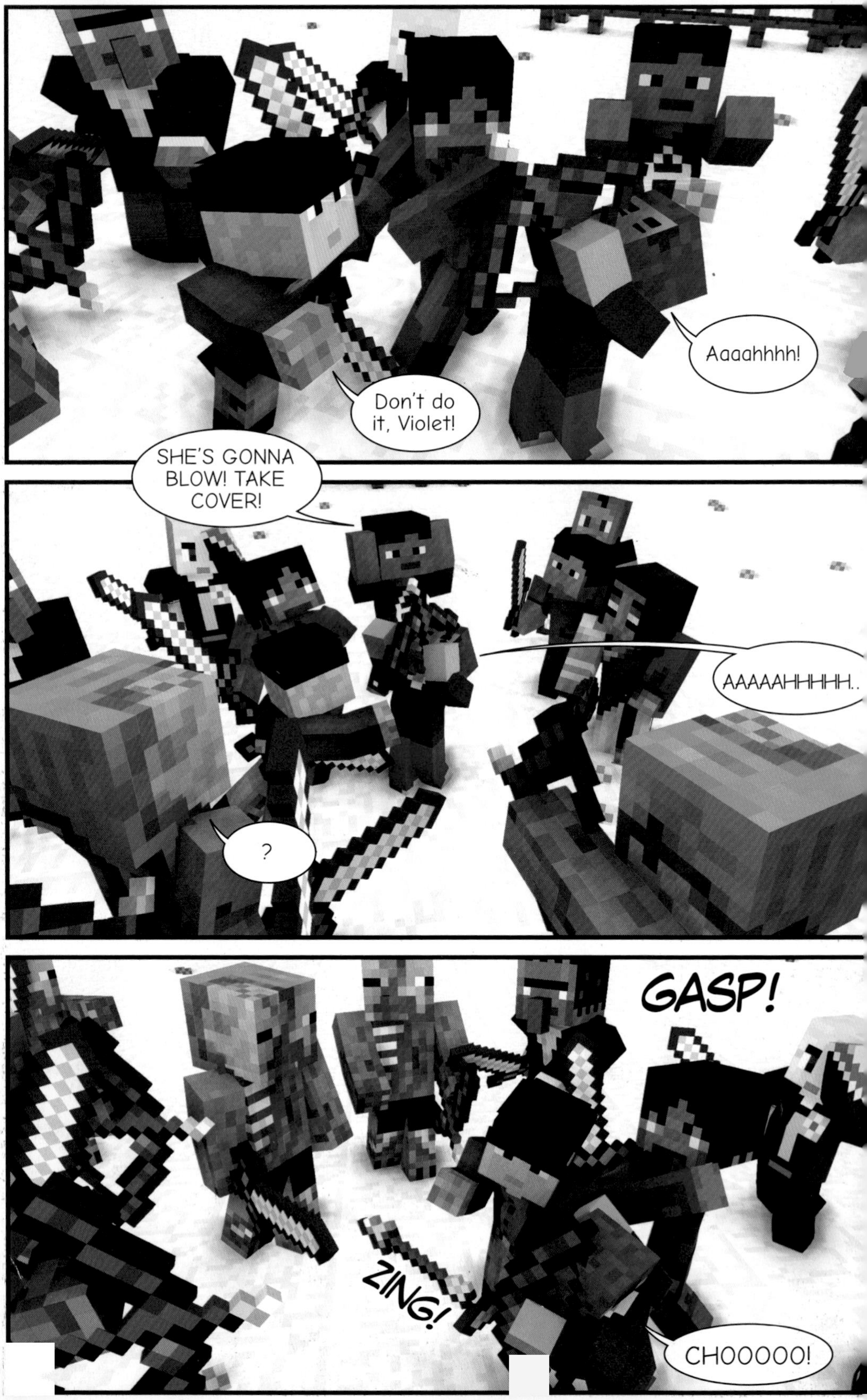
Aaaahhhh!
Don't do it, Violet!
SHE'S GONNA BLOW! TAKE COVER!
AAAAAHHHHH...
?
GASP!
ZING!
CHOOOOO!

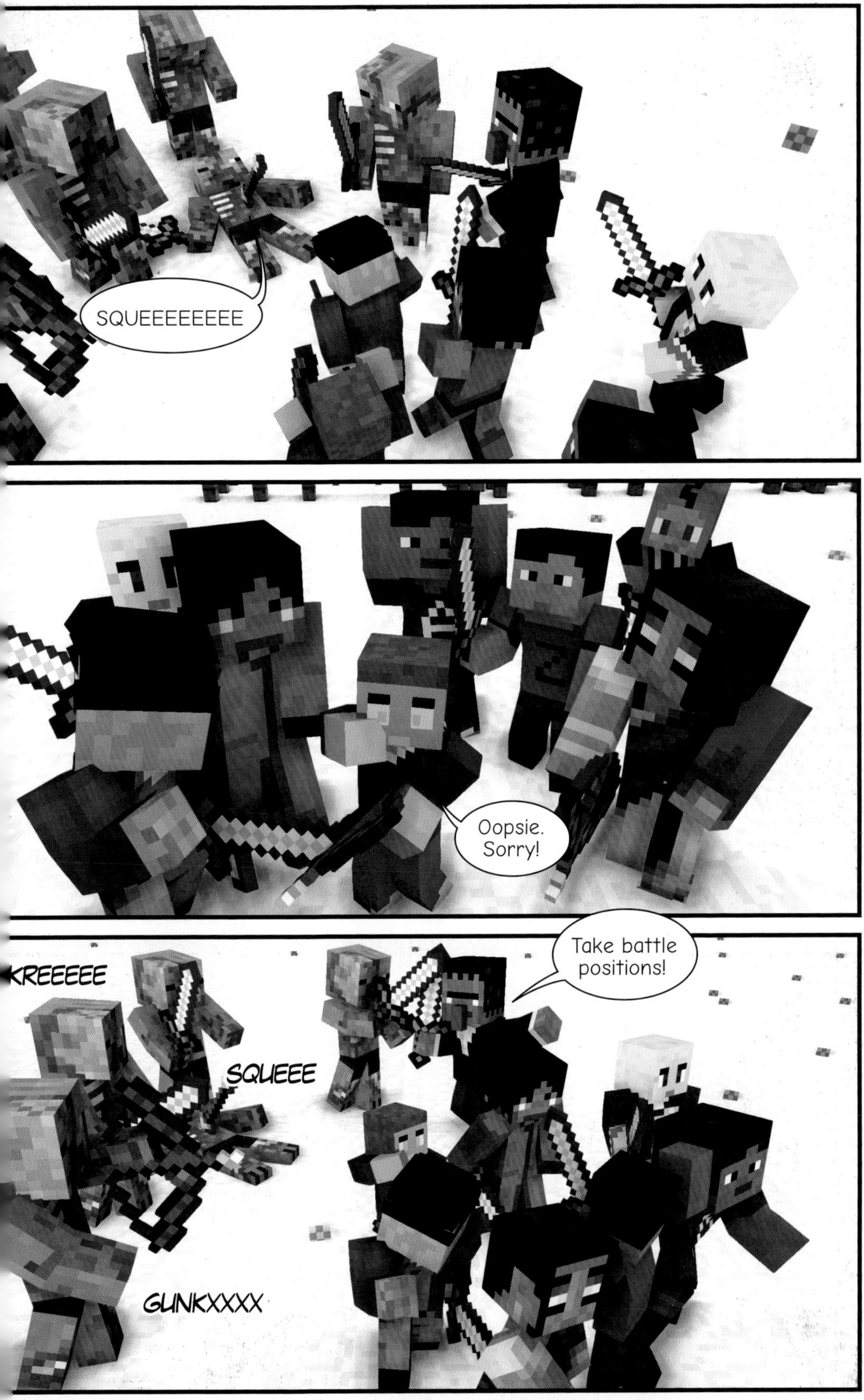
SQUEEEEEEEEE
Oopsie. Sorry!
KREEEEE
SQUEEE
Take battle positions!
GUNKXXXX

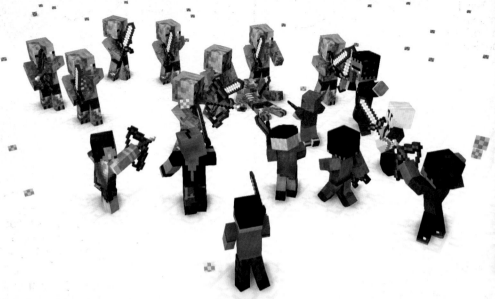

I sure hope that lightning strike doesn't do what I think it's about to do.

RATTLE

What is going on here? I took a quick power nap and woke up to the sounds of a battle. Where did all these pigmen come from?

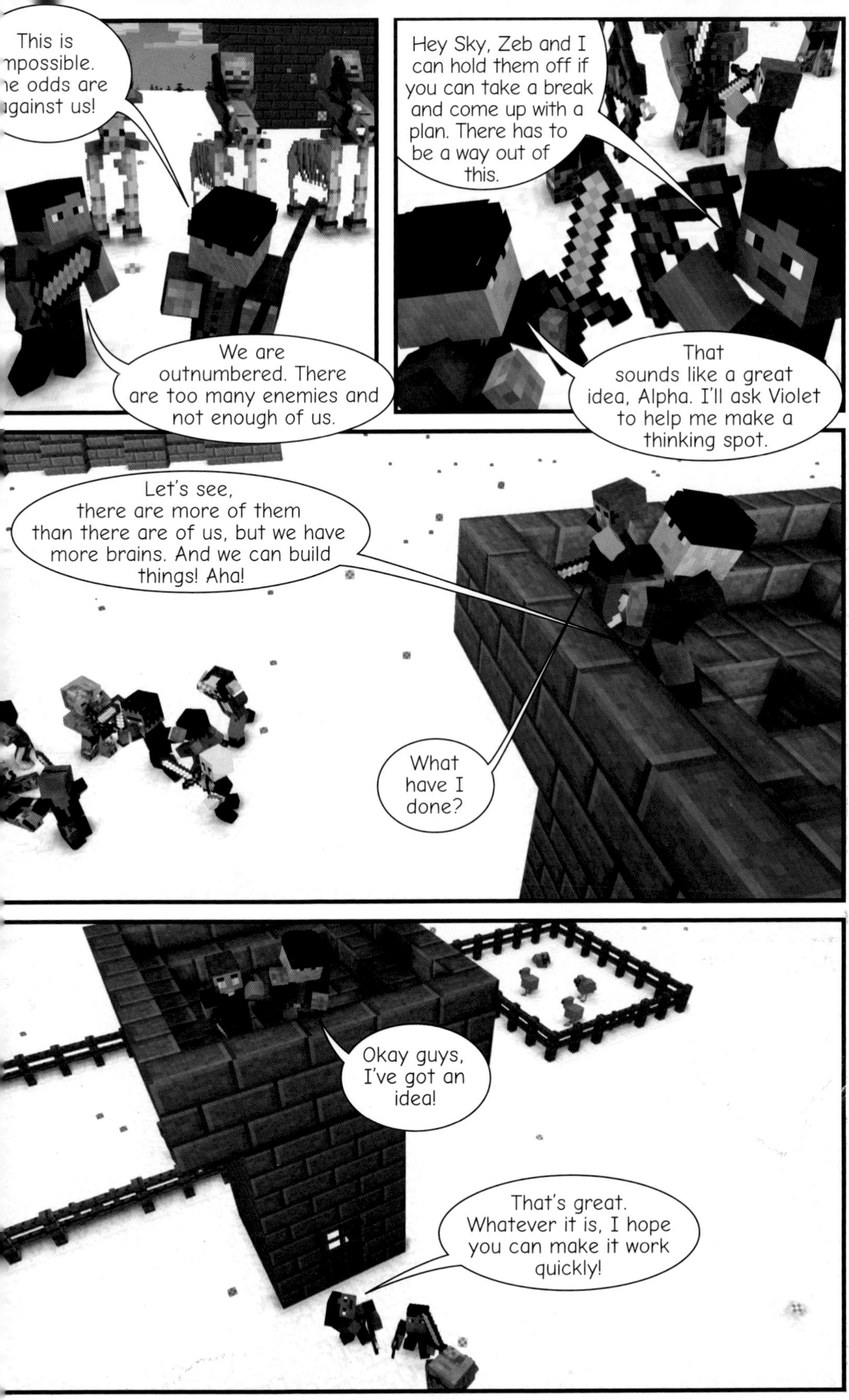
This is mpossible. e odds are gainst us!
We are outnumbered. There are too many enemies and not enough of us.
Hey Sky, Zeb and I can hold them off if you can take a break and come up with a plan. There has to be a way out of this.
That sounds like a great idea, Alpha. I'll ask Violet to help me make a thinking spot.
Let's see, there are more of them than there are of us, but we have more brains. And we can build things! Aha!
What have I done?
Okay guys, I've got an idea!
That's great. Whatever it is, I hope you can make it work quickly!

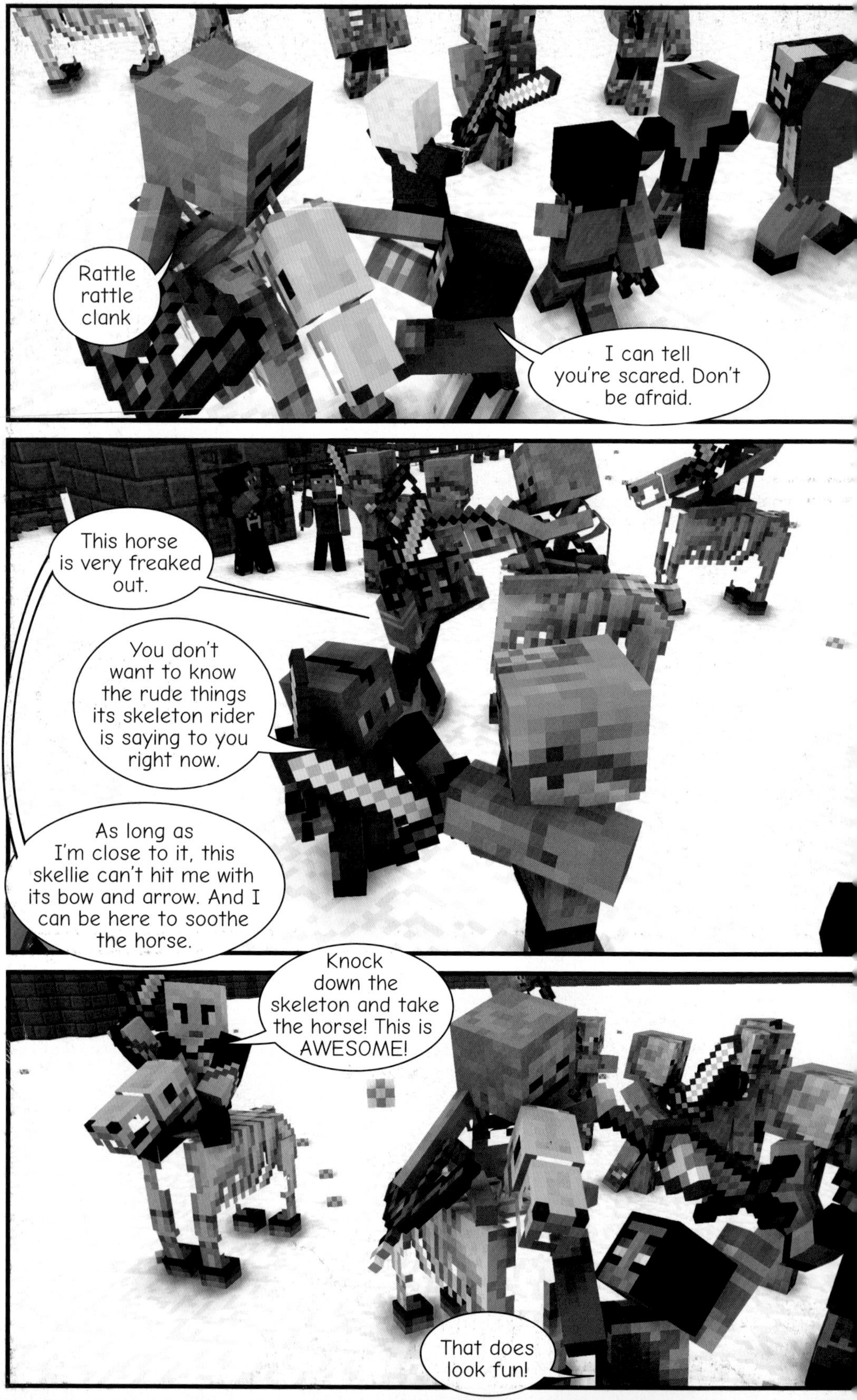
Rattle rattle clank
I can tell you're scared. Don't be afraid.
This horse is very freaked out.
You don't want to know the rude things its skeleton rider is saying to you right now.
As long as I'm close to it, this skellie can't hit me with its bow and arrow. And I can be here to soothe the horse.
Knock down the skeleton and take the horse! This is AWESOME!
That does look fun!

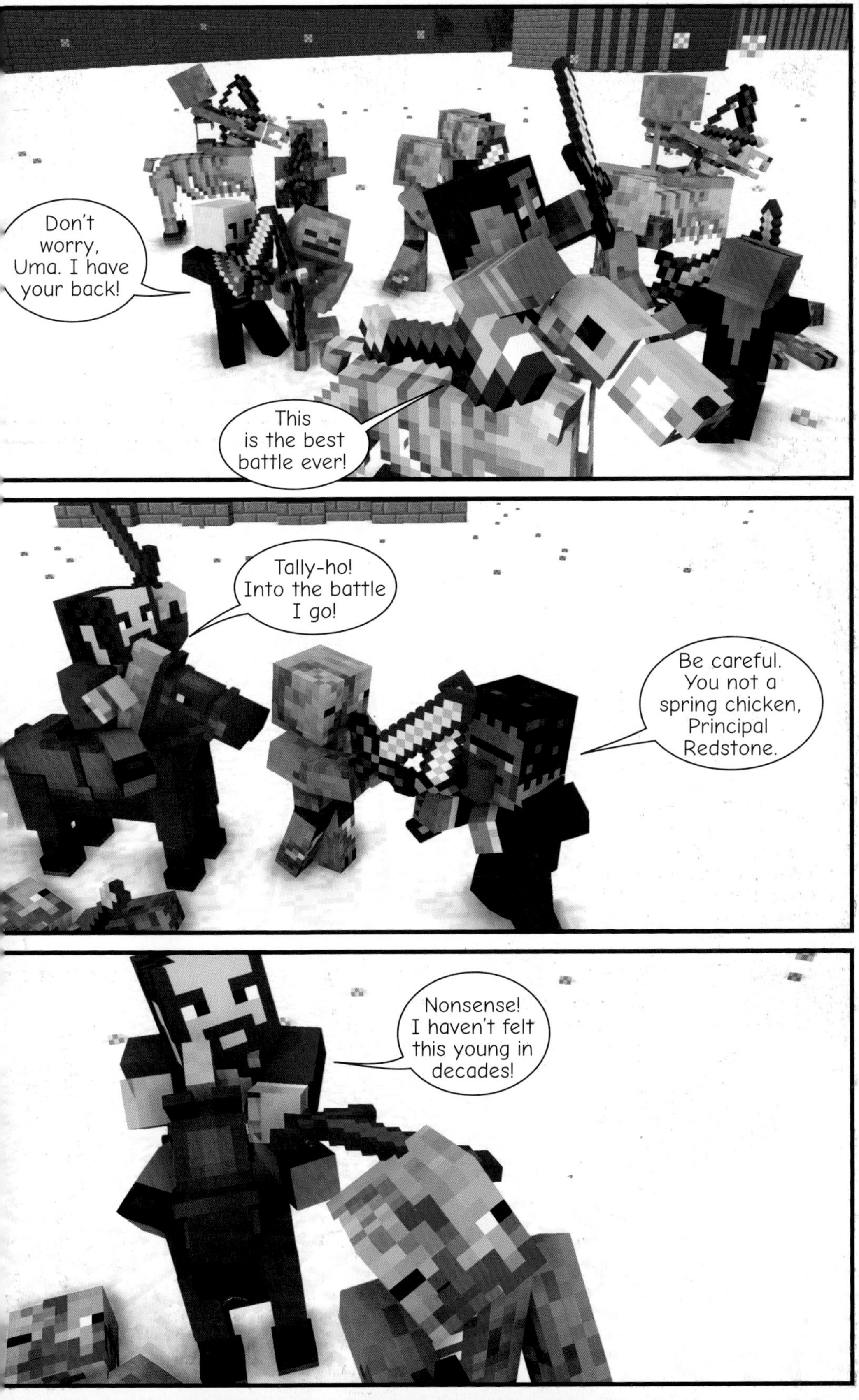
Don't worry, Uma. I have your back!
This is the best battle ever!
Tally-ho! Into the battle I go!
Be careful. You not a spring chicken, Principal Redstone.
Nonsense! I haven't felt this young in decades!

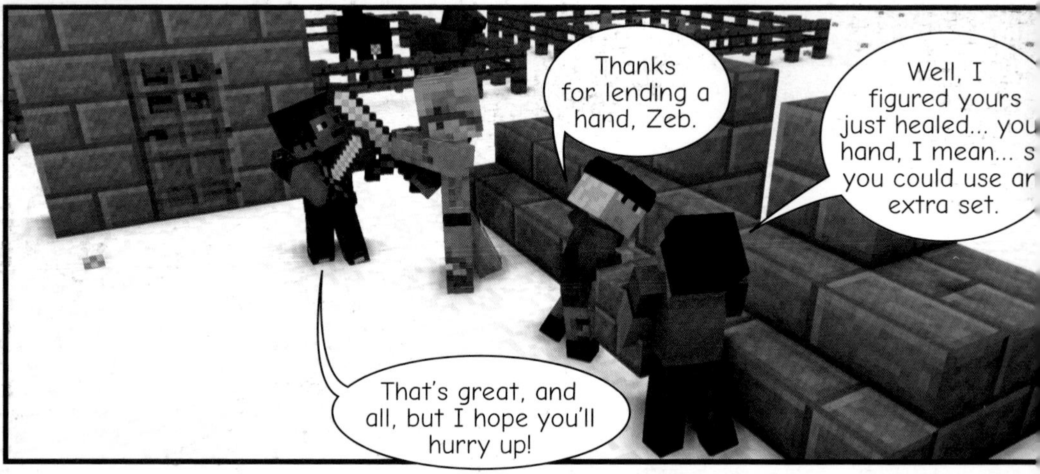
Thanks for lending a hand, Zeb.
Well, I figured yours just healed... you hand, I mean... s you could use ar extra set.
That's great, and all, but I hope you'll hurry up!

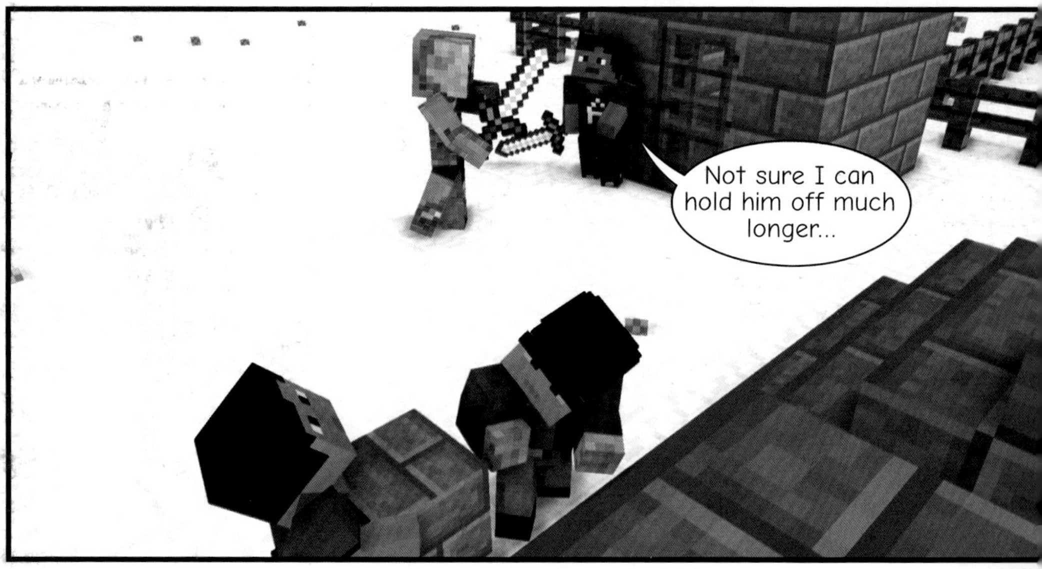
Not sure I can hold him off much longer...

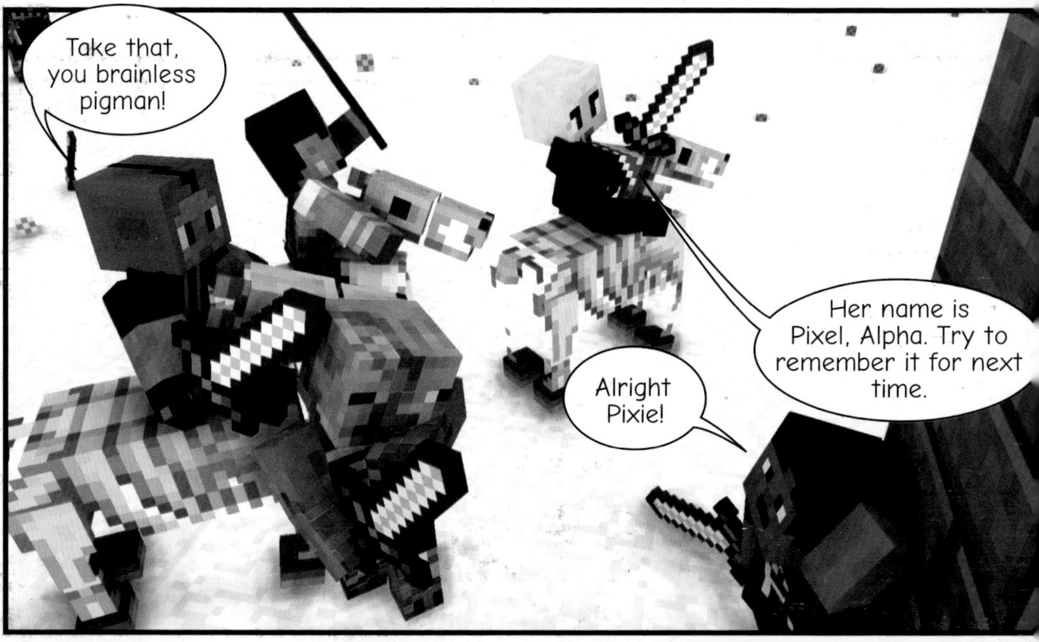
Take that, you brainless pigman!
Her name is Pixel, Alpha. Try to remember it for next time.
Alright Pixie!

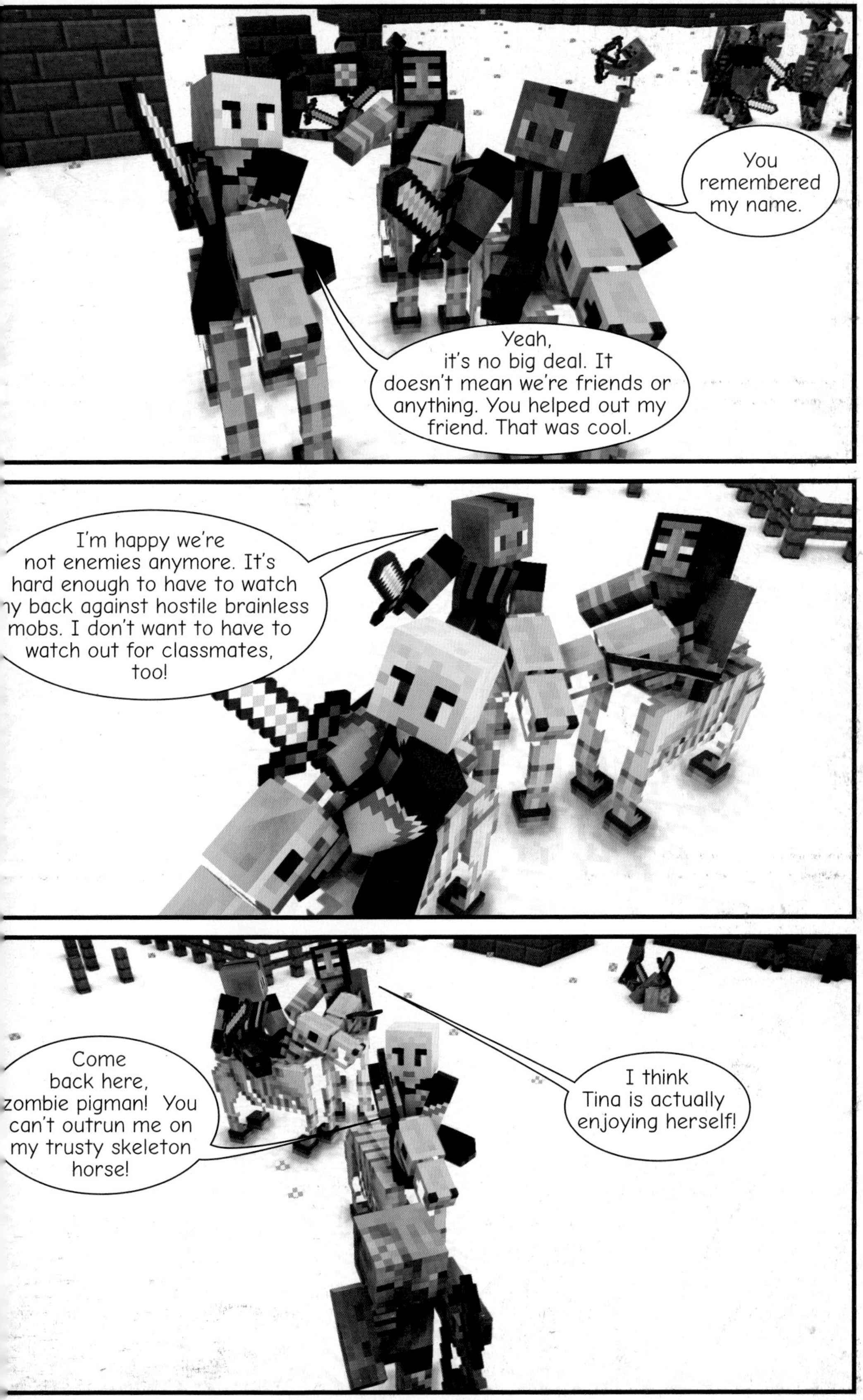
You remembered my name.
Yeah, it's no big deal. It doesn't mean we're friends or anything. You helped out my friend. That was cool.
I'm happy we're not enemies anymore. It's hard enough to have to watch ny back against hostile brainless mobs. I don't want to have to watch out for classmates, too!
Come back here, zombie pigman! You can't outrun me on my trusty skeleton horse!
I think Tina is actually enjoying herself!

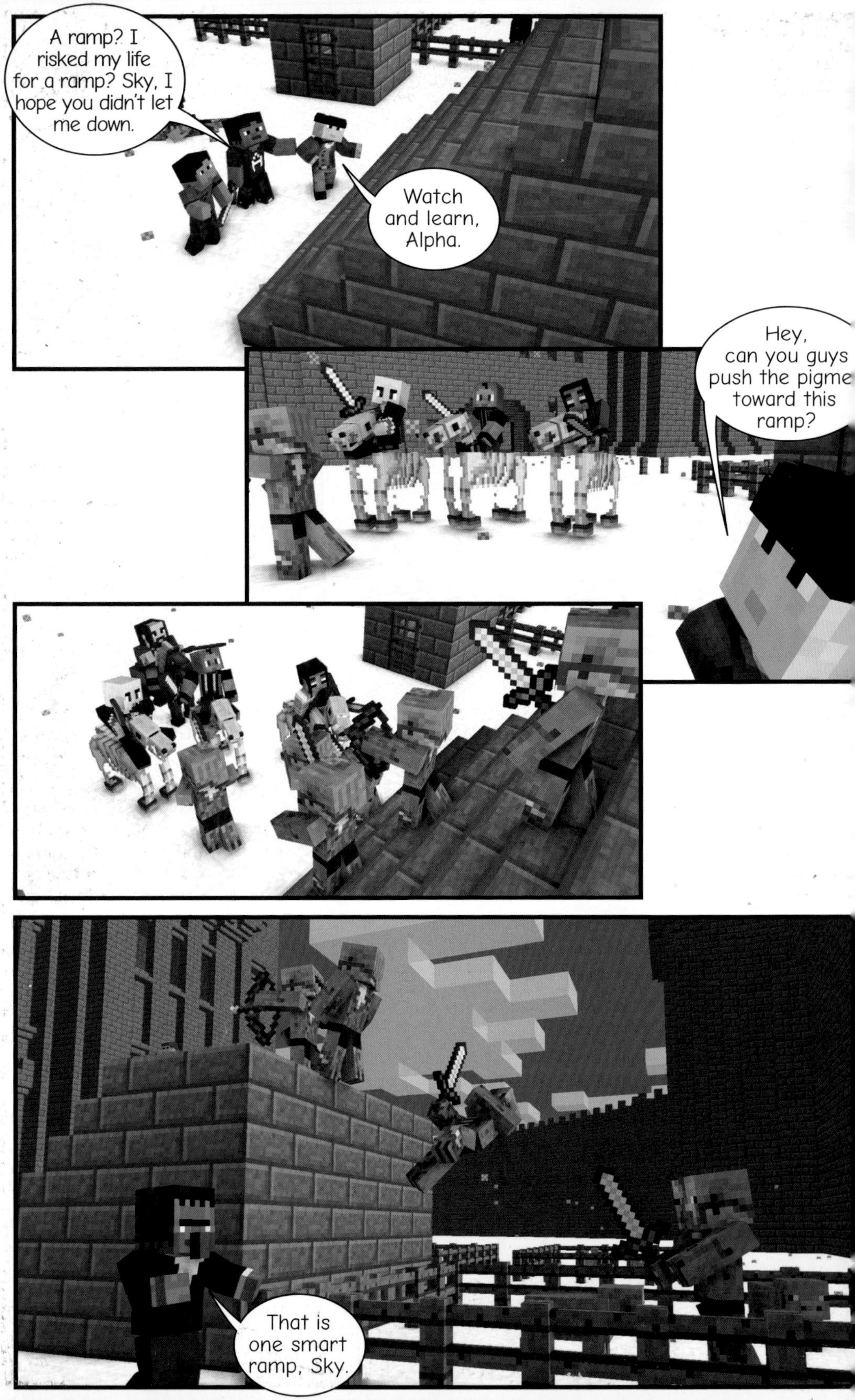
A ramp? I risked my life for a ramp? Sky, I hope you didn't let me down.
Watch and learn, Alpha.
Hey, can you guys push the pigme toward this ramp?
That is one smart ramp, Sky.

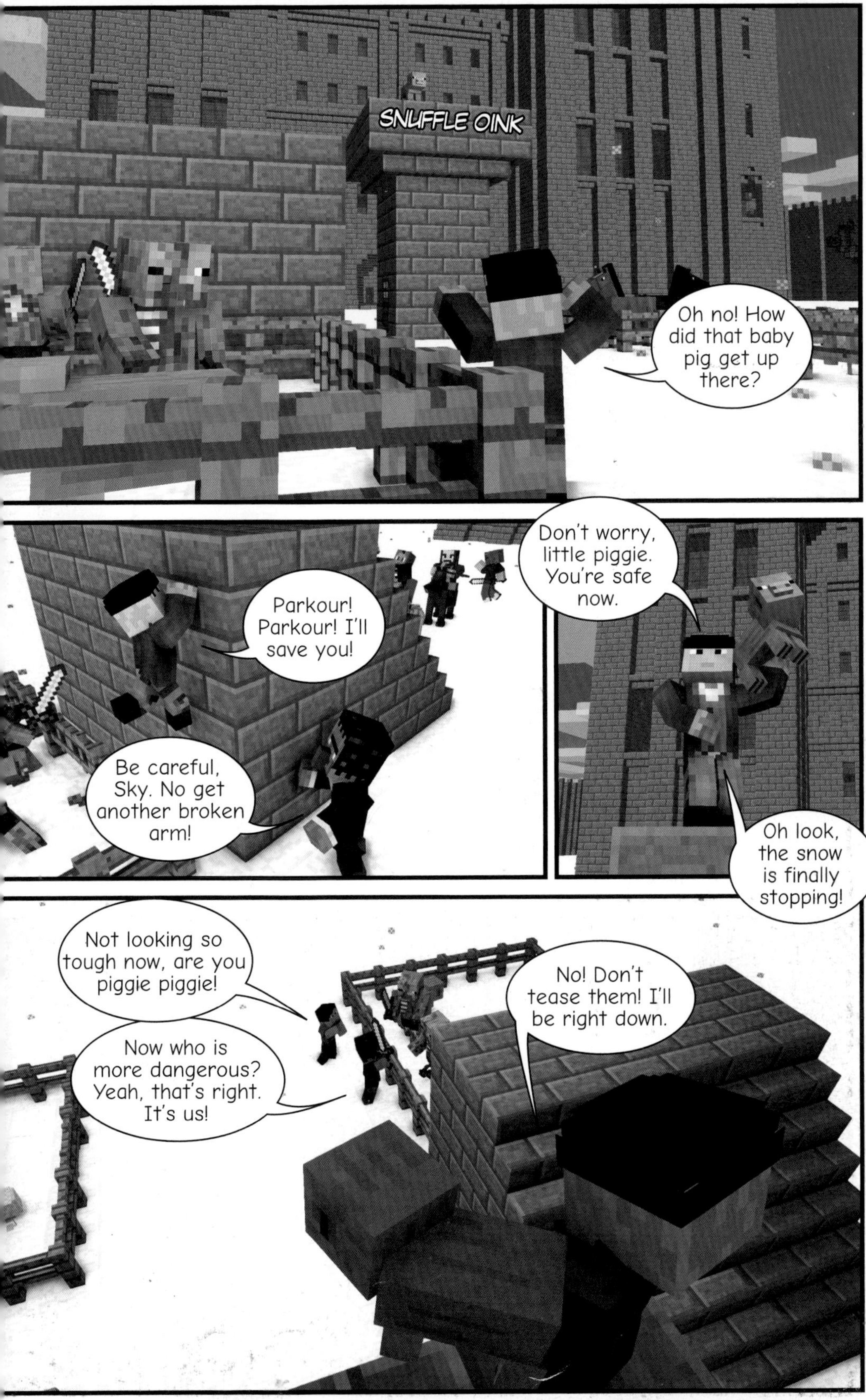
SNUFFLE OINK
Oh no! How did that baby pig get up there?
Parkour! Parkour! I'll save you!
Be careful, Sky. No get another broken arm!
Don't worry, little piggie. You're safe now.
Oh look, the snow is finally stopping!
Not looking so tough now, are you piggie piggie!
Now who is more dangerous? Yeah, that's right. It's us!
No! Don't tease them! I'll be right down.

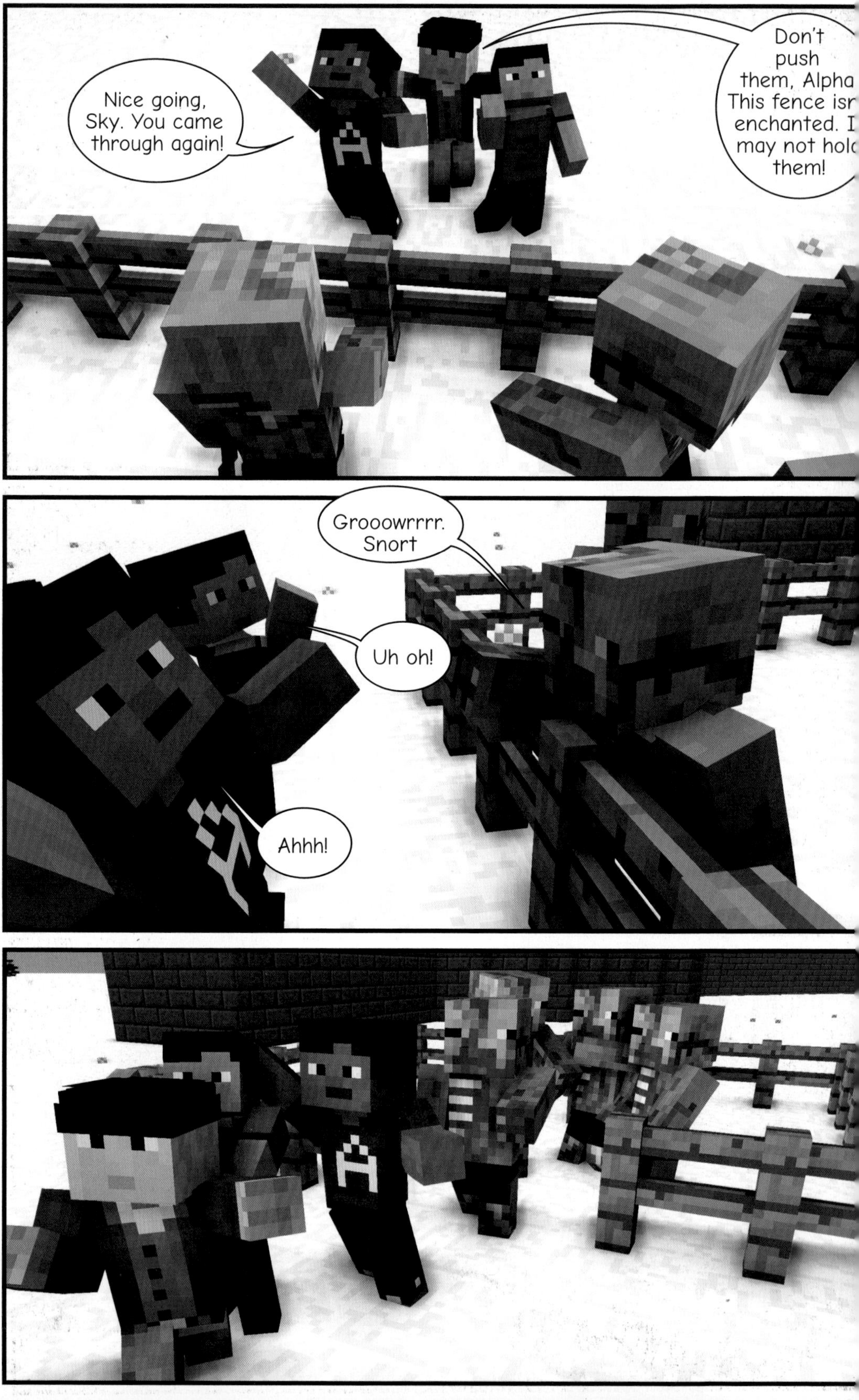
Nice going, Sky. You came through again!
Don't push them, Alpha This fence is enchanted. I may not hol them!
Grooowrrrr. Snort
Uh oh!
Ahhh!

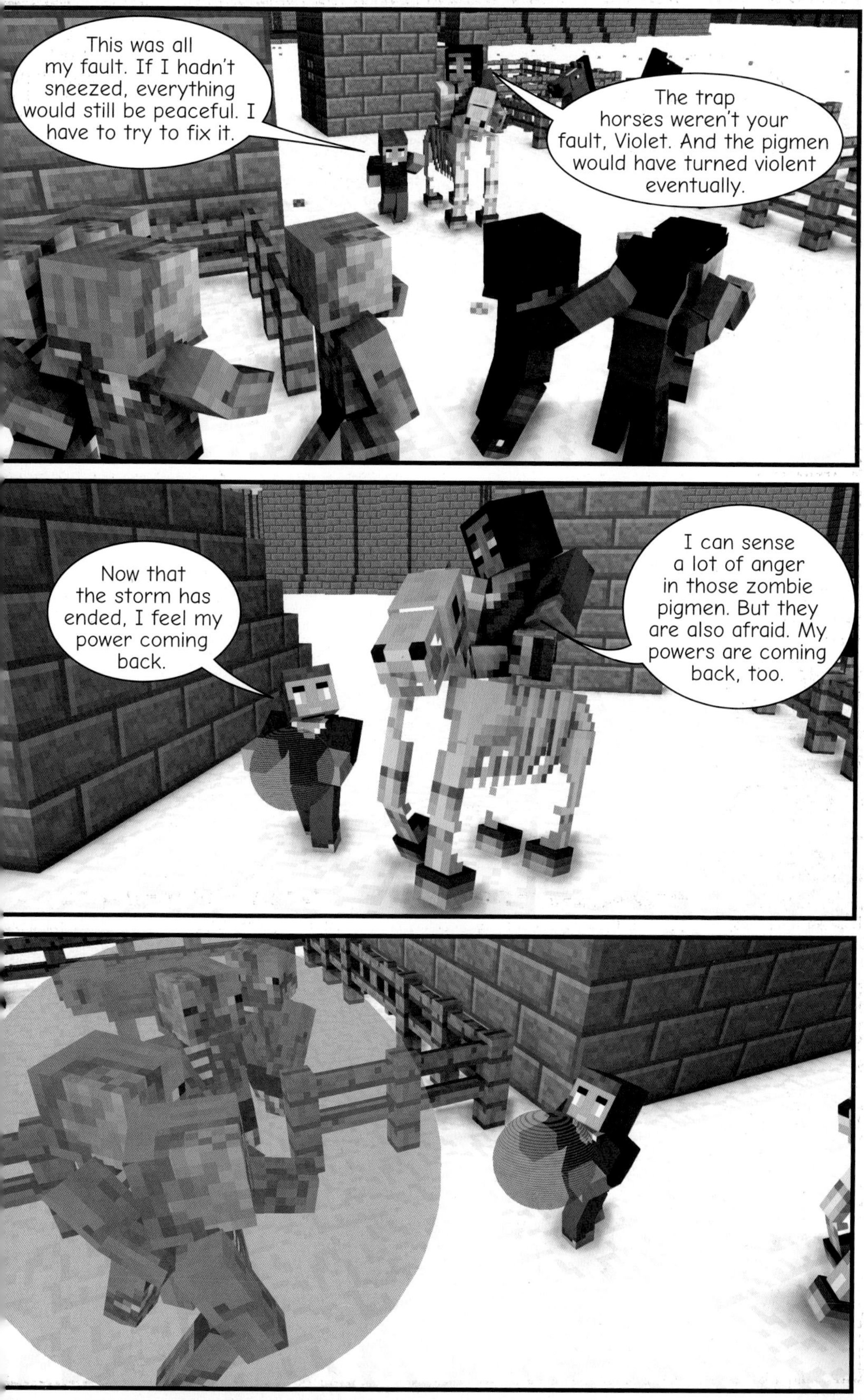
This was all my fault. If I hadn't sneezed, everything would still be peaceful. I have to try to fix it.
The trap horses weren't your fault, Violet. And the pigmen would have turned violent eventually.
Now that the storm has ended, I feel my power coming back.
I can sense a lot of anger in those zombie pigmen. But they are also afraid. My powers are coming back, too.

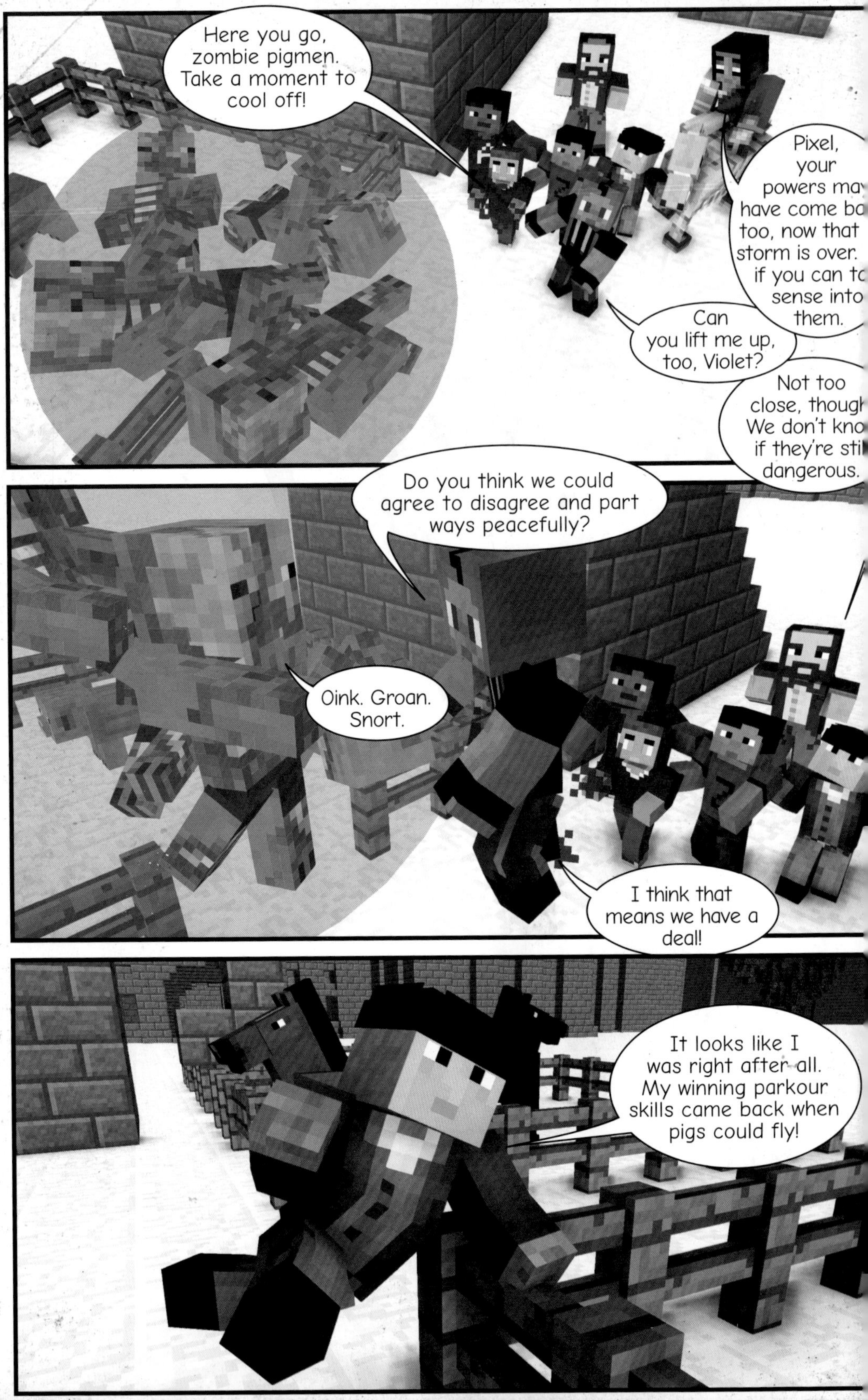
Here you go, zombie pigmen. Take a moment to cool off!
Pixel, your powers ma have come ba too, now that storm is over. if you can t sense into them.
Can you lift me up, too, Violet?
Not too close, thoug We don't kno if they're sti dangerous.
Do you think we could agree to disagree and part ways peacefully?
Oink. Groan. Snort.
I think that means we have a deal!
It looks like I was right after all. My winning parkour skills came back when pigs could fly!

CHAPTER 12

GRADUATION DAY

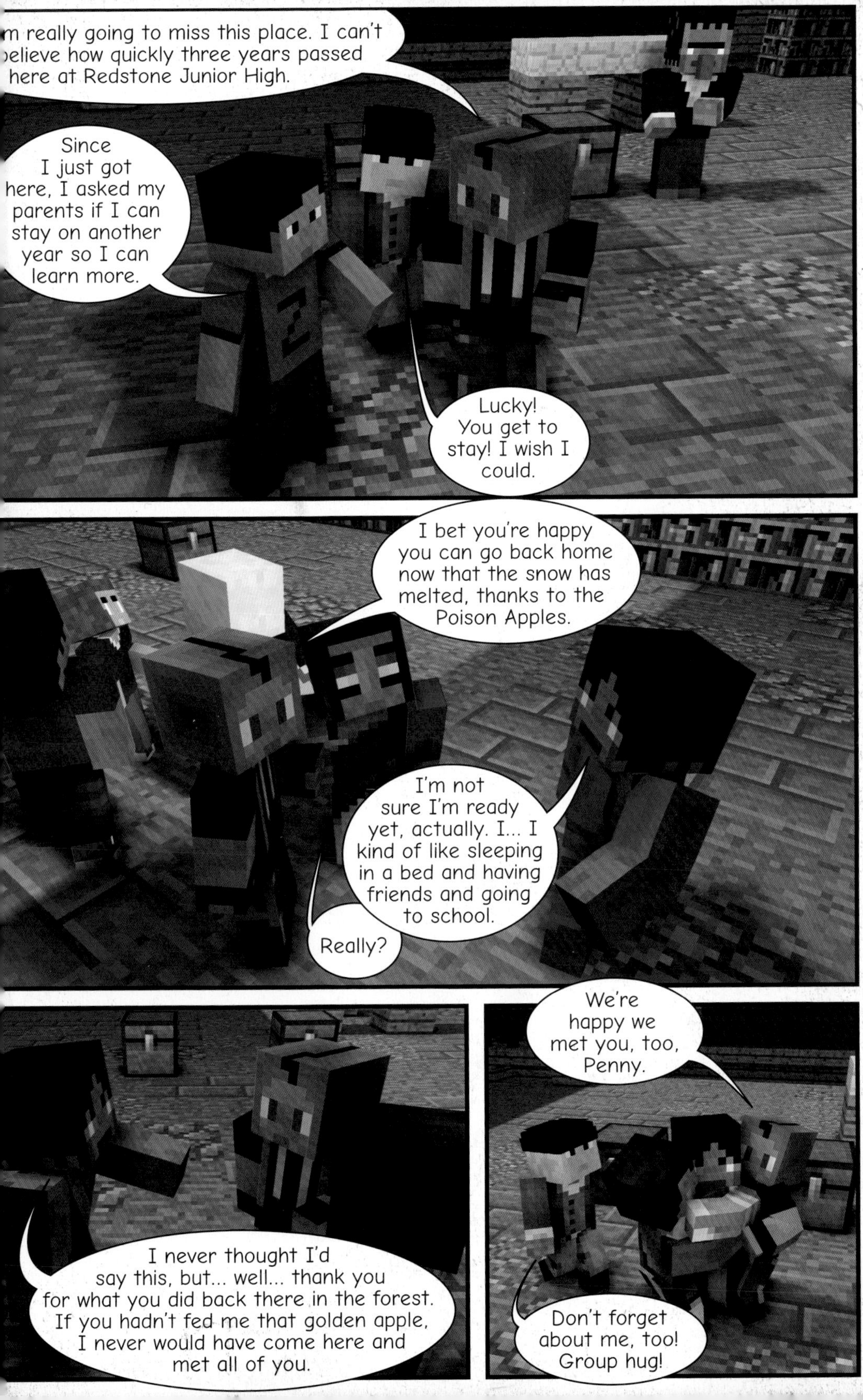
m really going to miss this place. I can't elieve how quickly three years passed here at Redstone Junior High.
Since I just got here, I asked my parents if I can stay on another year so I can learn more.
Lucky! You get to stay! I wish I could.
I bet you're happy you can go back home now that the snow has melted, thanks to the Poison Apples.
I'm not sure I'm ready yet, actually. I... I kind of like sleeping in a bed and having friends and going to school.
Really?
I never thought I'd say this, but... well... thank you for what you did back there in the forest. If you hadn't fed me that golden apple, I never would have come here and met all of you.
We're happy we met you, too, Penny.
Don't forget about me, too! Group hug!

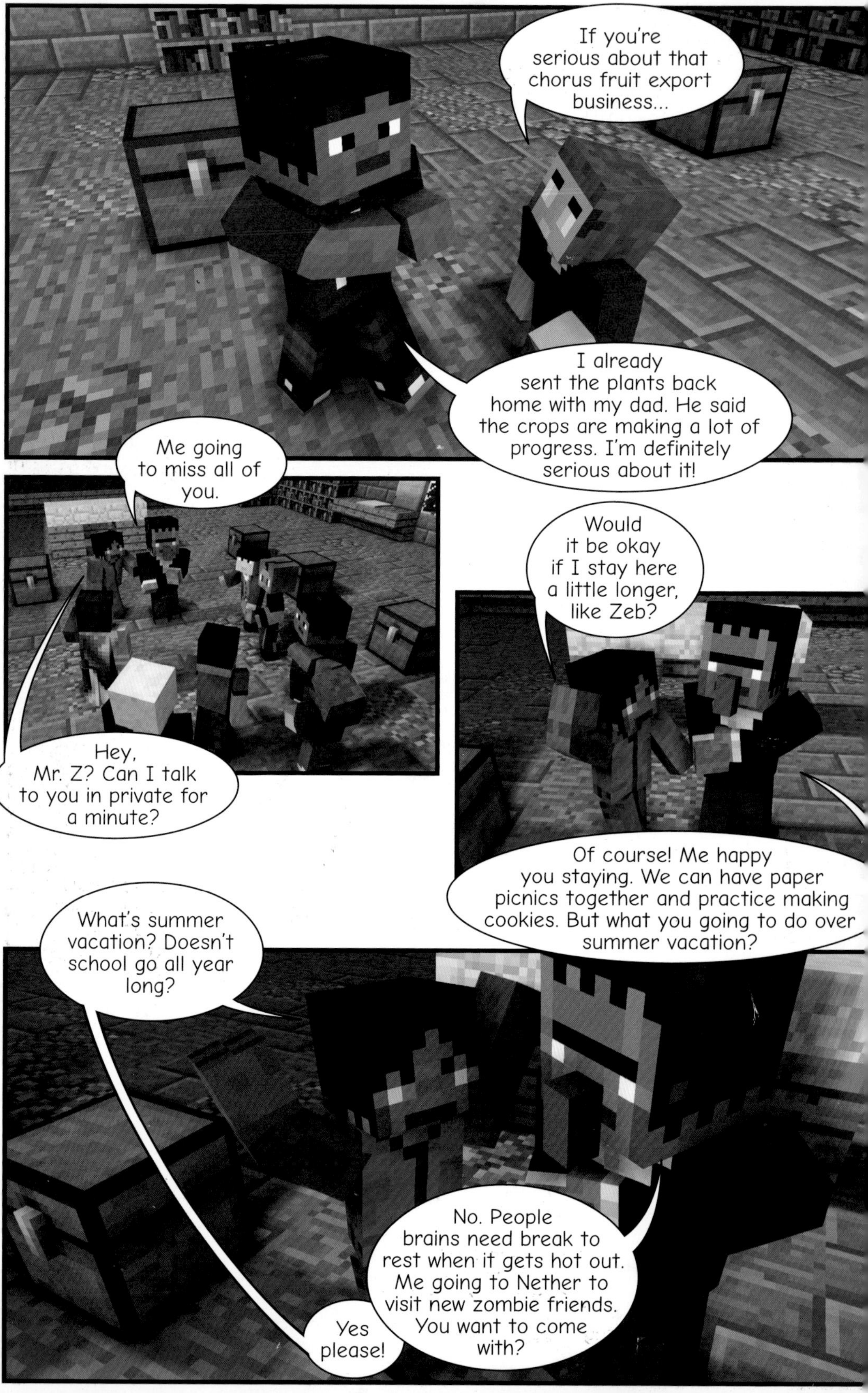
If you're serious about that chorus fruit export business...
I already sent the plants back home with my dad. He said the crops are making a lot of progress. I'm definitely serious about it!
Me going to miss all of you.
Hey, Mr. Z? Can I talk to you in private for a minute?
Would it be okay if I stay here a little longer, like Zeb?
Of course! Me happy you staying. We can have paper picnics together and practice making cookies. But what you going to do over summer vacation?
What's summer vacation? Doesn't school go all year long?
No. People brains need break to rest when it gets hot out. Me going to Nether to visit new zombie friends. You want to come with?
Yes please!

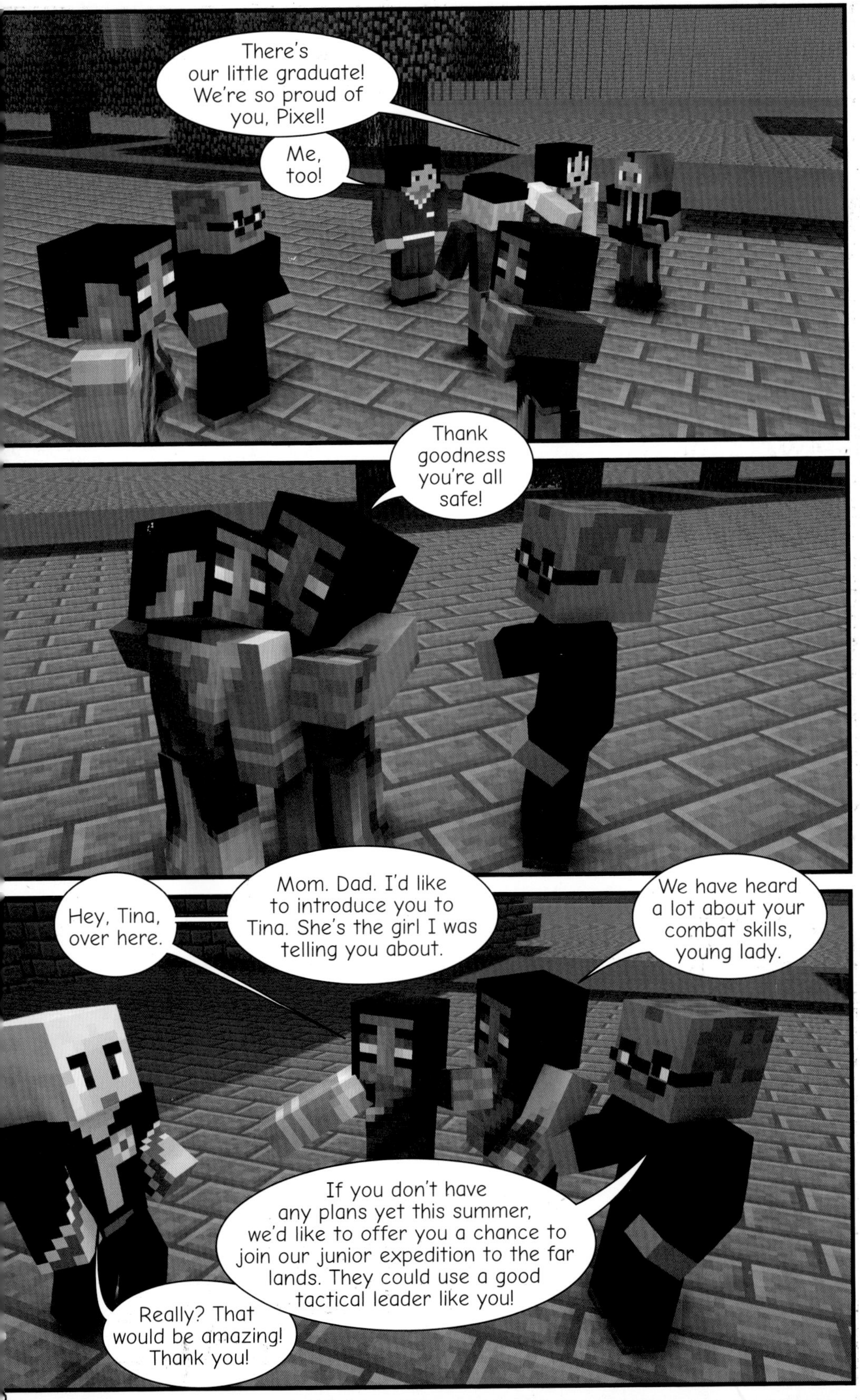
There's our little graduate! We're so proud of you, Pixel!
Me, too!
Thank goodness you're all safe!
Hey, Tina, over here.
Mom. Dad. I'd like to introduce you to Tina. She's the girl I was telling you about.
We have heard a lot about your combat skills, young lady.
If you don't have any plans yet this summer, we'd like to offer you a chance to join our junior expedition to the far lands. They could use a good tactical leader like you!
Really? That would be amazing! Thank you!

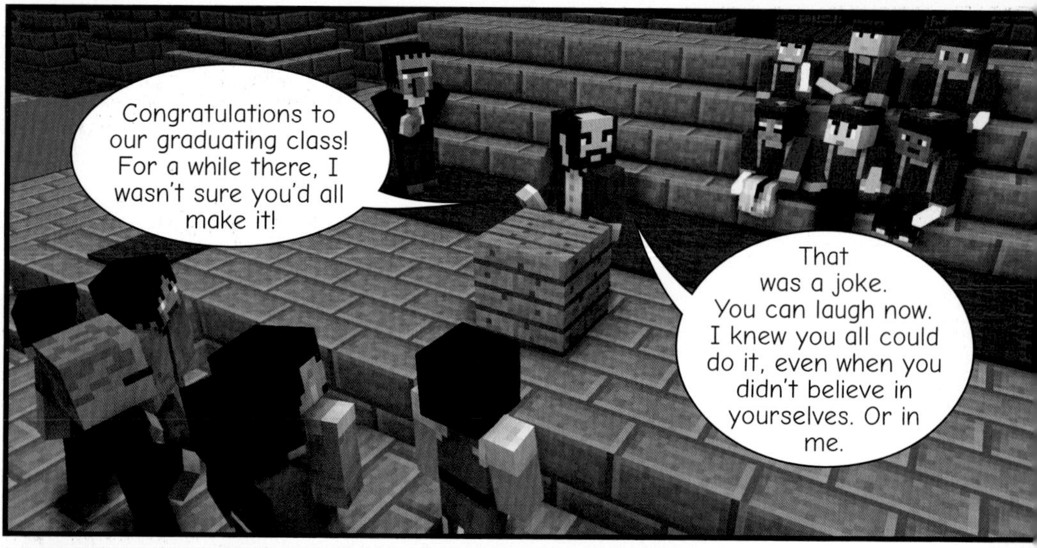
Congratulations to our graduating class! For a while there, I wasn't sure you'd all make it!
That was a joke. You can laugh now. I knew you all could do it, even when you didn't believe in yourselves. Or in me.

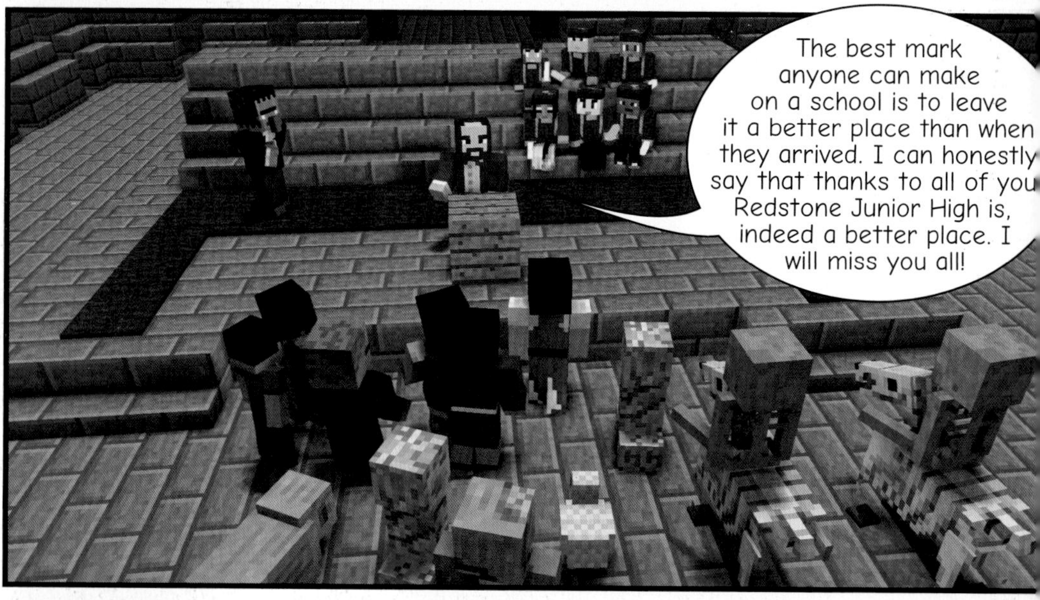
The best mark anyone can make on a school is to leave it a better place than when they arrived. I can honestly say that thanks to all of you Redstone Junior High is, indeed a better place. I will miss you all!

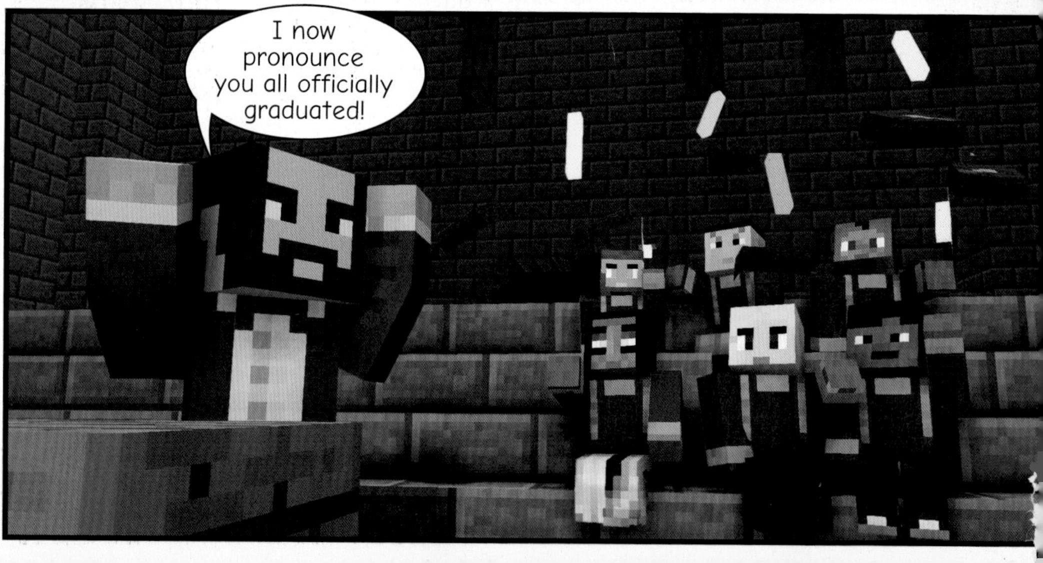
I now pronounce you all officially graduated!

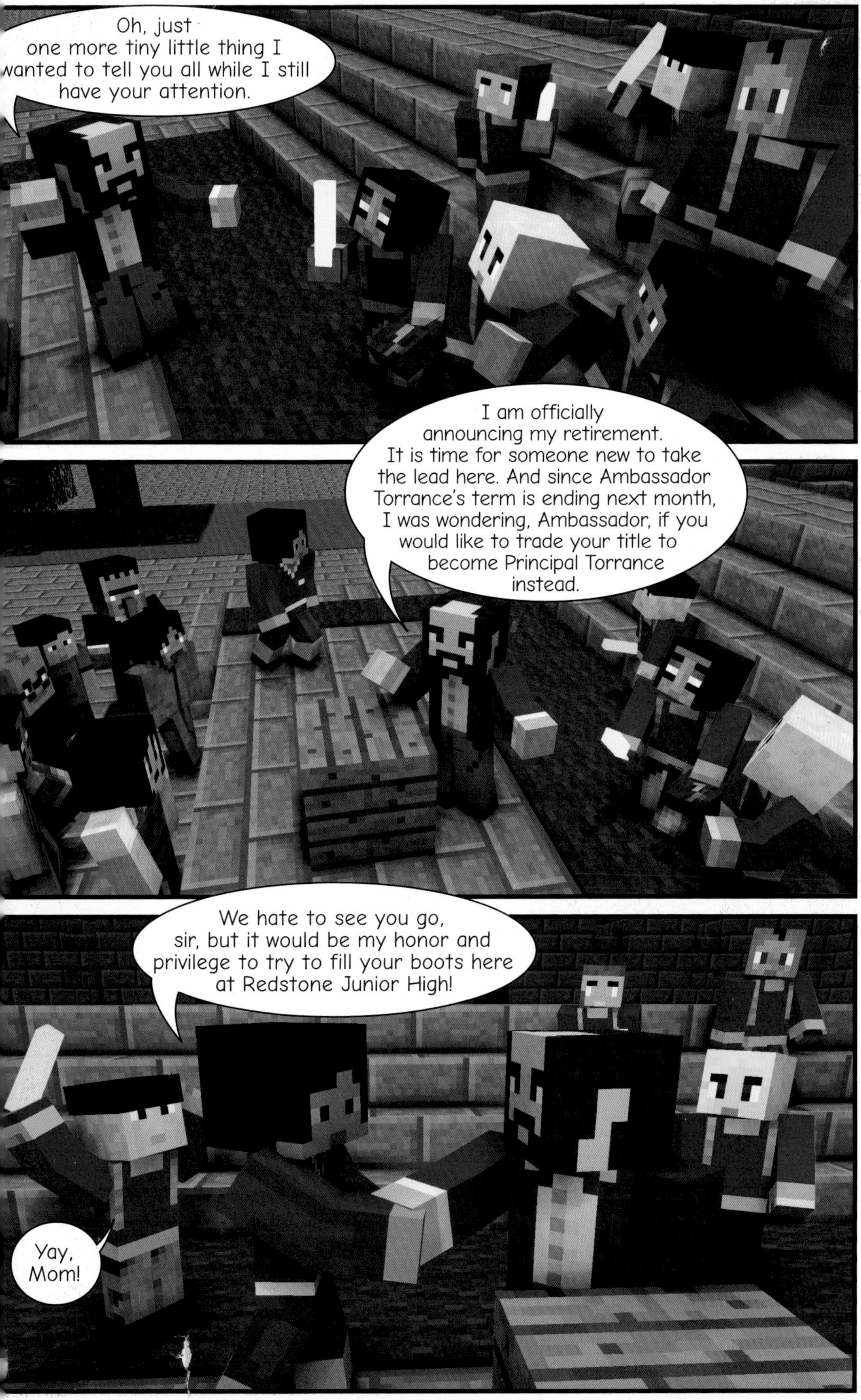
Oh, just one more tiny little thing I wanted to tell you all while I still have your attention.
I am officially announcing my retirement. It is time for someone new to take the lead here. And since Ambassador Torrance's term is ending next month, I was wondering, Ambassador, if you would like to trade your title to become Principal Torrance instead.
We hate to see you go, sir, but it would be my honor and privilege to try to fill your boots here at Redstone Junior High!
Yay, Mom!

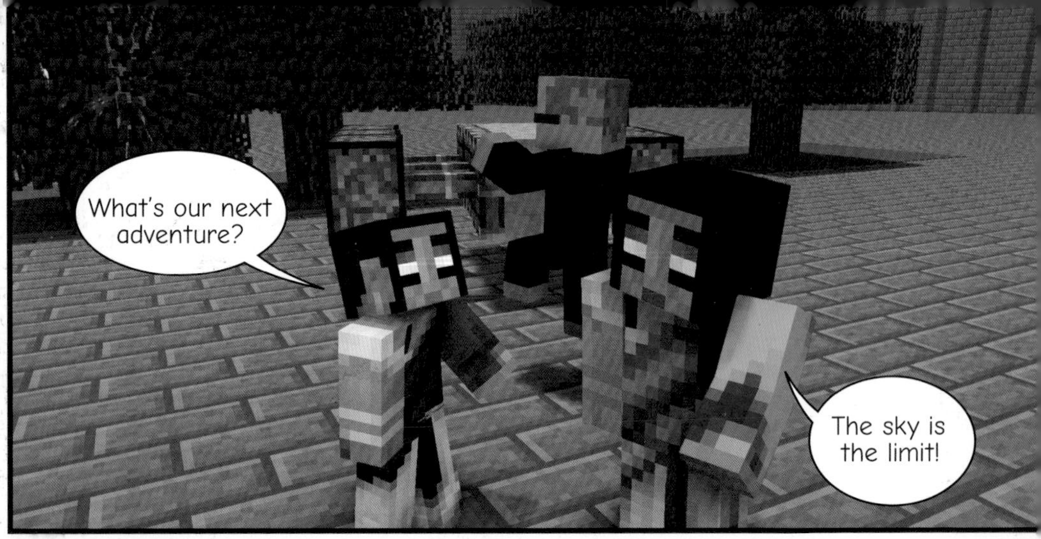
What's our next adventure?
The sky is the limit!

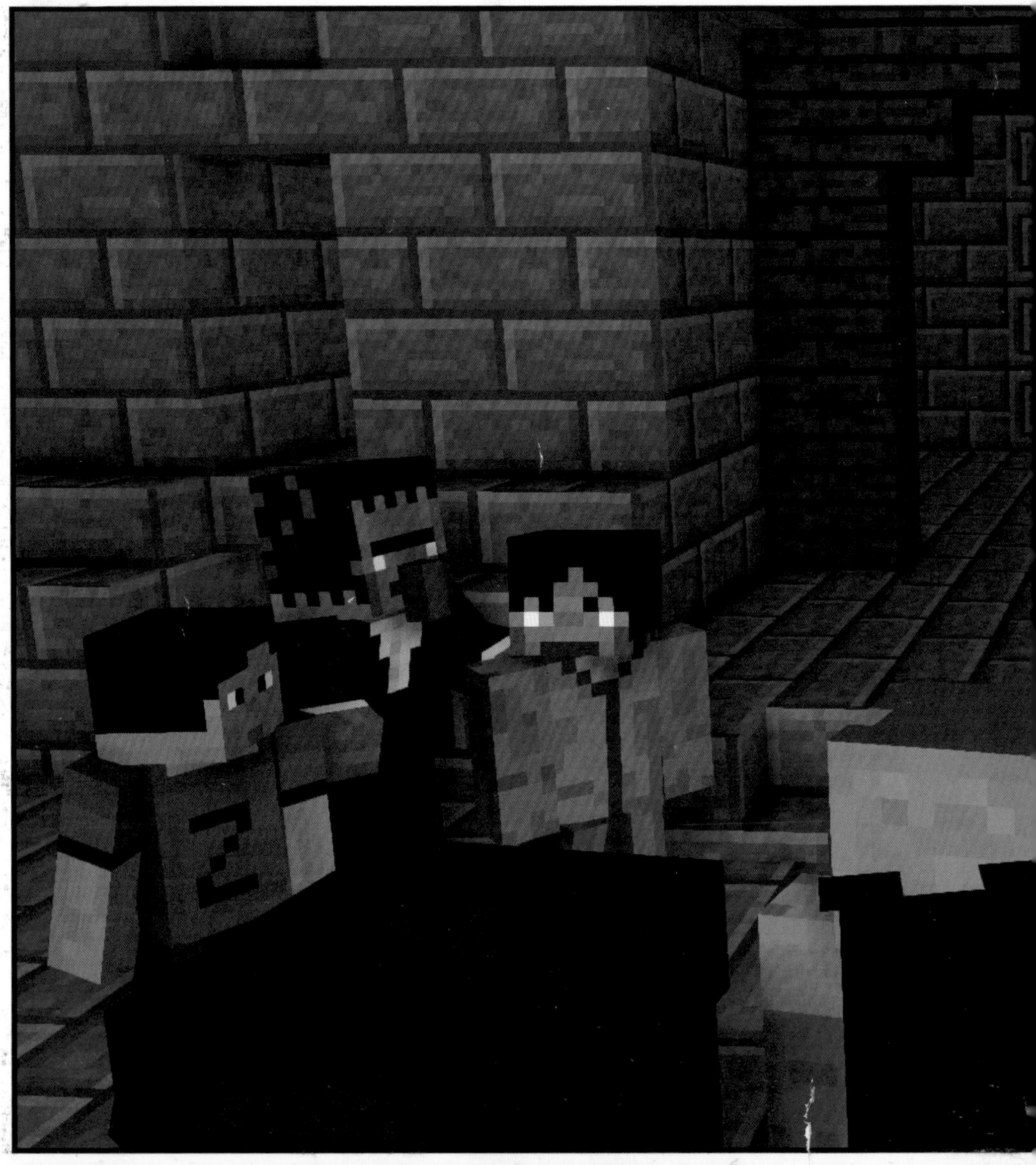

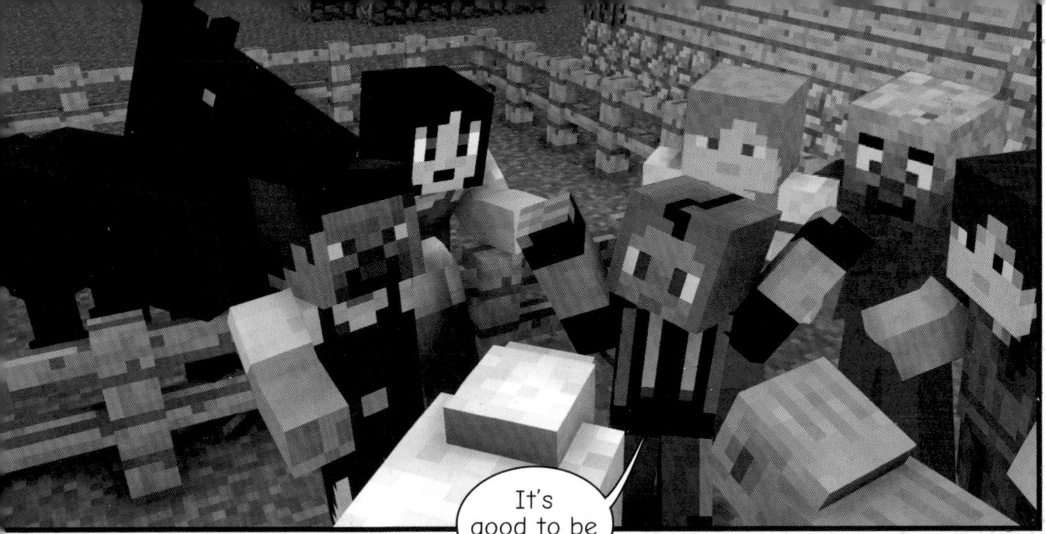
It's good to be home!

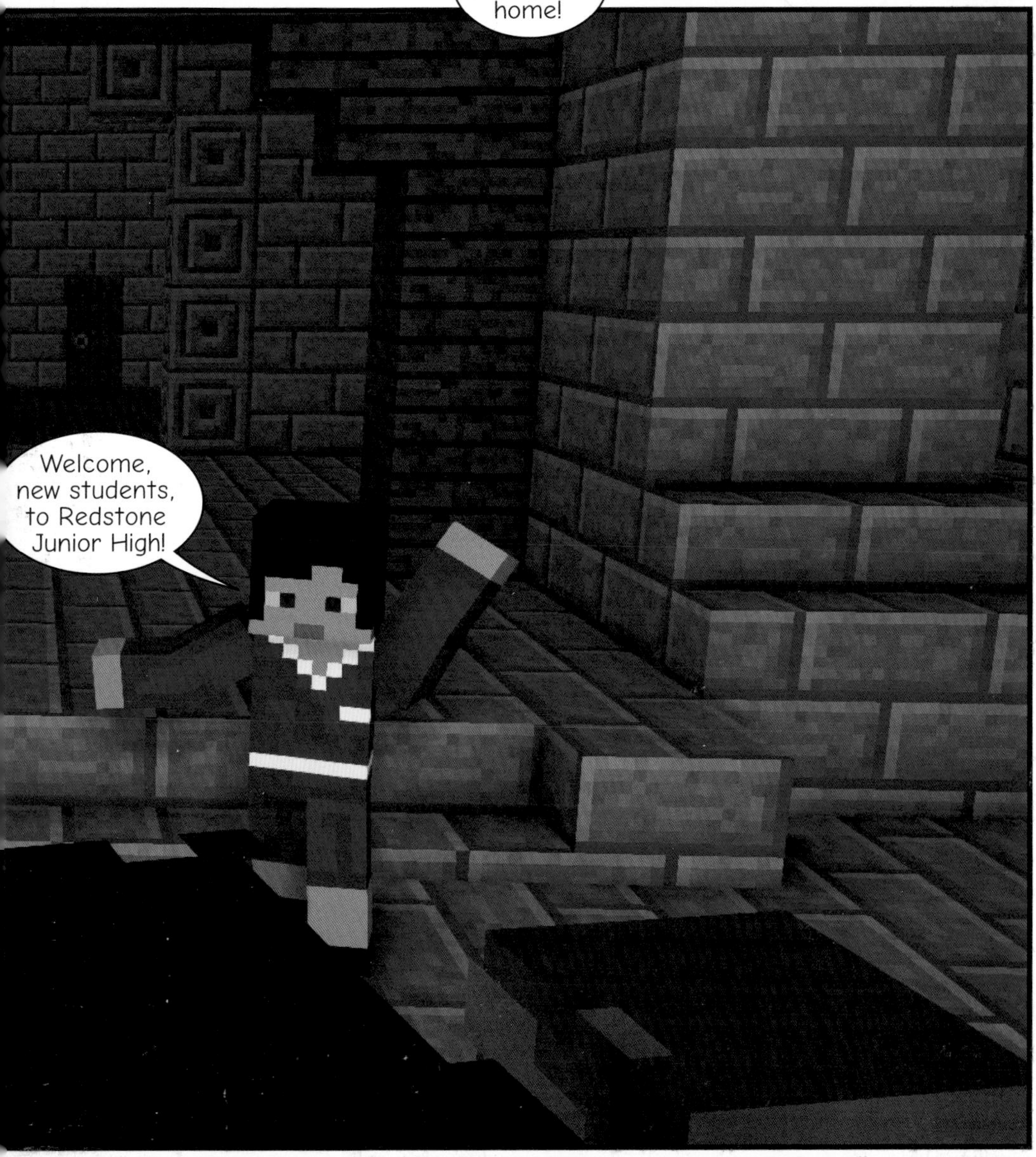
Welcome, new students, to Redstone Junior High!